PRAISE FOR GINA B. NAHAI AND
MOONLIGHT ON THE AVENUE OF FAITH

"A considerable talent. Nahai has achieved some wonderful effects, infusing everyday events with miraculous radiance."
—*The New York Times Book Review*

"A testament to the power and beauty of Gina Nahai's writing and the world she so brilliantly illuminates."
—*The Boston Globe*

"A novel of stunning beauty and power. . . . A supreme accomplishment. The magical realism so perfectly wrought by García Márquez has rarely been equaled, perhaps only by Toni Morrison in *Song of Solomon* and here in Nahai's novel."
—*The Plain Dealer* (Cleveland)

"A multigenerational story as intricate and richly hued as a Persian carpet. As she revealed in *Cry of the Peacock*, Nahai possesses an array of talents, all of which glitter in *MOONLIGHT ON THE AVENUE OF FAITH*. Nahai's writing recalls that of Gabriel García Márquez and Amy Tan, yet her prose bears its own stamp of inventiveness and vivacity. . . . A modern-day Scheherazade."
—*The Orlando Sentinel*

"A sprawling tapestry of a novel. . . . Clear testimony to her skill as a storyteller, Gina B. Nahai works in elegant contrasts, the spellbinding extremes of the best of the magical realist tradition, conjuring a story that glows as if lit by a subtle, internal fire."

—*Portland Oregonian*

"A nice addition to the canon of magic realism. . . . Ms. Nahai's lyrical command of her words carries through consistently. The book's effectiveness deepens into a powerful and surprising final chapter."

—*The Dallas Morning News*

"Lyrical, beautiful. . . . A languid, steamy read."

—*The Toronto Star*

"Absorbing. . . . Through the power of Nahai's language, the past becomes present. . . . This book is not a fairytale, not a poem, not a mystery story. Like moonlight, it is a little of each. So the Avenue of Faith is not just the novel's setting, but also the mindset that informs its characters—and readers."

—*The Virginian Pilot*

"*MOONLIGHT ON THE AVENUE OF FAITH* paves the way for Ms. Nahai to claim her place among other cultural women writers such as Amy Tan and Toni Morrison. Readers will not only gain some insight into a new people, but will also discover a storyteller who captivates an audience."

—*Baltimore Jewish Times*

"Spellbinding. . . . Marvelously compelling."

—*Publishers Weekly*

ALSO BY GINA B. NAHAI

Cry of the Peacock

Moonlight on the Avenue of Faith

Gina B. Nahai

WASHINGTON SQUARE PRESS
PUBLISHED BY POCKET BOOKS

New York   London   Toronto   Sydney   Singapore

This book is a work of fiction. Names, characters, places and incidents are products of the author's imagination or are used fictitiously. Any resemblance to actual events or locales or persons, living or dead, is entirely coincidental.

 A Washington Square Press Publication of
POCKET BOOKS, a division of Simon & Schuster Inc.
1230 Avenue of the Americas, New York, NY 10020

Copyright © 1999 by Gina Barkhordar Nahai

Published by arrangement with Harcourt Brace & Company

ISBN: 0-671-04283-1

First Washington Square Press trade paperback printing February 2000

10 9 8 7 6 5

WASHINGTON SQUARE PRESS and colophon are
registered trademarks of Simon & Schuster Inc.

Cover design by Claudine Guerguerian
Front cover photo of ocean © Jeffrey Sylvester 1990/FPG International

Printed in the U.S.A.

Alexander Shahin Nahai
Ashley Leila Nahai
Kevin Cyrus Nahai

believe in magic

Moonlight
on the
Avenue of Faith

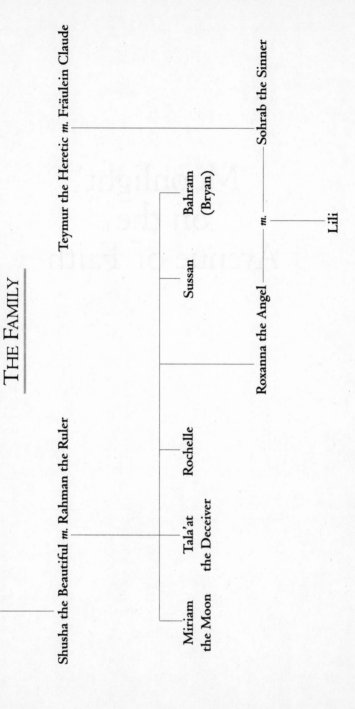

THE FAMILY

BeeBee

Shusha the Beautiful *m.* Rahman the Ruler

Teymur the Heretic *m.* Fräulein Claude

Miriam the Moon

Tala'at the Deceiver

Rochelle

Sussan

Bahram (Bryan)

Roxanna the Angel

Sohrab the Sinner

m.

Lili

Lili

AS I WATCH her now, three hundred and ninety-three pounds and gaining by the day, her frame so vast she has not been able to pull it upright in more than two months or to fit through any doorway without first having to take the door off its hinges, her breath so stormy it makes the dogs bark all the way up and down the street where she now lives with her sister in Los Angeles, and sets the piano in their neighbor's house playing mad tunes at odd hours of the night, it is impossible to believe that my mother, Roxanna the Angel, was once a young woman with watercolor eyes and translucent skin, that she could stop the world with her laughter and compel men, my father among them, to follow her across an entire city without knowing why they chased her or what they would do if ever she stopped and answered their calls, that she had been so light and delicate, so undisturbed by the rules of gravity and the drudgery of human existence, she had grown wings, one night when the darkness was the color of her dreams, and flown into the star-studded night of Iran that claimed her.

Back then, the entire city of Tehran had shaken with surprise at Roxanna's act. My father, who had loved her at the expense of all others, went into lifelong mourning and never emerged. I, who had been there, behind her, as she vanished into the sky, spent the rest of my childhood waiting for Roxanna to come back. Legends abounded about her whereabouts and fate. My friends, who suspected her dead and buried in the yard of our house on the Avenue of Faith, blamed my father and his parents for her demise. Roxanna's oldest sister, Miriam the Moon, who had raised her from childhood, made it her mission in life to find her, even against Roxanna's will.

Roxanna the Angel had kept flying, never once bothered by the pull of the earth or the sound of her loved ones calling her, never stopping to look behind at the devastation she would cause through thirteen years of absence, traveling from one city to another till she had crossed Iran and all of Turkey, living in un-marked houses and no-name streets where she was nothing more than an indigent woman with striking eyes and a languid, slowly vanishing beauty, and she would not have stopped or let any one of us find her were it not for the mysterious fluid that months ear-lier started to fill her body like a poisonous presence, that oozed out of the corners of her eyes, swelled her arms and legs till she had no more use of them and turned her once-magical voice into a gurgling whisper, and that, in the end, forced her to stop.

I was five years old when my mother left me, eighteen when she returned. My aunt Miriam the Moon tells me I must under-stand Roxanna's departure as the fulfillment of a destiny she could never control, that abandoning me was not Roxanna's idea but the result of forces that had been in motion for centuries be-fore I was born. She says that Roxanna had been a runaway be-fore she ever became a wife or a mother, before she came into existence, or was even conceived. That is how the world really functions, Miriam tells me, in the East as well as the West: Human beings are nothing more than the instruments of a callous Fate. Free will and conscious decisions are mere inventions of minds too feeble to accept the reality of our absurd existence. And so, she says, I must forgive Roxanna, forgive the fact that she left me without a word of farewell, that she heard me call her and never answered. I must forgive her because leaving me and my father was harder on her than it could ever have been on the rest of us.

And I must do this, Miriam insists, purely on faith—because even though she is back now, lying here in Miriam the Moon's spare bedroom on Veteran Avenue in west Los Angeles, even though she looks at me with her tear-filled eyes darkened with the knowledge of her own imminent death, Roxanna the Angel refuses to utter a single word of explanation to me.

Miriam the Moon tells me my mother's story.

The Ghetto
1938

SHE WAS BORN in 1938, the daughter of Shusha the Beautiful and her tailor husband, Rahman the Ruler. Her family lived in two rooms they rented from Shusha's mother—the terrible and terrifying BeeBee, who owned three houses in the Jewish ghetto of Tehran and who rented them room by room to anyone desperate enough to put up with her unreasonable demands and Draconian rules. BeeBee made no exception for her own daughter, and many were those in the ghetto who quietly whispered that she had never forgiven Shusha even a week's rent.

The rooms were unpaved and windowless, constructed of mud and clay and connected to the courtyard by a narrow wooden door made of loose planks nailed together into a lopsided, squeaky shape. The first room was where Shusha slept with her husband, and where he worked as a tailor during the day. The second room served as the family's dining and living room, and as the children's bedroom.

The children slept next to each other on the floor—five small bodies stretched out under a single comforter, limbs intertwined and skin so accustomed to the warmth of others, not one of them could have fallen asleep in a bed by themselves.

Once, when she was three years old, Roxanna awoke to a strange scent. She sat up on the sheet spread over the thin canvas rug that covered the dirt floor and that served as the only barrier between her and the insects that crawled in the dust. She was a tiny child, so thin and light her movement never disturbed anyone else. She reached over and awakened Miriam.

"I dreamt I was a bird," she said.

Miriam sighed and turned over. She was nine years old and had been caring for her younger siblings all her life.

"Does something hurt?" she asked without opening her eyes.

"No. But I can't feel my legs."

Miriam felt Roxanna's forehead.

"You're not warm," she concluded. "Go back to sleep."

An hour later, Miriam woke up scared. She saw that Roxanna was in her own place. The other children were also sleeping. But the room, she realized, smelled strange: instead of the usual scent of skin and hair, of leftover food and old clothes and dry, unforgiving earth, Miriam the Moon smelled the sea.

She lit a candle and looked around. Nothing appeared out of place. Then she saw Roxanna: her hair was wet, her arms stretched to her sides, and she was afloat in a bed of white feathers.

Roxanna looked so calm and beautiful then, so immersed in her dreams of faraway mountains and emerald seas, that Miriam thought she would die if anyone awakened her. So she lay next to her, on that bed of feathers so white they looked almost blue in the moonlight, and hoped to dream her dreams.

Miriam saw the feathers many more times, smelled the Caspian so often in their city thousands of miles away from the sea, she thought some nights Roxanna was going to drown. Afraid of what would happen if anyone discovered the feathers, Miriam hid them inside the comforter. She split the seam open with her fingers and stuffed the feathers on top of the existing fill of cotton that was yellowed with age and thinned from use. But after a while the weight of Roxanna's secret became too heavy for Miriam to bear alone. Once, when the air in their room had become so humid it had turned into beads of moisture and was dripping off the roof onto the children's faces and hair, Miriam went to call her mother.

Shusha came barefoot and sleepy, her chador wrapped loosely around her waist, and for a moment stood above Roxanna without noticing the feathers.

"Look!" Miriam grabbed a fistful and held them close to Shusha's face. "Many nights I wake up and find these in her bed."

Shusha gasped as if she had been struck by lightning. Her body shook, only once, but with enough force that Miriam had to pull away from the impact. She saw the color run out of Shusha till her skin was transparent.

"Who else knows about this?" Shusha asked.

"No one." Miriam wished she had not called her. "I've been hiding them. I'm sure no one has a clue."

Just then Tala'at, Shusha's second daughter, stirred in her sleep. She ran her hand over her neck and chest, rubbing the sweat off her skin as she whispered hoarsely to an imaginary lover. She was only eight years old and had never had any contact with men outside her immediate family. But even then she was driven by lust, by the raw, uncompromised passion that would rule her adult life.

Shusha looked away from Tala'at and went outside. She sat on the steps that led from the bedroom down into the courtyard, then signaled for Miriam to sit next to her. She was a stunning woman—dark skinned and dark eyed and so hauntingly beautiful she created a sense of confusion and sadness in anyone who saw her unveiled. But she had always seemed unaware, or perhaps ashamed, of her own beauty.

"Do you understand you can't tell anyone about the feathers?" she asked Miriam.

Miriam nodded.

"Do you know where they come from?"

Miriam began to answer, then stopped. They lived under a veil of silence then, a web of secrets spread over a thousand years, nurtured by a reverence for the power of the spoken word and a fear of its consequences. So Miriam did not speak, and Shusha did not tell Miriam what she knew so well: that the feathers in Roxanna's bed came from her dreams, that in them Roxanna was flying like a bird, or an angel, over a sea that was vast and limitless and that led her away from the tight borders of their ghetto, that the wings and the sea air spilled over the edge of the night sometimes, skipping the line between desire and truth, and poured into Roxanna's bed to speak of her longings.

IT HAD BEGUN, as tragedies often do, with a woman—the Russian wife of a Lubovicher rabbi who had come to Tehran at the end of the eighteenth century with the express purpose of educating the Jews in the ways of virtue and righteousness. To this end the rabbi had brought his wife, his four daughters, and a mule's load of books and scrolls, which he promised would serve as testimonial to his speeches and sermons. He set up a temple and pursued his mission with zeal. Before long he had managed to convince the Jews that he was the world's foremost authority on the nature of Wrong and on the manner of preventing it. Since women were most often the source of evil and the root cause of what he called "acts of moral turpitude," the rabbi had written his own bible on the proper codes of female conduct—forbidding them such luxuries as laughter, which made them light-headed, and requiring that they speak with one hand covering their mouths, so as not to tempt any man with the display of the pink and fleshy insides of their mouths.

To set an example that others would follow, the rabbi kept his own wife and daughters under the strictest watch. He wrapped them in suffocating layers of black cloth, never allowing them to talk, even in the presence of other females, never telling anyone their names. He even made the ghetto's bath-keeper open the bath two hours early every other week so that his wife and daughters were alone when they unveiled to wash themselves. The rest of the time they stayed at home, quiet and aloof and eerie in their isolation, communicating with one another through gestures for fear that someone other than the rabbi might hear their voices. To the people who came to the door or stood on the roof watching them, they looked like a tribe of deaf-mutes moving in a slow and interminable fog. Speculation ran rampant about their physical attributes, which the rabbi took such care to hide: the wife must be ugly, the Jews assumed, harelipped and pockmarked and probably even toothless. The daughters must have inherited her bad looks.

That was why the rabbi would not give them names—because he knew that an ugly woman would never get married and therefore had no business being alive. Behind the rabbi's back, the Jews called his family "the Crow and her daughters."

That is how the Crow lived for many years, and that is where her story would have ended, except that on Yom Kippur of the year 1800, she suddenly went mad. As always on that day, God had made the weather unseasonably hot—to make life more difficult for the Jews, who could not drink for close to thirty hours—and the legions of rats and scorpions that normally populated the surface of the earth had disappeared deep within its cracks in search of cold. It was almost noon, and the Lubovicher's temple was packed with worshipers repenting their sins. The men sat in the sanctuary, prayer books melting in their hands. The women stood in the courtyard outside, sweating under their veils and whispering to one another about the latest scandal in the ghetto. Then they all heard a sound and looked up.

Someone was singing. She had a soft, fluid voice, the kind of voice that drips off the lips and leaves a cool trail, that pours onto a man's body and makes his thighs burn. It was a harlot's voice, free and uninhibited, singing an old love song that only men of the lowest caste—entertainers—were allowed to sing. The women in the courtyard heard it first, then the men, and at last the rabbi. Then they all looked up, through the waves of yellow heat rising from the arid ground, and saw the Crow naked.

She was white as the river's foamy waters, blond from her head down to her feet, slender and curved and scented like every young man's dream of copulation. She walked into the temple with her eyes closed and her hands on the sides of her mouth, so that her voice would carry farther as she sang. She was followed by her four daughters, who were still veiled and who seemed entranced by her singing. The very sight of her made the rabbi turn black with rage.

Stop the Sinner! he wanted to scream, but his throat had shut down. In desperation, he watched as his wife went through the temple, circled the pulpit, then left. The women who saw her foamed at the mouth with envy, and the men memorized her every inch and passed the memory on to their offspring, and it was no wonder they all began to follow her when she walked out.

She went into the street, her daughters in tow, the congregation behind them. She went through the main square that until a moment ago had been empty but for a pack of yellow stray dogs, through the silent alleys and the stifled archways of the ghetto, past the sorry homes and the pitiful shops where her husband had forbidden laughter, until she finally reached the gates that connected the ghetto to the city of Tehran. At last she stopped singing and turned to her daughters. Her eyes were hollow, like a madwoman's, and when she smiled, her breath smelled like water.

Then she vanished into the unforgiving sun of the Day of Atonement.

Her departure, of course, would have been devastating enough to her family had it been an isolated incident that no one dared repeat. But it was especially harmful because it augured a series of escapes among the female members of every subsequent generation of the rabbi's offspring: The Crow's youngest daughter, for example, left home one morning at the age of fourteen and was never seen or heard of again. Her granddaughter ran away at the age of nine to join a band of Turkish gypsies who had camped out in the mountains outside Tehran. Other girls ran off with bandits, were abducted by nomads, sold themselves to traders of whores. One woman, Shusha's grandmother, threw herself in the Karaj River hoping it would carry her to sea. She ended up purple and bloated and rotting on the river's southern banks. Another one, Shusha's aunt, was caught by her father in midflight and brought home, where he kept her tied by the ankles to a brick column for the rest of her life.

Shusha the Beautiful was raised on stories of her wayward ancestors, many wandering naked and sorry through the deserts of central Iran, where even scorpions perished, wanting to return home and beg forgiveness but not being allowed to. As a child, she felt the humiliation of being singled out and despised, the fear of "remaining"—of becoming an old maid—and the suspicion that she, too, might someday run away because it was "in her blood." Her father died when she was two. Her mother, BeeBee, raised her in the back of the family's fruit and vegetable shop, amid rotting produce too old and rancid for the Muslims—the law stating that Jews should not have access to fresh produce. Harsh with her customers and cruel with Shusha, BeeBee thought nothing of denying a worm-ridden apple to the beggarwoman with the crippled child hanging at her breast, and taught Shusha obedience by beating her with the branch of a pomegranate tree till blood beaded on her cracked skin. To keep her from fulfilling her destiny and running away from home, BeeBee followed her own father's example and tied Shusha's ankles together when she slept.

Shusha grew up quiet and sad, so full of fear, she could hardly swallow the food her mother gave her, so convinced she would die alone and unmarried, she began to save shreds of fabric for her own shroud. It is true she did not have many suitors, her name having been soiled by the Crow's legacy, but her mother had told her early on that even if a suitor did emerge, she was not going to allow Shusha to marry.

"I am going to stop the shame," BeeBee had said. "If you marry, you will have a daughter, like I did, and she will run away, or her daughter will run away. I am going to keep you childless and, in this way, change our destiny."

At fourteen, Shusha was so beautiful BeeBee forbade her to look in a mirror, for fear she would become vain and disobedient. At sixteen, she had offers of marriage from brokers who worked for rich Muslims, searching far and wide for the most beautiful girls they could add to their harems. At eighteen, having finished her shroud and certain she would never become a mother, she cried bitter tears into a tear jar she had inherited from her runaway aunt, then drank the tears in a single gulp to mark her grief. It was the eve of the holiday of Shavuot, and BeeBee was away in Tehran looking for produce. The next day Shusha opened the shop at the usual hour—five A.M., before the man who sold drinking water had started his rounds—and spent the morning haggling with customers over the price of every vegetable. Around noon Rahman the Ruler walked in, just as Shusha was picking the bad leaves off a bunch of lettuce, and fell in love.

HE WAS AN apprentice at the house of the great tailor Alexandra the Cat—by far the most unique and enigmatic resident of the Tehran ghetto, patron of the arts and protector of no less than a hundred and twenty-one stray cats that had had the good sense to find their way into her house where they were treated with unholy care and heretical adoration. Alexandra had lived in the ghetto for eight years and still no one knew the exact truth about her past or the circumstances of her arrival. She had appeared on foot, alone and with no belongings, wearing only a satin ball gown, a fur stole, and twelve strands of pearls. Her hair, dusty and disheveled, had shown the remnants of an elaborate arrangement. Her shoes were high-heeled and narrow and so worn-out, they had melted into the soles of her feet.

She told the Jews she had come from Moscow, from the court of Czar Nicholas II, where she was married to his greatest general. One night, as she and her husband were leaving for the opera, the Bolsheviks had attacked her house. Her husband had been killed on the spot. Alexandra had grabbed her stole, into which she had already sewn all her jewels, and saved herself. Alone on the street, she had decided, with the courage that only madmen and children are capable of, that she was going to leave Russia. She had kept walking, through her own wealthy neighborhood and into the slums of Moscow, past soldiers and tanks and bloody, frozen corpses, in her satin dress with twelve strands of pearls around her neck, and every time her heels had hit the ground, she had thought that a hand was going to reach from behind and grab her.

But no one had stopped her, she said, and in time, she reached Tehran.

Forever skeptical of foreigners, especially of non-Jews and women, the people of the ghetto had remarked that Alexandra could not have escaped Russia undetected, that she could not have traveled thousands of miles in her high heels and her ball gown, that, at any rate, though she did have blue eyes and a Russian accent, she spoke Farsi far too fluently for someone who had just arrived in the country.

And yet her very boldness and the fact that she seemed to have access to large sums of money convinced the Jews to allow her among themselves. She bought a house, paid for it in gold coins, and announced she was going to occupy all seven rooms and the courtyard by herself. She furnished the house with strange and awkward objects: tables and chairs and a monstrous creature she called a "divan"—which in Farsi means "ghouls"—with a golden frame and a wine-colored velvet cover. She cut windows into the walls, installed glass so anyone could look right into her rooms, hung drapes the color of ripe pomegranates, with dark blue tassels and golden ropes. Then she hired a dozen men to drag an enormous animal with shiny wooden skin and bare teeth into her house. People lined up for three blocks to watch the spectacle.

She put the animal in her "drawing room" overlooking the street, unharnessed and cleaned it, then sat on a chair and put her fingers on its teeth. The beast let out a not altogether unpleasant racket.

"It's a piano!" She named her pet for the Jews. "My mother trained me as a concert pianist."

That is when the first rumors began to circulate that Alexandra the Cat was being supported by a male "benefactor": the workers who had helped the piano into her house later told the Jews that it was an antique purchased in Europe by an Assyrian merchant who had wished to remain anonymous. Confronted with the rumor, Alexandra held herself above the petty gossip and repeated, in ever more flowery detail, the original story of her escape from Russia. Then she settled in and hired Rahman.

Rahman the Ruler had worked for Alexandra seven years already, running errands and cleaning house, cooking her meals and helping her cut and sew the many ball gowns she insisted on wearing amid the dust and the poverty of the ghetto. Every morning, he walked to BeeBee's shop to buy vegetables for the day's meal. He had watched Shusha grow up but had never noticed her—because he was only two years older than she and himself an orphan and, for a long time, women had not featured paramount in his consciousness. Then all of a sudden one day, he saw her and felt his tongue grow heavy and dry, his hands become ice cold, and he became so confused, he left the shop without buying anything at all. All the way home, he kept thinking about Shusha, the way she had looked at him, the way her eyes had reflected every shade of light, and he was so immersed in this new sensation, he forgot to cook Alexandra's lunch.

For two weeks, he went to the shop every day, stood in a corner and stared at Shusha, then went home without a purchase. One night, as Alexandra sat down to dinner, he cleared his throat and asked if she knew BeeBee who sold vegetables.

Alexandra turned towards him with her rouged and powdered face, clearly annoyed at his impudence, and she was about to remind him that servants did not ask personal questions of their masters when she saw that Rahman had turned pale and was terribly nervous. She understood that he had something important on his mind. So she raised a painted eyebrow into a perfect arch above her lined eye, examined Rahman, and realized his predicament.

"So that's what it is." She smiled. "You've seen the vegetable seller's daughter."

Alexandra waited till Rahman had poured her wine, served the soup she had taught him to prepare, and withdrawn to stand in the back of the room—directly behind her, so he could anticipate her every need without intruding upon her privacy. Then she said, as casually as if she were commenting on the soup, "Go over to the shop and invite them to tea. Then I'll see if we can arrange some sort of an introduction in this savage and degrading tradition of courtship you people practice."

The next day, Alexandra wrote an invitation for BeeBee and sent Rahman to deliver it in person. He stood in the shop before the old woman, shivering with nerves, and because he could not read, he paraphrased Alexandra's words: "Come over to my house this afternoon," he said. "Have tea. Become acquainted."

At six feet three inches, BeeBee towered over Rahman even as she sat, and she filled the space inside the shop till he felt there was not enough air for both of them to breathe. As always, she was dressed in black taffeta, her face covered with a rough veil, her eyes shining through the fabric with all the intensity and forcefulness of a woman bent on avenging herself against the world. She took an eternity to answer.

"I don't like tea," she said. "And I don't need acquaintances."

Alexandra was insulted by the rejection. Ordinarily, she would have retaliated by ignoring BeeBee for the rest of her life. But she took one look at Rahman's dejected face that day, and decided to sacrifice her own pride for the sake of the boy's emotional health. She sent him back to BeeBee with another invitation.

"Come for a glass of wine, then," he paraphrased again. "There is a matter of importance we need to discuss."

"Only men and whores drink wine!" BeeBee responded.

Alexandra the Cat sighed with rage and decided to teach BeeBee a lesson. She went into her room and changed into a gown of lavender velvet, with three skirts and a short vest. She put on her silk shoes of matching color, and a necklace of purple crystal. She picked a purple lace parasol, dabbed herself with the essence of purple hyacinth.

"Let's go," she told Rahman, parting a way amid the swarm

of cats that snuggled around her shoes and rubbed themselves against her feet. "I'm going to have a word with that seller of rotten vegetables."

They found BeeBee smoking a water pipe in the back of her shop.

"This young man works for me," Alexandra said in her heavy Russian accent, looking down at BeeBee from above her exposed, corseted breasts. In the back corner of the shop, Shusha stood listening. "We are here because he has intentions towards your daughter, and has asked me to represent him."

The look BeeBee gave her made the vegetables wilt in their open boxes.

"Go away."

Alexandra breathed in so deeply, the crystals sang around her neck.

"There, now." She exhaled. "You have been made aware. Perhaps in the future you will be astute enough to recognize when luck calls upon you."

She marched out, swearing never to return.

When the Cat was gone, BeeBee reached over and slapped Shusha across the face. She sent her home to make dinner, told her that she must never wait on Rahman again, that she was not going to get married to him or to any other man, and might as well not tempt them with her eyes.

BeeBee kept the shop open till midnight, then carried a watermelon home to eat after dinner. The moment she cut open the watermelon, her room filled with the smell of purple hyacinths. She remembered the Russian pianist in her velvet gown.

She had to sleep in the courtyard that night—to escape the smell of Alexandra's perfume—and woke up the next morning with a headache. All day long in the shop, her customers complained that the produce smelled "like that crazy pianist with the cats." She closed early to go to the bath and wash Alexandra's perfume off her skin, but when she got home, the neighbors screamed that she had spoiled their dinner and made their children sick with the hyacinth she kept in her room.

BeeBee was forty-seven years old and a widow for sixteen years. She feared neither God nor the Devil nor even the Deevs of old Iranian mythology. But she did believe in the power of Destiny, and she understood that the pervading scent of hyacinths and the inescapable memory of Alexandra the Cat were a sign from above that marrying Rahman was Shusha's fate. So she left home without telling Shusha and walked straight to the Cat's.

"No wedding," she said the moment Rahman opened the door. "I will give no dowry and expect no milk-money. You can take her away Thursday night. I will not be there."

That is how Shusha the Beautiful married Rahman and went to live with him in the house of the Cat. Recognizing that he could not support a family on his butler's income, Alexandra set Rahman up as a tailor, and released him from her own service. Rahman and Shusha moved into two rooms they rented from BeeBee. Every other year, Shusha became pregnant with another child. Her mother never came to see her or the children, but she did send word every time a girl was born that Shusha must be careful, because sooner or later one of those daughters was going to shame her mother. And then, as if to please the gods of BeeBee's Destiny, Roxanna was born.

THE SUMMER of 1938 was unusually hot and dry. Dust blew over the ghetto from the surrounding desert and lined everything—even children's eyelashes and the blackened palates of old women—with a thin, gritty film. People woke up impatient and thirsty. Animals became restless and took to the streets. Men with golden suits of armor and sparkling silver swords rode their horses out of the folds of ancient fairy tales and into the back alleys of a ghetto forever longing for salvation.

Shusha was pregnant for the fourth time in eight years. She had become distant and distracted, uninterested in her children and in the daily routine of life. She sat in the courtyard all morning, till the neighbors thought she was going to get sunstroke and forced her into a room. Then she lay about, unaware of her children who moved around her, never lifting a hand to feed or wash them. Alarmed by his wife's behavior, Rahman the Ruler consulted the ghetto's best midwife, Zivar, who told him that Shusha was suffering from temporary senility brought on by her pregnancy.

"This happens when the infant's blood is hostile to its mother's," Zivar explained. "You will see what I mean when the baby is born. Your wife and this baby will never understand each other."

Every day, Shusha became more quiet and distracted. In her sixth month, she went seven days without talking to anyone. Panicked, Rahman called a leecher, who stripped Shusha naked from the shoulders down and applied four black leeches to her back. Shusha lay under the leeches aloof and undisturbed, obviously not feeling the pain of her pierced flesh, and when the leeches were removed, she sat up and dressed herself.

"I have been thinking of the sea," she told Rahman.

Rahman had never been to the sea. He knew of its existence only from the tales he had heard from Alexandra the Cat, who claimed she had once traversed it with her husband on a ship belonging to the czar of Russia. To him, the sea represented a world he feared would claim his wife.

"I have asked Alexandra the Cat," he lied to Shusha. "She told me there is no such thing as the sea. The sea is a lie gypsies tell children to lure them away."

Shusha looked at him in disdain.

"Tell Alexandra she is wrong," she said. "There is a sea to our north, and another to our south. In between, the earth is red and gold and magnificent."

She carried on in this way for another two months, and even the most optimistic observers gave up hope that she would ever return to normalcy. One morning in her eighth month, she woke up and called Miriam.

"Go to the butcher and buy me sheep's feet," she ordered. "And tell your father to fetch the midwife, because I am going into labor."

At seven o'clock in the morning, when Rahman stepped out of the house to fetch Zivar, he felt his skin blister in the sun. The heat had made a graveyard of the normally crowded ghetto streets, and for a moment, Rahman thought that the mullahs must have issued an order for a massacre and that all the Jews must be hiding in their basements.

He found Zivar the midwife sitting backwards on her midget mule, inside her room near the ghetto's seventh gate, applying mustard seeds and egg yolks to her swollen legs as she prayed for rain. She had been born with unusually short legs that made it impossible to walk more than a few steps at a time, and her very immobility had made her wide and heavy and shaped like a perfect square. To help her get around in her youth, her father had strapped Zivar onto the back of a young mule and trained the animal so it would move inside the house without trampling or breaking anything. The mule had become Zivar's most constant companion, so much a part of her that for decades now, she had not bothered to get off the animal except to use the toilet. She even took her meals on the mule, slept on its back with her eyes half-open and her head erect. Over time, her skin had turned the color of his coat and her voice had become hoarse like his, and she looked as if she were born half woman, half mule.

The beast, in turn, had proven his love for Zivar by not growing beyond the confines of her tiny home, and by staying alive long past its natural life span: Zivar the Midwife was sixty-eight years old the day Rahman knocked on her door, and she swore the mule was at least as old.

He told her Shusha was going into labor.

"We must stop it at any cost." Zivar abandoned her mustard pack and nudged her mule so he would get up on his legs. She had delivered more babies in her time than any midwife in the history of the ghetto, and she knew, as certainly as if it were written in the Torah, that any child who was born in the eighth month of a pregnancy would be deformed and retarded.

"The seventh month is all right," she explained to Rahman, her face shiny with perspiration, her mule dripping sweat into a puddle on the ground. "In the seventh month every baby is fully shaped. But in the eighth month it takes itself apart, moving limbs and organs around so that nothing is where it's supposed to be anymore. Then again, at the beginning of the ninth month, things move back till they're in the right place in time for birth."

The moment they arrived at Rahman's house, Miriam ran to them.

"Mother is sleeping," she reported eagerly. "I made her soup with the sheep's feet, to lubricate her uterus in case the baby starts coming, but I put her legs up and told her she must wait till the midwife gets here."

Zivar's mule did not need anyone to show him the way to Shusha's room. He went straight in and knelt beside the bed.

Zivar pushed up her sleeve, washed her gnarled and spotty hand in a bowl of water offered by Miriam, and felt inside Shusha's womb for the baby's head.

"False alarm." She pulled her hand out and washed it in the tub again. The mule got up and ambled back towards the courtyard. "This heat is playing tricks on people's minds."

All day long, the heat remained unbearable.

But late that night, a breeze blew across the ghetto, bringing the smell of moist air and cool waters, forcing fog—thick and white and impossible to see through—to rise from the torrid earth and travel into the houses full of sorrow where women, overcome by waves of desire, turned to their men in their sleep. At dawn, when the mist cleared, the sun rose over Tehran, but did not illuminate the ghetto within it: the ghetto remained still and quiet under a blue-gray sky—like the beach after a biblical flood—emitting a smell of fish so strong, it traveled all over the city and attracted the Muslims, who turned around at noon, when the heat was blinding, and discovered the patch of dawn that still lingered over the Jews.

Convinced as always that the "unbelievers" had practiced witchcraft to influence the heavens and the earth, the Muslims flocked towards the ghetto but stayed just outside its seven gates for fear of the sorcery that might entrap them if they stepped onto unholy ground. They remained there the entire day, while the Jews dreamt of the waters of the Caspian and the colors of eternal desire, and among them only Shusha lay awake, holding her newborn infant girl.

The sun came up at seven in the evening, and from that day on, the order of day and night changed forever in the Tehran ghetto.

EVEN BEFORE BeeBee had set out towards Shusha's house—black taffeta hissing around her ankles, crystal worry beads ticking in her hand, walking stick beating against the ground like the heart of a black ghoul—even before BeeBee had ever crossed the threshold of Shusha's room that night when the ghetto was surrounded by a sea of bewildered Muslims and the sun was rising fourteen hours late, everyone who had ever known the old woman swore she was going to declare Roxanna a bad-luck child.

They knew it with such certainty they did not need to examine BeeBee's reasons or wait for the evidence she might offer. It was one of those realities—like the existence of God, like the inferiority of women, like the fact that Alexandra the Cat had, since her arrival in the ghetto, been sleeping with an Assyrian phantom who paid all her expenses—one of those truths that did not need to be proven in order to exist: Roxanna had driven her mother mad during the pregnancy, been born under singular circumstances, and already had caused a near-pogrom in the ghetto. Of course she was bad luck. Of course BeeBee would say so.

She arrived at the house just as Rahman was pulling on his trousers, muttering to Shusha how he must have died and been resurrected—how else could he have slept through her entire labor?—and Tala'at the Deceiver was trying to force herself back to sleep, where for twenty-four hours she had been making love to a man with golden skin and purple eyes. Then the door burst open with the force of an apocalypse, and BeeBee appeared.

She was so enormous, she had to double over and squeeze sideways into the room.

She came up to Shusha and took the baby from her hands. Wrapped in old rags, Roxanna was small and pale, her lips round and pink, her eyes open and focused. They looked straight at BeeBee and made her shiver. She gave Roxanna back to her mother.

"This is the bad-luck one," she said. "Give her away if you can. Or else, kill her yourself."

ALEXANDRA THE CAT sent for Rahman on urgent business. During the years since he had married and left her service, she had fired servants faster than she hired them, never trusted anyone the way she had Rahman, and complained of a disease she called "ennui"—anguish, she explained to her illiterate neighbors, impatient of living among a people who neither understood nor appreciated her. She had spent most of her time alone, dressing up in ball gowns and playing the piano every afternoon, expanding her colony of felines and designing ever more elaborate and aesthetically appalling decorations for her house. For a while in the summer and fall of 1938, she had closed her doors and locked herself in without being seen even once. She had emerged again in the early months of winter, having lost her narrow waistline and her impeccable appearance, and started to buy enormous amounts of food and basic living supplies. She had stocked her house full of coal and sugar and oil, smoked fish and dried fruits and rice, and when she had filled every room and even the basement, she finally stopped and called for Rahman.

"A war is coming towards us," she warned him that day, sitting on her divan. Instead of her usual satin and velvet gowns, she wore a plain cotton dress that reached down only to her calves, and she had let her hair—white and yellow and dried out from years of being strangled into curls—down over her shoulders. Rahman had the feeling she was biting down on her lip to keep a secret from slipping out.

"I dream about the fires of Moscow every night," she told him with the look of a suffering animal ashamed of its own pain. "I see my husband's blood spilling onto the walls. We should all prepare for disaster."

He remained before her with his head bowed, his right hand gripping the left, and waited. For a while, it seemed as if she had said her piece, and she even looked at him with the impatience she had showed in the past when he had outstayed his welcome in her presence. Then suddenly she remembered why she had called him.

"About your child," she said, excited by her own powers of recollection, "the girl who was born last year, who brought all the rotting fish to the streets. I hear she has strange eyes."

She was looking straight at Rahman, but he, like a well-trained servant, was not looking up.

"Look at me," she commanded, full of disdain. "Over here." He raised his eyes to her.

"I've heard rumors about that girl," she said. "Terrible rumors. I wanted to tell you, you must watch out for her."

He did not seem to understand. She slammed her hand down on the arm of her divan and leaned towards him as if to drill the words into his skull.

"I hear your wife is going to kill that child."

The war did start in 1939, and by the time it reached the Soviet Union, it had caused widespread panic in Iran. Rahman's already scant business dried up, food became more scarce than ever, and for two years, the Jews did nothing but listen to the sound of the Nazis marching south from Russia towards them: Reza Shah, who was king at the time, favored Hitler over the Allies and allowed German spies into Iran. Ignoring repeated warnings from the British, he refused the Allies access through Iran to supply much-needed war materials to the Soviet Union. In 1941, the Allies invaded Iran.

They came at night, sinking Iran's few gunboats, flying uncontested over her skies, and in a matter of hours, they had occupied the entire country. They took over the fields and the factories, diverted all the food towards their own troops, shut down trade and commerce and travel. By Yom Kippur the following month, when they went to temple to repent for their sins, the Jews were thanking God for the Allies—who had saved them from Hitler—and praying that He now protect them from famine.

Roxanna was four years old that day, and despondent. Her parents had gone to temple and left her with Miriam. Everyone had to fast—even Shusha who was nursing a new baby, even Roxanna who did not understand why she could not eat or drink. As the day became warmer and her tongue began to burn in her mouth, she kept asking Miriam for water. In vain, Miriam explained to her the exigencies of being a Jew, and told her she had to wait till at least noon to drink. Roxanna stood by the door, waiting for the man who sold drinking water in a barrel strapped to his back. When he didn't materialize, she went into the street and sat by the dry gutter, waiting. Then she remembered the neighbor's house where there was a water storage tank, and went to look for it.

No one heard her fall in. Minutes later, Miriam looked around the house and realized that Roxanna was missing. By the time she found Roxanna floating in the neighbor's tank, a good twenty minutes had passed, and it was certain the child had drowned.

They dragged her out of the water all bloated up, and gathered around her to stare: Her skin was a diaphanous blue, her fingernails had turned purple, and an entire colony of white water-worms was crawling out of her hair and onto the ground around her. Then she sighed, like an angel coming to life, and burped a stream of clear, cool water that sprang out of her mouth and splattered everyone's shoes. Her eyes, when she opened them, were fluorescent.

"Mother said I should drink," she said to Miriam.

IN 1943, smallpox came to Tehran. The husband of Sun the Chicken Lady was the first victim, but he died so fast no one could know for sure what had killed him. In three days he got the fever, the boils, and the death shivers. On the fourth morning, his wife came into the room and found that he was already stiff. She went out into the yard, where they raised chickens and roosters for sale to the kosher butcher, and saw that all of their animals were also dead or dying. She tried to warn people of the danger of a communicable disease, but no one paid attention to her. Sun the Chicken Lady had been one of the first to take advantage of the new law allowing Jews to live outside the ghetto. She lived in a barn in the northern hills surrounding Tehran, in an area so remote no one thought her husband could have passed his illness to others.

But a few days after the husband's burial, the doctor who worked in the army hospital fell ill with the same symptoms Sun had described, and then the sixteen-year-old bride of Rahman's only remaining customer got the boils. Suddenly, an epidemic was running loose in the ghetto.

Roxanna was five years old. She heard her parents talk of the latest victims, of hospitals being filled over capacity and turning patients away, of doctors and nurses treating the sick till they themselves fell ill. She became aware of the threat of the disease, its smell warm and hideous, like the breath of a terrible beast. She saw the bodies, naked and pale, wrapped in cheap canvas shrouds and strapped onto the backs of mournful relatives who carried them to the Jews' cemetery. After a while, she thought she could smell the illness in her own house.

"It smells like that disease in here," she confided to Miriam, who admonished her for her foolishness.

"Smallpox does not have a smell," Miriam retorted. "I heard it comes from the water."

Even so, Roxanna insisted she could see the fever in various parts of the house, pointed to the spots where she said the smell was strongest. In the spring of 1944, Rahman fell ill.

Shusha took him to the Savior's Hospital, then came home and, following instructions from his doctors, burned all his clothes. The children gathered in the courtyard and watched as their father's belongings went up in flames. The neighbors whispered that Shusha had gone mad, that she was practicing a sort of witchcraft, that contracting smallpox was an act of God and could not be stopped if a person burned herself out of house and home.

They must have been right, because that same night, Shusha's only son fell ill, and in the morning, Sussan got the fever. Certain she was going to lose everyone unless she acted fast, Shusha gathered up her nerve and sent for the one person in this world she thought might scare even Death away.

BeeBee walked through the front door in her stiff taffeta skirt and threw only a sideways glance at Roxanna.

"It's *her* fault," she declared without formality. "*She* brought that disease in here."

It was true, Shusha admitted to herself in despair: Roxanna had summoned the disease by talking about it. Maybe she had wished it on her family members. Maybe she had picked it up in her sleep, on those nights when she flew unrestricted into strange lands Shusha had never even heard of, and brought it back to give to others.

"You'll have nothing but bad luck as long as *she's* around," BeeBee predicted, and went to work.

She nailed all the doors shut and ordered the healthy children to stay away from the sick. She put the stricken children in a room and locked herself in with them. Because a shortage of medication made obtaining a vaccine or an antidote for smallpox impossible, she nursed the sick only with medicinal herbs and daily leeching. To cast Roxanna's evil luck off of Shusha's house, she lit a brazier full of coal, wrote Roxanna's name on a raw egg, and placed the egg on the coal, hoping it would burst. She burned wild rue seeds till they created a thick, odorous smoke, then forced the smoke into Roxanna's face till the child's eyes teared and she gagged. She took salt in her fist, circled her hand around Sussan's and Bahram's heads, then threw the salt at Roxanna.

For her part, Shusha prayed and cried and even undertook the making of almond tears—a long and laborious process designed to procure miracles when all else had failed. A week passed. On the eighth day, BeeBee emerged from the sickroom looking tired but victorious, and announced that the sick would survive.

"Go to Sun the Chicken Lady's house and buy a rooster to sacrifice," she ordered Shusha. "Take that evil child with you and make sure she watches the blood being shed. Then bottle up the blood and bring it back, with a prayer the Chicken Lady will write for you. We will hang the bottle outside the children's rooms."

Shusha stood pale and despondent before her mother. Her eyes were locked into BeeBee's, her lips moving as if in confession of a crime she had not yet committed. She was already planning to kill her own child.

They walked to the edge of the ghetto, then hired a horse-drawn wagon that took them all the way to Sun's barn. Shusha had wanted to take only Roxanna along, but Miriam had insisted that she and Tala'at accompany them. Now they saw Sun's house from far away—a shack in the middle of a dirt road, disfigured by a single room that had been added to one side of its roof and from which a lone figure now waved at them. As they approached, the figure vanished from the window and burst out minutes later through the front door: She was short and thin, dressed in a man's white shirt with the sleeves rolled up. Western-style trousers were tied around her waist with the help of an ordinary rope. On her head she wore a military hard hat that she had bought from an Allied soldier and decorated with paper flowers around the rim.

"Come in, come in." Sun beckoned everyone with pride. There were a few chickens in the yard. The ground was covered with a two-inch layer of feathers mixed with dried bird droppings. Sun led Shusha up to the barn, then started to climb the ladder that ran along the outside wall. She climbed to the roof of the barn, then up to the room she had built above it, and finally onto the roof of the added room. She stood on top like a straw puppet in boy's clothing and motioned to Shusha and the children:

"Come on," she yelled. "The view up here will make you crazy."

She saw that the children were afraid to climb the ladder.

"Come on." She laughed. "It's only scary if you look down."

The roof was flat, three stories above ground level, furnished with a straw mat and wide pillows, a brazier, a water pipe, and a coal samovar. Sitting cross-legged next to the samovar, Sun smiled at the children with her toothless mouth, and poured black tea into finger-long glasses. She asked about Rahman and BeeBee, gave her best advice on caring for the sick children. As the evening wore on and the sun began to set, she drank glass after glass of steaming black tea, and settled into her own life story.

Her parents had raised chickens all their lives. Her husband had met her when she was only thirteen, and married her in spite of his parents' objections. His father had disowned him. His mother came to the wedding wearing a black veil, and carried a bundle of ashes, which she kept pouring on her hair as indication of her grief.

Sun the Chicken Lady had borne five sons, each one healthier and smarter than the last. She had sent them all to the ghetto school, then to high school in Tehran, where they won scholarships to study in France. Now they were all doctors, too busy and important to come back to the ghetto.

She talked through the evening and into the night, her voice sweet and girlish, her mood light and playful, as if in celebration of Shusha's company. Watching her talk as the sky grew darker, Roxanna lay on her stomach next to Miriam, and slowly fell asleep.

A hand pulled Roxanna to her feet. She opened her eyes and saw that the other children were already descending the ladder. Sun was still talking, bouncing around as she gathered her rug and put out the fire in the brazier, telling Shusha they should stay the night, really, that traveling in the dark, even now that Reza Shah had installed military rule in the country, was too dangerous an undertaking for a Jewish woman with three daughters.

"Over here." Shusha pulled Roxanna's hand. "Let's go down."

It never occurred to Roxanna that she should escape.

Years later, as she recounted the events of that evening, Miriam the Moon would feel an ancient sense of dread, and tremble with the force of relived emotion: the sky was crowded with stars, the moon like a mirror over the earth. Against it, Roxanna was pale and small, her eyes half closed, her hair falling around her face in loose curls. In her old dress of faded blue cotton and her hand-me-down shoes that were two sizes too big, she looked like an aberration of nature—an angel, Miriam thought, that had fallen from the sky and landed on Sun's roof.

Just then something stirred. There was a breeze, like the breath of a Deev, or a jinn—one of the many who inhabit the night—rolling over in his sleep and upsetting the balance between dreams and reality. In one instant, the chickens in the yard began to scream and bat their wings, and a flock of pigeons appeared in the sky like a gray cloud, shedding their feathers and blocking out the moon. Shusha pushed Roxanna off the roof.

"Stop!" Miriam screamed, but it was too late.

Roxanna fell backwards into the night, descending slowly, her arms outstretched and her legs loose—like a swimmer floating on water. She sank silently, losing her shoes, her eyes open but not frightened. Just as she was about to hit the ground, she began to move her arms, up and down, like a bird that was flying for the first time—finding its balance, tasting the air, loving its freedom. Then she moved with more certainty and rose higher, backwards and up over the wall of Sun's yard, away from Shusha's shadow and the touch of her murderous hands, away from Tehran and its fears, towards the snow-covered summits of the Elburz Mountains and beyond them, to the everlasting waters of the Caspian Sea.

AFTERWARDS, everyone's recollection of what they had witnessed that night would be different. Miriam the Moon claimed that Roxanna had grown wings—swan's wings with silver and white feathers—and had flown north until she became a white spot on the horizon and vanished. Her story was confirmed by Tala'at, and by some neighbors down the road who had been awakened by the sound of frightened doves and seen a girl with white feathers fly over their roof. Sun the Chicken Lady did not recall having seen any wings. She said that Roxanna had flown like a ghost—one-dimensional and using only her arms to keep her airborne—and that she had been awake and alert and conscious of what she was doing all along. Sun's version of the story especially frightened Shusha; she was not sure Sun was wrong. But Shusha insisted that Roxanna had simply been carried off by a strong current of air formed by the sudden and massive flight of doves.

Yet even Shusha could not deny that Roxanna had disappeared for five hours that night, and that when she finally did come back, it had been to a place of her own choosing: the steps outside the Savior's Hospital, where she had gone to look for her father. Roxanna was barefoot and frightened, her dress torn into shreds and covered with leaves, her face smeared with dust. Her pupils were so enlarged, she looked like a sleepwalker suddenly brought into light.

The nurses told her that they did not allow visitors, because of the risk of contagion, and that at any rate, a child of her age had no business being out in the city alone at that time of morning. Roxanna stood on the landing outside the main entrance, argued and screamed and pushed her way into the lobby till the head nurse had to grab her from the back and hold her down. Roxanna bit the woman's forearm through to the bone, and freed herself. She ran up the stairs, a host of guards and nurses behind her, and by the time they caught up with her on the second floor, she had already screamed Rahman's name many times and sent the other patients into frenzied fits of fear.

The military police who guarded the city were called in to help. They came on foot—their cars having run out of gas days earlier. They wore faded uniforms that hung loose on their emaciated frames and brandished outdated weapons they did not know how to use. After much struggle, they managed to calm Roxanna and carry her home. By then Shusha and the children had also returned, exhausted from their futile search for Roxanna up and down the dirt roads and the barren hills surrounding Sun's barn.

When she saw Shusha, Roxanna ran to her instinctively to seek solace. Then suddenly she stopped and pulled back. For a moment she remained stunned. Her lips turned white. Then she dropped her head.

"I know what you did," she whispered.

From that day on, Roxanna, who had been entirely tame all her life, became possessed with a thousand demons. Perhaps she had stared Jebreel, the Angel of Death, in the face and could not forget him. Perhaps her brain had been jolted as a result of her fall. Or maybe she could not live with the knowledge that her own mother, who seemed to love her, had tried to kill her. Whatever the cause, Roxanna became so restless after her flight, she could not sit in the same place for more than a moment at a time, so driven by the need to guard herself against real and imaginary dangers, she barely slept anymore.

At home, she disobeyed Miriam and Shusha, hit back when they tried to beat her, ran away when they tried to lock her up. She returned hours later, bloody and disheveled, her shoes completely wet, her clothes torn to pieces, so ready for a fight no one dared challenge her. When Rahman came home from the hospital, she calmed down temporarily. The fear that had gripped her the moment she had realized that Shusha had pushed her—not just from the roof that night but also earlier, that Yom Kippur, into the well in their neighbor's house when Roxanna was thirsty—that fear subsided when Rahman came home, but not for long. Roxanna knew that Shusha feared her, that she cried secretly and whispered to Rahman, "Give her away. I'm afraid of her." She saw this, and her own doubt—that she was indeed evil—drove her mad.

Two years passed. The war ended, but the Allies continued to occupy Iran. Rahman was destitute. His children were hungry. His wife lived in constant fear of the ruination that Roxanna was going to bring upon them. Rahman himself dreaded Shusha's next attack on Roxanna.

And so it was not altogether unexpected, the year Roxanna turned eight, that her father would decide to save his family and Roxanna's life at once—that he would find a taker for Roxanna, wrap her up like a bad gift, and give her away.

ALEXANDRA THE CAT summoned Rahman to her house and told him she was looking for a servant again. She had tried three dozen butlers in the last twelve years. This time, she said, she wanted to hire a woman.

"Men are dense and slow and naturally reluctant," she told Rahman. "Go to the village of Sabzevar, and buy me a nice young girl I can educate in my service."

Alexandra was not asking Rahman for anything unusual. Peasants had always sold their children into labor at the homes of wealthy townspeople. Alexandra was prepared to offer a more-than-generous fee for a girl with natural intelligence. But in her request, Rahman recognized an opportunity he dared not squander. Instead of a peasant girl, he asked the Cat hesitantly, might she consider hiring one of his daughters?

"You can keep her as long you want," he said, without disclosing which child he had in mind, "and you don't have to pay me a dime. All I ask is that you allow her to go to school a few hours a day."

It was twelve noon, and Alexandra was having breakfast in the courtyard of her house, under an umbrella she had erected for the sole purpose of shielding her delicate skin from the ravages of the sun. She was dressed in one of her ball gowns again, having lost the excess weight from around her waist and hips, and she had curled her hair into a cone-shaped production that rose twenty inches above her head and stayed in place with the aid of a hundred pins and a gallon of English beer she had bought on the black market to wash her hair with. As always, she had set the table with starched linen and expensive china, and had laid her opera glasses next to her plate. She picked up the glasses now and used them to examine Rahman.

"I want a girl I can keep for life," she challenged through stiff lips. Her eyesight, never perfect, had been steadily worsening since the Occupation, and now she needed the opera glasses just to see more than a hazy outline of any object. But she was too proud to admit she needed glasses, and she still carried herself with her usual confidence, so that even Rahman, who had seen her in better days, did not discern her near-blindness.

"You can have her for life," he said, suddenly turning red with shame and dropping his eyes to the tips of his shoes.

Alexandra put the glasses down and released Rahman back into the white cloud that had recently surrounded her. She thought of how comforting it was not to have to see anything she did not want to see. She sipped her coffee, moved her chair back a bit under the umbrella.

"You're giving me the one they say is a bad seed," she declared.

His head was still bowed.

"I heard your wife pushed her off the roof to kill her."

He would not look up at her.

"You should have known better. I warned you."

It disgusted her that Rahman had not protested, that he had stood by and let such horror take place.

"Shame on you," she declared, and Rahman bristled.

Alexandra had had enough.

"Fine." She stood up. "Bring me the girl and I'll have a look."

Thursday afternoon, Rahman took Roxanna to the bazaar and bought her a new chador, a loaf of sweet bread, and her first pair of new shoes. He told her that she should not wear the shoes on the street, where they would become dusty and scratched, but that she should carry them in her hands and put them on when she arrived at her destination.

Beside herself with joy, Roxanna did not know what she had done to deserve her father's kindness, but as she walked out of the bazaar with Rahman that day, she resolved to redress all the wrongs she had ever committed and to make herself worthy of the gift she had received.

Instead of their own house, Rahman took her to the Cat's.

Alexandra was sitting at her piano when they came in. She looked up and saw two silhouettes, one taller than the other, and realized Rahman had brought his daughter. Fumbling on the piano for her glasses, she remembered she had left them in her bedroom. So she peered at Roxanna with all the strength in her cataract-ridden eyes, and that was the beginning of her troubles, because instead of the child with the brown ringlets and the transparent skin smiling at her through the fog, Alexandra saw herself.

She had been born in the town of Orumiyeh on the Russian-Iranian border. Her mother, blind since birth, had been a piano teacher. She had gone around with a strip of white lace covering her eyes, tiny cowbells ringing around her ankles to announce to anyone on her path that she could not see. She had never been married to Alexandra's father, had no other relatives or friends. Forever fearful that she would not receive a decent burial, she had spent her youth saving up for the moment of her death. She denied herself and Alexandra the most basic of comforts, saved every penny and hid the money in the piano for her funeral.

Alexandra the Cat was twenty-two years old when her mother died. All she had ever wanted in life was to leave Orumiyeh and marry a rich man. Now she was faced with the choice of burying her mother the way she had willed, or leaving her and using the money to escape Orumiyeh. She left the corpse exposed and unburied in the house.

She ran away in the night, thinking that she would forget the old woman soon enough, that she must not waste money on the dead when it was so badly needed by the living. She told herself that she would go back, once she had met a rich man and married. She would find her mother's corpse and give it the kind of burial she had wanted.

In Moscow, Alexandra married a general in the czar's army. He died not at the hands of the Bolsheviks, as she would later claim, but in a fight over a gambling debt. Alexandra was alone again, and again she was forced to save herself.

She met another man—an Assyrian merchant with a small imagination and a rich wife. The wife, of course, realized that all men have biological urges which make monogamy impossible. But she was rich, and rich women do not care about biology as poor ones do. This meant that the Assyrian, who did not wish to incite his wife's wrath and thereby lose access to her money, had to keep his affair with Alexandra secret.

He brought her to live in the Jews' ghetto. It was far enough from the Assyrian neighborhoods that he figured his wife would never get wind of their affair. He counted on a short-lived affair with Alexandra, betting he could walk away the moment he sensed danger or she became too old. But Alexandra charmed him with her European sophistication and her opera singer's makeup, lured him into her cocoon of fantastical stories and unreal habits till he could not find the way out. Every night when the ghetto slept, he crept through the alleys into the house, and made love to her till dawn. No one saw him, not even Rahman in the seven years he worked for her, not even Shusha in the short while she lived with the Cat before they moved out on their own. The whole thing would have turned out fine, really, except for a small indiscretion that led to the birth of a green-eyed monster with yellow hair and no heart.

The year before the war, Alexandra became pregnant from the Assyrian phantom. When she told him, he suggested she throw herself down a steep set of stairs and kill the fetus, but Alexandra refused. So he told her to lock herself up in the house—to hide her pregnancy. When she had delivered her own baby, he took it away to raise in his own house. He told his wife his daughter be-longed to a distant relative who had died. His wife believed him.

They hired a nursemaid and let the child grow up in the house without interfering with anyone's business.

Alexandra the Cat never asked her lover what their daughter's name was or who she looked like. She had never been ashamed that she'd given the girl up, because she was smart enough to understand she had had no choice—no real choice—not when the stakes were so high and the game so deadly: It was the baby, she realized, or the lover, without whom Alexandra would be poor and alone and abandoned. The day Rahman brought her Roxanna, the Cat looked at the child before her and recognized herself: a girl with no options.

"Leave her," she said, and waved Rahman back into the fog.

ROXANNA stayed easily at first, fascinated by Alexandra, by the way she looked and smelled and carried herself in that house haunted by cats and the memories of dead czars. With her starched laces and painted satins, her perfumed hair and blackened eyelashes, Alexandra looked like the china dolls that Blue-Eyed Lotfi had sold from the basement of his house before he got himself a shop on the Avenue of the Tulips.

Roxanna was amazed by the silence over which Alexandra reigned, by the sound of her own footsteps echoing in the hallway, the rooms that sat empty, the furniture that was never used. Cats stared at her from every corner, lay on Alexandra's bed, licked the gold-leafed tips of the piano's legs.

Every day, Alexandra slept through the morning and woke up only when Roxanna came home from school to serve her coffee. She spent the next three hours before her dresser. She wrapped her hair in tiny curlers and plucked her eyebrows till there was nothing left of them and she could paint on a new set, squeezed her body into tight corsets and agonized over which gown to wear with which set of pearls. By the time Roxanna had finished the afternoon session of school, the Cat would be dressed and ready.

She ate her lunch at three o'clock, took her coffee at five, and entered the music room shortly before sunset. At that hour, the room was filled with light, the black lacquer piano in the center shimmering like a jewel on display. Roxanna opened the curtains to reveal her mistress to the audience of ragged children and jobless old men who regularly gathered outside the window. Alexandra faced them with regal poise, curtsied, and sat down. Then all at once she was the master pianist of the court of Czar Nicholas II, his most beautiful courtier, giving the performance of a lifetime before a full house at the Moscow Opera.

Waves of music rose against the light, filled the room, lapped at the walls like a tide. Alexandra gave a signal—an almost imperceptible nod of her head—and Roxanna would open all the windows to let the music pour into the ghetto. It flooded the alleys, ebbed against the half-crumbled walls of houses where it awakened the Jews from a two-thousand-year sleep of surrender and instilled in them, for a moment, the longing to fight back.

Alexandra played Chopin and Beethoven and Schumann, and no one could tell what she was playing or if she was any good because they had never heard that kind of music before and did not know what to expect. Yet they came back every day, in the hot sun or the drenching rain, skipping the hour of their siesta or forsaking the pleasure of drinking hot tea in a cool coffeehouse, only to watch the spectacle of this strange woman with her many cats and the madness of a distant world.

After dark, Alexandra retired into her bedroom and lay on a divan that she had named after a woman—Josephine—and read until midnight. She told the Jews that Josephine was a woman who had been loved by a great warrior—Napoléon Bonaparte—and that he had made her empress of France. Years later, Roxanna's sister Rochelle would name her own daughter after the sofa in Alexandra's bedroom, hoping she would grow up to marry an emperor.

Before going to bed, Roxanna walked around the house, lighting the candelabra, humming the tunes Alexandra had played, feeling them resonate in the dark.

Roxanna saw her sisters at school, but did not dare ask about her parents or why she had to stay in Alexandra's house indefinitely. She understood she was being punished for being rebellious, for the feathers that filled her bed, for the bad luck that followed her. She knew she was not the only girl who had been forced to leave home in childhood: Many were sent off to work in distant towns, and never saw their parents again. Many others were married off before the age of puberty, or given to relatives who could not bear children.

Still, Roxanna could not help feeling that her mother despised her.

"It's not your fault," Miriam told her once. "Mother is afraid of her own life. She thinks she can change our luck by giving you away."

By then, an anchor had been cut loose, setting Roxanna alone and unguided at sea.

She realized Alexandra's was the only home she would have. She took her work seriously, tried her best not to be distracted by thoughts of her parents or by the people and places she saw in her dreams. Yet she woke up every morning with her eyes full of the golden light of the sun rising over the green waters of the Caspian, and when she left her room, she ran right into Alexandra's memories: they walked around the house, in flesh and blood, more real than life itself.

Roxanna saw Alexandra as a young woman, dressed in poor clothes but always with an air of superiority. The woman kept talking about a coffin she had left behind and a corpse that was alone and unburied, she said, in a city she could not return to because its name had been changed and its borders had been destroyed and its streets no longer existed except in old people's memories.

Roxanna also saw Alexandra's mother: She sat next to Alexandra when she played the piano, and kept time by tapping her fingers on her lap. She wore leper's bells around her ankles, cheap rings on her fingers.

Only the phantom lover never showed himself to Roxanna.

He was tall, Roxanna surmised from the creaking of the floor when he arrived. He always came after Roxanna had gone to bed. She could tell the Cat was afraid he would leave her someday, go off in the morning and never come back: every night, before he arrived, Roxanna could hear Alexandra's heart beating in every room in the house. When he did come, Alexandra would sigh in relief, and her cats moaned resentfully as they were chased off her bed. A moment later something light and metallic, like a ring, chimed against the porcelain top of the night table.

Six months after Roxanna arrived at the Cat's house, the phantom lover stopped calling.

One night Alexandra waited for him till morning. She paced through the house and the courtyard, opening and closing doors, then opening them again. She was still waiting the next day at lunchtime, and again that evening. He did not come.

On the third night, Alexandra stood by her window from midnight onwards, refusing to budge for fear she would miss his shadow crossing the courtyard, and when morning came and Roxanna went to the fishpond to wash her face, Alexandra was still peeking through the folds of her bedroom curtain, too proud to show herself.

Roxanna dipped her hands into the water and broke up the reflection of a familiar ghost—a green-eyed girl with patent-leather shoes. She scooped water into her hands and poured bits of the ghost's image onto her face.

"Go away," she told the ghost distractedly. She was so used to the spectral images, she never bothered to check if they were real anymore. "The Cat's in no mood to see you today."

The image of the girl remained in the pool. Next to her, Roxanna saw the reflection of a man she had never seen before.

He was tall, with a bald head and lips that were too red. He wore a European suit with a vest and a watch chain. His legs were too fat for the rest of his body.

Roxanna turned to see the man and the girl standing before her.

"Alexandra tells me you can fly," he told Roxanna.

His voice was soft, like a woman's, and he leaned forward

when he talked. He put one foot on the edge of the pool, rested an elbow on his thigh, and smiled.

"This is my daughter," he said, pointing to the girl with the white shoes.

"You two must be almost the same age," he said. "She's going to stay with you."

The girl wore a starched white shirt with a navy-blue skirt, white socks with a stiff lace trim, shoes that looked as if they had never been worn before. Next to her on the ground, Roxanna noticed a brown cardboard suitcase placed upright in the dust.

"Her name is Mercedez." The man wet his red lips with the tip of his tongue. "She doesn't speak any Farsi yet, just Assyrian, but she'll learn soon enough."

He looked down at his own reflection in the fishpond.

"In the meantime," he said, "you're going to have to give Alexandra a message from me."

All at once, the fish began to swim in a mad frenzy. Roxanna looked up at the Cat's bedroom window. She knew Alexandra was looking at them through her opera glasses.

The man was tentative.

"Tell her I can't keep the child anymore," he said. A sweat stain had begun to spread from around his neck down onto his white shirt collar. He looked over at Mercedez, then at the bedroom window, then back at Roxanna.

"Tell her"—he swallowed—"I can't come back anymore."

The fish dove deep into the water and did not emerge. The man exhaled, straightened, then forced himself to walk over to the girl. He whispered something in a strange language, touched her face with the back of his fingers. Mercedez recoiled but did not look at him. In vain, he repeated himself, nodding towards Roxanna as he spoke, pointing to the house. The girl never answered.

Roxanna thought the girl was strong, terribly strong, to be able to withstand the will of an adult in that way. When he took out a handkerchief to wipe the sweat off his hands, she saw the gold wedding band on his left ring finger.

"Good-bye," the Assyrian said to Roxanna, trying to force a smile that did not materialize.

All morning, Roxanna and Mercedez watched each other.

Mercedez remained next to the pool—there in her rich-girl's clothes and her spotless socks, so perfect in her white straw hat with the wide navy-blue ribbon, she looked positively untouchable. Before her Roxanna was small and helpless, clearly aware that she would lose any contest against Mercedez, wanting nothing more than to please her, if only so she would stop looking at Roxanna with loathing in her eyes.

Around noon, Roxanna remembered that she had missed school and that she had not seen Alexandra all day. She went to her door and knocked, but there was no answer. She waited, afraid to knock again.

"Not now," Alexandra's voice came through a moment later. "I'll call when I need you."

Roxanna went into the kitchen and looked through yesterday's leftover dinner. She arranged the food on a plate, swallowing her own hunger, and took it outside to Mercedez.

"Here." She put the plate on the edge of the pool, beaming with the pride of her own generosity. "It's all for you."

The moment Mercedez looked at the food, Roxanna felt herself cringe with shame: what had seemed fresh and appetizing a moment ago became stale and inedible under the green flare of the rich girl's eyes. Roxanna stayed glued to the ground, unable to decide if she should remove the plate. After a while, when Mercedez looked away, Roxanna reached forward and quietly took the plate.

Later, she found Mercedez sitting at the edge of the pool. Her knees were almost touching her suitcase, and her back was straight and determined against the world. By nighttime, she still had not moved.

"You can come inside to sleep," Roxanna told her in vain.

The courtyard was dark, filled with the sounds of the ghetto's evening—murmurs drifting in from the street. Shadows floated on the fishpond; the multicolored fish glowed fluorescent in the moonlight. Roxanna missed her parents' noisy house, her sisters sitting down to eat or doing their chores, Shusha nursing a baby or working on one of Rahman's orders. Looking at Mercedez with her yellow hair and her white clothes, Roxanna felt her own loneliness more than ever, wished she were strong like Mercedez, wished her mother had wanted her.

She fell asleep on the floor outside Alexandra's bedroom and dreamt of Shusha all night. The next morning she awoke with only a faint memory of the events of the previous day. She saw that she was lying on the ground without a cover, that she was still wearing her school uniform, that Alexandra's door was still locked and her curtains were still closed. So Roxanna got up and went to check in the courtyard. There she was, the green-eyed daughter of Alexandra the Cat and her married phantom, sitting at the edge of the fishpond in her navy-blue skirt with the razor-sharp pleats, looking exhausted and pale but still—still unbeaten.

MIRIAM THE MOON hated Mercedez the moment she laid eyes on her, right there in the middle of Alexandra's courtyard, so defiant she had made Roxanna cry without uttering a single word. Unable to convince Mercedez to move into the house, or to coax Alexandra out of her bedroom, Roxanna had gone to school to ask for Miriam's help. They had waited till school was over and the principal, Mrs. Wisdom, had dismissed everyone. Then they had walked together to the Cat's house, and all the way there, Roxanna had held Miriam's hand.

Miriam was a beautiful girl—tall and slim and prettier than any girl in her age group, attractive enough to have suitors even in spite of her family legacy. So far, the suitors had all been flawed men who realized they needed to make a compromise in order to find a wife. Miriam, with her gentle ways and her superior looks, appeared so wasted on them that her parents could not bring themselves to give her away.

Miriam did not question her parents' judgment, of course—though she was fifteen years old already and getting close to the time when girls became "decayed" and unmarriageable. She had a natural sense of obedience that compelled her to accept any lot handed to her. She was also humble, as a woman should be, and knew better than to believe that her good looks should afford her passage into a happier life. She studied hard at school and obeyed her teachers, never flaunted her knowledge or even spoke of her secret wish to continue studying after high school. Even in her youth, Miriam believed that endurance—the power to accept life's disappointments without breaking down—was man's highest quality: she dressed in severe black and sorry brown, kept her hair in a tight braid that she hardly opened, went about with the air of a young woman ready to accept old-maidenhood. She took on more responsibility than anyone imposed on her, denied herself even the smallest pleasures for fear of letting her body and her mind become spoiled, always prepared for the worst.

That is why she hated Mercedez so suddenly and for so long after they met.

They stood glaring at each other in the Cat's yard—Mercedez worn-out from her day-and-a-half-long sit-in, Miriam astonished by the vision of this golden girl whose resplendence she had not counted on—and after a moment Miriam realized she had to attack at once or accept defeat.

"It's the Devil in shiny white shoes," she declared like ice.

She circled Mercedez, looking for a weak spot to attack, and found the suitcase.

"Must be her father was dying to get rid of her," she speculated out loud.

She opened the suitcase without asking permission, sifted through the pile of starched and folded fabrics—all white laces and smooth cotton, three extra pairs of patent-leather shoes (one white and two black, their soles barely scratched) that made Miriam's hands grow cold with envy. She sniffed in disdain.

"Huh," she said to Roxanna. "This stuff'll get ruined the first time she wears it on our streets."

Mercedez was so enraged, she let her guard down and blurted out a string of insults at Miriam. The words poured out of her mouth and hung in the air like carcasses of birds in the butcher shop. Spoken in Assyrian, they were incomprehensible to Miriam—and therefore inconsequential. They proved only Mercedez's vulnerability, her defenselessness against these people whose language she neither spoke nor understood.

Miriam had won the round.

"Let's go see the Cat," she told Roxanna.

They knocked twice on Alexandra's door.

"Your Excellency," Miriam called, careful to address the old woman with respect. "There is a matter of utmost urgency that requires your attention."

There was no answer.

"Your Excellency," she called again. "There is a strange young girl in your courtyard with a suitcase full of probably stolen clothes, and your servant, Roxanna, and I do not know what to make of her."

In the end, they opened the door and went in.

Alexandra sat upright on her Josephine. Her hair was done in a half-crumbled chignon, her arms were almost dried onto the divan, and she still wore the pearls she had put on three nights earlier to wait for the lover who had not come. When the door opened, she drew in a breath, as if suddenly awakened from a long sleep, and pushed her chin into the air. She wanted to keep her poise in spite of the makeup that had run in streaks all over her face, and the eyes that were bloodshot and half-closed. But she must have known that the damage was already done—that the icon, heretofore intact, had suddenly turned into a pillar of salt—because she extended a hand towards the two girls and let them help her up. They walked her to the vanity mirror, unfastened her dress, and freed her of her corset and her shoes. Then they put her to bed.

She stayed in bed for eleven days, having confused the darkness that had set into her eyes with the blackness of sleep, and she so enjoyed her peace, so cherished the freedom not to set eyes on reality's petty reminders anymore, that she would have remained in that state of silent rapture had not Roxanna and Miriam kept boiling rice and pouring the murky water down her throat so she would not starve. In the end, she did get up, but she never again felt the obligation to concern herself with anything but her fantasies, and never lamented the fact that she had gone completely blind.

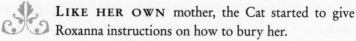 LIKE HER OWN mother, the Cat started to give Roxanna instructions on how to bury her.

"Have your father sell my piano, and use the money for a grand funeral," she said. "Invite my lover. Put my green taffeta dress on me, with my long pearls, and paint my lips bright red. Bury me near a stream of clear water, and visit my grave every time it rains."

She said this sometimes with tearful self-pity, sometimes with the coldhearted indifference of one who recognizes that history repeats itself only because God is a creature of small imagination, and she was so absorbed in her own thoughts, she did not understand the kind of desperation Roxanna felt at the possibility of losing her.

More than anything else, more than the taste of hunger that tainted every bite of food she ever ate or the fear of Shusha coming in the night to kill her, Roxanna the Angel dreaded the time when Alexandra would die.

That is why she took such excellent care of the Cat, why she fed and changed and bathed her like a child, why she was so patient with Mercedez: tolerating first her anger, then her indignation, approaching her every time with a smile and a token of peace until slowly, slowly, Mercedez let go of her hatred and allowed Roxanna her friendship. They were alone but for each other, abandoned by their parents, depending on Alexandra for survival. Still, Mercedez laughed at Roxanna's attachment to the Cat.

"Stop acting like she's some national treasure no one else has discovered," she told Roxanna in the flawed Farsi she learned after a year in the ghetto. Her voice was rich like velvet, tainted with anger. "I myself pray that she croaks as soon as possible. Then I'll get out of this ghetto and never look back."

Mercedez felt no guilt for wishing death on this woman who had brought her into the world only to give her away, who had never wanted her and now pretended she did not notice her presence. She saw no reason she should feel connected to Alexandra, or to wish, as Roxanna often fantasized, that her own father would come back and take her home. All the time she lived in the ghetto, Mercedez had a single agenda that she followed tirelessly and finally achieved: to leave as soon as possible, on the back of a rich man stupid enough to give her not just money but also freedom, so that she could go out into the world alone and unencumbered, never again counting on another person only to be let down.

She figured out her strategy before she was old enough to implement her plan. She knew, for example, that she was exceptionally pretty, that her body, even before it had reached puberty, gave off a sinful hint, an aura that made boys panic every time she ambled up to them in her brown school uniform. She hated the rough fabric of the uniform, and she refused to put on—Mrs. Wisdom be damned—the black tights, thick as oilcloth, that were required for all girls. She wore little white stockings instead, let her hair loose over her shoulders till Mrs. Wisdom grabbed her at assembly one morning and, with her dark hands, dipped that golden mass into a bucket of muddy water, then braided it so tightly Mercedez could almost feel her skin splitting above her nose. Mrs. Wisdom promised to cut the hair off the next time Mercedez came to school "unkempt," and she must have managed to get her message across that time because Mercedez began to wear her hair in a ponytail. Even so, she swung the ponytail from side to side when she walked, giving it a thrust and a bounce that made the hair every bit as suggestive and unsettling as it had been before.

As the years passed and they grew older, Alexandra's girls became the talk of the ghetto. Roxanna had pale skin and caramel-candy eyes, fine bones and that look of innocent wonder as if she never quite existed in her own world. She wore faded dresses that she created out of Alexandra's old, discarded fabrics, dresses that were always too long and too loose because she cut them straight, like a sack. She also wore the old shoes Miriam brought for her from Shusha's house. When she walked to school with her books in her hands, a stream of venomous gossip followed behind her. Next to her, Mercedez strutted like a prize horse—chest pushed outwards and eyes full of disdain—and railed against every old woman who dared make a comment about her.

"It's not their fault," Roxanna told her. "They're mean because they're old, and sorry, and afraid they're going to die."

"High time they should die." Mercedez let go of the fight only reluctantly. "Poor people have no business living long lives. Only the rich should be immortal."

Because she wanted wealth and immortality, Mercedez focused on the boys. She did not wait for them to approach her first. She went to them instead, trying out her powers, carving out a territory no other girl in the ghetto would dare transgress. At twelve, she drove boys to despair merely by the gleam of her panther's eyes, the bounce of her breasts, the parting of those amber lips, and the way she had of walking right up to boys—so close she could feel them trembling in their patched-up uniforms—and sighing ever so lightly, so that her white breath dusted their dark and sunburnt faces and for a moment they felt a happiness greater than any they would ever feel again in their lives. Then she turned around and walked away as if from a heap of dust.

At fourteen, she made boys weep in their mothers' laps and drove married men, belittled by the flirtation that she had extended to them, home to beat their wives.

At sixteen she stopped going to school altogether and spent her time mostly in Tehran, hunting for a rich Muslim man who would be her ticket out of the Cat's house. She did not give a damn about the Jews who called her "whore" before she had ever slept with anyone; she laughed at Roxanna's warnings that the men she was seeking out would use and then discard her. She was using them more than they used her, she said, and showed Roxanna the money and presents they gave her as proof that no one had taken advantage of her.

Seven years had passed. Roxanna, who had full charge of the house, had sold off every valuable except the piano, and still barely stretched the funds to cover the cost of their meals. She got help from Miriam, who had finished high school and started work as a first-grade teacher. Miriam spent most of her salary on her parents and younger siblings, but sometimes she managed to save part of it for Roxanna. Mostly, it was Mercedez's money that kept the Cat and Roxanna alive.

Some nights Mercedez did not come home at all. The next morning the peddlers who set out in the dark for nearby villages would see her slide out of a shiny car and walk, sleepy but defiant, through the narrow streets of the ghetto, humming foreign tunes and smiling as if to a secret.

At home, she would undress slowly in the twilight, slip out of the silk stockings she had bought from Blue-Eyed Lotfi's shop on the Avenue of the Tulips, and the skin-tight dresses she insisted Roxanna make for her. She told Roxanna about her boyfriends in Tehran: they were older men, she said, because the young ones had no money to spend and often expected "real love" in return for the smallest gift.

Roxanna did not understand her friend's aversion to being loved.

"Me, I *want* a man to love me," she would confess to Mercedez. "I don't care how much money he has, as long as he will take me home and never leave me."

Then she would lean back against her pillow and describe the man of her future as if she had already seen him, cast in stone and waiting for her.

"He's going to be young, and kind, and together we'll have a daughter that the whole world will love because she will be prettier than anything anyone has seen—prettier than Miriam the Moon, or even you. And what's more, she will be smart. You'll be able to see in her eyes how smart she is, and even Mrs. Wisdom won't dare stop her from going to university because she'll know, everyone will know, that my daughter will someday make my whole family proud and undo every shame that I have brought."

They would remain quiet in that room that would slowly fill with the magic of Roxanna's dreams, the images so alive Mercedez could extend her hand and touch every one of them, and for a while their joy would be palpable. Then at last Mercedez would force herself free of the madness.

"You're stupid like all the others." She would laugh. "The man you marry will spend his money on other women, and keep you at home to raise his children. You will be cleaning rice and daydreaming about how your daughter is going to conquer the world, while I will be riding high on someone's back."

Sure enough, Mercedez found her man.

He was a wealthy Muslim called Amin who owned a string of weaving factories in various cities around Iran. The factories had been small operations, equipped with rusted machines that had remained quiet all through the Occupation, but after the Allied withdrawal, Amin had started them up again, turned them into modern, profit-making ventures. To run his factory in Tehran, he had hired a manager.

The manager was neither wealthy nor sophisticated, but he was in a position of power because he had the right to hire and fire people, and this, in spite of his well-worn suits and the scuffed heels of his shoes, gave him the audacity to approach Mercedez with only a slight fear that she would laugh at him. He found her in Blue-Eyed Lotfi's shop, looking through a case of imported lipstick, and asked if she would go with him across the street to have a glass of hot tea.

Mercedez only saw the man's dusty shoes and the wrinkled cuffs of his pants, and she knew better than to waste her time.

"I don't drink tea," she answered, then smiled conspiratorially at Blue-Eyed Lotfi. "I only drink arrack."

Encouraged, the manager asked if she would go to his house

instead, to a gathering he had arranged in honor of his boss, the famous Amin who owned, the manager explained with excessive pride, all the cotton fields and weaving factories in the country except the ones stolen from him by the Shah.

"You can drink all the arrack you want there," he insisted. "And you can even smoke opium."

Mercedez went home and changed into her white satin dress. She had seen the dress in a magazine that was already a year old when she bought it, then insisted that Roxanna make the dress for her. The result was less than perfect: The dress was longer on one side than the other, and the sleeve holes were too tight. But in it, Mercedez looked every bit the movie star she knew she was going to be someday.

The manager waited for her in his car outside Blue-Eyed Lotfi's shop. He said she looked stunning.

We'll see if your boss is worth the trouble I've put myself through, Mercedez thought as she lit a cigarette in the car.

The guest of honor was fifty-some years old, with two wives, seven grandchildren, and a host of lovers and concubines whose names he never bothered to remember. He had more money than Mercedez had counted on, but beyond that he was a man of honor and good intentions who never imagined, that night when he saw Mercedez smiling at him from across a room full of men in shirtsleeves drinking shots of arrack, the kind of annihilation she was going to bring into in his life. He sat with his legs crossed in front of a water pipe, eating sweets and smoking the opium that was a staple in the daily lives of many Iranians. All night long she stood with her back against the wall, smoking cigarettes and staring at Amin. At the end of the evening, when Amin got up to leave in his chauffeur-driven car, she ambled over to him and asked if he wanted to take her home.

"What about our host?" Amin asked, actually amused at her audacity.

Mercedez the Movie Star stared at Amin with her eyes so warm, he felt he would sink into them and never emerge. Then she extended her hand, and with the tip of her forefinger circled the diamond dial of his gold watch. She walked out three steps ahead of him, under the hate-filled glare of the manager, who saw his boss take his prize woman and dared not object for fear of jeopardizing his position at the factory. The moment Amin sat in the car, she wrapped her legs around his waist and slipped her tongue into his mouth.

For four months in the summer of 1955, Mercedez the Movie Star did not return home to the ghetto. Roxanna waited for her a few days, then a week, and then, fearing that Mercedez was in danger, went into Tehran to look for her. She found Blue-Eyed Lotfi's shop on the Avenue of the Tulips.

"Don't bother waiting for her anymore," Lotfi advised. He was a kind man, too short to look masculine, but with clear blue eyes and a conciliatory manner than made everyone like him. "She's found her gold mine, and she won't give it up if she has half a brain behind those green eyes of hers."

Roxanna did not believe Lotfi.

"Mercedez wouldn't leave without telling me first."

She stood her ground even as the months passed and there was no word from Mercedez, even as false rumors circulated that Mercedez had married Amin, that she was pregnant with his child, that she was living in the same house with his first wife. Without the money Mercedez had brought home, Roxanna and the Cat went from being poor to having nothing at all, so much so that some of the Jews who were aware of Alexandra's predicament went to see Rahman and suggested that he help his daughter.

In the house, Alexandra dressed in tattered gowns and walked around all day, shouting orders at the imaginary servants of her

Russian palace. "For dinner we'll have braised lamb with tarragon, saffron rice with dill, red wine, orange sorbet. Don't burn the tarragon like last time."

They ate Lavash bread, white rice with olive oil, cucumbers, and walnuts. It was always the same food, lunch and dinner, and for breakfast, sweet tea with last night's stale bread. Yet Alexandra, her wrinkled breasts pushed up in a low-cut gown she had not changed in a week, danced pirouettes around her husband in his general's uniform, and sat down to a meal of young Cornish hen marinated in white wine with shallots and leeks.

In Tehran, Mercedez lived in one of Amin's many houses. She was waited on by a host of servants, went around town in a chauffeur-driven Studebaker, spent money as if she had just robbed a king's treasury. She demanded nothing of Amin—neither his time nor his love, nor any promise that he would look after her at least until she found her next man. It was not out of consideration for his family or social status that she kept herself out of his way. It was only because she knew, from the way his hands turned cold every time she walked away from his bed, that he had stepped into a hole and was falling faster than he knew.

She stayed with him exactly four months, then packed a bag with the dresses and jewels he had given her, and announced she was leaving. He laughed, of course, certain that she bluffed, that she had no other man to keep her and could not return, now that she had so compromised her reputation, to the ghetto where the Jews would stone her to death if they dared. Still, when she walked out the front door, he panicked enough to suggest a compromise.

"Stay," he said, "and I'll marry you on a temporary contract of six months."

Shiite Muslim law allowed men four permanent wives, and as many temporary ones as their virility could manage. It was an honorable way for a man to have lovers without breaking God's law against adultery. But the woman who was a temporary wife lost her virtue and, after that, could claim no right to her husband's name or money.

Mercedez the Movie Star did not even turn an eye towards Amin as she left him.

She went back to the ghetto, with her suitcase full of clothes, looking every bit as elegant as the rich man's whore she had become, and even the dust that covered her expensive leather shoes did not detract from the dazzling effect she created merely by her presence.

"Almost there," she whispered to Roxanna with the cool irony of a woman who knows she has achieved her end. "You can come stay with me after I'm married."

Amin would have laughed at her presumptuousness, of course. He was a man of many means, and she, only a hungry young girl with no family ties and no prospect for advancement in life except her looks. For nine weeks he went around convinced that he was over Mercedez. He even took another lover, one who at least pretended to care more about him than his money. Then one morning, sitting in his barber's chair, he caught a glimpse of himself in the mirror and went mad. Instead of the proud young man who owned many factories and many more women, Amin saw an aging creature with a white stubble and a sagging chin, who had just about run out of time. Something screamed inside his head—so loud he was sure everyone in the shop heard it—and when the noise had settled, he realized he wanted Mercedez back because she was his youth and his ambition, and the very breath of his wheezing lungs.

He sent his car to the ghetto for her, but she turned it away.

He sent her a pair of hand-painted satin shoes with ruby-studded clips. She took the shoes but did not respond to his message.

So he went to see her, one early evening, in the house of Alexandra the Cat, and she told him the only way he would ever have her again was to divorce all his wives and marry only her.

Mercedez the Movie Star left the ghetto on the morning of March 21, 1956, in a white wedding dress Amin had bought for her from Tehran's most celebrated tailor, under the glare of hundreds of people who lined the streets to watch her go. All the way to the gates of the ghetto, the Jews saw her ride in Amin's car, and for the first time in ten years everyone, from the most forgiving to the most judgmental, remained speechless.

The City
1956

THE DRIVER of the bus had blue skin.

He sat on the dirt floor outside the station—an enormous creature with no hair and muscles so huge, they gave him an other-than-human appearance. He had on wrestler's clothes: baggy pants that reached only below his knees, a tight, sleeveless shirt that left most of his upper body exposed. His eyes were dark and wet, like fish; his eyebrows were so perfect, they looked as if they had been painted onto his face. But his entire skin, from the tip of his shaved head to the ends of his crooked toes, was covered by tattoos—so that when Roxanna first saw him, all she could think was that he was blue, like a seal.

She had walked to the station from Alexandra's house, equipped with a few paper bills and a small bag in which she had stuffed her only good dress. She was wearing her school uniform, and she carried her notebooks as if she were headed for school. Instead, she was going to catch a bus into Tehran, and all she had for a destination was the name of the man Mercedez the Movie Star had married.

It had been inevitable, Miriam the Moon now tells me—because she believes in Destiny and in the independent logic of events— that Roxanna would one day follow Mercedez into Tehran. The strange part was not so much that Roxanna finally left the ghetto but how long she waited before doing so—and that it had happened, albeit indirectly, because of Miriam.

In 1956 Miriam the Moon was twenty-four years old—an old maid even by the Jews' more modern standards—and her chances of getting married were close to nil. She had worked as a first-grade teacher for five years, and although her mother still insisted that she was only eighteen, it was clear Miriam had no more hopes of finding a husband. Nevertheless, her own predicament did not seem to concern her as much as that of Tala'at and Rochelle. A younger brother and sister—Bahram and Sussan— were still in school and therefore spared the question of what they were going to do with themselves once they became a drain on the family's resources and a noose around their father's neck. But Rochelle, thin and nervous and always expecting the worst, was convinced she would be stuck in line—behind Tala'at and Miriam—and never marry. Tala'at, who wanted nothing but to make love to a man, lay in bed all day, crying into her pillow and threatening to run away—like her aunt and Mercedez the Movie Star—and become a whore just so she could sleep with someone.

And so that day when Miriam came home, arms full of first-grade dictations she had to correct, and found a group of grim-faced women sitting in the courtyard, she did not think for a moment that any of them might have come to seek her. The women sat talking to Rahman as Shusha served them tea and sweets, bread from her own underground oven, cherry nectar with water and ice. It was clear who the most important guest was: the woman with the two gold front teeth, to whom Rahman spoke most directly and whom Shusha served most eagerly.

The woman was seeking wives for two men. One was her son, an unemployed twenty-five-year-old who had had one year of schooling before he went to work in a bottle factory in Esfahān. His mother had named him Mr. Charles, after British royalty, and she sincerely believed, though he was illiterate and without a job at the moment, that, given the right spouse, Mr. Charles had the potential to become a great man with enormous power and eye-catching wealth. She was less enthusiastic about the second bridegroom-to-be: he was her brother, Habib, not handsome but hardworking. He was thirty years old and owned a silver shop in the bazaar.

Miriam found Tala'at and Rochelle in the bedroom, peeking out at the visitors.

"Someone's got a suitor," she told them, and went to work on her dictation papers.

The women in the yard stayed through the afternoon. They

called Rahman's daughters one by one, starting with Miriam and ending with Sussan. They told the girls to laugh—so they could examine the girls' teeth—to talk, and to walk across the yard and back—to prove they were still virgins: girls who had given up their virginity walked with their thighs far apart, Mr. Charles's mother explained, because they had nothing left to protect.

Afterwards, the girls were sent back inside, and negotiations began. Miriam fell asleep waiting for the results. Tala'at threatened, as always, to run away and become a whore unless she was picked as a bride. Rochelle sat at the door, peering out, swallowing her anxiety.

When it was all over, Mr. Charles's mother had picked Miriam for Charles—because Miriam was pretty, and Mr. Charles's mother wanted good-looking grandsons. And she picked Tala'at for her brother, Habib, because Tala'at was so clearly panting for a man, she would keep any husband satisfied.

The fact that the girls were already old maids would serve as a weapon—every mother-in-law needed a weapon—that Mr. Charles's mother planned to use against them all their lives.

To begin with, she demanded that Rahman pay for the wedding, which was traditionally the grooms' responsibility. She also insisted on a decent dowry for each girl—let Rahman borrow if he had to—and thereafter felt no shame in claiming that Mr. Charles, who could not even read his own name, was studying to become a doctor. About her brother, Habib, she did not have to lie, only to omit the rather curious truth that at thirty he still had an exaggerated aversion to any form of physical intimacy.

Rahman did, of course, borrow money to finance his daughters' wedding, but in the end it was worth it just to see Miriam and Tala'at married off. He held the wedding at home, and invited Roxanna and the Cat. He even bought Roxanna a new dress.

Roxanna came holding Alexandra's hand, shy and ill at ease in this house from which she had been driven. She had given her new dress to Alexandra to wear because she did not want to see the old woman ridiculed in one of her tattered and outmoded gowns, and the end result was devastating for both of them: having found nothing better to put on, Roxanna was wearing her school uniform, while Alexandra, old and wrinkled and with her face painted a dozen colors, paraded around in a white cotton dress with French pleats becoming of a twelve-year-old.

The two of them made such a sight, they stopped the wedding the moment they walked in. The men in the party frowned at Alexandra and cursed the bad luck that had set such an old and depressing creature in their field of vision. The women sighed in genuine grief over Alexandra's not-so-distant youth, and their own not-so-improbable future. Mr. Charles's mother complained out loud about the caliber of Shusha and Rahman's guests, and did not approve when Shusha kissed Alexandra on the head, then seated her in a place of honor near the grooms' family.

Miriam called Roxanna over. "I will come see you all the time," she tried to reassure her sister. "Mister Charles's mother won't let me work outside the house anymore, but I will bring you money one way or another, and I will look after you even after I have my own children."

Roxanna just looked down at her shoes and nodded. It was clear she did not believe Miriam.

The wedding proceeded smoothly—except for Habib's nephew, an anxious-looking eight-year-old with his hair shaved against head lice, who planted himself in front of Tala'at and stared at her with such obvious greed, there was no mistaking his intentions. The force of his virgin lust created enormous pressure in the inside of his thighs, so he had to run outside every few minutes and urinate against the wall of Rahman's house just to relieve the aching in his penis.

Sometime near midnight the two brides and grooms were summoned by Mr. Charles's mother, given a blessing, then set on their way to their new homes. Tala'at and Habib were going to live in a rented room near Sar Cheshmeh. Miriam and Mr. Charles would live with his mother.

The guests followed the two brides out of the wedding and through the ghetto towards their new homes. Shusha and Rahman went with them, of course, as did Rochelle and Sussan. But Roxanna stayed behind, because she could not take Alexandra along and could not leave her in the house by herself.

That is why Roxanna was alone, with only a few very old people still in the house, when she went to call Alexandra and found that she was cold and stiff and dead as a mummy.

She knew better than to alert anyone to the death at that moment: a broken mirror at a wedding meant an unhappy union. A death, especially a sudden one, meant that the bride was the bearer of bad luck. So she let Alexandra stay there, sitting up with her back against a cushion, eyes open in her now-familiar blind-woman's stare, red lips barely parted, fingers adorned with cheap rings, clasping the pleats of her young woman's dress. Watching her, Roxanna felt a mild sadness—like someone remembering a loss she had already suffered once—but none of the terror she had expected. Rahman would have to sell the piano, she thought, to pay for the burial. Someone would have to alert the phantom lover. Roxanna would have to find Mercedez and tell her.

They buried Alexandra in Beheshtieh—the Jews' cemetery, which the Muslims had not allowed to expand, so that for centuries corpses had been placed one on top of the other. Hundreds of Jews came. Alexandra's cats sensed her loss and followed her smell to the cemetery. The phantom lover also showed up—in his three-piece suit with wide legs and watch chain—proving himself at once as gallant as the man Alexandra had loved, and as cowardly as the one who had left her. He brought his wife, his children, even his father-in-law. When he saw Alexandra's body wrapped in a white shroud, he fell to his knees, there before all the Jews and his own family, and cried as if he had never recovered from loving her and did not care who knew it.

It was a moment of great vindication, perhaps, or just another one of life's useless ironies, that the phantom lover had finally acknowledged their relationship when Alexandra was not there to benefit from it. But then he went up to Roxanna, right there as the grave was being filled, and told her that she would have to return the house to him. He was its rightful owner, and he wanted to sell it, now that the Cat no longer occupied it. Roxanna, he suggested kindly, should go back to live with her own family, under her father's roof, where—if he might be so bold as to suggest—all girls belonged till they got married.

Roxanna the Angel did not have to leave the ghetto once the lover evicted her from Alexandra's house. Miriam would not have refused her a roof. Tala'at might have taken her in. A man might even have married her. She left because she had been told, since before she could understand language, that it was her destiny.

"All you have to do," Alexandra had said, "is not look back."

THE BUS STATION was a brick room where the drivers ate and slept in between shifts and where passengers could wait during rain and snow. A single bus—beaten, empty, its tires smooth as skin—sat outside like a loyal dog.

The driver saw Roxanna approach, of course, because she was the only person out on the street that day, but he did not acknowledge her because he was a Luti, part of a breed of men who prided themselves on their physical strength and their dedication to protecting the rights of the weak. He was trained not to address a woman, or even set eyes on her, unless she had talked to him first. She came up to him, knees quivering, and stopped.

She was holding a paper bill between her fingers, like those girls he sometimes boarded on his bus, the ones who had slept with boys, become pregnant, and were running away from their fathers' wrath. He wondered if she knew that day was a Muslim holiday—a day to commemorate the assassination of one of the Prophet's disciples. All over Tehran, Shiite believers were walking in processions. They were dressed in black shirts, which they tore in grief in order to flagellate themselves and their young children with metal chains. They wrapped the chains around their wrists and slapped their bare backs, their faces, their heads, till they had broken skin and bone and bled unconscious. In each procession, the man who hurt himself most violently was believed to be closest to God.

The bus driver did not believe much in self-flagellation, and he did not like to cut himself because once the skin healed, the shape of his tattoos would change. He ignored Roxanna and busied himself with his lunch. He had a bowl of soup—beef shank with onions and potatoes, white beans and yellow garbanzos. Dipping a blue hand into the soup, he fished out all the solids and placed them in a small mortar next to the bowl. Then he put the bowl to his lips, snapped his head back, and poured the soup down his throat in a single, breathless stream. When he was done, he belched, smacked his lips, and praised Allah.

She was still standing there.

He turned to the mortar and began mashing the beans and meat from his soup. When he had created a pasty blend, he scooped it out with his fingers and spread it over a loaf of flat Lavash bread. He put a raw onion in the middle of the bread, then rolled the loaf around it. Folding the roll twice, he praised God again and, in a feat of oral artistry for which he was famous among the Lutis of Tehran, fit the entire morsel in his mouth at once.

Roxanna just stared at him.

He poured himself a shot of raisin arrack and downed it in a single gulp. His next belch made his skin turn a darker blue, and burned Roxanna's feet.

"We don't care that you're a Jew, sister," he finally said, referring to himself in the plural as was the custom among all Lutis, "but you should let a man drink his arrack in peace."

From his skull a dragon exhaled blue flames down over his eyelids.

"I want to buy a ticket for the bus," Roxanna said weakly.

He laughed.

"Don't you know it's a day of assassination?" he asked. "Did you want us to drive the bus through the processions?"

She looked so perplexed, he actually felt sorry for her. She drew her hand back with the money, and for a moment he thought she was going to go home. Suddenly, he was certain she was running away.

"Sister, do you have a husband?"

She shook her head.

"How about a father? A brother? An uncle who's looking for you?"

"No."

Her voice was like water. Her eyes, too, were fluid.

"My friend is married to a man called Amin," she explained.

"I am going to Tehran to find her. I need to tell her. You see, her mother died."

He was looking at Roxanna's eyes, and the more he looked, the more he felt that looseness in his legs, that warmth in his groin which he felt every Friday morning as he prepared to visit his whore, Fariba, the one and only woman in his life, who fed him broiled lamb's testicles and blew opium smoke in his mouth till he felt he had the power to conquer the world and lay it at her feet.

He went to see Fariba in her own house because she was a woman of discretion and did not practice her trade, as others did, in one of those places where a hundred men were received in a single day. In those houses, there was a courtyard where the men sat in single file, and there were two cubicles, each furnished with only a bed and a curtain. Early in the morning, the prostitute would enter the courtyard in the veil and chador she wore in observance of the Islamic rules of decency. She would say a quick hello to the men, and send the first two customers into the cubicles. She would spend ten minutes in the first cubicle, get up from the bed without bothering to clean or dress herself, and move into the second one. Ten minutes later, she was back in the first bed, which was now occupied by a different man. She would do this till she ran out of customers.

Fariba, on the other hand, was an exemplary homemaker and a devoted mother. Her children, whose fathers she had never known, played in the yard while she entertained her "friends." Sometimes they appeared at the bedroom door while the bus driver was in the middle of his business. They would complain of aches and scratches, report fights and lost toys. But they were never hungry—the bus driver admired this about Fariba—or dirty, or even bored.

She took as good care of her "friends" as she did her children. On Friday mornings she lit a water pipe and placed a piece of brown opium paste on the coal to heat. She also lit the brazier and skewered four dozen lambs' testicles that she had already marinated in garlic and onions the night before. She put arrack on ice, and started her date with the driver by pouring the arrack over his body till his skin felt like hot ice. Then she rubbed him down as he smoked the opium and drank the arrack. She brought him the lambs' testicles right off the brazier. The skewers were so hot, they singed his fingertips when he picked them up (always with bare hands, because that's the kind of man he was) and then, in a single swoop, slid half a dozen testicles into his mouth at once.

But it was only Tuesday, and Fariba had a strict policy against out-of-turn visits.

He downed another shot of arrack, then pulled his canvas slippers onto his tattooed feet.

"Go find whoever it is you're looking for, sister," he told Roxanna. "As for me, I'm going to sleep right here today."

He slept five hours. When he woke up, Roxanna was sitting in the bus, alone, with her money still in her fist, waiting. He laughed at her persistence.

"Do you think I would run the bus for only one person— and a Jew at that?" he yelled at her from his bed. She got up from her seat and came to the door.

"It's dark," she told him, careful not to offend. "The processions have ended."

He realized she was not going to quit. Suddenly angry, he swore on the holy spirits of the Prophet and all of his disciples, summoned the blessing of the Koran and of the Invisible Imam. In the end, he dragged himself off the ground and sat behind the wheel. "Which station?" he asked, looking at her in the rearview mirror.

He was not at all surprised to see she could not answer.

"Uptown." She forced a look of confidence. "I'll know where to get off."

On assassination days in Iran, the entire population stayed indoors except for the processions. Everything shut down, even the radio, which replaced its regular programming of state-controlled propaganda with broadcasts of wailing mullahs chanting prayers from their local mosques. Finding himself alone on the uncontested road, the driver floored the gas pedal. He raced the bus at such speed, it threatened to topple over at every turn. Watching her in the rearview mirror, he could see that Roxanna was frightened, that he was going so fast, it was impossible for her to find the street signs, much less read them. But he was riding high and getting a thrill at not having to stop at any of the stations, and he did not much care what happened to his passenger.

"Let me know when we get there," he yelled back to her halfway uptown.

They drove to the end of the line, past the city and into the Vanak area, and finally stopped when there was no more road. He pulled the parking brake and turned towards Roxanna.

"End of the line."

She slid off her seat and stood up. She was bone pale, trembling a bit, obviously scared. When she came up to him, he realized she was going to pay the bus fare. Suddenly, he was ashamed.

"Keep your money, sister," he mumbled.

He watched her get off the bus.

"None of our business," he said, careful to avoid her eyes. "But whatever you've done, you know, it can't be so bad you'd rather stay out here, in this night, than go home to your man."

Roxanna watched the bus pull away, the driver's color blending into the night. As soon as he was at a safe distance, she started to walk towards the area where she had seen the last of the paved road. Something about the darkness, about being out in the unknown, so far from the ghetto even God could not find her, was exhilarating.

She had walked barely ten minutes when she heard a sound from behind and turned to look. She saw a car—long and dark and shiny—gliding on the road like an eel in black water. Its windows were tinted, reflecting first the various shapes of darkness, then, as it approached her, Roxanna's own image. She moved to the side of the road to let the car pass. It slowed down, almost stopped, then picked up speed and pulled away.

She walked faster now, suddenly concerned that she would arouse suspicion on the street or be arrested by the military police. She came to a street named after the first Pahlavi king, the Shah's father, who liked to erect monuments to himself. He had been a half-literate soldier the British had picked to rule Iran on their behalf. When he disobeyed their orders, they had removed him from the throne and put his son in his place. Still, in the short while the two Pahlavis had been in power, most of the streets of Tehran had been named or renamed in their glory.

At the end of the street, there was a small square adorned with the statue of Reza Shah riding on horseback. Roxanna saw a bench near the statue and sat down to rest. She heard the car again.

It entered the square from the opposite direction, circled it once, then twice. It moved so slowly, Roxanna could feel the people in the car looking at her, hear the wheels churn against the asphalt. Frightened, she began to run towards the street that led away from the square. The car followed her. It pulled up. A window rolled down.

"Just a moment!"

Roxanna dropped her bag of clothes and ran.

She ran with all the strength in her legs, aware that they were no contest for the animal she was racing, and all she knew was that she should not stop, no matter how long she had to run or how far the car pursued her, because stopping would mean certain capture and death.

The car passed her.

It pulled a hundred feet ahead of her, turned slightly to the left, and blocked the street. Roxanna let out a cry and turned to the opposite direction. The car's doors opened. Two men in black suits got out.

"Just a moment, miss!" a voice, different from the first, called out. "Just a word, if you please."

She was panting, shaking with fear, unable to turn and face the man.

"One word."

She tried to run, but couldn't.

Don't turn around, she told herself.

The man walked towards her.

Don't look back.

He came within five steps of her and stopped. He was waiting—waiting, she thought, as if his life depended on seeing her. *Don't turn around.*

But she did.

LATER, when the sorrow had already destroyed them both, Sohrab the Sinner would still recall with delight the moment in Freedom Square when Roxanna had turned towards him for the first time.

He was a quiet man, forlorn almost from birth—though his mother, Fräulein Claude, would later blame his melancholy on Roxanna. He spoke little about himself, even less about his feelings. But he talked of meeting Roxanna with all the tenderness of a man forever in love.

He was twenty-one years old, out of school and working for his father. The family had been on vacation in the village Teymur the Heretic owned near Gorgān, by the sea. Sohrab had returned to Tehran earlier than the others. On the way home, he had seen Roxanna.

He thought at first that she was lost, and asked Mashti to slow down. When she turned away to hide her face he became curious, but he was too well-mannered to stop someone who did not want to be disturbed. So they sped away and, a moment later, reached Freedom Square.

Sohrab the Sinner had always thought that Freedom Square was the place where he started to have memories. The first time he went there, he was seven years old and in second grade. His class had been studying the latest version of Iran's history, the one just dictated to historians by Reza Shah. As with every rendering before it and all the ones that would follow, this version spoke of the horrors of previous dynasties and of the greatness of the current one. But it also professed a new idea—that of personal and political freedom, of the rule of law according to a constitution, of the need to extend the same rights to everyone. Over dinner one night, Sohrab had tried to impress his parents by repeating for them what his teacher had said about freedom.

Fräulein Claude had praised him, of course, because Sohrab was the apple of her eye and could do no wrong. But he could tell that his father was displeased by his new finding, because he did not once raise his eyes to meet Sohrab's, and did not acknowledge hearing him. For many nights after that, Teymur had scanned the evening paper looking for something. One night he found it.

"We're leaving home early in the morning," he had told Sohrab. "I'm taking you to see an execution."

The evening paper always announced executions open to the public: there would be murderers and opium dealers, foreign spies, and, most of all, political enemies of the crown. Reza Shah had hung enough men, Teymur said—so many of them Shiite clergy—that the dead in Tehran were soon going to outnumber the living.

All night long, Sohrab felt his father awake and pacing in his first-floor drawing room. At four in the morning, Teymur nudged him awake.

"Come along," he said. "You might as well see what freedom looks like."

In the car, Sohrab tried to hold his father's hand, but Teymur pulled away. He looked straight ahead, like a man who knows he is about to commit a terrible act.

Around Freedom Square, the air was like sand—rough and grainy and so cold it hurt the chest. Hundreds of people had come to watch the execution. They were mostly men with pallid faces and black circles around their eyes. But there were also women in the crowd, most of them sobbing quietly into their chadors. Here and there children perched in their mothers' arms.

Sohrab saw four rows of makeshift gallows, five in each row. They were guarded by soldiers who stood against the crowd with their rifles drawn.

At five-thirty, a military truck pulled into the square. It deposited soldiers who then proceeded to unload the condemned men. Some of the prisoners walked out willingly. Others begged for their lives and had to be dragged by the soldiers. A few just held their hands over their faces and prayed.

One by one, Sohrab watched the men hang from the noose.

The bodies were left on the gallows for an entire day, so that as many citizens as possible could see for themselves the results of opposing Reza Shah. They dangled from the ropes like statues of lead—heads fallen to the side, eyes protruded, tongues swollen. In the center, riding his horse to save the world, Reza Shah's statue never turned around to watch his victims fall.

"Remember this!" Teymur told Sohrab. "This is the freedom your teacher told you about. This is the price you will pay if ever you believe her."

Sohrab the Sinner could never walk or drive through Freedom Square without feeling the nausea, the terrible sense of panic that had gripped him during the executions that day and for many months later. The night he found Roxanna, he had closed his eyes as the car moved through the square, and meant to open them only when they had cleared the area. But in the dark space behind his eyelids he had seen her again, remembered her face during the split second before she had turned away from the car in Vanak. He told Mashti to go back and look for her.

In the place where his most bitter moment had come to pass, the place where his childhood had ended and his faith had been destroyed, Sohrab saw a field of light so radiant, he felt as if he had opened his eyes for the first time.

SHE TOLD HIM she was looking for a friend, a girl her own age who had recently married a man called Amin.

Sohrab said that he knew Amin, that Amin was a friend of his father's. He said Amin was in Europe, traveling with his new wife.

Roxanna shook her head.

"That's not possible," she said.

Sohrab could tell she had nowhere else to go.

"I happen to know this for certain," he insisted.

He took a step towards her, hoping it would not scare her off.

"They've been gone for three months. Amin's sons are running the business. No one knows when he and Mercedez are coming back."

Roxanna looked so confused, it made him feel as if he had just betrayed her.

"With your permission, sir," the driver, Mashti, intervened. Having raised Sohrab from infancy, he felt a responsibility to steer him clear of danger. And he could see, just by the way Sohrab had not blinked since he set eyes on Roxanna, that the girl was dangerous.

"Perhaps I could take the young miss back to her house."

Roxanna balked.

"No," she said directly to Mashti.

Sohrab realized that she was about to run again, that he would have to chase her once more, hunt her down like a scared deer, because he could not stand to let her go.

"Come home with us, then," he told her so suddenly that even Mashti did not understand him at first. "I don't live far from Amin's. Spend the night, and in the morning you can go look for your friend."

Mashti panicked.

"But, sir," he pleaded.

Roxanna was tentative.

84

"Sir," Mashti interfered again.

Sohrab took her hand and led her towards the car.

In the car, Roxanna sat with her hands clasped together on her lap, and refused to look up. Mashti watched her in the rearview mirror. Something about her—the way her skin was so light he felt like touching it just to see if it was real, or the way she seemed completely alien to her surroundings—scared him. Next to her, Sohrab was so beside himself with joy, he had become unrecognizable.

From a distance, Teymur's house loomed over the Avenue of Faith like a monument. The car went through the back gates of the garden and up the cobblestoned driveway, past the fruit trees in full bloom and the sleeping flower beds, into the clearing outside the main building where all the walls were covered with creeping vines of jasmine. Seven marble steps led from the yard up to a pair of etched-glass doors two stories high. A servant, Mashti's Wife, saw the car's headlights through the glass and ran out to greet Sohrab. Since her employers had been away, she had not bothered to wear the dreaded uniform imposed on her by Fräulein Claude—the long-sleeved white shirt and the long black skirt with the white apron that was required for all the maids. Instead, she was wearing her chador, draped over her head and wrapped around her waist so that her hands were free to do her work, and she was barefoot. She balked when she saw Roxanna.

"May God strike me dead!" she shrieked, immediately covering her eyes with her hands. "I believe it's an Englishman."

Mashti's Wife had once had a name, to be sure, but it had not been used for so long, even she did not remember it anymore. She had been a young girl when Mashti married her in their village and brought her to Tehran to work for Teymur. Nowadays she was the most senior servant in the house and Fräulein Claude's right-hand woman, the person in charge of all the other maids except the hussy Effat, whom Mashti's Wife refused to supervise, on moral and ethical grounds. Effat had been employed at Teymur's house for seven years already and, in all that time, had never picked up a broom or a dusting rag. She had slept with every gardener and butler and salesman who happened to walk through the back gates of the house, and created such an atmosphere of corruption and sinfulness in the house, Mashti's Wife threatened to quit every day.

In truth, however, Mashti's Wife objected to much more than Effat's vagaries. For although she had spent most of her life in Teymur and Fräulein Claude's employ, she had a violent distrust of all people and things foreign, of bloodsucking Jews and whiskey-drinking Armenians, black-skinned Arabs and barefoot gypsies and, above all, that most atrocious of species—the blue-eyed animal responsible for all of the world's suffering, the beast that all the mullahs said had invented poverty and lack of faith, the snake that slept in every king's bed and curled under every Jew's pillow—the Englishman.

Mashti's Wife had never known an Englishman in flesh and blood, and could not even imagine what one looked like outside the human guise the mullahs said it assumed in order to fool believing Muslims. Many times, it had come to Teymur's house, of course, as a guest at his parties or on business, but on those occasions Mashti's Wife had heeded the advice of her local mullah and stayed hidden in her room. Any believing Muslim who laid eyes on an Englishman, the mullah had said, would immediately go blind. Anyone who did not go blind was simply not a real Muslim.

But the fact that she had never seen Englishmen and refused to look at pictures of them made it impossible for Mashti's Wife to distinguish them from people of any other race or religion except her own, and so she spent her life in a state of perpetual anxiety. It was bad enough that her employer, Teymur the Heretic, was a half-Jew who had lived in the West for the first twenty years of his life, and that his wife, Fräulein Claude, claimed to have been born and raised in Germany. Every mullah worth his salt had always told her it was a sin for a Muslim to work for Jews, to step under their roof, to eat their food. Mashti's Wife had subsisted for years on a diet of hard-boiled eggs and sweetened rose water, believing that eggshells provided some level of protection from the contamination caused to food anytime it was touched by an infidel. She washed herself five times a day, before every prayer, and made two pilgrimages a year—paid for by Teymur and Fräulein Claude—to the holy city of Mashhad, where she threw herself at the gates of Imam Hussein's burial grounds and begged forgiveness for the sin of taking money from Jews.

She never bothered to hide or even disguise her hatred for Jews and foreigners in general, and for her employers in particular. This may have seemed strange anywhere else in the world, but in a country that was a vast patchwork of different nations brought together by the force of history, where dozens of languages were spoken and each province believed itself a separate nation, living with the enemy had long since become a habit no one wasted time examining. For Mashti's Wife, the hard part came when a new person—a Sunni Muslim, a relative of Teymur or Fräulein Claude's, a friend of Sohrab's—entered the household. Then she felt the old fire re-ignite and, because she had no power against the infidels, directed it at Mashti.

Stepping out of the car, Roxanna lowered her head before Mashti's Wife in respect, and whispered hello. The old woman stepped back, her hands still over her eyes, and let Sohrab guide Roxanna into the house.

A long hallway paved with black marble led to an enormous drawing room with three crystal chandeliers and heavy wooden furniture. At the end of it, French doors opened onto a veranda with wrought-iron railings intertwined with purple lilacs.

Roxanna walked in slowly, without looking at anything on her way, without seeming impressed or overwhelmed or even surprised by the lavishness of her surroundings. She had seen this kind of house before—smelled those lilacs, stood on this veranda—or others like it. They had been in Alexandra's memories, those palaces where Alexandra had danced with her husband, those gardens where she had dined as a young woman before the phantom lover had brought her to hide in the ghetto.

Mashti's Wife was acting as if the world had come to an end.

"God strike me dead for all my sins," she repeated over and over to her husband. Whenever her cheeks got flushed like that, Mashti knew he was in for a night of suffering. "This girl is either a Jew or an Englishman or both, and I don't even want to know how she ended up in your car."

She turned around and headed straight for the servants' annex behind the main building. She found the hussy Effat packing fresh dough into her brassiere and licking her lips to give them a shine before she got into her uniform and showed herself to Sohrab.

"Get out there and see to Sohrab Khan," Mashti's Wife ordered, so repulsed was she by this woman who had made a career out of keeping her legs open. "No doubt he's going to want dinner. And he's brought some Englishman he wants to put up for the night. Keep an eye out so she doesn't steal anything."

Effat walked out, smiling so broadly, Mashti's Wife had to look away just to avoid seeing every last one of her teeth.

She was the only maid Teymur had ever hired directly, and the only one he would not allow Fräulein Claude to get rid of. He had even sent her to school, where clearly the only subject she had learned was how to string men along by the hem of her skirt, and from then on, it was makeup and perfume and fake breasts, birth-control pills and abortion-inducing remedies, until Effat ruined her insides and was told by a doctor that she could not have children even if she tried.

She was so shameless, she once went out of the house to buy a loaf of bread, dressed in her house clothes and with no shoes on, and came back a month later claiming to have married and divorced an American soldier stationed in Tehran. He had stopped in front of her to stare at her bare legs, and she had gone off with him, though neither one of them spoke the other's language, and they had lasted together as long as they could make love without needing to speak, and then they had separated. Back on the street and still barefoot in spite of her month-long escapade, Effat had turned up at Fräulein Claude's door with a bouquet of red roses and a smile for an apology.

For years she had also pursued Sohrab, parading in front of him in short skirts and bare feet, her toenails painted red and, when Fräulein Claude and Mashti's Wife were not home, without even a bra. She had gone into his room after midnight with one excuse or another, sat on his bed and told him about her lovers and all the things she did for them, how she liked to dip her nipples in honey before she made love, how she wore nothing under her chador and walked on the street with her lovers, so that from the outside she looked covered and only they knew exactly how naked she was under her chador. She had done all this with no result, drawing at best an indulgent smile from Sohrab, who listened only out of politeness and then walked her to the door, leading her to believe, against her own heartfelt wishes, that the boy did not have his instincts in the right place.

Still, Effat's hair had retained its unusual luster and her laugh had remained resonant as a dozen bells and she had gone on sleeping with men as if she were guaranteed eternal youth.

In the hallway, Mashti was pleading with Sohrab.

"Sir," he tried, careful to keep his voice low, "you don't even know this girl's name. We could go to sleep tonight and wake up to find she has set the house on fire."

But Sohrab was barely looking at Mashti. When he saw Effat, he looked relieved, as if he had found a natural ally, and asked her to show Roxanna to a room.

"Sir!" Mashti tried, more fearful of his own wife's anger than of anything Roxanna could do to them, "I must protest!"

Roxanna heard him and came into the hallway.

"I will only stay one night," she said, so gently Mashti felt his palms sweat with shame. "I can sleep anywhere you like. I promise I won't take anything."

She followed Effat into the guest room on the ground floor. It was smaller than the upstairs bedrooms, but it was at a safe distance from Sohrab's bedroom, Effat figured, and close enough to the servants' annex to keep Mashti's Wife satisfied. Roxanna said good-night quickly and closed her door. Then she lay on her bed, still dressed, and listened.

Hours passed. Roxanna lay awake, reliving the day's events, wondering about her parents, and Miriam, and what they would feel and think once they discovered that Roxanna had left the ghetto. Something about the house she was in—something both new and familiar—made her uneasy. When she thought everyone was asleep, she got out of bed and wandered out.

She walked along the hallway, up the staircase, into lavish, empty bedrooms with painted wooden closets, bathrooms adorned with mirrors and shiny-gold-and chrome faucets where water ran the color of diamonds, through glass doors that opened onto round balconies overlooking the garden. She saw Sohrab sleeping in his bedroom with the door half open, peeked into Fräulein Claude's room, then Teymur's. Roxanna felt invisible, so light no one heard her footsteps, so free she could have opened her arms and flown off any balcony if she had wanted to.

Downstairs, the kitchen was a sea of white walls and cabinets, connected to a smaller room with a rectangular table that seated eight. In between the two rooms was an alcove—small and poorly lit, furnished with a low stool, a brazier, a water pipe.

A man sat on the stool. He was dressed in a dark brown suit, a brown felt hat, brown leather shoes. He had on a white shirt with a starched collar but no tie. His eyes were all white, with no pupils, and yet Roxanna had the impression that they could see her.

Immersed in that strange yet familiar silence, smelling the opium and feeling the old man's blind stare, Roxanna the Angel realized that she had walked into a house of wonders, that she had come here by mistake and would never find her way out.

FRÄULEIN CLAUDE would curse that day as the worst one of her life—Saturday morning when she returned from Gorgān with Teymur and found her house overtaken by that runaway from the ghetto, Sohrab so infatuated with her, he carried her image all over his eyes and in his smile, Effat so intrigued by her, she followed Roxanna from a distance of ten feet, and swore the girl was a jinn—one of the many spirits who inhabit the nights of Persia and who have the power to transform themselves into human shape. Roxanna had only been in the house for three days—having confirmed for herself on Thursday that Mercedez was away in Europe with her new husband—and after that she had come back to Sohrab because she had nowhere else to go and no intention of returning to the ghetto.

Fräulein Claude threw one contemptuous glance at Roxanna, and knew she had to leave.

"Enough is enough," she said to Mashti, without even addressing Roxanna. It was seven in the morning, and Roxanna was standing on the steps outside the main entrance to the house. "Give her fifty rials and put her on a bus downtown. We're not running a boardinghouse here."

She left her coat on the railing downstairs, and began to climb towards her bedroom in the high sandals with needle-thin heels that made her look as if she were about to topple over with every step. Behind her, she could feel Roxanna frozen outside the house, sensed her embarrassment at being dismissed like the worthless creature that Fräulein Claude knew she was. She went into her bedroom and closed the door. What she did not expect was that Sohrab would follow her.

"Let her stay," he asked.

Fräulein Claude shook her head.

"Just a few days," he persisted, "till Amin comes back with his new wife. Roxanna is here to see Mercedez. She says they lived together in the ghetto."

Fräulein Claude was indignant: it did not help the girl's case that she had lived with the woman who had ruined Amin's family and good name. It further annoyed Fräulein Claude that Sohrab called her by her first name.

"So much more the reason we should get rid of her as soon as possible," she said.

They had left Gorgān in the dark, at three A.M., so Teymur could get to work early, and Fräulein Claude had to get up at two o'clock to get ready. Now she was tired and sleepy and more than a bit distressed by the way Sohrab, who had never challenged his parents' decisions, was reacting to Roxanna. Fräulein Claude would have liked to lean back in her chair, take off those sandals that had left deep red marks on her skin, put her feet up on the ottoman, and sigh in relief. She would have liked to take the pins out of her hair, detach the bits of horse hair, dyed blond, that she added to her chignon to make it look fuller, wash off the mascara that was weighing down her lashes and making her eyes water this early in the morning.

But she could not relax until Sohrab had left the room. In twenty-six years of marriage, she had never allowed anyone— not her husband, not her son, not even the servants, except for Mashti's Wife, who helped her bathe—see her without makeup and high heels. It was the secret of every successful marriage, she believed, for the wife to present only her best to her family, even if it did take a bit of extra effort, even if her son was twenty-one years old and pestering her in her own bedroom.

Suddenly, Sohrab raised his voice at her.

"You can't throw her out!" He yelled at his mother for the first time since he was a child. "I won't allow it."

She stood up and caught her breath.

"It wouldn't be proper," she explained. "She's a young, unmarried girl with no relation to us. Sooner or later her parents will come looking for her, and they will blame us for whatever it is she's trying to hide from them. Or she will develop expectations—from you most of all—and it will be so much harder then to make her leave."

He was not interested in her logic.

"You're going to have to reconsider," he said. "I'm not letting her go."

Fräulein Claude would think about that day a thousand times in the years that followed. In retrospect, of course, she should not have allowed Roxanna to stay even one minute longer. She should have called the police or the National Guard, sent Mashti to buy rat poison and mix it in Roxanna's food, told Mashti's Wife that the girl was a genuine Englishman who deserved to burn at the stake. Had she known what would happen next, Fräulein Claude would have piled firewood in the yard and lit the fire under Roxanna's feet herself. But right then, with Sohrab in her room, defying her for the first time in his life as he demanded permission for this girl to stay, Fräulein Claude gave in to the weakness she had always felt for her son and to the ache in her tired ankles, and she told herself that perhaps it was not so bad, that Sohrab was, after all, a man who needed female company, that they could keep Roxanna a few more days, till he satisfied whatever need was driving him to this foolishness, or until Teymur, who had not even taken an interest in the situation, interfered on Fräulein Claude's behalf.

Every day that went by, Fräulein Claude would regret her decision more.

It was not as if Roxanna were some magnificent beauty the likes of which Sohrab had never seen before, or that she acted provocatively or demanded anything from anyone. But there was something strange and unsettling about her—the way she sounded different from all the other Jews Fräulein Claude or Sohrab knew, the way she moved as if unimpeded by gravity. She observed her surroundings with those eyes that were almost hollow, went about without saying a word or making a sound for hours at a time, till Fräulein Claude had almost forgotten her existence, and then, all at once, she would laugh her three-year-old's laugh—tiny bits of musical joy springing out of her like pink cherry blossoms—and everyone in the house would stop whatever they were doing and look up as if to see the color of her smile. There she was, small and young and strangely confident, standing in the servants' yard with her feet bare as she helped Effat wring the sheets they had just washed, the lavender bleach water beading on the sides of her powder-white forearms and sliding onto her thin, childish legs. Or she was in the kitchen, careful to keep out of Fräulein Claude's way, talking to Jacob the Jello, whom everyone knew did not see or hear reality anymore, except that with Roxanna, he managed to hold entire conversations and even laugh at the right times.

It made Fräulein Claude boil with anger that Roxanna had managed to reach Jacob in the place he had lost himself. It was true that Jacob spent most of his time hallucinating. But his dementia also served the very useful purpose of making him forgettable, so that he could observe his surroundings—the servants, the houseguests, even Teymur—and, once in a while, in a rare moment of lucidity, report to her on events she would never have discovered on her own.

Fräulein Claude put up with Roxanna for a week, then went to Teymur. One morning she put on her red wool suit and her rhinestone-studded sandals, and went into the kitchen before Mashti's Wife had time to prepare breakfast. Roxanna was sitting at the table drinking tea with Effat. She had changed out of her school clothes and into something shapeless and old that Mashti's Wife had given to her. The moment Fräulein Claude walked in, Roxanna stood up with Effat and sewed her eyes to the ground.

"Good morning." Fräulein Claude smiled at no one in particular. In the alcove, Jacob the Jello was deep in his opium sleep, moving only occasionally to swat ten-foot-long flies from his face and head. Fräulein Claude went to the samovar and poured a glass of hot tea and one of hot water, covered the bottom of a silver tray with a starched, embroidered linen napkin, placed the glasses on the tray alongside a plate of dates and a single pink rose. She went to the mirror above the sink and checked her makeup, her hair, the lines around her lips. Then she picked up the tray and headed for Teymur's bedroom.

"Good morning, good morning." Her singsong voice trailed down the staircase and made Mashti's Wife frown in disapproval. Inside his bedroom, Teymur sat at his desk, reading last night's newspaper. He raised his eyes when she walked in, smiled, then went back to reading without a word.

She laid the tray on the desk, put the glass of tea before Teymur, sat down across from him with her hot water. It was their routine whenever she had something of importance to discuss. Only this time, Teymur did not seem in the mood for talking.

Fräulein Claude cleared her throat. After almost thirty years of marriage, she still felt her heart race whenever she was close to Teymur.

"This girl Sohrab has brought home," she began, "it's been eleven days. . . . We don't know a thing about her except some story about a Russian woman her mother gave her to. I think we should let her go."

Teymur had not touched his tea. She cleared her throat again.

"Sohrab wants her to stay, it seems." She spoke more to prevent her own creeping panic than to state what must have become obvious to Teymur by now. "But I don't see what her place would be among us, and I'm concerned about future problems."

She paused, took a sip of her hot water, watched Teymur. His eyes were on the paper but not moving, not reading anything, just avoiding her.

"At any rate, I thought I would send her off today after you and Sohrab leave for the office. You might mention it to him once you're both out of the house, let him know it was your decision as well as mine, so he won't resist me."

Suddenly, she thought that she should not have come, that she should not have brought up the subject with Teymur at all. She stood up abruptly and rubbed her hands together.

"There," she said, trying to leave before Teymur had a chance to speak, but it was too late.

He looked at her. She thought he was darker than she had ever known him, sadder, more alone.

"Let her stay," he said, and Fräulein Claude could hear the pieces fall out of her life.

TEYMUR THE HERETIC was the nephew of Muhammad Ali Shah, grandson of the prince Zil-el-Sultan, great-grandson of His Majesty Nasser-ed-Din Shah Qajar—the King of Kings, the Shadow of God, the Light of the Universe. Teymur's father, Solomon the Man, had been a Jewish singer blessed with irresistible good looks and a legendary charm that made him a favorite in the royal circles of his time. His mother, Tala the Qajar, was a Muslim princess who fell in love with the Jew and married him against the will of her father. She took Solomon to live with her in the Palace of Roses in Tehran, among the walls of diamonds and the pools of sapphire and the everlasting rose gardens of the Shah. There they lived for twenty blissful years, making love and producing children who were raised comfortable and self-assured, unaware of the war that raged outside the palace walls and the revolution that was closing in on them.

Teymur the Heretic was his parents' last son. The year he was born, in 1907, the Constitutional Revolution overthrew the Qajar dynasty and sent the royal family into exile. Teymur's mother followed the deposed king to Russia, children in tow, and left behind her husband, who refused to leave Iran. They stayed in Russia until the Bolshevik Revolution, then moved to Europe, and eventually to Turkey. They changed addresses every few months, lived off the ever-shrinking salary determined for them by their deposed uncle. Tala entrusted her children to the care of a house tutor, Mirza Muhammad the Muslim, who made them memorize facts and numbers till their minds were numb. Her older sons grew into bespectacled gentlemen of high education and impeccable manners, living in genteel poverty in France and England, spending most of their lives calculating the wealth they had lost because of the Constitutional Revolution and Reza Shah's coup d'état. The younger ones, Teymur and his brother Morad, remembered nothing of their mother's lost wealth, and therefore shared none of her nostalgia. All they wanted was to stay in one place long enough to belong.

In 1927, Tala the Qajar announced to her children that they were going to move again—from their house in Paris to the home of a distant uncle in Saint-Cloud. It would be their eleventh move in ten years.

Teymur the Heretic was twenty years old that year. He had been thinking of leaving his mother's house for a long time. He wanted to disassociate himself from the futile anger that drove her. He knew that she would not accept his departure, that she would not forgive his disobedience. Still, having weighed his options, he went to see his mother.

"I am not going to Saint-Cloud with you," he told her in the drawing room of her house.

Tala was standing under the enormous portrait of her grandfather, Nasser-ed-Din Shah. She had commissioned the portrait in order to prove to all those haughty Europeans who thought she was an imposter—claiming a right to royalty when it was clear to them she was just a poor émigré with a bloated self-image—that she was indeed a princess. Once a great beauty, she had become old beyond her years. Her skin had yellowed with the bitterness of exile, her lips had darkened from the tobacco that she smoked incessantly and that made her thin and feverish, forever surrounded by the scent of French cigarettes.

"You have no choice," she told her son. "We have no other place to go."

Teymur told her he was going back to Iran.

"Never!" She slapped him across the mouth. Blood gushed out of his nose. Tala despised the nation that had rejected her family's rule, the people who had removed her uncle from the throne. More than anything else, she hated Reza Shah, this man who had called the Qajars immoral and accused them of stealing the nation's wealth, only to adopt their throne and began stealing himself.

"You are a Qajar. Reza Shah will find a reason to kill you before you even reach the capital."

It was true that every reigning monarch in recent Iranian history had made a habit of eliminating the descendants of the ones preceding him. But Teymur, after all, was also the son of a Jew who had died unnoticed in Tehran.

He told Tala he would take his father's name, tell everyone he was Jewish, build a life separate from the bitterness and the longings of his mother's family.

"That is heresy," Tala fumed. "A Muslim who changes his religion is automatically condemned to death."

She could not stop him.

Teymur the Heretic dreamt of his mother's fury all through the journey back to Iran. He traveled alone, with only the sound of Tala's vengeance in his ears, riding on trains and aboard ships, arriving in Tehran two months and thirteen days after he had closed the last door of the last house in the last European city where she had gone to hide from her fate. To the innkeeper at the main caravansary in the Tehran bazaar, he said only that he was the son of a Jew, raised abroad by a Muslim mother. He found a job at the Ministry of Foreign Affairs as a translator to French and German and English diplomats. With his salary, he bought a house on Phoenix Avenue in Tehran and hired Mashti and his wife as chauffeur and maid. Then he met Fräulein Claude, and maybe it is true what she always said about herself—that it was she who brought Teymur his good luck.

SHE WAS THE daughter of Ruhallah from Shiraz, the man who owned the fabric shop at the back of Tehran's smallest bazaar. Ruhallah had come to Tehran in the early years of Reza Shah's rule and, soon after, had brought his wife and children from Shiraz. They had six sons and one daughter, a girl named Golnaz ("Fair Flower"), who thought it her mission in life to care for all the men in her family. Shortly after they arrived in Tehran, Ruhallah's wife ate a sour melon and died overnight of a stomachache. The doctor said the cause of death was a ruptured appendix.

Like all the men and women of his generation, Ruhallah of Shiraz knew better than to supplant centuries' worth of common sense with an outlandish diagnosis made by a young man barely out of his mother's womb who had done a five-year stint at some university, and suddenly thought he could speak the language of God. Ruhallah determined the cause of death to have been the sour melon and only the sour melon, and he did not hesitate to tell the doctor how much he resented the man's callousness, attributing such a defect—having body parts capable of rupturing on a whim—to a woman who was dead and could not defend herself. Ruhallah demanded an apology, since the diagnosis would reflect negatively on the desirability of his children for marriage, and the doctor quickly obliged. The truth was that, although he had no money and even less social standing, Ruhallah of Shiraz was a popular man with an extensive list of friends all over Tehran, and he could make or break a young man's career merely by talking about him over a plate of broiled calf's liver with onions, and a few glasses of aqua vitae in the Shah's Cafe downtown.

After her mother died, Golnaz left school to take care of the men in her family. One by one, she saw her brothers through school, married them off, and found them jobs as petty government employees obligated to take bribes in order to make ends meet. She ran the house, managed Ruhallah's accounts, gave him a daily allowance to spend playing backgammon with his friends. Every year, she found herself unmarried, getting older and—she had no illusions about this—less attractive.

Not that she had ever been much to look at, what with her kinky brown hair, that razor blade of a profile, those enormous breasts standing up over her incredibly thin waist. She did have long, shapely legs, it is true, and they could have looked exquisite were it not for the heavy, square hips that rested on them like a commode. Still, as time went by and life became more difficult, Golnaz also understood that a "correct" marriage was her only chance at improving her life and saving her brothers from their poverty. And as if that weren't hard enough, she went one step further and fell in love with Teymur.

In truth it wasn't love so much as total adoration, or awe, that she felt for Teymur. She had seen him around town, in the days before the war, when he was still working at the ministry. Few people owned cars then, so she recognized Teymur's Ford from far away. Perhaps it was his bizarre good looks—that dark, dark skin with the light green eyes that gave him the air of a threatening animal—or the legend that preceded him, about his *tar*-playing Jewish father who had sung, one drought year when the world was overrun by ants and locusts, and coaxed rain out of the sky. Perhaps it was because he looked so sad, so alone, every time she saw him, sitting in the back of the car driven by Mashti, smoking a cigarette and reading over his papers. Even his hands, she thought, looked sad. Beggars mobbed his car, and he gave money to every last one of them, even paid the little boys with the shaved heads and already rotten teeth without taking the junk they were trying to sell to him. He never refused anyone. If he did not smile at them, if he hardly said a word, it was because of his sadness, she thought, and not because he was cruel.

And so, like every other stupid woman in this world who has

ever walked willingly into an already spoiled life thinking she will be the Angel of Mercy, Golnaz decided she was going to marry Teymur and make him happy.

In 1933 she was twenty-eight years old—two years older than Teymur—with only six years of schooling and no knowledge of things fine and refined. She knew that Teymur had never noticed her, that he would not notice her if she appeared naked at his doorstep on a rainy night. But Golnaz was a woman who would not shy away from taking a drastic step if she felt the need. So she went to a loan shark and put up her father's shop as collateral on a loan, set her brothers in charge of the business, and bought two tickets—for herself and Ruhallah—on a ship bound for Germany. They were leaving for good, she told her friends, and they had no regrets.

Six months later, Ruhallah came back to Tehran wearing a padded wool suit, a full-length cashmere overcoat, and a hat that made him look every bit the Christian millionaire gentleman he was trying to personify. On his arm he had a young lady with platinum-blond hair and shaved eyebrows who bore an uncanny resemblance to Golnaz, but who introduced herself as Fräulein Claude. She spoke only a broken Farsi marred by a harsh German accent, claimed to have lived in Frankfurt all her life, where she had studied "the arts." And she persisted in her role so forcefully and for so long that after a while all her old friends wrote her off as a lunatic and played along with her story.

Fräulein Claude rented a house on Phoenix Avenue, down the street from Teymur's. She took long walks with her father in the afternoon, wore hats with little strips of gauze lowered over her eyes, tight cashmere sweaters that she belted at the waist so that her breasts looked like two huge sugar cones laid horizontally. She also wore impossibly high heels that made her legs look longer and her hips less heavy, shook hands with all the men her father introduced her to, drank anisette and smoked cigarettes, left enormous tips, spoke of buying a car. At the end of two months, as her borrowed money threatened to run out and her expensive new clothes began to look worn from frequent use, Fräulein Claude made her move on Teymur.

One afternoon she put on a gold lace dress, high-heeled gold sandals, a beige coat, and marched off with her father to Teymur's house.

"He is not home." The servant woman shoved the door in their faces, closing her eyes so she would not be contaminated by the sight of what she suspected might be an Englishman. Fräulein Claude pushed the door back and walked right in.

"We'll wait," she announced like a girl who is used to having many servants. "Bring us some anisette and two cups of Turkish coffee."

An hour and a half later, when Teymur came home, he found Ruhallah of Shiraz greeting him with a wide smile and a warm hand.

"Your new neighbor," he introduced himself.

He put a hand on Teymur's shoulder, and turned him towards the chair where Fräulein Claude sat with her back straight and her legs crossed at the ankles, her torso turned slightly sideways so that the peaks of her breasts were maximized.

"My daughter, Claude," he said. "Here from Germany to interview prospective spouses."

Teymur smiled at their presumptuousness, of course, but he was too polite, perhaps even too lonely, to ask them to leave. They sipped anisette and talked about the wonders of civilized Europe. Fräulein Claude admired Teymur's taste in colors, commented that the servant, Mashti's Wife, could use some training. Then she stood up and extended her hand to Teymur.

"I enjoyed our visit," she said. "I promise we'll be back."

Three afternoons a week for two months, Fräulein Claude, formerly the Jew from Shiraz and Tehran, visited Teymur without an invitation, thereby terrorizing Mashti's Wife, who would spend that evening and the following day washing the floors where Fräulein Claude and Ruhallah had stepped, in the hopes of neutralizing their contaminating presence. Fräulein Claude annoyed Mashti with her obnoxious requests for everything Teymur did not have in the house—French cognac, German chocolate, seven-day-old pigeon eggs—and she certainly tried Teymur's patience with her affected manners and her jarring accent, to the point where he often declined to receive her. Still, she sent her father back to the loan shark twice for more money, and spent it on clothes for herself and gifts for Teymur. Finally, one afternoon, she asked him if he knew how to waltz.

"Why?" Teymur asked.

She smiled at him indulgently.

"Just to observe the custom," she said.

He did not understand.

"What custom?"

"At our wedding," she answered, "I would like to open the dance with a waltz."

There was a moment—a single moment stretched out over all of Teymur's loneliness and all of Fräulein Claude's desire, a moment when he realized not only what she had asked him but just how far she was willing to go to get it—when he looked at her colorless smile and saw the tips of her fingers turning blue from the fear that he might laugh at her, and he understood that she loved him, that she had remade herself in order to be loved by him, and that if he turned her down now, she would sigh, right there before his eyes, and turn to dust.

"Very well, madame. We will open the dance with a waltz."

That is how Fräulein Claude married Teymur and came to live with him on Phoenix Avenue, how she paid off all the loans on her father's shop and set her brothers up in business, how she supported her father in grand style till the morning he was found dead in the Shah's Cafe holding a glass of cherry maraschino. She had only one child, Sohrab, who was born in the year 1936 and who was so beautiful, Fräulein Claude often refused to show him to visitors for fear that he would be struck by the evil eye. After that she never became pregnant: either, as Mashti's Wife insisted, because she was too old or, as Mashti speculated, because Teymur spent too many nights in his own separate bedroom.

In the years before the Second World War, when Reza Shah was building Iran's first modern factories, Fräulein Claude convinced Teymur to leave his job at the ministry to work as a metals broker, then to buy and sell the metal himself. Right before the war, someone told him to buy rubber: "a lot of it. And make sure you don't sell for a long time."

It was the rubber, during the Allied invasion of 1941, that would bring Teymur and Fräulein Claude their incredible fortune: The Americans needed rubber to make tires for their military vehicles. They would pay enormous sums, quickly and without questions. Teymur took the money and invested it in everything from metals to cement to basic food products. Then he bought the land on the Avenue of Faith and built the house that became the envy of the entire city.

The day she moved into her new home, Fräulein Claude thought she would never know grief again. For years, she proceeded to live in a state of uninterrupted bliss, adoring her husband and her son, relishing her wealth and social respectability to the point where no disaster, small or large, ever drew so much as a frown or a sigh of disappointment from her. As Sohrab grew older, she filled her time with select gatherings and society events, hired an ever-growing staff of servants, traveled to Europe and America. At one point, she even moved her brother Mr. Jacob into the house to live with her and Teymur.

Mr. Jacob had the ill fortune of liking opium so much, he preferred its company to anyone else's. For years he had done nothing but smoke while Teymur paid his rent and the cost of his children's education. One day his wife grew tired of caring for her dysfunctional husband, and sent him off to Fräulein Claude's. Teymur did not object, because he was a generous man who did not concern himself with ordinary matters of the household, but Fräulein Claude was so afraid of losing face with her society friends, she hid Jacob away in a guest room with the door closed. To the servants, she claimed he was ill from a nervous condition. To everyone else, she denied he was there at all. And she kept up the pretense until Teymur remarked that Jacob was going to die one day with the opium pipe in his mouth, and that he would do so alone, because Fräulein Claude refused him human company.

After that, she moved Jacob into the alcove between the kitchen and the servants' dining room. There, Mashti's Wife named him "the Jello" because of his constant shaking, and the other servants avoided him because they believed he was possessed by evil spirits. So Fräulein Claude was in no position, some years later when Teymur's brother showed up unannounced at their door, to complain about relatives invading her privacy.

Morad the Mercury had not seen Teymur for fifteen years.

"Mother died cursing you," he told Teymur. "She said she never forgave you in life for leaving, and she will not forgive you in death. She will be looking over your shoulder all your life, to deny you peace and take away anything that matters to you."

Fräulein Claude disliked Morad the moment she saw him. She hated the news he brought. More than that, she hated the way Teymur held his brother close, patted him on the back, smiled at him as she had never seen him smile at anyone else. Morad, she had heard Teymur say, was a gigolo who lived with many women at once, and had never worked a day in his life. Of course he accepted Teymur's invitation to stay in Tehran and live with them for a while.

She put up with Morad for close to a year, until Teymur had bought him a house and given him a job that he never held, living instead off of Teymur's generosity and gifts from his various girlfriends. Fräulein Claude even found him a wife, a naive peasant's daughter from some undeveloped province, who proceeded to give him no less than three sets of twin boys, which Teymur also ended up supporting. Still, Fräulein Claude was glad to have Morad out of her way, if only to satisfy the jealousy she felt every time she saw Teymur talk to his brother as if he were the only person in the world he could trust.

She told herself—on those occasions when she noticed Teymur's love for Morad and understood that he had never felt anything like it for her—that a man did not need to love his wife in order to find happiness, that the secret to a good marriage was compatibility and not passion, respect and not intimacy. She knew Teymur had never regretted having married her. She also knew that her son, Sohrab, was going to marry the girl Fräulein Claude chose for him—a girl so perfect and refined, so well connected and beautiful, she would outshine Queen Sorraya and all her jewels. A girl, also, who could not compete with her for Sohrab's love. A girl he would not love nearly as much as he loved himself, or his mother.

Instead, of course, there was Roxanna.

ROXANNA THE ANGEL believed that nothing was real until it had been named, that no one existed until they had been spoken of, out loud, before a witness who could hear their tale. All the rest, she thought, even pain, was illusion.

And so she began to keep the secret that year—of her own strange influence over that house, of the light that surrounded her wherever she was, that mesmerized Sohrab till he could not stop looking at her and unnerved Teymur so he could never set eyes on her. She kept the secret even as it came to life and grew, even as it walked and breathed and spoke to her in its own familiar tongue, even as it stared at her like her own shadow. It was the secret, she knew, that made Sohrab deaf to Fräulein Claude's warnings about her. It was the secret that made Teymur silent and hard and impossible for Fräulein Claude to reach. And it was the secret, above all, that kept Roxanna from leaving Teymur the Heretic's house.

The first thing she noticed about Teymur was that he would not look at her, that he made a point of not looking at her. That first morning when he arrived from Gorgān with Fräulein Claude, Roxanna saw him step out of the car, thank Mashti, come up and shake hands with Sohrab. Teymur was a lion, she thought—old and weathered but still magnificent. She knew he had seen her, but all the time she stood before him, he kept his eyes away and refused to look at her.

He went past her a few more times that day, happened upon her in the hallway and the yard. He heard the servants talk about her as if she were some novelty just arrived from Farangh, saw Fräulein Claude turn red and furious every time she was mentioned. He saw Sohrab watch her in the halo of Jacob the Jello's smoke, and all the while, Teymur never set his eyes on her.

It made Roxanna uneasy that he ignored her in this way. No one, not even her grandmother BeeBee, who had so despised her, had ever refused to see her. She wanted to go up to Teymur and stand in his face, lean over till she saw herself in the whites of his eyes. She wanted to call his name, ask him if it was true what Sohrab had said, that Teymur's mother had branded her servants' feet with a hot iron, that his grandfather had boiled his enemies alive in a pot of oil.

"Then he, too, has no pity," she had told Sohrab, and it had frightened and intrigued her at the same time.

At night, Roxanna walked through the house and stopped outside Teymur's bedroom. She heard the silence—the same one she had heard long ago in Alexandra's house when the Assyrian lover had called. She knew that Teymur was awake and alert, his senses magnified, his eyes focused on her in the dark like a predator on its prey. Frightened, she rushed back to her own room, closed her eyes, and tried to force his image out of her mind. But she knew that Teymur had seen her better than any-one else ever could, that he had watched the halo of her bare feet against the shiny black marble floor, felt her skin grow cold with fear as she stood outside his bedroom, her shadow floating against the white plaster of the walls as she ran away. She knew he could hear her body whisper against the sheets, feel her eyes burn with the rush of blood to her head.

And so she began to understand what no one else would sus-pect for many years yet: that Teymur the Heretic did not look at her because she was already in his eyes, from before he had ever met her, before she had even left the ghetto; that he did not have to stand close to her because he knew she smelled like the seas he had already sailed; that he did not have to touch her because he knew she had no weight—like sleep, or desire. And then she un-derstood that he had seen her wings—those transparent feathers that grew color only at night, against the blue sapphire sky of her longings. That is why Roxanna stayed in the house on the Avenue of Faith—because from the day he first saw her till many years later, Teymur the Heretic never looked at her.

SHE WAS STANDING in the servants' yard, before a barrel of red grapes just picked by the gardeners to make wine. She was barefoot, her white dress stained purple, elbow-deep in the grapes she was helping Effat squeeze. When Sohrab walked up to her, she smiled, then looked down at the barrel again. Effat could tell Sohrab wanted to be alone with Roxanna, so she stayed on, talking fast and making it clear she had no intention of abandoning the fort. In the end, Sohrab asked Effat to leave.

"My father has given me permission to ask you this," he told Roxanna once Effat was gone. His hands were shaking with nervousness, and a prayer teetered on the edge of his smile.

"I wonder if you would like to be my wife—marry me, that is—and live here with us in this house."

Startled, Roxanna pulled her hands out of the barrel of half-crushed grapes and wiped them on the front of her dress. Purple lines formed across the white fabric.

"I told my father I am not a wise man," he said, "but I do have immense feeling for you. I will tell you now that you are free to decide, but that I hope you will agree, and that, someday, you will love me."

She stared at him. The summer-afternoon heat rose in waves off the brick floor, sat on Sohrab's forehead, dripped off Roxanna's wet arms.

She thought of Teymur, of the way he had walked past her that morning, faster than usual, as if to cut off her hold on him. At the door, he had paused, his hand resting on the etched-glass panel, and for an instant she thought he was going to address her.

Was he watching her now? Did he know what she was going to say to Sohrab? Did he want her to marry his son, stay in his house, sleep in Sohrab's bed?

She told Sohrab it was entirely his decision—if they got married or not—because she was just a runaway from the ghetto with no place to go and no choices to make. Then she told him what she thought he deserved to know—that she was a bad-luck child, that she came from a line of women who had dishonored their families, that she was destined to run away, from her parents or her husband, or perhaps from both, that for this reason, her mother had tried to kill her and her father had given her up to a woman who lived with ghosts.

Sohrab laughed and told her Destiny was a lie.

Roxanna was shocked at first—at his impudence to the established rules of the universe. Then she looked at Sohrab's yellow eyes full of adoration for her and, for the first time in her life, thought that perhaps she had found a way out of her own destiny. She remembered the conversations she had had with Mercedez—about the man Roxanna said would love her, the child she would bear. She saw that child now, the girl who would be born into wealth, not poverty; love, not fear; optimism, not Fate. In that house far away from the ghetto, among these people who were immune to the powers of God and nature, Roxanna the Angel thought she could have a girl and perhaps give her, instead of her mother's sorrow, a new destiny.

They set a date, Sohrab and his father, and only then informed Fräulein Claude. Even the maids found out before she did.

For a few days, Effat had been going around with a long face, talking about how she had squandered her one chance at happiness by acting too "ladylike" around Sohrab, and saying that the next time she saw a man worth his name, she would take him to bed without asking his permission. She also spoke about the dress she was going to make for the "big affair." She did not mention what the affair was, and Mashti's Wife cursed and bit her lip every time Fräulein Claude walked in on their conversation, so that it became clear to Fräulein Claude they were hiding something serious from her.

She went into the kitchen and awakened Jacob. "What are they talking about?" she asked him.

"The nationalist insurrection," he responded with laser-sharp lucidity. "The CIA has paid people to back the Shah. Their tanks are coming down the street shooting at everyone in their way."

"What else?" Fräulein Claude persisted, trying to be patient. But her heart was beating in her throat.

"During the last insurrection, your husband's great-uncle sent an executioner to blind the people of an entire city with his dagger. So stay inside. You never know."

Fräulein Claude was livid.

"What is Effat saying about 'the affair'?"

Jacob frowned at her as if she were stupid.

"Your son's wedding, of course. Effat is making herself one hell of a dress."

FRÄULEIN CLAUDE tried to stop the marriage, of course. She fought a bloody battle to the finish, schemed, plotted and cursed, threatened suicide, staged a heart attack the day Sohrab came to her asking permission to get married. She threw herself in front of Teymur's black Ford, saying she would rather die suddenly than after a life of slow suffering, even took her maternal responsibilities to their logical end and tried to poison Roxanna: She ground the pearls from one of her own necklaces in a tiny mortar used for making powdered saffron, and had Mashti's Wife pour small amounts of the powder into Roxanna's food every day. It should have worked, too, forming a harmful sediment in the victim's digestive system that would make it increasingly difficult for her to eat, thereby causing death by starvation. Other women Fräulein Claude knew had tried it with great success. But Roxanna just swallowed an entire pearl necklace without so much as developing a case of indigestion, and even seemed to be thriving on the powder. Exasperated, Fräulein Claude consulted the best witch doctors and fortune-tellers in the city, complained to Tehran's martial-law commander and the head rabbi, donated money to the Muslim shrine of Shah Abdol-Azzim, asking the Holy Spirit to intervene on her behalf.

In the end, however, it was not Sohrab who defeated Fräulein Claude. And it certainly was not Roxanna: Fräulein Claude had overcome greater obstacles in her life than an eighteen-year-old runaway with no money and no relatives to speak of. In the end—and this was the hardest fact to accept—it was Teymur who prevailed upon her.

He wanted this marriage.

Fräulein Claude did not know why and she did not manage to make him explain himself. It is true that he had always been less concerned with the matter of Sohrab's personal happiness than was Fräulein Claude. It is also true that, having endured his own mother's ruinous preoccupation with family lineage and social standing, Teymur despised all such distinctions (why else would he have married Fräulein Claude?) and mocked his wife's consistent efforts at forming the correct social alliances. But in the past, he had understood Fräulein Claude's need to control her household, deferred to her petty concerns and her grand schemes, kept the peace by indulging her to the point where she sometimes mistook his lack of interest for a distant, passive kind of love.

He seemed to have done the same with Roxanna: he had remained quiet and uninvolved, ignored her existence until Fräulein Claude had pushed it in his face, and then, inexplicably, he had sided with Sohrab. After that it was one setback after another until Sohrab had gone to Teymur confessing love for Roxanna.

The only explanation Fräulein Claude could think of, the only possibility that made any sense, was that Teymur had never loved his son and did not care what happened to him or their family.

For this, too, Fräulein Claude blamed Roxanna.

July 17. The date loomed in Fräulein Claude's nightmares and drove fever into her blood.

A doctor came to the house every day to administer shots. Designed to calm her nerves, they only made her more edgy, and produced blisters in her mouth that burned every time she ate or drank. In response, Mashti's Wife soaked Fräulein Claude's feet in buckets of cold water mixed with salt and alcohol, applied mustard packs to her forehead, fed her fresh coriander and the juice of sweet lemons. Fräulein Claude stayed in her bedroom, and no one but Mashti's Wife was allowed in to see her without makeup and a proper hairdo. Mashti's Wife told the others of Fräulein Claude's deplorable health, of her broken heart and bitter disillusionment.

Still, the wedding plans moved ahead uninterrupted, confirming Fräulein Claude's worst fears that, with Roxanna's arrival, her own existence had become suddenly superfluous. The last straw was when Sohrab contacted Roxanna's family in the ghetto and invited them all to the wedding.

They arrived en masse, like a cloud of locusts descending on a wheat field, only more destructive—twenty-seven ghetto-dwelling Jews smelling of mothballs and cardamom, with under-nourished faces and patched-up clothes, children hanging onto them like shipwrecked sailors to bits of rotting wood—and Fräulein Claude did not have to meet them to know she wanted every last one, even the children, dead and buried in the ghetto's Pit so they could never set foot inside her house.

Mashti's Wife held Fräulein Claude's hand and walked her to the window of her second-floor bedroom so she could watch the procession. There were five men, ten women, twelve children. The men had dressed in bazaar-merchants' suits that they wore like a burden—the sleeves too long, the pants bubbling around their ankles, the shirts buttoned up all the way to the collar but with no tie. They had two- and three-day-old beards, yellow teeth, lips darkened from tobacco smoke. The women all looked as if they had dressed up to cover some terrible crime. They were wrinkled and dry and, all except for Tala'at, without makeup.

Tala'at had pulled her dress down so much, half her chest was showing through the neckline, and she wore a wide-brimmed hat—something pink and green and horrible with wilted paper flowers, like a Parisian whore out on her last stroll. Next to her, Miriam the Moon had the air of an undertaker come to take away the corpse, and her mother, the one they called "the Beautiful," sported a face so full of shame, she could not even hide it under a chador.

Once she had helped Fräulein Claude to the window, Mashti's Wife ran away to hide in her own room from the dangers of fatal contamination by Jews. All the other servants had been sum-moned by Teymur and asked to line up on the steps outside the main building to greet the family.

The guests hesitated as they approached the reception line. Then Rahman pushed himself ahead of the pack. Obviously feel-ing inferior even to the staff, he shook hands with Mashti and the gardeners, and bowed before the maids.

Teymur and Sohrab came to the door and welcomed them. The relatives remained stupefied, as if carrying millstones around their necks, appearing not to comprehend the strange and inexplicable thing that had happened here, thinking that it was all a mistake—the news that Roxanna was to marry Sohrab, that she was going to live in this house.

Only Miriam managed to keep a semblance of objectivity. She looked at Sohrab and his father suspiciously, like someone inspecting the wreckage of a lost ship for signs of human misconduct. Then she went into the house.

"Where is Roxanna?" she asked.

Roxanna came out of her room, smiling shyly, dressed in the new clothes Sohrab had bought for her. Everyone stared at her. Even the children, too young to understand, seemed aware that something of great import had happened to her.

Miriam went up and embraced Roxanna. Shusha followed, then Rochelle and Sussan. Tala'at did not move. Rahman just kept rubbing his hands together nervously, like someone who is late repaying a loan. He called Roxanna *khanum*—"lady"—as if her impending marriage had already elevated her to ranks much higher than her father's.

Effat showed everyone to their rooms. She noticed that Miriam walked with an air of dissatisfaction, looking suspicious instead of impressed, insolent instead of grateful.

"This house has ghosts," Miriam whispered to Mr. Charles.

Upstairs in her bedroom, Fräulein Claude took off her nightgown and ordered a bath. Her temperature was still high and she felt weak, but she was not so sick that she could not endure a house call by her hairdresser and a visit by her seamstress. Now that she could not stop the wedding, she decided it was time to emerge from hibernation and show those barbarians from the ghetto that she was still mistress of her own house.

THE NIGHT OF the wedding, the sky was cobalt blue, the moon so large it rose over the earth as if for the first time and turned the darkness into a soft, fluorescent glow. All over Tehran, torches burned the length of every major street, illuminating the city from its northern borders south to the gates of the Jewish ghetto and beyond, to the desert where men and women, drawn by the lights of the city, were traveling towards Tehran. In the residential neighborhoods and around the main bazaar, night watchmen paraded in new uniforms, calling, "All is safe in His Majesty's shadow," as they looked at their pocket watches—gifts from Teymur and Fräulein Claude.

Along the Avenue of Faith, ushers in white uniforms bowed as wedding guests drove past them in open carriages and shiny automobiles. At the gates of the house, women stood in long white gowns, their faces veiled, holding tiny braziers of green and turquoise enamel in which the coal burned amber. As the cars passed by them, the women poured wild rue seeds onto the coal and guided the thick white smoke—a harbinger of purity and good fortune—towards the guests.

Inside the garden, paper lanterns hung alongside the walkways. Two hundred trees, each lit from the trunk up, beamed in the night like incandescent spirits. In all the flower beds and along every pool, gardeners had planted new flowers for that night, so that the scent of perspiring jasmines and the white of blooming camellias would forever be linked in the memories of Tehran's inhabitants with the sound of Roxanna the Angel's name, and the legend of how she came to be the most envied woman in all of Iran.

Along the white satin runner that stretched from the gates into the reception area, violinists played the music of Mozart. Young women with faces out of old Persian miniatures led each arrival into the garden. As they walked, their steps rang with the chimes of the gold coins that hung around their ankles, and faded into the hushed murmur and the stunned laughter of the thousand guests who stood on the main terrace facing the house.

In his beige tuxedo with tails, Sohrab looked every bit the prince he would have been had the British not overthrown the Qajar dynasty. Fräulein Claude rose to the occasion in a gown of gold taffeta that blazed with the reflection of yellow rhinestones. On her head she wore a tiara of canary diamonds purchased in India and assembled in Paris. She had dressed Jacob in a new suit—black wool with a vest and a watch chain—and moved him out of the kitchen alcove into an armchair in the main drawing room. He spent the evening calling out to every servant and tugging at every guest's jacket, asking for his water pipe and brazier.

Morad the Mercury had left his wife and children at home, and was seducing every rich woman who came within arm's reach. Even Effat had put on a long gown of white silk and decorated her hair with white rosebuds and baby's breath. She went around the party introducing herself as a "close relation of the groom's," drank martinis with old married men, and shrugged off Mashti's Wife, who kept eyeing her in warning.

"If you sleep with an Englishman, you will turn into one," Mashti's Wife predicted before retiring to her room for the night.

"I hope so," Effat retorted. "Englishmen are better than you and I, or God wouldn't have made them English."

At ten o'clock the violins stopped playing. A choir of twenty-four castrati sang the traditional Persian wedding tune. Then a boy, barely three feet tall, walked out of the darkness and to the top of the walkway leading directly into the house. He took a flute from his pocket and began to play a tune so gentle and melancholic, it hung in the air, note by note, and stirred the sleeping shadow of desire in the heart of every guest. As he played, the boy looked at the house, at the far left corner of the top floor, and he looked for so long and with such intensity that everyone else followed his gaze and then they all saw, there behind the beveled-glass window, the radiant blaze of white that suddenly appeared.

The light moved slowly past one wall and then another, illuminating every room, becoming brighter as it crossed the third floor, went down the staircase and through the second, then onto the ground floor, so that by the time it was at the front door, the entire house was lit—like a golden ship rising out of dark waters—and opened its arms to reveal Roxanna.

Her skin was pale, her dress made of lace woven by Italian nuns, her veil a single sheet of silky gauze that stretched over her face and her entire gown. She walked down the pathway strewn with white roses—so beautiful with her gossamer step and her eighteen-year-old's smile, everyone who saw her at that moment swore she had been touched by the hands of God.

Sohrab the Sinner bowed before Roxanna. His eyes were yellow, like a tiger's, with rays of a darker brown shooting from them. They kissed her every time he looked at her.

Under a *huppah* of white gauze and camellias, surrounded by candles, Roxanna the Angel sat next to Sohrab and listened to the rabbi who pronounced the marriage vows. Afterwards, Teymur gave Roxanna a gift—a necklace of dark blue sapphire, which he hung around her neck himself. She raised her eyes at him and murmured thanks. He did not look at her even then.

Watching Roxanna at that moment, Miriam the Moon once and for all brought faith to the inevitability of Destiny. Tala'at the Deceiver spewed tears of rage and envy that poured down her meaty painted cheeks and gathered in a salty puddle above her breasts, in the space around the cleavage she so shamelessly laid bare every chance she got. She had been sulking all day long, ignoring her children and showering her husband with humiliating insults, and as soon as she saw Roxanna's necklace, she let out a sigh of desperation and broke into sobs so loud her brother, Bahram, had to remove her from the scene just to save face. In the struggle that ensued, Tala'at broke a heel, and after that she was forced to sit down all night, at her assigned table with the rest of her family, whom she could never tolerate from that night on, and though she did make a heroic effort at keeping her feelings suppressed, she broke into tears again sometime between the soup and the lemon sorbet.

Hours later the sun came up and the lights faded in the house on the Avenue of Faith. The last of the guests drove away in a stupor of exhaustion, and the servants closed the doors and drew the shades. Rahman the Ruler took his daughter's hand and gave her to Teymur: "My daughter is your slave," he repeated the traditional prayer expected of the bride's father. "Treat her with kindness."

Feeling her fever return at that moment, Fräulein Claude escaped to her bed with a handful of sleeping pills and a jar of chilled cucumber juice, hoping to wake up later and find out it had all been a bad dream. Tala'at limped on her broken heel towards a life she could never again share with her husband. Miriam vowed to get rich enough never to envy another woman's good fortune. And Rochelle decided she would go home and marry her only suitor—the little man with the bulging eyes and the melon-shaped head who kept eyeing every woman he passed on the street.

In his bedroom afloat in the morning light, Sohrab watched Roxanna before the mirror.

"Where did you come from?" he asked.

Roxanna did not answer him. She was looking at herself in the mirror. She could still hear the music of the violins, see herself move through the crowd. She could feel the hands that had reached out to her all night, that had touched her face, her back, her shoulders—all those people who had wanted to know her and own, perhaps, a piece of her luck.

She turned before the mirror three times and, every time, uttered a prayer:

"Eternal sunlight.

"Everlasting youth.

"A daughter with yellow eyes and a destiny of greatness."

FOR YEARS, the music did not stop.

There were intimate parties and formal receptions, trips to the Caspian shore, visits to the seamstress and the fabric store. Hairdressers came to the house to dip Roxanna's hair in ice-cold beer and roll it into tiny curls that fell around her face and made her look even younger than she was. Beauticians boiled brown sugar and lemon juice over a slow fire for ten hours straight, then poured the resulting warm, golden wax onto her skin. They let the wax cool, then removed it with strips of linen cloth, leaving Roxanna's legs bare and hairless as a child's. Manicurists soaked her fingers in soapy water and painted her nails amber. Effat asked her if she knew what to do with Sohrab in bed, and gave her the fruits of her own ample experience with other men. Sohrab loved Roxanna every moment of the day. Even Fräulein Claude tried to make peace with her, to swallow the hatred and accept Roxanna's presence, because anything less would cause the destruction of the family she had so carefully nurtured.

Teymur watched her.

He did not frighten her then—not like later, when his eyes became her prison, when she realized that he would never allow her out of his field of vision, because to do so would mean he had given up his last hope. In those days his eyes were indulgent and protective. There was understanding in them, a silent complicity with Roxanna over the secret they shared. Sometimes Teymur's presence induced in her an overwhelming urge to cry. Sometimes she woke up thinking he was standing above her, watching her sleep. Sometimes she turned around, when she was alone and he was far away, feeling he had said her name.

Two months after the wedding, Amin returned from his honeymoon, having spent a hundred thousand dollars and, in the process, lost his wife. They had traveled across Europe, and from there, Mercedez had wanted to go to America. In Los Angeles, she had bought a house on Sunset Boulevard, in between the homes of two movie stars, and declared she was staying for good. She was too young to spend her life with Amin, she had told him, too beautiful to be a mother and a wife. She wanted to become a star, like those women who lay around the pool at the Ambassador Hotel with their dark sunglasses and their bleached hair, making love in the afternoon and drinking themselves to sleep.

Dejected and shamed, Amin tried to save face in Tehran by denying that Mercedez had left him. He told his friends that she was staying in America temporarily, that the mansion on Sunset Boulevard was really just a vacation home where he would join her every few months. To prove it, he made frequent trips to Los Angeles and had himself photographed in white suits and linen shirts, standing with his arm around Mercedez's waist, their shadows floating on the blue water of the swimming pool. He tried to persuade her to come back by giving her jewels, to keep her from sleeping with other men by sending her more money than anyone else could give her. She never went back to Iran—not even in 1966, when Amin died of a bleeding ulcer, or afterwards, when Roxanna wrote to her asking that she return at least once, if only to lay a flower on the grave of Alexandra the Cat.

"No need for flowers," Mercedez wrote back. "The least I can do is to live honestly."

Roxanna saved her letter in the box where she kept her wedding ring and the other gifts Sohrab had given her. With a red pen, she circled the part of the envelope where Mercedez had printed her return address.

THE CHILD, of course, came in 1966—the daughter with the yellow eyes, the one Roxanna named Lili, who was going to relive a thousand lives and make each one free of loss. There would be others, Sohrab had thought, but none ever came.

Like my mother, I would be raised alone. Like Roxanna, I would be despised by my grandmother, Fräulein Claude, who saw me as final proof that Sohrab had thrown his life away.

Teymur the Heretic came to the hospital when I was born, and spoke to Roxanna for the first time in years. "Your child looks like you," he said, and his lips quivered with regret.

Miriam came to see Roxanna with her own daughter, a one-year-old with ruby red lips and jet black eyes who kept bursting into great cascades of laughter every time someone smiled at her.

Rochelle came with her husband, the man with the roving eye, who sat in the room smoking his pipe and inviting Sohrab to his weekly backgammon game.

Shusha and Rahman waited till after dark, when they knew they would not run into Sohrab and his family, then arrived with apologetic eyes and a plate of homemade halva designed to help the mother recuperate after childbirth.

Tala'at the Deceiver sent word that she was not coming because she had had three children of her own and had never once received a call or a visit from Roxanna.

But among them all, it was Effat whose life would be most directly affected by my birth. She did not come to the hospital the first day, because Fräulein Claude had burdened her with too many insignificant chores, and Effat had not had time to set her hair just right. She spent the next day doing her hair and shopping for a dress: Servant or not, she had told Mashti's Wife, she was not going to look any less attractive than any of the mothers who reclined on their hospital beds like queens on the throne of India, and who acted as if they had accomplished a task of real significance just by fulfilling nature's call. On the third day she headed out for the hospital and ran into the man of her dreams.

He was, literally, an Englishman.

He had come to Tehran to advise on the construction of a dam. He stopped Effat on the street and asked her the way to Queen Elizabeth's Boulevard.

"Yes, Your Excellency." Effat offered him the only three words she knew in the English language. She had learned them from her American boyfriend of long ago, who had insisted she answer him in that way every time he wished her to perform a sexual act. To the American soldier, this was only a harmless joke, but it would change Effat's life forever. She gave the Englishman her best smile.

"Do you speak English?" the man asked.

"Yes, Your Excellency." She shoved her breasts closer to his chest.

"Can you direct me to the English embassy?"

"Yes, Your Excellency."

She could tell the Englishman was getting impatient. After Roxanna had so deftly snatched Sohrab away from her, Effat had sworn she would never again waste a moment in the journey towards happiness. So she went forward that day and took the stranger by the arm. He thought she was going to lead him to the embassy. She called a cab, and instead took him to "New City," where her sister ran a whorehouse for American and British soldiers. She took a room and showed him her bare breasts. The Englishman with the pale face and the buck teeth squirmed a bit and tried to protest. Then he gave in.

After the first time they made love, he tried to make polite conversation—to prove he was no barbarian—but Effat signaled that talking was not the object, and so they spent the next four days making love and eating lamb kebob, drinking arrack, and smoking opium together. By the time Effat remembered Roxanna and the circumvented visit to the hospital, mother and child were already back at home. Effat took the Englishman to meet Teymur at his office.

"May God strike me dead," she pleaded with Teymur, "I must ask you for this one favor if it kills me. I have told this man you are my father—from another woman, because I know the Fräulein would never play along with this. At least I think I've told him you're my father. Some of the whores in my sister's house say they speak English. They translated for me."

Teymur laughed good-naturedly. Encouraged, Effat pressed on. "What I want is for you to tell him this is true, because he's English, you see, and no Englishman will want to sleep with a common maid if he can help it."

She thought Teymur was going to be furious. Instead, he told her she could tell the Englishman anything she wanted. She was so relieved, she grabbed Teymur's hand and kissed it.

"Your wife doesn't deserve you," she told him nostalgically, meaning every word. "Only I deserve you."

For the next few months, Effat dated the Englishman in spite of Mashti's Wife's warnings that she was copulating with the Devil. She brought him to the house when she knew Fräulein Claude was not home, and played hostess. She borrowed Roxanna's best clothes, and wore them with as much confidence as any rich girl on her best day. She took English language classes and typing lessons, and practiced her elementary skills of reading and writing in Farsi. Then one day she announced she was leaving Iran—for Kent County in England, she said, where she was going to marry the Englishman and have many sons.

Mashti's Wife spat at her. "You will burn so bad in the fires of Hell, even your ashes won't be found. Your sons will be born with horns instead of penises, and your daughters will have no anal opening through which to empty themselves of their English feces."

Years later, after she left Iran and married the Englishman, Effat would send Teymur a letter. It would be postmarked in England, written in Farsi but with the Latin alphabet. In it, she would claim that she was happy, the mother of two sons and a daughter, and that as much as she had checked her children, she had found no tails or tiny Devil's ears anywhere on their bodies.

Hers would be the first of many departures.

TEN YEARS after her wedding, Miriam the Moon was still living in the ghetto—because Mr. Charles's mother refused to leave the house where she had given birth to her crown prince, and Mr. Charles could not contemplate living anywhere without his mother. But Miriam had used her considerable talents and energy in making the best of a deplorable situation. And she had managed to find her husband a job that produced an income: She bought cheap silver trinkets from Tala'at's husband at cost, buried them underground for a while, then dug them up and knocked them over with a hammer till they looked antique. She gave the "antiques" to Mr. Charles, who sold them on the street to foreign tourists and rich housewives, swearing they were recently unearthed in the ancient city of Hamadan.

Miriam had conceived of the idea herself, but she refused to do any selling. "I can't lie about that kind of thing," she threatened Mr. Charles every time he tried to get her to help. "You know if I see someone being stupid with their money, I have to set them straight."

She made enough money managing Mr. Charles that by the early sixties, she could buy a share in Habib's silver business. Then she convinced Charles and Habib to give up the shop in the bazaar and move uptown, to one of the trendy antique shops along Ferdowsi Avenue. It was a shrewd and timely move, one that should have provided great happiness to all involved, but as things turned out, it was the beginning of real trouble, because in the frenzy of expansion and moving that followed, Tala'at's husband lost control of his household, and woke up one day to find that his children were neglected and his wife was sleeping with his nephew.

In 1969 Tala'at was thirty-six years old and the mother of three children. She slept with her husband at least twice a week, and certainly every Friday night after she had fed him meat-and-garbanzo balls packed with ground pepper and cardamom to increase virility. But theirs was a passionless affair that was over almost before it had started, and it always left Tala'at feeling angry and dissatisfied and certain she had been cheated. Perhaps this is why she took The Nephew as her lover. Then again, she always had been like a dog in heat.

The Nephew was always around, watching Tala'at's children for her so she could tend to her chores, helping her with anything he could, even while he should have been at work. Tala'at, of course, was not as obtuse and short-sighted as people seemed to think, but even she could not have predicted The Nephew's sudden transformation from infatuated little boy to rabid young man. On the morning of his twenty-first birthday, The Nephew wore his father's only good suit without his permission, stole his mother's bath money, and with it bought a box of candy so old, the sugar had crystalized on the inside of the lid. Then he pulled out a handful of geraniums recently planted on Pahlavi Avenue as part of the Shah's efforts at beautifying the city, wrapped the flowers—dirt-laced roots and all—in a newspaper, and at eleven o'clock in the morning knocked on Tala'at's door ready to give up his life.

At that moment Tala'at was sitting in her bedroom, sweating in the heat and wondering how she could get her husband to make love to her more often. When she heard the knocks on the door, she knew it was The Nephew, and the thought of him made her so hot between the legs, she had to fan herself before she could even get up.

The moment she opened the door, The Nephew gave a desperate cry—at once pathetic and exhilarating—and fell onto Tala'at's breasts with a thirteen-year-old hunger he had finally come to satiate. The geraniums dropped from his hand, and the candy spilled all over Tala'at's feet, sticking to her bare legs and to his father's leather shoes, but The Nephew did not notice. He kept sobbing and kissing Tala'at's breasts, and he would not have thought twice about making love to her right there in the yard, before the eyes of her three young sons, except she pulled him into the bedroom, closed the door, and tore the suit off his back with her teeth.

Noon came and went without a sign from either Tala'at or The Nephew. Frightened by the scene they had witnessed and the sounds escaping from their mother's bedroom, Tala'at's children knocked on the door and asked to be let in. They received no response. In the afternoon, they yelled that they were hungry, but Tala'at did not hear them. When it got dark, they went to a neighbor's house and stayed till their father, Habib, came home at nine o'clock.

"I think Mother is dead," the oldest son reported to Habib.

They found Tala'at lying in bed, alone and strangely satisfied.

For three months that summer, Tala'at the Deceiver allowed The Nephew into her husband's house and made love to him till he was exhausted and spent and shivering like a man about to give up his soul. He told his father that he had a job in Tehran, that he had to walk a long way, that if he worked hard enough, the job would lead him to great places. Every day, he put on his father's suit, which had become wrinkled and sweat-stained and shapeless in Tala'at's smoldering embrace. He also wore a cologne he had bought from Blue-Eyed Lotfi, with money Tala'at gave him from her weekly household allowance. It smelled like fresh lavender, she told him, sniffing every crack of his body. It made her want to eat enormous portions of food, throw herself in a fire, run naked through the ghetto square.

The smell of cologne trailed The Nephew out of his parents' three rented rooms and through the ghetto, past the square and up to the top of the alley leading to his uncle Habib's house, where The Nephew waited with his hands in his pockets and his heart in his mouth until he saw the poor man leave home. Then he rushed forward, knocking on Tala'at's door as if to announce that war had broken out in the capital. Together, they would vanish into the bedroom, and no one saw them till the late hours of the night.

Week after week, the neighbors saw Tala'at's children wandering alone and unsupervised in the streets, telling everyone who asked that their mother was "sleeping in her bed with Cousin Solomon," but even the most suspicious of minds could not conceive of a scenario as shocking and ghastly as the reality of Tala'at's transgression, and she was able to continue her affair with impunity.

By the end of July, The Nephew's mother was getting dizzy from the smell of lavender all over her house. She complained to her friends that her son was working too hard, that he was losing weight by the day and becoming forgetful and angry, "like those boys," she said without knowing how close to reality she had arrived, "who get bewitched by sorcerers and whores." One Sabbath evening in early August, she dropped by her brother-in-law's house just after The Nephew had left, and smelled her son's cologne all over the courtyard and even on Tala'at. The next day, she followed The Nephew up to Habib's door, and when she saw Tala'at open it and take the young man into her bedroom, she was still incapable of believing the facts that stared her in the face. She followed him every day for a week, but she never dared confront her son for fear of what he might answer. Then at last she went to Habib and Charles's new store, sobbing, and dragged them back to the house to show them what she could not describe.

Tala'at was sitting naked on the floor of her room, feeding bits of halva to The Nephew with her fingers. When she saw that she had been discovered, she stood up, wrapped a sheet around herself, ordered The Nephew to dress. She was strangely calm, even jovial, as she told Habib that she would rather burn in the fires of Hell with The Nephew than live another day with Habib. She told him she was willing to leave that moment, vanish into the void that was the city, and never call on him or his children again—as long as he did not order her stoned to death.

Habib shook with rage and remained speechless. Her children sobbed and held onto Tala'at's skirt. She walked out without a second thought.

In the ghetto, the rabbi declared a day of mourning.

Habib locked his sons into the house, painted the doors and the windows black, and sat shiva for an entire year. He would emerge only to change his name and move his broken family to Palestine, where he hoped no one would know their past.

Miriam the Moon followed Tala'at and The Nephew to their hiding place in a remote part of Tehran, and tried in vain to bring them back to their senses. They left a week later for Shiraz, where Tala'at had heard that moral corruption was tolerated.

Behind them Shusha the Beautiful, who had tried all her life to avoid infamy, boiled three scorpion tails in a pot of cowslip tea and drank the poison in a single gulp that induced cardiac arrest before she had had time to take the glass away from her lips.

THE NIGHT BEFORE Shusha killed herself, Roxanna dreamt of her burial.

They were walking in an endless procession—Roxanna with Sohrab, Miriam and Rochelle and all the rest of the family, dressed in black. Men carried a body wrapped in a shroud. In the Jews' cemetery, they placed the body in an open grave. Someone sang the Kaddish. The men—only the men, because women were not worthy of burying their own dead—began to throw dirt on the body. Finally, Roxanna approached the edge of the grave and looked inside: the body, shroud and all, was crawling with black scorpions.

She sat up, panting, and opened her eyes. She was numb with fear, her extremities ice cold and covered with perspiration. She turned on a light and saw that Sohrab was asleep next to her. She went across the hall, into my room, and watched me sleep. She was thirsty: the scorpions from her dream had poisoned her throat. She went down to the kitchen for water.

Jacob the Jello was sitting immobile on his stool in the alcove. As always, he was dressed in his brown suit and hat. His eyes were wide open, showing no pupils, and it was impossible to tell if he was asleep or awake. Roxanna poured a glass of water from the refrigerator and sat down at the maids' table. She rubbed her eyes, hoping to erase the image left in them from the dream. When she looked up, she saw Teymur.

She stood up, suddenly terrified, and knocked the chair down behind her.

"I heard a sound," he said. She felt that terrible sense of elation—that sweet, terrifying ache she always felt in his presence. For one instant, she thought she should run. Then his eyes caught her and she was eighteen again, standing barefoot outside his bedroom door, naked but for her desire.

They remained still, in the darkness filled with the white of opium smoke, their images reflected in Jacob the Jello's eyes, realizing they had already gone too far and would not go back.

Roxanna grasped that she was about to give up the life she had come to this house to seek—or at last claim the one she had really wanted.

She thought about the threshold that she was going to cross, that she had already crossed years earlier, the first time she saw Teymur and wanted him, or when she married Sohrab, knowing it was his father she loved.

She thought about how it would feel to press herself against Teymur, to lean away and let his hands run up and down the front of her chest, close her eyes and feel him look at her as he had wanted to do—as she had wanted him to do—for so long.

She went to him.

She put her fingertips on his lips and parted his mouth. Then she took his hand and put it on her cheek, where he had always imagined he would touch her—to see if she were real, if her skin would not decompose on contact. Something ice cold and fluid— like a stream of wine—poured out of his hand and into her body. She leaned back against the wall.

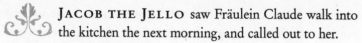 JACOB THE JELLO saw Fräulein Claude walk into the kitchen the next morning, and called out to her.

"Over here," he said, waving a trembling hand. "Your husband was screwing that girl from the ghetto last night."

Thus began the end of all of our lives.

Jacob the Jello exhaled a cloud of sweet, musky smoke, and in one telltale breath blew away the house of his sister's bliss. It was as if a breeze had stirred the earth, awakening the evil spirits that inhabit the night.

Fräulein Claude reached over and slapped Jacob then—so hard she threw him from the stool where he was sitting, and smashed his water pipe into a thousand sprinkles. She screamed that he was an old addict better dead than alive.

Mashti's Wife was passing through the kitchen. She stopped when she heard Fräulein Claude.

"What's happened?" she asked. "What did he do?"

Fräulein Claude did not answer her. She left Jacob on the ground and, trembling, went upstairs into her bedroom. She came back almost immediately to ask Jacob if he was certain of what he had seen.

Mashti's Wife had picked him up off the ground and was feeding him sugar water to stabilize his blood pressure.

"God help me," she told Fräulein Claude, "he's been saying disgusting things about your husband all morning."

Fräulein Claude took the glass of sugar water from Mashti's Wife and began feeding Jacob herself. The minute he recognized her, he started his story again.

"They were at it half the night," he said. "You'd think they'd been practicing all their lives."

It was true. Fräulein Claude could see the image still preserved in the whites of Jacob's eyes. She threw the sugar water at his face.

He thought he had been hit by a tidal wave, and began to flail his arms. He was drowning in the gray waters of the Gulf of Oman, with only Fräulein Claude nearby to help him, and all she did was stand by and watch as he struggled for life. He called out to her over and over, but she did not move—she who had been his closest friend and most devoted caretaker, who had trusted him with her secrets and raised him like her own child. She was looking at him and thinking that he was a stranger—like Teymur, and Sohrab, and everyone else she had ever loved—that he was separate from her, that he had betrayed her.

Her rage turned to hatred.

She went to look for Teymur, to attack him with her own hands, kill him if she could. She looked for him in his bedroom, in his study, back in the first-floor drawing room. Mashti's Wife stared at her with suspicion.

"Your husband is gone," she finally said condescendingly. "He left in the dark. Woke Mashti up and said they were going away for a while." She paused, studied Fräulein Claude. "I thought you knew."

She could tell that Fräulein Claude was stunned, that for the first time in her long and sinuous life, the Fräulein was truly confused. When she had first heard Jacob's story, Mashti's Wife had assumed that it was made up—like the white Mongolian horses he said had gone on a stampede through the kitchen during siesta time, or the naked women, wives of Ottoman emperors, he swore lay at his feet in hundred-degree heat, making love to one another because Jacob the Jello would not touch them.

But now, seeing Fräulein Claude before her, Mashti's Wife was not so sure that Jacob had lied about Teymur and Roxanna.

"It's enough to make any Muslim cringe with shame," she said, turning her lips up in disgust, "but you people know no god and no prophet, so it's possible that this thing actually happened with your husband and your son's wife. Maybe you should find the girl and ask her if it's true."

She took Fräulein Claude by the elbow and pushed her

towards the staircase. On the second floor, Sohrab was still asleep. Roxanna was nowhere to be found.

"Let's look upstairs," Mashti's Wife suggested.

Roxanna stood on the terrace of the third-floor ballroom. Her body leaned against the terrace railing, her hands gripping the metal. When she heard Fräulein Claude, she started, as if coming out of a deep sleep, then turned around. She was pale, almost transparent—a figurine made entirely of glass except for the tears that fell from her eyes. She moved her mouth, but no sound came from her throat. She tried again, but in vain. So she put her hand out, towards Fräulein Claude, and called her forward. Fräulein Claude did not respond.

Mashti's Wife went ahead and put her ear to Roxanna's mouth. She turned purple with disgust.

"What did she say?" Fräulein Claude asked her when Roxanna had finished.

"'Forgive me,'" Mashti's Wife repeated. But already, it was too late.

Roxanna did not wait for Fräulein Claude to tell Sohrab. She woke him up herself, in her gown that still smelled of Teymur, and told him what she had done.

She told him it was always meant to happen, that it had started to happen the moment she saw Teymur, or he saw her. She said that she never should have come to this house, that she should not have married Sohrab when she wanted his father, that she should not have stayed when she knew she was going to ruin them all. She knew now her mother had been right: Roxanna was bad luck; she brought shame wherever she went.

Sohrab listened.

They could hear Fräulein Claude sobbing in her bedroom.

They could smell the wild rue seeds that Mashti's Wife was frying on the stove—to chase away the evil spirits that Roxanna had brought to the house.

Sohrab looked at Roxanna in the early morning light and listened to her every word.

She told him that she would go away, that she knew he would want her to, that *she* wanted to go. She said she would leave everything—even her child—because she knew that no woman had the right to take a man's child away from him. She wanted to run, she said, wanted it more than she wanted her child, more than she wanted forgiveness.

She cried on Sohrab's hands. Her tears were heavy, like lead, and he thought they were going to crush his bones.

When she was done talking, Sohrab stood up and began to dress. He did not wash his face, did not shave. His suit, newly pressed before he put it on, wrinkled immediately against his skin, so that by the time he was finished dressing, he looked as if he had not changed in days. She thought he was going to work. Instead, he lay back on the bed, face up, eyes open, hands folded on his stomach.

They stayed in the room all day, Roxanna crouched on the floor with her back against the side of the bed, Sohrab lying awake and silent.

Fräulein Claude waited for Teymur, who did not come back and did not call.

Morad the Mercury stopped by to see his brother, then left, knowing he had stumbled onto a grave situation.

Night fell slowly. The same maid who had dressed me in the morning fed me dinner and guided me to Roxanna before bed. Three years old, I put my arms around Roxanna's neck and kissed her. Then I went to Sohrab and asked if he would carry me into my room. He picked me up and walked me over. Roxanna watched him. He was young, she thought. And sad. And he loved his daughter.

When he came back, he finally spoke to her.

"You can't leave," he said.

THE NEXT MORNING, I woke up to the sound of wood creaking, of metal grinding against metal, nails scraping against brick, moaning as they were pulled out of the walls. My room was still dark. I ran barefoot into Roxanna's.

"It's Mashti's son." She took me into her bed. Her sheets were cold, as if she had not lain in them all night. "He's taking the doors down all over the house."

We lay still and listened to the noise. Roxanna smiled at me.

"Don't be afraid," she said, but I could see her own fear in the lines around her eyes. "It has nothing to do with you. It's about me."

We got up and walked to the top of the stairs. Fräulein Claude was waiting for us.

"My son's orders." She attacked Roxanna immediately. Her face was chalk white and drawn, her eyes swollen and red. "He figures this way he can watch you every moment of every day and night."

Roxanna dropped her eyes to the ground and tried to pull me back into her room.

"Just a minute." Fräulein Claude stopped us. I pressed myself closer to my mother. Fräulein Claude approached.

"My husband has slept with many women since he married me," she said. "It's not as if I haven't known. But it doesn't bother me because he knows they're all whores, there for his taking. So I don't blame *him* for what happened. I blame *you*. And my son, too, blames *you*."

I could feel Roxanna's terror. Fräulein Claude moved closer.

"You may think my son has allowed you to stay because he still wants you," she hissed.

"You may think he decided to keep you because this girl needs a mother. "But I know my own son, and I will tell you that you're here because he wants *revenge*.

"And he will get revenge.

"I will help him."

All day long, Roxanna and I stayed in her room. In the evening Mashti's Wife came and called me to dinner. I pulled on Roxanna's hand, trying to drag her out with me, to take her downstairs, where she would be a buffer between me and Fräulein Claude, but Roxanna refused. I went downstairs alone. Fräulein Claude and I sat at the table. She did not look at me while we ate.

I sat still for as long as I could. Sometime during dessert, I stood up and asked if I could be excused. Fräulein Claude raised her eyes at me for the first time all evening. I remained there, small and terrified, wrapped in the frozen stare of this woman who had always hated me.

"Know one thing," she said.

"You are your *mother's* child, not my son's. One day soon, your mother is going to leave this house, and then you, too, will have to go."

I ran out of the dining room and into the hallway.

"Mama!" I called, racing up the stairs and towards the safety of Roxanna's arms.

"Mama!"

I tore up the staircase, through the hallway, towards her room. Suddenly, I stopped, turned, and looked behind me.

The hallway unraveled before me like a roll of bright, gleaming silk—smooth and flat and inviting. With the doors gone and the rooms all connected to one another, airy and without secrets, my view was unobstructed, as if in a dream.

"In here," Roxanna called.

She sat upright at her vanity table. She wore a gown of light, almost faded pink. Her hair fell around her face in large, loose curls. Her skin glowed. I saw her and thought, as always, that she was perfect.

She opened her arms and embraced me like a flower. She smelled of rain.

"Now I can see you even in my sleep," she whispered.

MIRIAM THE MOON came to Teymur's house to deliver news of Shusha's death.

"I've been trying to reach you every possible way," she told Roxanna at the etched-glass doors of the entryway. She had brought her daughter, who played on the ground near her. "I've called and come by, but your mother-in-law has left instructions with the help that they should not let me in. That woman, Mashti's Wife, was only too glad to oblige."

She waited for Roxanna to express surprise, or to explain what had happened, but all she got was a slight nod of the head and evading eyes. She realized that Roxanna was not about to invite her in, that Roxanna was afraid Fräulein Claude would happen upon them and disapprove. So she looked around, at the yard full of ancient trees and flower beds, and drew in a breath before she spoke.

"Mother boiled some scorpion tails and drank the poison," she said without warning.

"It was quick," she went on, "because no one even heard her gasp, but it must have burned quite a hole in her insides. She started to bleed from the back. Sussan found her, foaming at the mouth and still in the death throes."

Roxanna's knees buckled under. Miriam grabbed her arm and helped her sit down on the steps directly outside the house. A life of hardship and responsibility had made Miriam tough, uncompromising, intolerant of weakness. But with Roxanna she was always more gentle than with others. She let Roxanna catch her breath.

"We buried her a week ago today," she said softly, then put her hand on Roxanna's head and caressed her hair. "It's all right, you know. She was tired and wanted to stop. I think Tala'at's craziness was the last straw."

Just then, Fräulein Claude came outside and saw Miriam. She turned pale with anger.

"Stop trying to sell your cheap silver at my door," she told

Miriam with unadulterated hatred. "Go away and take your dirty, retarded child with you."

Miriam's daughter, Sara, stopped playing. She came up behind her mother, afraid to look Fräulein Claude in the face, and pulled at Miriam as if to indicate she wanted to leave. Roxanna did not look up at either one of them.

Slowly, Miriam the Moon adjusted her scarf on her head and retied the knot under her chin. She stared at Fräulein Claude, then at Roxanna, then back at Fräulein Claude.

Then she looked past Fräulein Claude into the hallway, and noticed that all the doors were gone.

"Something happened here," she said matter-of-factly. "You people are up to something, and I can tell it's no good."

Even Fräulein Claude was taken aback by Miriam's frankness.

"Whatever it is," she went on, "be careful. There are ghosts in this house that have been asleep for a long time. One false move, and they will all wake up and haunt you to the grave."

That is how it happened. Miriam the Moon spoke of the robber ghosts of the house on the Avenue of Faith and, by so doing, brought them to life.

At first, they stole insignificant items: a pair of scissors, a stack of sheets, a pot of food. Sohrab's papers disappeared from his desk, and Fräulein Claude had trouble remembering where she had last seen her reading glasses. The maids accused each other of losing the laundry, and Mashti yelled at his wife for throwing away socks she claimed she had darned.

But then Roxanna took off her wedding band to wash her hands one day, and when she reached to put it on again, she saw that it was gone. Certain she had left it by the side of the sink, she looked around the bathroom and under the rug, inside the medicine cabinet and in the folds of her own dress. She put a knitting needle down the drain and into the toilet, turned the bedroom upside down and, in the end, came up empty-handed.

Fräulein Claude noticed that the ring was gone. She declared, in front of Sohrab and Mashti's Wife, that it was typical for a woman of lax moral standards to lose her wedding band. At that time Teymur was still away on his trip, and Sohrab was spending more and more of his time at the office, so Fräulein Claude was the uncontested ruler of the house. She declared that Roxanna was not to be trusted at all, that she had lost her wedding ring on purpose so as to attract men who would not suspect she was married, and that the only way to keep her on the right track was to watch her all the time.

"You may not leave this house without my permission and without a chaperon," she warned Roxanna.

Roxanna accepted her punishment quietly. Sohrab had not spoken to her for weeks. He did not seem angry or vengeful, as Fräulein Claude had said. Mostly he looked sad, and on the few occasions when Roxanna had tried to speak to him, he had offered only a polite word and then silence.

She went to him again.

"Your mother does not want me here," she told him as he lay in bed with his eyes open one night. "I know you can't live with me anymore, and I can't live with myself. Let me go."

He closed his eyes then, knowing that she was looking at him, that she would have touched him if she dared, to heal the scars she had left on his soul. He thought of his own loneliness—vast and gray and eternal now that he knew she did not want him.

"I know I can't take Lili," Roxanna went on, pleading like a small child. "You wouldn't give her up and I wouldn't want to take her anyway—not the way I am, so unlucky I will smear my misfortune all over her destiny. All I ask for is my own freedom."

He was thinking of the night he had first seen her, how she had run on the street, surrounded by a translucent glow that left a trail of light through the darkness.

"If you don't let me go, I will have to run away," she said. "It will be without warning, without a word to you or Lili."

He opened his eyes, suddenly furious, and tore at her.

"Go, then!" he screamed. "See how far you will get before I bring you back. Go and see how long you will last on the street."

It was the first time she had ever seen him so angry.

"In this part of the world, no woman can get beyond a city's borders without her husband's written permission. I will call the police and have you arrested. I will have my father call out the National Guard to bring you back."

He turned away from her, slid off the bed, and walked to the window. A moment later he looked back and saw she was still sitting there—small, helpless, trapped. He felt sorry for her.

"If I let you go," he said, softly now, but still furious, "you will be lost. You will have to run all your life, and you will be alone. Someday Lili will ask me where you went and why I let you go, and I will have nothing to say and no excuse for what I did."

He could tell she did not believe him. He was not certain he believed himself.

Teymur came back at the end of four weeks, quiet and severe, looking much older than he had before. He did not ask for Sohrab or Fräulein Claude's forgiveness, did not explain where he had been or why he had gone away. He avoided Roxanna any way he could. Confronted by Fräulein Claude's hatred, ashamed of his own weakness—the arrogance that had allowed him to take a woman as his son's wife when all he had wanted to do was to hold her naked against his own skin—he closed himself off, and abandoned Roxanna to Fräulein Claude's revenge. In the years that followed, he would take many lovers, travel on long and unnecessary trips, speak to his son only when it was absolutely necessary. But at night, every night, he stayed up in his bedroom that had no doors, and listened to the sound of Roxanna's breathing.

He had run his hand down the center of her chest, from the hollow of her neck between her breasts and onto her stomach, and his fingers had drawn a pale, icy line on her skin.

A FEW DAYS after Teymur's return, Fräulein Claude lost her turquoise earrings with the diamond settings. It happened during a house call from her hairdresser, a woman she had known for a decade, and yet Fräulein Claude did not hesitate to draw the obvious conclusion.

"That woman is a thief," she declared to all of her society friends, telling and retelling the story of how she had taken off her earrings, laid them on the table before her, and then, suddenly, not seen them anymore. In a matter of days, she managed to ruin the hairdresser's reputation and rob her of all her best customers. The hairdresser asked for a meeting, to try to clear her name, but Fräulein Claude contemptuously declined.

Immediately after she fired the hairdresser, Fräulein Claude lost two pairs of sandals, and fights broke out among the servants over personal belongings that each accused the others of stealing. Teymur gave up on looking for his cuff links every morning, and Sohrab stopped bringing papers to the house to review. Then Roxanna confessed to having lost her sapphire necklace.

"It's the new maid!" Fräulein Claude declared. "I always thought she was crooked."

The new maid was sixteen years old, a distant relation of the washerwoman who came three times a week to help with the laundry. When Fräulein Claude called her in and demanded a confession, she sobbed on Fräulein Claude's shoes, begged for her life as if it had been threatened, swore she had never stolen a thing. If her family found out she had been accused, she said, they would flog her to death in her village.

"Tell me where you put everything," Fräulein Claude answered coolly, "and I will dismiss you without trouble."

The girl was not forthcoming. So Fräulein Claude ordered Mashti to light a fire in the servants' yard, tied the girl by the hands and feet, and threatened to burn her at the stake unless she confessed. She stopped just as the girl's feet began to blister, of course, never having intended to go through with her threat, and

returned the maid to her family with a detailed account of everything that had been stolen.

She had not always been cruel. She became that way, Fräulein
Claude, once she had lost to Roxanna everything that had
mattered.

The servant girl's departure should have meant the end of all the
trouble, except for the six-foot Persian rug that suddenly vanished
from under a coffee table in the third-floor sitting room, and the
twenty-nine-piece china set—a wedding gift to Roxanna and
Sohrab from Fräulein Claude's friends—that was taken from a
locked cabinet without so much as a whisper.

"It's the cook!" Fräulein Claude decided, and fired the man
without ceremony.

"The washerwoman!" Mashti screamed, and she, too, was
gone.

The gardeners took the blame for the four-hundred-year-old
painted-glass candelabra in Teymur's drawing room, and the
woman who did the ironing found herself accused of having
stolen Sohrab's leather-bound books. Every day, all day long,
Roxanna and Fräulein Claude looked for items they had lost.

By the end of that year, Fräulein Claude had fired every
servant in the house except for Mashti—who was beyond suspicion—and his wife, who quit in a fit of rage when questioned
on the whereabouts of yet another priceless antique. Fräulein
Claude was so certain of each person's guilt, she did not even
change her mind after firing them had proved futile in the war
against the robber ghosts. New servants lasted a few days at
best, and after a while, Fräulein Claude decided to stop hiring
anyone at all—the house could succumb to dirt and disorder
for all she cared—until she had located the source of the
trouble.

Then she turned against her family.

She had already told Roxanna that her relatives could no

longer visit even for a moment, because they were obviously thieves. Now she told Sohrab that he was not allowed to invite anyone to the house. She asked Jacob's wife and children, on one of the rare occasions when they came to see him, if they would not mind opening their bags so she could search them. She called her friend of twenty years, the wife of the minister of war, and asked if she had not happened to take a Baume and Mercier watch by mistake on her last visit. Those who were not accused directly heard stories of Fräulein Claude's mad suspicions, of her dust-filled house with the empty cabinets and the bare floors where nothing lasted more than a few weeks, of Roxanna forever looking for lost items, and of me, her child, who was afraid to be alone anymore, because it was possible—Fräulein Claude had warned me many times—that the same people who stole everything else would grab me when I least expected it.

They heard the stories and stayed away, certain that bad luck was catching.

ROXANNA went to Teymur, one afternoon when the strain of her confinement and the weight of Sohrab's sadness were too much to bear, and told him she wanted to leave. It was a Friday, and Teymur sat in his study sipping tea and reading the paper. Fräulein Claude sat across the desk from him, as always overdressed, and even she could not hide her shock at seeing Roxanna walk in.

Roxanna was thinner than before, more pallid. Her eyes looked larger. She had grown up, Fräulein Claude realized, become more beautiful, more threatening.

"I have come to ask your blessing." She addressed Teymur directly.

Fräulein Claude watched him as he looked at Roxanna. His eyes had turned to stone. His hand held the glass of tea in midair without so much as a tremor.

"I want to leave this house," Roxanna said, looking at him. "I have told Sohrab I will ask for nothing but my freedom. I need you to let me go."

Fräulein Claude forgot how to breathe. She was staring at her husband, praying to him with her silence, asking him, begging him to say what he should have said from the first day—that Roxanna could leave, that she *must* leave, that Teymur would let her leave and thereby give Fräulein Claude her life back.

He put his glass down and stood up. He had never feared anyone or backed out of a fight. But he did not dare look at Roxanna.

"You are my son's wife," he said. "I could not take you from him even if it were my wish."

That night, for the first time in many years, Roxanna the Angel dreamt again that she could fly. She woke up and checked her bed: Her sheets were clean, her pillow was still dry. But all around her bed, the black marble floor was spotted with long blue-white feathers.

MORAD told Teymur they must resort to drastic measures to protect themselves against the thieves.

"Do whatever you want," Teymur told him, uninterested. "You're not going to stop anything."

So Morad went to Sohrab, and together they called Teymur's friend the army general in charge of Tehran's security. He ordered additional men to guard the house, planted half a dozen informants up and down the Avenue of Faith. They drew barbed wire along the top of the wall surrounding the garden, replaced the iron gate with solid blocks of metal. Then they bought four guard dogs. They ordered Mashti to keep the dogs chained all day and let them free only at night, to feed them raw calf's liver, and to beat them till they became rabid.

Mashti kept the dogs in the greenhouse so the heat would make them more angry. At night, they ran free around the house, charging every shadow, attacking everyone except Mashti, who fed them. After a while, when the robber ghosts had not backed down, he let the dogs loose during the day as well as at night—to make certain no one sneaked in from the yard. They barked all day, tried to jump the fence that separated the servants' yard from the rest of the garden, to attack Roxanna and Fräulein Claude as they were doing the laundry. Instead of saving the house from the robber ghosts, the dogs became its jailkeepers—like the doors Fräulein Claude had taken down, the servants she had fired, the soldiers who guarded the street.

Every day, Roxanna felt more trapped.

THE NIGHT OF my fifth birthday, Roxanna told me that she would go away, one day when no one was watching, and that neither the land nor the sea would ever hold a trace of her tracks.

We were lying in her bed, in the second-floor bedroom she still shared with Sohrab. Sometimes, when Sohrab stayed up late in his study, she brought me into her bed and talked to me past midnight.

"They will come looking for me," she said, "a thousand men with a thousand lanterns, and though they will search the earth and all of its rivers, they will never find me."

Helpless, I listened to her and tried to keep my fear from choking me. I realized she was confiding in me because I was her only friend, the only person in that house who loved her unconditionally. I never understood why she wanted to leave.

"Teymur the Heretic will call up all the generals in the Shah's army, and your father will summon all the soldiers in the barracks," she said. "They will ride the mountains and descend into the valleys, but I will be far away, beyond everyone's reach, and this time—this time I will not look back."

She must have realized she was hurting me. She held my face in her hands and kissed my eyes. I inhaled the smell of the sea in her hair, held my breath so I would not cry.

"It's going to be hard for you," she said. "I know. I, too, lost my mother when I was young. But you must survive, just as I have, and just as I know you can. You must survive because you have a future here, with your father. I will not take it away from you."

In my dreams at night, I walked barefoot in the desert, a lantern in my hand, surrounded by a thousand children—my own shadows—calling Roxanna the Angel's name.

FRÄULEIN CLAUDE called a family meeting. She summoned Teymur and Sohrab, Roxanna and Mashti, even Morad and Jacob the Jello. She did not defer, as she would have done a few years earlier, to her husband.

"I have spoken with numerous experts in the field of security," she said, "and they all agree that the thefts in this house are inside jobs."

She paced the room as she spoke, her hands on her still-tiny waist. She looked composed, in control, more powerful than anyone else in the room. Teymur's betrayal had given her the tacit right to be in charge.

"Someone living in this house has brought us bad luck." She did not have to name Roxanna for everyone to know who her target was.

Jacob the Jello waved his hand up and down as if to awaken his body.

"Nothing to do with bad luck," he said. "It's those two men who come to the house and carry everything away."

No one listened to him.

Aware that she was being attacked, Roxanna sat next to Sohrab and looked at Fräulein Claude. By then she fully believed in her own corrupting influence—the ill fortune that surrounded her like a halo and spread to anyone she touched.

"I think it's important that we know the enemy," Fräulein Claude went on, "and that we protect ourselves against it and its offspring."

Sohrab looked up. Teymur, who had paid no attention so far, suddenly turned towards Fräulein Claude.

"This house is haunted," she went on. "We should move—the immediate family, that is—and let the rest stay on."

Morad raised an eyebrow, full of sarcasm, and wondered just how far Fräulein Claude would go.

"And the immediate family would be?"

"Teymur, Sohrab, Mr. Jacob, and myself."

Even Jacob was stunned.

"What would you do with Roxanna and Lili?" Morad asked. Sohrab stood up to leave. He walked out alone, without a word to either his mother or his wife. Teymur, too, went to his desk and sat down before a pile of documents, which he began to read.

"No need to move." Jacob struggled to be heard again. "All you have to do is stop those men from carrying everything away. I call out every time I see them, but it's no use. I can hear myself all right, but my voice doesn't seem to carry these days."

Tall and lean and forever the gigolo, Morad the Mercury traversed the drawing room in his tailored black suit, and addressed his brother as if Fräulein Claude were not present.

"Time to do something about your wife," he said, rubbing his hand over his freshly shaven skin. "She has been going mad before your eyes and you haven't even noticed."

Fräulein Claude caught up with Morad and slapped him across the face.

"Watch yourself!" she tore at her brother-in-law. "You have lived off my husband's charity for twenty years. If he ever cuts you off, you will starve in the gutter like the stray dog that you are."

So Morad got this idea—late in life, when it was already clear to everyone except himself that he would never amount to anything more than an educated dandy—that he was going to prove his business savvy to Fräulein Claude and stop depending on Teymur for financial support.

The first thing he did that day was go home and tell his wife and sons they should no longer call at Teymur's office for their monthly allowance. Then he went to the bank and checked the balance on his savings account.

"Thirty thousand rials." The manager, who knew him, smiled helpfully. "But, of course, you could always draw against your brother's credit."

Morad shook his head. In 1971, thirty thousand rials would buy him dinner with a few friends at a cabaret, not including the alcohol. As investment capital, it amounted to less than the price of goodwill.

He withdrew the money and asked the bank manager to dinner. They had vodka and caviar, coq au vin, profiteroles filled with vanilla ice cream and topped with chocolate sauce and whipped cream. Over dessert Morad asked the manager for a loan—not against Teymur's account, he stressed, but in the name of their new friendship. The manager agreed over a glass of port and a handshake, gave Morad a limitless line of credit, quietly assuming that Teymur, as always, would be the guarantor.

Then he told Morad he knew of a great investment that would make him rich in no time. An air-force general with actual blood ties to the royal family owned a thousand acres of prime cultivated farmland in the north. He had bought the land in partnership with one of the Shah's brothers, but His Majesty had not approved of the deal. So the general had been told he should sell his land—before the Shah lost patience. He was in such a hurry, he would gladly take a big loss if it meant the buyer was good for the deal.

They had another glass of port. Morad was moved by the bank manager's expression of trust.

"Who better than yourself—with your family lineage, your sophistication, your honesty—to become partners with His Majesty's brother?" the manager encouraged Morad.

A hundred million rials—a little over three hundred thousand dollars—and Morad would be on his way to great fortune.

He went home and told his sons he had made them all rich in their own right. He sent word to Teymur that he would not be needing his charity anymore, that he had made connections in high places, that all was forgiven between brothers. Teymur called the bank's owner. The land Morad had bought, with money he had borrowed against Teymur's credit, was indeed prime real estate—so prime the Shah's sister, acting as head of the so-called Pahlavi Foundation, had already announced she was going to confiscate it in the name of state security. That is why the general had to find a buyer fast—to get at least his own money out before the Shah's sister had stolen everything.

Teymur sent for Morad. He came beaming and exuberant, dressed in new clothes he had also paid for on credit now that— he explained to Teymur casually—he was a partner of the royal family's. Teymur laughed. He opened a drawer and wrote Morad a money order.

"This is your month's expenses," he said gently. "The land deal was a hoax."

He was not angry with Morad. He did not expect the news to hit his brother so hard. He never imagined it would kill him.

Because it did—Miriam the Moon is certain of this: Morad the Mercury died of Sorrow, his doctors' subsequent and very useless diagnosis notwithstanding. Grief welled up in his body—so hard he could touch it under his skin—and poisoned his cells. Grief can do that, just as it can drive a person's blood sugar up so high, he slips into a coma without knowing what has happened. It can attack a person's nerve cells till it has landed its victim in a wheelchair. In the West, doctors and scientists have given names to grief's creations: Cancer. Diabetes. Multiple sclerosis. They claim no one knows what causes these illnesses or how to cure them. But in the East, people have been dying of Sorrow since the beginning of time, and it had never been a mystery to anyone until the doctors arrived on the scene. There is even a name for it in Farsi—*Degh*—which means, literally, "to get sick and die of Sorrow." That is what happened to Morad—the doctors and all of their scientific failures notwithstanding.

Morad sat in Teymur's drawing room that day—the sun blazing against the window as it went down in the west—and did not say a word for close to an hour. Then he asked for a glass of water, drank it down, and realized he had a violent stomachache. He went home, and for many days ate nothing but ice water and plain, homemade yogurt. Still, the burning that had started in the pit of his stomach would not go away.

His wife told him he should go to the doctor. Morad slammed the door in her face and lay face down on the bed, listening to the state-controlled radio broadcast pro-Shah propaganda. A few days later, she found blood in his stool and suggested that he had contracted an incurable disease from the rich woman he had been sleeping with. Morad became furious. To punish his wife, he went to see the rich woman again.

For the first time since he had reached puberty some forty years earlier, Morad's body did not respond to his desire.

He did go to a doctor then. He told the man that he had lost fifteen kilos recently, that he was always cold, shivering even in a warm room. The doctor observed that Morad had a fever. He ran tests. The trembling, he diagnosed, was from pain Morad was trying to deny. The pain was from a tumor, probably malignant, that had lodged itself in his stomach.

Morad ran to his brother for help.

Teymur the Heretic summoned the doctor to his office and cross-examined the man as if he were a petty criminal caught in the midst of committing a great crime. He took Morad for a second opinion, then a third. He asked to see the test results for himself, paid other doctors to interpret them independently.

"My dear sir," an X-ray technician whistled from under his spectacles, "judging by the size of this tumor, I suggest you operate tomorrow, or resign yourself to the fact that your brother is going to die."

Black with rage, Teymur slammed his hand down on the technician's table, and declared war.

"The hell with dying," he said. "I will take Morad to America."

The flight for New York, via London, was scheduled to depart at 7 A.M. June 18, 1971. Morad would be accompanied by Teymur and Sohrab. It was the earliest they could travel, having bribed various officials to obtain passports and visas without the usually lengthy wait.

By then Morad had lost another few pounds, and his wife came to Teymur's house every day, crying that she was going to be a widow if something was not done very soon. Teymur watched his brother tremble and sigh, sigh and tremble.

He promised Morad that the doctors in America were going to cure him of the tumor, that they would not even operate, probably, because surgery was the last resort of barbaric Eastern doctors who were not up to the latest advances in medical science. No doubt they would give Morad some pills, prescribe the right foods, perhaps even decide there was no tumor to remove.

Stinging with remorse over what she had done to Morad, Fräulein Claude brought a mullah to the house, sacrificed a sheep, and poured a few drops of its blood in a tiny bottle that she gave to Morad.

"Hang it around your neck till you come back from America," she ordered, and Morad, who had laughed at superstition all his life, obeyed dutifully.

They left for the airport at three in the morning. I woke up with Roxanna to watch them go.

Morad's wife sobbed on his shoulder till his jacket was wet and sticky with her tears.

Fräulein Claude held him close, her face against his, and cried real tears.

Roxanna waved at him from the top of the staircase: she was wearing a long, pale blue nightgown, her hair loose on her shoulders. She looked like a candle, I thought. If she leaned forward one more inch, she would tip and fall over the railing, down onto the black marble floor of the entryway, and break into pieces.

When they were gone, Roxanna took my hand and led me

back towards my room. Fräulein Claude caught up with us in the hallway. She was slightly disheveled. Her makeup, always perfect, was smeared around her eyes. She grabbed Roxanna on the shoulder.

"It's just you and me," she hissed. "Make a move."

DAYS WENT BY that summer without a visit from any one to the house. Claude locked the doors, let the dogs loose, and told Roxanna and me we could not leave—not for a day, not for an hour. She spent her own time doing her hair and her nails, cooking and taking care of Jacob the Jello. Roxanna and I cleaned house and sat together in the kitchen, read fairy tales in her bed on the terrace, ate together in her bedroom. I was frightened of Fräulein Claude, worried that Roxanna would make good on her promise to escape the house and leave me—or that a robber ghost would indeed snatch me away from her. I followed Roxanna into every corner of the house. I listened for the sound of her footsteps, learned to sleep lightly, woke up if I could not hear Roxanna breathing nearby. Often, I spent the night awake, watching Roxanna at her bedside, guarding against Claude and the robber ghosts.

I wanted to tell her—my mother, who thought of nothing but her own need to leave—how much I wished that she would change her mind and stay with me. I wanted to say that Roxanna was my only friend, that being with her—even in that house full of fear, even during that summer so charged with heat and danger—was the closest I had ever come to feeling safe.

"Take me with you if you go," I wanted to say. But I was afraid that Roxanna would refuse, that she would tell me, again, how she was going to escape and vanish so no one could find her.

I never spoke.

The only person who still called at the house was Bahieh the Sponge Woman. She was short, almost as wide as she was tall. Her legs were like two streams of moving fat, and she walked barefoot because no shoe had ever fit her wide feet. Her soles, therefore, were three inches thick, and black as leather. Her hands were so callused, she could not make a fist.

Bahieh the Sponge Woman was too poor to buy a cart or a

donkey to carry her wares. She put her merchandise—cleaning fluids, soaps, powdered detergents—in two enormous bags which she flung across her shoulders when she walked. She came to our door early every Saturday morning, before the sun had become too hot, and refused to go away until she had sold something. Fräulein Claude's accusations of theft and treachery did not frighten her. Mashti's threats to call the police fell on deaf ears. Even the dogs could not keep her away.

"Staaaaaand baaaaaack!" she screamed at them so hard that tiny hairline cracks appeared in the brick pavement beneath her feet. The dogs retreated before her with nothing more than a moan. She dragged her body across the garden and up the three steps of the entryway.

"Look at you," she said when I answered the door that summer, "so privileged it makes me puke. I was younger than you—not even four—when my mother brought me down from our village and put a saddlebag on my back. She gave me walnuts to sell by the kilo. If I didn't sell, we had nothing to eat. The other kids my age just begged. My mother begged, too. But no one would give me anything for free, because I was ugly."

She repeated the same story to Roxanna, told Fräulein Claude she did not care whether we needed anything that day, that we had to buy from her because we owed it to her, because we were rich, and could spare the dime.

"If you don't," she warned Fräulein Claude frankly, "I'm going to stay here forever. Or else I will curse you, and take away any bit of luck your daughter-in-law has not already spoiled."

With that Bahieh would sigh, pick the bags off her shoulders, and turn them over on the floor.

Out poured a fountain of brilliant, beautiful colors—dozens of bright green and orange and red sponges, bottles of indigo bleach, bars of pink soap, boxes of perfumed detergent that sprang out of her bag like jewels from the mouth of a terrible beast and lay at my feet on the floor—the light that came through the etched-glass doors falling over them in long white shafts and transforming my world full of fear and sorrow into magic.

"Look at all this." Bahieh would smile like a god before her creation. "Pick out what you want."

I knelt on the floor and dug my hands elbow deep into the pile, hoping to keep those colors forever.

THERE WAS NO sound, only the touch of a cool hand, a brisk motion sliding me through the sheets and pulling me upwards to a sitting position. Someone was putting shoes on my feet, a coat on my back. I smelled the sea and opened my eyes. Roxanna smiled at me in the dark.

"Shhhhh!" she whispered, almost mouthing the words. "Don't talk."

She picked me up off the bed and walked towards the window. She was barefoot, carrying her shoes in her coat pocket. Her feet were so light, they sounded like raindrops against the stone floor. At the window she stopped and looked into the yard.

"We're going to go down the ladder," she said, her lips grazing my hair. "You must hold on to me and not let go. When we get to the ground, I'll take your hand and we'll run."

She put me on her back and wrapped my arms around her. Five years old, I was almost too heavy to be carried anymore, but Roxanna moved around as if she did not feel my weight.

When she climbed onto the windowsill, I buried my face in the space between her neck and shoulder, and did not look down.

The outside shell of our house was made of yellow bricks and white stone. Roxanna was going to climb down two stories— from my bedroom to the yard—using a built-in ladder that served only repairmen and chimney sweeps.

"What about the dogs?" I asked.

"They're dead." Roxanna sighed with relief. "The Sponge Woman poisoned them."

It was early November. Morad the Mercury was still in America with Sohrab and Teymur. I had started kindergarten, but Roxanna was still confined to home, guarded by Fräulein Claude, allowed no freedom.

"Fräulein Claude is asleep," she told me. "We'll be back before she wakes up."

The night air was cool and light and startling. Roxanna

breathed it in, trying to contain her excitement, and when she exhaled, she was like a child with no sorrows.

I had always imagined that the world outside our house was as silent after dark as my bedroom. Now I stood on the sidewalk, holding Roxanna's hand, and, for the first time, watched the night bloom before me into a thousand buds of light: Men strolled past us in work suits, chatting as they smoked. Beggars wrapped in torn blankets called from every corner, and cursed when Roxanna did not give them money. Children with scabbed faces and bare feet pulled at my coat sleeve, shoving boxes of gum, packs of red Marlboros, folds of lottery tickets in my face.

Music spilled out of the open windows of passing cars and washed over me like water. An old man wrapped in newspapers for warmth held a monkey on a leash and searched for a spot to put his animal on display. The monkey wore a satin vest, sequins on the edges of his shorts, a fur hat. When the old man called him, the monkey turned around and looked at his owner with disdain.

A flower vendor, her arms wrapped around a bunch of garden roses, bumped into the old man inadvertently. The roses fell out of her arms, loose petals paving the sidewalk.

"Look!" Roxanna yanked my hand.

A woman was crossing the street. Her white chador billowed in the wind to reveal her long, lean legs. She wore no stockings— only a pair of red patent-leather boots that reached up over her knees. Her appearance confused the drivers on the street. Cars screeched to a stop, sliding on the icy road, honking furiously as they tried to avoid her. The woman threw her head back, the chador slipping down to her shoulders, and laughed a clear, resonant laugh that echoed through the street and dimmed every other sound. This was Pari-with-the-Boots, Roxanna told me, Tehran's celebrated prostitute, known for her beautiful long legs and her preference for wearing only boots.

A taxi stopped an inch from Pari's feet. It was packed with passengers—seven people in a tiny orange car—but the driver stepped out and insisted that they must leave. The passengers protested, demanding to be taken to their destination. The driver was adamant.

"Pari Khanum here needs a ride," he told his passengers, referring to Pari with the reverence due a lady. Around them traffic had become gnarled and furious. People left their cars to scream at the taxi driver that he must pull aside so they could pass. Pari-with-the-Boots just stood with her chador down on her shoulders, black hair shiny and soft, bare legs showing no sign of being cold, and laughed. Even from the distance, I could smell her perfume, the tobacco that had made her young fingertips yellow, the cold, dry steam that blew out of her mouth every time she laughed.

We walked to the next street. Roxanna tried to call a taxi, but in vain: they were all full, carrying many people to different spots along the same route. In the end, Roxanna opted for one of the passenger cars that operated illegally as taxis.

"If anyone asks," she warned me, "don't tell them our name. Everyone in this town knows your grandfather. They may tell Fräulein Claude they saw us."

Only then did I realize that I was still in my pajamas, my coat covering them to my knees.

We drove along a wide and crowded street, northbound in a car full of strangers, and it was all I could do to keep my eyes to the ground and my heart from bursting out of my chest with excitement. When the car finally stopped, Roxanna pulled me onto a sidewalk full of people and music. Red and blue and orange lights flashed in my eyes.

"This fair is here all year round," Roxanna told me. "It's open every night, and often I have wanted to bring you here, and to come myself."

The man in the ticket booth had a blind eye that was completely white, with no pupil.

"You shouldn't be on the street without a man," he said as he handed Roxanna our tickets.

We stood in the Ferris wheel line. When we sat in the chair, Roxanna squeezed my hand and smiled. I watched as the ground pulled away from us, the people getting smaller, the music sinking away, then coming back, drawing away, and back again. Roxanna took my chin in her hand and tilted my head upwards.

"Look *up*," she said. The sky washed over me like water.

"I flew there once," Roxanna said. "I was six years old, still living with my mother. One night, I grew wings and flew."

She saw the stunned look on my face.

"I don't know how it happened." She shrugged. "Maybe I only dreamt it. Maybe I'm different that way.

"But from that time on, I could never stand the feel of my feet on the ground anymore."

MORAD THE MERCURY came back from America on a stretcher, a plastic bag hanging from the side of his stomach. Behind him walked Teymur, a storm in his eyes, a box full of painkillers in his hands. America, he told Fräulein Claude, was the promise of fools.

The doctors had given Morad two to six months to live. He died within thirty days of returning home.

Fräulein Claude was afraid to hold the wake in the house: with so many people going in and out every day, the thieves would have free reign over her belongings.

"But there's nothing left to steal," Teymur pointed out bitterly, looking around at the empty drawing room, the dusty outlines of missing frames on the walls.

During the week of shiva, I stayed home from school, wore black, and watched as people filed in and out to pay their respects. Teymur's friends came with their wives, gawked at the emptiness of the house, told each other it was true, what Fräulein Claude had said about the daughter-in-law who had brought bad luck. Morad's many lovers came alone or with their husbands. They were pretty women in tight dresses and black silk stockings. They wore too much makeup, too many jewels. They shook hands with everyone and then sat there crying nobly into their tissues, careful not to smudge their mascara, while checking the room for potential new lovers. They smiled at Teymur and Sohrab, offered their sympathy—any time of day or night—their phone numbers, their warm embraces.

Rochelle came twice, sat in her fur coat with her legs barely reaching the floor, and watched her husband try to impress the women Morad had left behind. Every few minutes, she went to the bathroom to check her makeup and smoke a More cigarette.

Sussan came once, and told Roxanna about her fiancé—a man with dusty shoes and a wrinkled jacket who said he was an architect. He had lied to her about his age, pretending he was younger than he really was. He lied about anything he could, and she knew if she married him, he would let her down someday when it mattered most. She asked Roxanna what it was like to be the wife of a rich man who loved her.

"I don't know," Roxanna replied quietly. She had not noticed that I was looking at her, that I had heard Sussan's question and would feel, once again, the twinge of betrayal at my mother's response. "Like I'm living someone else's life."

All week long, Roxanna sat in the room directly across from Teymur. He never looked at her. She knew that Sohrab and Fräulein Claude were watching her. And yet, being near Teymur—knowing that he felt her instinctively, that his body, all his nerves were tuned in to hers—knowing this made her desperate with longing.

Over and over, she saw herself walk up to him, there in that room with all the men and women watching them, black drapes hanging by the windows and on mirrors, tables overflowing with funereal white orchids. She saw herself walk up to Teymur in one last journey of salvation, stand before him, and look into his eyes. She bent over, slowly, and let her face touch the side of his cheek. With her lips she grazed his skin, the outline of his jaw, his mouth.

"One more time," she whispered, oblivious to the consequences, unafraid of the pain she would cause others. His eyes bored into her. She took his hand and let it part her dress. Her skin was bare and cold and ravenous. He touched her breasts, her stomach, the inside of her thighs. She sighed, and opened her legs. She sat on his lap, facing him, wrapped her legs around his waist.

In the room, people cried and spoke and said prayers for the dead. Roxanna never moved from her chair.

Miriam the Moon came on the last day of the wake.

She was a beautiful woman still, but she had adopted the serious and unflinching look of a sour-mouthed schoolteacher. She dressed only in dark colors, believed neither in makeup nor in setting her hair. She worked twice as hard as any woman Roxanna had ever known—raising children and managing her husband's affairs, dealing with family issues on all sides, trying above all to meet life's challenges head on.

She gave Roxanna a glass bottle: it was green, with a long, narrow neck and a round bottom.

"Mother's tear jar," she explained without drama. "She cried into it after every major loss in her life—after her sister ran away, after she gave you to the Cat, after Tala'at took off with The Nephew. She gathered her tears and, when the jar was full, drank them to prove her grief."

Roxanna took the bottle and stared at it absently. Miriam watched her.

"It's the only thing Mother left us," she said. "I thought it's only fair, since she gave you away so young, that among all her children you should inherit her one belonging."

Roxanna gripped the bottle so tightly, it seemed she was going to crush the glass with her hands.

"You're getting thinner every time I see you," Miriam told Roxanna. "I know there's something wrong in your life."

She waited for a reaction, but Roxanna would not look up from the bottle. Miriam drew her own conclusions.

"Charles and I have finally moved out of the ghetto," she said. "We had to wait for his mother to die first because she wouldn't agree to live anywhere else. But now we live on Persepolis Avenue. Number 108."

She leaned forward and whispered her last words.

"If ever you manage to sneak away from the Dragon Woman over there"—she nodded towards Fräulein Claude—"come by and tell me what's wrong."

Roxanna opened the tear jar. Inside, she could see the salty residue of Shusha's tears lining the glass. She thought about the irony of what Miriam had done—brought her their mother's tears, given her the legacy of sorrow and shame to keep. For a moment, Roxanna thought she should destroy the bottle. Then she closed its top again and took it into her room.

That night she dreamt of sapphire elephants.

They were dark blue and luminous, larger than life and clear as glass. They stood around her bed, staring at her with crystal eyes, and she was so mesmerized by their brilliant color she did not realize at first that they were alive and moving. She reached out to caress one, but the very touch of her hand made it shatter into a million pieces. She touched another one, then another, and every time, the elephants exploded into a shower of blue, shimmering glass. The sound of their bodies being pulverized and dropping onto the marble floor was making her deaf. She woke up.

Sohrab the Sinner was leaning over her.

"You were dreaming," he said, and touched her hair. "Don't be afraid."

She waited till he had gone back to sleep, then got off the bed. She saw a single white feather on the ground and quietly shoved it with her foot against the wall. Sooner or later, she thought, Sohrab was going to notice those feathers, ask her where they came from, know her secret.

She went to the sink at the end of the bedroom and washed her face. She was thinking of the elephants in her dream, of the sapphire necklace that Teymur had given her the night of her wedding. She remembered how his hand had touched her neck when he hung the stones around it. She felt drops of water, cool against her skin, run the length of her neck and onto her bare breasts.

She caught sight of her own image in the mirror: thirty-three years old. Trapped at the end of her own life.

She knew Teymur was awake. He was watching her in the mirror, waiting for her, wanting her. She leaned forward, towards her own image, and let her breath cast a foggy shadow on the mirror. She kissed him in the fog.

"Take me away," she told him. "Let me sell my soul."

She went to the window and looked into the yard. She had to leave that house before she gave in to Teymur again.

She came into my room and watched me sleep. She kissed me on the forehead, turned my hands over, and kissed my palms.

"Sleep tight," she said.

I heard her but did not open my eyes. For years now I had slept in a state of semi-awakening, forever conscious of my mother's movements, forever watching her. I loved her nearness, loved the weight of her eyes—even the sadness in her movements. When she left the room that night, I got up and followed her.

The hallway was dark, but I could see the white of Roxanna's gown like a bright shadow. Unaware that I was behind her, she went to the top of the stairs, listened for Teymur. For a minute she thought she was going to call him, open her jaws that had been shut so tight for so long and scream his name till she had awakened the entire household and smashed the silence—the constricting, virulent silence that had imprisoned all of us, that kept the peace at the cost of quelling every instinct and every desire. She could already hear her own voice—sharp and resonant and for once daring to demand. She would call Teymur from his brutal distance, Alexandra the Cat from her blind madness, Mercedez the Movie Star from her benign, flippant neglect. She would call Shusha—her mother who had left her only tears—and demand that she take them back, call her father and scream that he should have been there, that night a lifetime ago on the roof of Sun the Chicken Lady's house. He should have been there, between Roxanna and her mother, stopped Roxanna's fall, saved his daughter.

Instead of screaming, Roxanna pressed her teeth so hard into her tongue, blood filled her mouth and dripped onto the front of her gown.

She turned around, towards the upper floor, and though her eyes rested on me in the darkness, she did not see me. She climbed the stairs.

The entire third floor of our house was a ballroom with many connecting doors where Teymur and Fräulein Claude had entertained guests in wintertime. Once adorned with Italian furniture and French silk drapery, it had become empty and full of dust, robbed of everything but the enormous chandelier that Fräulein Claude had bought in Germany while on her honeymoon with Teymur. Full-length doors of etched glass lined the outer wall of the room and opened onto a wide terrace with wrought-iron railings laced with intertwining white and pink jasmine. It was here, through these glass doors, that Roxanna had first appeared to the guests on the night of her wedding.

Now she crossed the ballroom and walked onto the terrace. Behind her, a breeze swept over the crystal droplets of the chandelier, releasing tiny streams of dust into the air and ringing the crystals like chimes. I heard them and shivered.

Roxanna climbed onto the railing.

"Mama," I called her hesitantly, and advanced into the ballroom. I was afraid she would be angry that I had followed her. Then I realized she had not heard me.

She stood on the railing, in her bare feet and white gown, and instead of looking down, she stared up at the sky.

Suddenly, I knew what she was going to do.

"Mama!" I called. "Mama!"

She turned and looked back. Her eyes rested on me but did not see me. I was invisible to her—one ghost among many, a voice she would not hear.

She opened her arms and leaned into the night.

My CRIES TORE through the house.

Sohrab ran upstairs. He found me reaching over the railing, screaming so hard he thought the veins in my neck and forehead were going to burst. He grabbed me, but I fought him with mad strength. He picked me up and carried me, still screaming, to the sink. The cold water he splashed on my face only shocked me more. I was yelling Roxanna's name, heaving in terror. Fräulein Claude came upstairs, followed by Teymur, then Mashti.

"Give her some opium," Mashti advised.

They carried me into the kitchen, held me down, and let Jacob the Jello blow puffs of smoke into my mouth. I fought for a while, then gradually grew limp. My muscles gave out, my head fell back, and I went silent in midscream.

Sohrab thought I had had a heart attack, from the opium, and panicked.

"Leave her be." Fräulein Claude pulled him off me. "She just passed out."

They stood around me, unaware of what I had witnessed or even of Roxanna's absence. I breathed in short, panicked gasps that gradually became slower and more relaxed. For a while, the only sounds in the house were my breathing and Jacob's puffing on his pipe. Then Fräulein Claude noticed that Jacob was trying to speak, waving his hand in the air for attention, as he often did when his voice failed him. Realizing that his blood pressure was down again, she mixed some sugar water and fed it to him by the spoonful till he got his strength back.

Just as she was about to walk away from him, he looked up at her from under his hat.

"I saw that girl," he said. "Your son's wife. She had white wings, and she was flying outside the kitchen window."

They searched the house, the maids' quarters, the garden. Sohrab and Mashti got into the car and drove the streets in a ten-kilometer radius. In the morning, Teymur called a friend, Tehran's military police chief, and gave him a description of Roxanna. "A young woman," he said, "with a child's body and very old eyes."

The police chief assured Teymur that Roxanna would be found. No one, he swore, least of all a woman in a nightgown with bare feet and no money or papers, was going to evade His Majesty's armed forces for long.

"She will be home in time for dinner tonight," he promised, and hung up.

We waited. Teymur made more calls. Sohrab searched the city from noon to night. They asked me questions: What had I seen? What time had Roxanna left? Had she told me anything before she jumped out the window?

I wanted to help them—even if it meant betraying Roxanna, bringing her back against her will into this house she had wanted to escape for so long. I wanted to tell them how Roxanna had told me she could fly, how she had warned me for months that she was going to leave. I wanted to describe what I thought I had seen: Roxanna flying like a bird, moving away from the house, never falling to the ground.

Would they believe me?

The doubt choked my voice.

Teymur and Sohrab searched the city from door to door. They went to Miriam's house and followed every lead she gave them, appeared at Rochelle's and Sussan's, even Rahman the Ruler's in the ghetto. The police brought Roxanna's family in for questioning, planted spies around them to report any contact with her. They searched Tehran's bus and train stations, stopped taxis at every intersection in town, broke into safe houses for Communist spies and drug-dealing scum. They checked fingerprints and footprints, raided the whores' district and paid off the pimps, walked the maze of the bazaars' sinuous alleys and dark back rooms. Every day, they became more zealous in their pursuit, warned more people of the consequences of hiding Roxanna from the long reach of the Shah's police. They found nothing.

Rumors abounded about her disappearance. Her picture landed in the nightly paper and the weekly women's magazines. There was talk of foreign lovers who had spirited her away in the dark, of manifest witchcraft that had made her vanish like all the other objects in Teymur's house.

Miriam the Moon checked with me every few days. Her questions made me cry. I wanted to help if I could, but my pain was so onerous, my fear so paralyzing, I could not talk.

Miriam never gave up.

"One way or another," she said, "we are going to find her. I know this because I know your mother. I raised your mother, and I know she is not going to leave her child alone for long."

My skin blistered at the mention of Roxanna's name—little drops of sadness that emerged at night and itched until dawn.

The Exile
1971

WHEN SHE OPENED her eyes, Roxanna was standing in the Karaj River, waist deep in water and surrounded by darkness. She was ice cold, miles away from Teymur's home, fighting the strong current that threatened to wash her almost-weightless body away at any moment. She looked for the shore, but all she saw were tricks the night played on her eyes. Blindly, she began to walk, aware that a wrong step might send her tumbling into a deep pocket from which she would not emerge. But instead of fear, Roxanna was filled with a sense of relief so deep and liberating, it made her feel omnipotent.

She saw some rocks, then shrubbery, then a rough shoreline. Pulling herself out of the river, she realized that she had no shoes on and that her feet were cut and bleeding. Far in the distance, she saw the blue peaks of the Elburz Mountains, which separated Tehran from the lands of the north and the Caspian rice fields. She thought of the story Alexandra the Cat had so often told, of how she had escaped Russia: walked out one night in her high heels and pearls, walked and walked and never looked back till she reached Tehran.

"I have seen the Caspian white tiger," Alexandra had boasted. "It is the most magnificent animal in the world, so rare the queen would give anything to have one trapped and brought to her. I have sailed in handmade boats with their bottoms rotting out from under me, eaten fish fried live on the end of a stick. I have slept in the emerald jungle, in a rice field, aboard Russian smuggling ships. And I have done it all because I was not afraid of exile."

Roxanna, too, was not afraid of exile anymore. It did not matter to her that she was alone and nearly naked, about to freeze, and lost on her way to nowhere. It did not matter that she would never see Teymur again, that Sohrab would try to hunt her down, that she had left her child crying out to her in the dark. She had saved herself and was not about to look back.

She sat on the river's bank, waiting for daylight so she could find a road or determine her direction. After a while, when her ears were accustomed to the sound of the river, she managed to detect the sporadic noise of trucks' engines gasping uphill in the distance. At dawn, she saw the gray outline of a dirt road that snaked away from the river, towards an arid plain with no vegetation and no other sign of life.

She followed the road. A truck passed by, the driver slowing down but not stopping. An hour later, a small blue bus, carrying a load of young theology students with brown turbans and bearded faces, dragged itself up the hill. The men stared at Roxanna through the bus's dirty, scratched windows. She saw their lips move as they wondered out loud who or what she was, saw their eyes chase her even through the cloud of dust that billowed around the bus.

She kept walking. Peasant children passed her on the backs of mules. Stray dogs barked at her from beyond the road, but dared not approach. The sun was high up now, but the sky remained murky. With her bare, bleeding feet and her white transparent gown, Roxanna looked like a vision dreamed up by sleepy travelers and dying men. She sat in the middle of the road. The next car that passed by would take her away.

The next car was a moss green Peykan with a shattered windshield that had been covered with a sheet of plastic held in place by duct tape. It stopped ten feet away from her. The driver bent forward across the steering wheel and squinted through the plastic. Not believing his eyes, he leaned to the right and lowered the passenger-side window to get a better look. Roxanna watched him—dark eyes, narrow nose, day-old beard. He shivered when the cold air entered his car. Cautiously, like a man who was himself afraid of being detected, he opened the door and stepped out.

He wore a heavy coat with gloves, a ski hat, a scarf wrapped around his neck and covering his mouth and chin. He stared at her but would not approach. Roxanna went towards him. Her feet left a bloody trail on the sand.

"You can take me where you're going," she told him when she was closer. Her lips were white, her hands blue. Her gown, wet and frozen in the cold, was paper stiff. "Don't be afraid."

The car's passenger door was jammed. She went around the back and opened the driver's door, climbed over his seat and into the one next to it.

The man looked stunned.

"It's all right," she said. "I'll get out wherever you want."

They drove towards Qazvin. The man chain-smoked Marlboros. He was young, no more than twenty, and it was clear he did not know what to make of Roxanna. He studied her from the corners of his eyes, but did not speak to her, not even to ask the most basic questions. If they talked, she would ask her own questions, ones he did not want to answer.

He had two cans of gas in the back of the car, a basket of food, two blankets, water. He stopped outside Qazvin to eat lunch out of the basket: smoked whitefish, pickled garlic, Lavash bread. Roxanna watched him. He asked if she was hungry.

"Just thirsty," she said, without smiling at him. Their eyes locked for a long time. Then he looked down at his hands and kept eating.

Two hours past Qazvin, they stopped outside a teahouse. It was a filthy shack along an unpaved road, lit by two kerosene lamps and warmed by a portable heater. The man left Roxanna in the car and went inside. He came back with a tall glass of black tea, three sugar cubes, a plate of fried eggs floating in oil.

"Eat this," he said quietly. "It's going to be a long night."

When they started on the road again, a heavy fog made it impossible to see the road beyond the car's headlights. The man reached into the backseat and gave Roxanna a blanket.

She thought that he, too, was running away, that he felt in

danger and feared being discovered, that a woman, probably his mother, had packed him that lunch of smoked fish and garlic, knowing she would never see him again.

"How far do you want to go?" he asked near midnight.

"As far as I can," she answered.

He snickered.

"That wouldn't be very far, judging by the way you're dressed."

"I ran away from my husband's house," she said, and watched him for a reaction. "I left my daughter. She's five years old. I will never see her again."

He kept looking at the road. His hands clutched the steering wheel. A cigarette burned between his lips.

He had been a student at Tehran's oldest university, the son of middle-class parents with small possibilities and even smaller ambitions. He had gone to college to study engineering. Instead, he had met a group of left-wing students and professors bent on undermining the Shah's dictatorship. He had attended a few meetings, passed out a few leaflets. One of his friends, the most ardent of the Communists, had turned out to be a mole. He gave a list of names to the Shah's secret police. The young man's name was among them. In two days, twelve of his friends were arrested. They were tortured with electric needles inserted into their genitals, injected with truth serum, thrown alive out of a helicopter into a salt lake that sucked them down and never spit out their bodies. The young man had escaped before he was caught.

"I'm going to Turkey," he said to Roxanna without revealing any more. "I'll take you to the border."

They went from Qazvin to Zanjan, then to Mianeh and Tabriz. They drove on mountain roads that were unpaved and unlit, stopped only at the most out-of-the-way teahouses where he did not chance running into the agents of the military police.

He drove all night, pulled off the road around midday, and slept a few hours at a time. His friends had told him that if he ever needed to run away from the country, there was a safe house in Van, near the Turkish-Iranian border, where he could take refuge.

Wrapped in the blanket, Roxanna never went into the tea-houses with him. She understood that he had kept her against his own better judgment, that he knew she might be a spy, or police, or that she might betray him the moment he let her out of the car. But he was also alone and afraid, and her presence soothed him.

Once, when he had pushed the seat back and was trying to sleep, she reached over and touched his mouth. He shook as if with an electric charge, grabbed her hand so hard she thought he was going to break her wrist. Then he saw that she had not intended to harm him, that her fingers were cool and light and healing, and he let go.

She parted his lips, gently, and touched the inside of his lower lip. Then she slid out of her gown and climbed onto him naked. She was so white, he thought, that his hands would stain her skin if he touched her. She sat with her back to the steering wheel, knees planted on the sides of his hips, and she never closed her eyes even as she leaned forward and kissed him.

She made love to him in broad daylight, in a car exposed on the open road, in a land where a woman accused of indecency could easily be stoned to death or thrown into a deep well to rot. She made love to him over and over, at every stop, in every village, without asking his name or offering her own, without loving him, without being ashamed.

"I don't feel shame anymore," she told him once, when he warned that they could be seen, naked and intertwined, by others on the road. "I gave up my whole life, my daughter, so I wouldn't feel shame."

In Marand, he paid a peasant woman for a change of clothes and a pair of handmade canvas slippers that he gave to Roxanna.

In Khvoy, he counted all his money and gave her half, enough for her to live on for three days, maybe five, by herself.

They crossed the border at night, without realizing they had entered Turkey: There were no guards, no fence, no line separating the two countries. No one checked for passports or identification papers. The landscape remained constant. The trucks that traveled on the highway still bore Iranian license plates. But at dawn, they saw the Turkish military police in their marked cars and then a faded sign announcing that they had entered the city of Van. He stopped the car and told her she must leave.

"The people I'm going to," he said apologetically, "would not understand why you're with me and would turn us both away."

She slipped out of his car as easily as she had entered.

SHE WAS IN an old frontier town—a dusty, violent place with a harsh landscape and mountains bearing down on it. The mountains were honey colored and naked, with sharp black slopes—like spears—that gave the town an added sense of austerity and brutality. An immense citadel of rock, shaped like a ship, rose in the distance out of the plain. A narrow outcrop of limestone, this Rock of Van was believed to have been the biblical ark of Noah, the natural boundary between the old and the new city of Van.

The new city was modern, bland, impoverished. Populated mostly by Kurds, it was a collection of shops and houses bordering narrow streets crammed with cars and pedestrians. Old men with weather-beaten faces and cracked fingertips, survivors of old wars and bloody rebellions, carried rough Turkish rugs on their shoulders and knocked on every door, hoping to make a sale. Younger ones, angry and threatening, leaned against walls and light posts, chain-smoking American and Russian cigarettes, plotting new battles. One of Turkey's oldest cities, Van had been the capital of the ancient Urartu kingdom, home of various tribes and nations, site of many a great war and endless carnage. Its men were fierce, cold, hopeless—raised on memories of loss and defeat, forever betrayed by foreign schemes and stronger nations.

But there were no women here. On the streets and in the shops, in doorways and in cars, Roxanna saw no women. Van had the feel of a city under siege, of women and children hiding from the enemy.

A carload of men stopped her. They were members of the military police, underpaid and untrained and forever on the lookout for an extra source of income. Roxanna had been in Van for barely two hours. They could tell she was a foreigner by her clothes, by the way she walked around as if unaware that a lone woman out on the street was only begging for trouble. They asked in Turkish for her papers.

She answered in Farsi that she had none. They put her in the car and took her to the station—a one-room cement building populated by rabid-looking policemen sporting dark mustaches and too many weapons. Most of them spoke enough Farsi to communicate. They were not interested in Roxanna's origins or her business in Van; they wanted to know how much money she had. They took all of it, then put her into a Jeep and said they would take her to a "hotel for runaways."

They drove towards the Rock and, beyond it, the old city of Van.

Old Van was a vast graveyard of dust and rubble, spotted only with a few broken minarets, haunted by the memory of centuries of war and bloodshed: here, King Sargon II had once beheaded an entire army, then piled the severed heads at the gates of the city. Here again, during the First World War, Turks had massacred three million Armenians.

But beyond the old city was the lake.

It sat across the arid plain—an immense, quiet horizon of turquoise blue against brown, white-capped mountains and a lava beach hugging an inland sea astonishing in its beauty but even more so in its solitude. Its water, too alkaline to be used for drinking or irrigation, allowed almost no animal life and therefore no fishing. Its shores were bare and rocky and forbidding.

This was not the sea Roxanna had so often seen in her dreams, the one she had flown to and back from in the ghetto. That sea had been green—the color of old emeralds—surrounded by lush jungles, teeming with life. It had smelled of gentle rains and early dawns. Seals had swum up to its shore. Birds had flocked to its beaches.

She had lost that other sea. Now she was here, by this lake that had outlived millions of innocents and many an empire, and these men with dark mustaches and dirty hands were driving her towards a house that sat alone on the farthest point on the horizon.

The house was made of dark wood—a ramshackle construction with nothing around it but rocks. There was no gate, no pathway leading up to the entrance. Roxanna had often heard of the whorehouses in Turkish border towns, places so cheap and desperate they employed eleven-year-old virgins and fifty-year-old grandmothers. Now, even with the door closed, she could smell the scent of rotting limbs and dried cow dung, of cold semen and fresh sweat and bruised limbs rubbing against unwashed sheets.

A woman answered the door. She was in her thirties, with shiny jet black hair and black eyeshadow. When she saw the policemen, she smiled, revealing two rows of perfectly lined gold teeth.

"Brought you something," one of the men announced. "She just arrived here. Doesn't speak a word."

The woman threw Roxanna a threatening glance, moved away from the door enough to let her squeeze in.

"Wait in the hallway," she said.

And Roxanna, who had lived all her life in fear of becoming, in the words of her mother, "a woman of ill repute," walked at last into the whorehouse.

"GIVE HER UP," Fräulein Claude warned Teymur and his son early one morning. Two months had passed since Roxanna's escape.

"She has been gone too long. You will never find her now, even if she *were* alive, in this country that's as wide and as varied as Hell. Give her up and know that she left *both* of you."

Fräulein Claude was standing in the doorway of Teymur's bedroom. She had watched him all night, from her own bed across the hall, through the empty doorway that had framed him as he stood by the window, staring at the sky. She had felt sorry for Teymur then. For the first time since he had betrayed her with Roxanna, since that morning when she had come into the kitchen and heard Jacob retell their secret, Fräulein Claude had felt her husband's suffering and wanted to soothe him.

But in the morning Sohrab had gone into his father's room, whispering that there was no news, that the secret police had called to let him know—because a general in high places had asked for their help on Teymur's behalf—that all of their inquiries had revealed nothing about Roxanna's whereabouts. In horror, Fräulein Claude had watched Sohrab and Teymur confer as if on a matter of vital importance. They had become allies, she realized, these two men divided all their lives by personal differences and later by their love for Roxanna. They had developed an unholy bond, become united by their need to find the woman who had destroyed them both—who had destroyed Fräulein Claude.

So she went to them, armed with her hatred, and said the truth.

"By now she has probably rotted," she said, and did not care that Sohrab bristled. "Or else she's sleeping in someone else's bed, eating out of his hands the way she ate out of both of yours. So enough drama already. Tell Lili what happened to her mother, tell everyone else to stop looking, and let's move on."

Alone in my own bedroom, I sat at the small table where Mashti had placed my breakfast, and heard every word.

———

When I came home from school that afternoon, I found chaos.

There were men in the yard armed with electric saws, cutting down the trees. They screamed at one another over the incessant noise of the machines, moved back, and watched the trees fall with the impact of small earthquakes. In a fit of rage and disappointment so overpowering it would burn his spirit to ashes, Teymur the Heretic had ordered his garden destroyed.

For days, the trees fell. Police came to the house, threatening to fine Teymur for disturbing the peace, and walked away with bribes. Men from the Ministry of the Interior called to warn Teymur of dire consequences if he did not stop cutting his trees. Because of the city's serious smog problem, they said, His Majesty had declared it a felony to cut down trees. They left when Teymur offered them jobs in his companies.

Mashti cried when the trees fell. These were ancient trees, much older than the house itself, and every time one of them fell, a window shattered in the house and cracks opened across the length of the marble floor.

Mashti's Wife, who had not stepped inside the house since Fräulein Claude had accused her of stealing, remained at the main gates and warned that all the shaking of the ground would disturb the dead already buried in it.

In her upstairs bedroom, Fräulein Claude dressed in a red velvet gown and her best high-heeled sandals, and savored the triumph of her endurance over the girl who had come from the night and vanished back into it like a thief.

Teymur did not see Fräulein Claude, or anyone else. He stood on the landing outside the front door, in the spot where he had seen Roxanna for the first time—that day when he had set eyes on her and thought that she was not real, that she was going to die young, or live forever, like an angel.

AT SCHOOL, the teachers stared at me and whispered to one another about my mother. The janitor uttered protective prayers under his breath every time I went past him, and told the teachers they must do the same—to ward off the bad luck I was sure to spread. The children repeated for me what their mothers said at home—that Roxanna had not run away, that she was locked up by her husband or his family, wasting away in a dark cellar or behind a heavy door, crying for help, starving to death.

Even the principal of the school was not immune to curiosity. She called me into her office, as if on school business, and asked me why Teymur had destroyed his garden.

"It's because of the thieves." I made up my own explanation. I sat with my hands folded on my lap and my feet reaching halfway to the ground. I felt hollow, like my words, held together only by a breath.

"My grandfather thinks this way the thieves can't hide in the garden during the day and come into our house when we're sleeping."

The principal walked around the room with her hands clasped behind her back. She was an attractive woman in her sixties—a distant cousin to a fallen prince—and she hung on to this honor with all her might. She had followed the story of Teymur the Heretic with particular zeal.

"What does your grandfather say about your runaway mother?" She smiled through the layers of powder and rouge that covered her face.

My hands trembled on my lap.

"He doesn't say anything about her."

I was fighting tears, fighting the urge to put my face into my hands and sob.

"But my mother is coming back," I said.

The principal took long pelican steps around the room. Raised by a French governess who had taught her all the fine manners of European women, she believed that ladies should walk like dancers—with their legs stretched forward so they touched the ground first with their toes and then with their heels.

"No doubt she will," she answered without conviction. "Most mothers would."

The governess had also taught her to be frank.

"But I've been hearing, you see, that your mother is dead." She pranced around the room.

"I heard she threw herself out a window and your father buried her in the yard.

"That's why they poured concrete all over the yard: to keep the body from being discovered."

MIRIAM THE MOON came to the house again, this time flanked by Rochelle and her short, cigar-smoking husband, and demanded to see me. Four months had passed since Roxanna's flight. No one in our house mentioned her name anymore.

"You people may have given up," Miriam argued with Fräulein Claude, "but I certainly haven't. People don't vanish off the face of the earth like a drop of water. Either you killed her, or she ran away. If she's dead, I want to see the body. If she ran away, I am going to find her and bring her back."

I was alone in my mother's room, standing before her vanity in my blue-and-white school uniform. I came here every morning to comb my hair, rushed back every afternoon as soon as I got home from school. I spent every evening, every weekend in this room. I stood before her mirror, in the place I had found her that evening when Mashti's son took the doors down in the house, when she had turned to me and said I would always be able to see her. Now I looked for her in the room and saw only my own reflection—the pale face with the frightened eyes, the skinny legs, the white socks stretched up to my knees. I was lost and afraid and without power. I had known that Roxanna was going to leave but, as much as I had wanted to, had not been able to stop her. She had not heard me when I called, did not even see me when she turned around and looked.

I had been invisible to the one person I loved most.

"Do what you want," Fräulein Claude shouted back at Miriam in the hallway downstairs. "Bury her or find her or name your grandchildren after her. I don't care, as long as I never see her or the rest of you again."

Even as Fräulein Claude spoke, Miriam was pushing past her and forcing her way into the house.

"I need to talk to Lili," she told Rochelle and her husband.

I did not know if I should run to her or hide from her. Then she was there, in my mother's mirror, her image superimposed on my own: she had on a pair of thick glasses, no makeup, a man's watch.

She put one hand on my shoulder and turned me around.

"It's all right," she whispered, and the very sound of her voice, the knowledge that she was the only person still looking for Roxanna, made me cry.

She would have hugged me then, but she herself had never received that kind of affection and did not know how to show it. Instead, she patted me on the back, pushed my hair, the same color as Roxanna's, away from my face.

"Jacob the Jello swears to me he sees your mother," she said. "If she comes to *him*, then she must also come to you."

I shook my head. Tears choked me. I had failed again. Roxanna had not come to me.

Miriam let go of my shoulder and adjusted her scarf. She looked at Roxanna's makeup on the vanity, looked around as if to feel her sister's presence among those belongings: There was her bed, her clothes, her house slippers paired up and waiting next to her chair. There was the tear jar Miriam had given her.

"At any rate"—she drew in a breath and forced herself to be strong again—"I want you to be on the lookout. Watch for her. Wherever you are, no matter what anyone tells you, know that Roxanna is coming back. It's up to you and me to find her."

For years after that visit from Miriam, I would lie awake, listening in the darkness for the sound of my mother knocking on a closed door. I would look into crowds, follow strange women on the street because they bore a resemblance, however tiny, to Roxanna. I would search yards and streets paved with cement, imagine my mother's body trapped underneath the cement and rotting alive. At school, I broke into sweat and fits of panic, certain that Roxanna had gone to our house the moment I had left and was looking for me, certain that she was calling me, that she would leave before I got home. At home, I sat in the kitchen, next to Jacob the Jello, who claimed he still saw Roxanna outside his window, and I waited for her. I stopped before every mirror and every glass, turned and prayed to see Roxanna looking back at me. She was never there, of course. She had told me she was not coming back, just as she had promised that she would run away. She was not there and she would never be there, and yet I would look for her, from house to house and year to year, look for the window that would open, one night when my hope was more solid than reality, and give me back my mother.

IN THE House of the Eastern Star, the men went to bed with knife in hand, ready to cut each other in a fight or to slash any whores who disobeyed them. They were underpaid soldiers and long-distance truckers, peasants out on the town for the first time in their lives, smugglers of Iranian hashish and American whiskey, Kurds embittered by a history of stunted rebellion. Most of them suffered from gonorrhea or syphilis. Many fathered children who would be raised in the house and who would—the boys as well as the girls—enlist in the owner's service before they were twelve.

The owner was an Azerbaijani Turk who ran a string of twenty such houses up and down the Iranian and Russian borders with Turkey. He came to the house once a month, to collect his profits from the woman he had left in charge. She was the one with the golden teeth, herself a prostitute, tougher on her employees than any pimp could ever be. She ordered the lashing of young boys and girls who refused to sleep with customers, kept the whores in a constant state of hunger so they would know their limits and obey her orders, allowed the men to cut up anyone they did not like, then commanded the victim to clean up her own blood.

She told Roxanna the rules.

"You will work here as long as I want to keep you," she said. Her breath was yellow and cold, like the metal in her mouth.

"If you try to escape, or disobey a customer, I will have my boys knife you in the face. If you get sick, I will let you die."

Her conditions were no better or worse than those of any other brothel within a hundred miles. Looking around her, Roxanna recognized the house from her own nightmares, from the stories she had heard Shusha tell of what would happen to runaway girls, where they would have to live, how they would die. She remembered the stories of the runaway aunt who had gone blind with syphilis and the one who had been drowned in a lake by a lover she had shunned. Roxanna had no reason to be-lieve that her own fate would be any different.

And yet it was not fear, that first day when she saw what her life was going to be like, that shook her up so much. It was the realization of how fast and easily she had come to fulfill her grandmother's prediction, and how free she was going to be, now that her actions could no longer harm anyone but herself.

She was assigned a cubicle with a bed and a change of sheets. She would receive customers whenever the manager told her to. The rest of the time, she would help the other women cook and wash and do household chores. Her first customer was a young man from Van who lasted less than a minute, then kissed her hands and told her he loved her. The second one beat her till she threw up in her bed. After that she stopped keeping count.

She was going to escape, she knew. She just had to wait for a chance.

LITTLE NOORI the Tax Man had been visiting Teymur at home twice a year for three decades. He had come on the first day of spring—the Persian New Year, when gift giving was a tradition—and on Christmas Day, when he reminded Teymur that all of the "civilized world" was in a generous mood. In 1972 he came a third time, in July, when the heat drove madmen into the streets and the sea took dozens of victims every day. His wife was about to leave him, he knew, because she had waited twenty years for him to buy her an apartment and she was tired of waiting. Little Noori needed a bonus, some extra cash to use as a down payment on an apartment, or his marriage was doomed for sure. He had gone over the list of his "clients" and picked Teymur—not only because he was rich but also because, given the recent rumors about Roxanna's disappearance, he figured Teymur would be in a vulnerable mood and not eager to fight.

Little Noori was short and bald, his head shaped like a cantaloupe, his right leg shorter than his left one and twisted inward, so that he walked with a pronounced limp. He had had the limp all his life, but he was too ashamed to accept responsibility for his own defect. Up until three years ago, he had attributed the limp to poor circulation caused by a lifetime of sitting behind a desk and not getting enough exercise. Then Fräulein Claude's dogs had bitten him, taking off a piece of his right thigh as he made the dangerous journey across our yard, and thereby giving him a new story to tell.

"I got this limp in the line of duty," he recounted to all his so-called clients, "at the mansion of His Excellency Teymur Khan. It really is a splendid property, its bad luck notwithstanding. I would hate to see it confiscated by His Majesty's government in payment for back taxes."

In a country where the government's annual budget was determined not by the taxes it collected but on the basis of what was left once the Shah and his relatives had helped themselves to the national wealth, in a place where government employees were sustained purely by bribes, Little Noori the Tax Man and thousands like him went around collecting not taxes but payoffs.

That day, he came unannounced, at noon, carrying a green briefcase under his arm. His suit was creased, with large oil spots on his leg where he had rubbed sheep lard to help his circulation. After years of following the same routine, he did not wait for an invitation or a greeting, but headed straight through the hallway and into Teymur's drawing room. In the days before the robber ghosts, he had ordered Effat to bring him a glass of Oxymel sherbet on ice. Now he just sat down, dry mouthed, and hoped Fräulein Claude would offer him at least water.

She did not.

Little Noori sighed and opened his green briefcase. He took out a stack of ledgers, a small notebook, memos from various governmental agencies, handwritten notes he had made to himself about Teymur's affairs. Having barely sneaked past the new pair of dogs Fräulein Claude had recently bought, he tried to ignore them as they barked at him through the window, charging him so their bodies slammed against the glass and their nails scraped it. He cursed them under his breath, repeating a three-year-old litany of how he had lost the use of his leg because of their attack. They instilled such fear in him, he perspired through his jacket.

An hour passed. Little Noori went to the doorway and called out, but no one answered. He came into the corridor and saw me sitting at the top of the stairs, legs hanging through the openings in the railing, looking down at him.

"Go call your grandpa," he said, but I did not move. Teymur was in his room, lying down to a sleepless rest, and I knew better than to disturb him for Noori.

At three o'clock Little Noori was still sitting in front of his ledgers in his jacket. With the windows closed because of the dogs, and the sun beating against the glass, the room had turned into an oven. Furious, he drew a magazine out of his briefcase and began to leaf through pictures of naked women with enormous busts and tattooed behinds, puckering their lips at him. It was a back issue of *Hustler* magazine, which he obtained once a month through a client who had a subscription. Looking at it, he turned pale and sheepish, a smile dangling from only half his mouth, and he was so immersed in pleasure, he did not hear Teymur till it was too late.

"You're six months early." Teymur towered over him.

Little Noori scrambled to put his magazine away, tried to stand up and shake hands, then recognized the futility of his attempt and sat back down. He pulled his chair closer to the table, to hide his erection, and complained about Fräulein Claude's hospitality.

"I've been here three hours and no one's offered me a glass of water."

Teymur was unmoved. Little Noori shook his head and observed aloud that rich people were the least compassionate sort in the world and therefore deserved all the bad luck that befell them. Then he opened his notebook to a marked page and began to read over his notes. He started to tell Teymur how much he owed in back taxes, plus interest and penalties for evasion, plus court costs and accountants' fees if he decided to fight the assessments, and how deplorable it was that we had to pay taxes in a country so rich with oil and other resources, but it was the law, after all, and Noori was just a government employee on a fixed salary with no benefits and four children to feed . . .

"How much do you need?" Teymur stopped him.

Little Noori looked like a man who had gone to buy diamonds and was offered instead a bag of rotten tomatoes.

"I beg your pardon, sir." He smiled reproachfully. "We're not here to talk about *my* needs."

It had always worked in the past. It was like a dance that had been rehearsed a thousand times, except this time, Teymur was moving out of step. He put his hand in his jacket pocket and took out a stack of bills.

"This is it." He threw the money on the table in front of Little Noori. "Come back in December."

The cantaloupe skull turned beet red. Little Noori looked at the money, then, without bothering to count it, began to put his papers back in his briefcase. He could tell Teymur was in a bad mood. But his own marriage was about to break up over a thousand-square-foot apartment he could not afford no matter how badly he wanted it, and so he was not about to be cheated out of his payoff by a man who lived in a palace he could not even keep occupied.

He snapped the briefcase shut.

"I need five hundred thousand rials." He came clean. "You have till tomorrow to prepare it."

Right then, Teymur decided he was going to pay his taxes.

He called four accountants to his office on Ferdowsi Avenue. They were young men, educated in America, eager to make a name among Iran's businessmen. When he told them he had not paid taxes in thirty years, they smiled and said they understood. When he said he intended to pay it all now, because he was tired of threats from petty bureaucrats with green briefcases and girlie magazines, the accountants shook their heads and rubbed their chins as if to say Teymur had gone mad.

He took them into the basement of his office building—a dusty, airless chamber with no windows and twenty years' worth of papers stashed away without order.

"This is it," he said. The accountants had the impression they were looking at their own graves. "Sort through all the records and come up with a figure that will stand up to government scrutiny."

One of the accountants ventured a response.

"You realize, Your Excellency, that paying your taxes in no way guarantees you will be free of people asking for bribes." He was wearing white shoes and a pair of white linen pants already dirtied from the dust in the basement. "You know better than to think the system will work on honesty."

Teymur did not react. The accountant felt emboldened and pressed on.

"Besides," he said, "no one is going to like your coming forward and volunteering to pay taxes after all these years. Questions will arise: How come the tax inspector never caught up with you? How rich can you be to actually volunteer this kind of money? His Majesty is suspicious of anyone who works against the system. You're only asking for trouble."

Teymur's answer terrified the man.

"Trouble," he said, "is just what I want."

SOHRAB THE SINNER told me I had to go away. It was May 1972, five months after Roxanna's disappearance. I was having dinner with Sohrab and Fräulein Claude on the terrace of the second-floor dining room. Below us in the yard, Mashti was crying as he watered the cement floor where he had once tended his beloved garden. Without any trees or greenery, the yard had been covered in snow and ice all winter, then turned into a furnace of heat and dust over the summer. Every night, Mashti would wash the cement down with a hose, raising waves of steam that surrounded him till he was almost hidden from view. Then he would tie the hose into a loop, roll down his pant legs, and curse the night Roxanna had ridden home in his car for the first time.

Sohrab was eating a salad of roasted eggplant with tomato and garlic prepared by his mother. Fräulein Claude had set the table for three—because Teymur never came home for dinner anymore—and she sat directly across from Sohrab in a high-backed chair that only accentuated her shortness. She watched as Sohrab tried to break my silence, asking me questions about school that I answered in short, quiet sentences, hardly raising my eyes to meet my father's. I had grown taller over the past few months, Fräulein Claude remarked. I had my father's yellow eyes, his solemn look, even his way of talking.

That was another reason why Fräulein Claude despised me: because as hard as she tried, it was impossible to pretend I was anyone other than Sohrab's child.

So she wanted me out of the house—out of the country and away from sight. With Roxanna also gone, Fräulein Claude thought, she could start her life all over again.

She had told Sohrab that I needed proper supervision, that it was in my best interest to leave the house where my mother had vanished, the school where my friends and teachers would not stop talking about Roxanna. She had told him that he owed it to me to give me a new start, that by sending me away, he would free me of Roxanna's legacy.

"Send her to America," she had insisted. "It's so new and so large, no one from this life will ever catch up with her. Send her while she is still young and can adapt easily."

It had not been difficult to convince him. In a country where universal education was still more an ideal than a reality, it was not unusual for wealthy parents to send their children abroad to study. Most children were sent off in their early teens—to European boarding schools where they learned the languages and the manners of the "civilized" world, and where access to a college education was not nearly as difficult as it was at home. But Fräulein Claude did not want to wait till I was older, and she considered Europe too close to Asia. That is why she picked America—the country that had killed Morad—and why she picked that year.

"Send her to America for first grade." She had convinced Sohrab. "Let her learn to read and write in English rather than in Farsi. It will be easier for her, and easier for you."

In March, Sohrab had called up the doctor who had operated on Morad's cancer. With the man's help, he had enrolled me in a Catholic boarding school near Pasadena, California. Sohrab had never been to Pasadena and had no intention of visiting it before he sent me there. He only knew that it was a small town, and quiet, and far from Iran. He had waited till May to tell me.

"I have decided to send you abroad to boarding school," he said that night without warning.

Fräulein Claude had cleared the salad and served her roasted chicken with saffron and potatoes. Even she was shocked at the abruptness of Sohrab's announcement.

"You have been enrolled for next September. You will leave late August."

I stared at Sohrab, my fork raised in midair, my eyes glassy.

"Your school is run by Catholic nuns," he continued, steeling himself against my glare. Sweat beaded on his forehead and the back of his lip. "I chose it because they are conservative, like ourselves, and their values are similar to ours. I have told them that you are Catholic—they wouldn't take you otherwise—but that you have no religious training. They have agreed to teach you everything from scratch."

I should have known, I thought. I should at least have had a suspicion of what was to come. Fräulein Claude, after all, had never made a secret of her desire to send me away. But all those times, especially after Roxanna left, I had heard her talk and told myself that Sohrab would never agree.

"I thought you might want to say good-bye to your friends before school is over this year." He now dragged out his words under the heat of my stare. "I know it seems like a difficult thing right now. But I think it's best for you. You will be happier growing up away from this house."

I was crying now, begging that he change his mind. Sohrab reached for me. He may have held me. He may even have cried with me—I don't know. All I could think of was that Roxanna would come back, out of the same night that had swallowed her, and with me far away in America, she would not know where to find me.

ROXANNA stayed in the House of the Eastern Star for eight months. She slept with hundreds of men, ate leftover food, drank raisin arrack mixed with distilled alcohol. She bathed in the lake that was cold and harsh and that left a residue of salt on her skin, washed her clothes in the same basin of dirty water used by the other women in the house. She became sick with malaria and typhoid fever, survived only because the manager of the house knew Roxanna was popular with the men. She grew thin and yellow and dirty, her skin dried up from fever and strange men's sweat, her teeth hollowed from malnutrition, her face lined from the effort—the constant, all-consuming effort—of not thinking about what she had left behind.

She had to escape the house, she knew, but to do so, she needed money and a man who was willing to help her. Without that, out on the open plain between the lake and the Rock, she would be spotted in a matter of minutes, arrested by corrupt Turkish police, brought back to the house, and slaughtered before the eyes of the other women, who must learn from her example.

Every week, the young man who had been her first customer brought his savings and spent them on a few minutes with Roxanna. She was the only whore he ever wanted to sleep with, because she was not cruel to him, and he was convinced he loved her. It was true that she hardly ever spoke to him, that she seemed revolted by his body and always looked away when he professed his everlasting love for her. He was willing to wait, he told her, as long as she didn't reject him, and in time, perhaps, she would develop some feeling for him.

In July, Roxanna contracted malaria again and spent two weeks in delirium. Coming out of the fever, she realized she would die unless she left the house. The next time the boy arrived for his session, she spoke to him.

"I want to run away with you," she lied. "Help me escape, and I will be yours and yours alone forever."

His eyes lit up with joy. Then he became frightened.

"But they'll catch us," he said. "They'll kill you and cut off my testicles and put them in my hands. That's what they do with anyone who helps one of you women run away."

She asked him again the next time he came, told him he had to help her because she would die if he didn't, promised she wouldn't tell the owners who had helped her if she got caught. Week after week she chipped away at his fear and filled him with false hope. In the end, he stole money from his father, bought two bus tickets to Ankara, clothes for Roxanna, a new pair of shoes for himself. One early morning in August, he took his father's car and waited for her by the lake.

She got out of bed at five o'clock. The manager had just gone to sleep. The other women were still in their rooms. Roxanna slipped slowly through the door and found the boy in the designated spot.

They drove to the bus station and abandoned the car. It would be too easy, the boy had reasoned, for the police to catch them in the car. Once his parents had reported it stolen, the license plates would give them away immediately.

They told the bus driver they were husband and wife, off to visit family in Ankara. All the way from Van to Erzurum, the boy held Roxanna's hand and smiled at her adoringly. In Erzurum the bus stopped in front of a teahouse where the passengers could eat and stretch their legs. The boy went to urinate in the outhouse. When he came back, Roxanna was gone.

She had taken the money, the bus tickets, the clothes. She could not have gone far to hide—just down the road and behind some boulders pushed there by an avalanche the previous winter. But the boy was afraid that if he looked for her, he would be arrested for having helped a prostitute run away. He waited in the teahouse.

The bus left without him and the next one would not pass for another three days, but he did not budge from his place. He was sure Roxanna would come back if she could, worried she had been caught and whisked away by the police in the short interval he had left her alone. In the end, the teahouse's owner took pity on him and told him he had been taken for a fool.

He got on a bus going back to Van, and told the driver he would pay for his ticket when he arrived home and could beg his father's forgiveness.

Roxanna walked from her hiding place ten hours to the next teahouse. On a bus again, she told everyone that she was a widow with no children, off to live with her husband's parents in Istanbul.

Erzurum had been cold, wild, sparsely populated. Riding now towards Trabzon, Roxanna stared out the window at the great distances of treeless plains and bare, rocky mountains—the earth cracked from extremes of temperature, the road almost empty for fear of the bandits and rebels that stopped cars and buses to rob or murder the occupants.

Trabzon, by the Black Sea, was a modern city full of cars and pedestrians, run-down houses and poor shops. There was a harbor and a huge Russian bazaar. An old woman with many bags got on the bus there and told Roxanna the city was full of seedy brothels and Russian prostitutes. She chain-smoked Turkish cigarettes. She said Trabzon had been the land of the Amazons, the ancient race of women warriors. She asked Roxanna where she was headed.

"To Istanbul," Roxanna answered, then looked away towards the window.

"That's far away." The woman coughed and rearranged her bags around her seat.

Roxanna did not answer her. Alexandra the Cat had once told her that Istanbul was a city between two seas, the farthest point of travel in Asia, a bridge to the European continent.

———

For most of the journey between Trabzon and Istanbul, the Black Sea coastline was rimmed with thickly wooded mountains and scattered farming towns. There were fields of tobacco, cherry orchards, white beaches along a sapphire blue sea. There were the hazelnut plantations in Giresun, the port at Samsun, the town of Sinop, where, at the start of the Crimean War, British and French forces had fought the Russians. There were long stretches of empty road, the black asphalt stark against the blue of the sea. And then, many days later, there was Istanbul.

On its outskirts were the slums and the shantytowns inhabited by peasants who had migrated to the city in search of jobs. Built at night alongside the ocean, the makeshift homes took advantage of an old law that protected a house whose roof had been built during the hours of darkness. The houses were dirty and overpopulated and rampant with disease, forever lingering on the edge of destruction. Sooner or later, government bulldozers would come— they always came—to raze the towns and make room for new high-rise buildings. The peasants would then sift through the rubble, salvage what they could of their belongings, move a few miles farther along the coast, and build new shacks in the dark.

The city itself was set at the point where Asia faces Europe. Between the two continents lay the turquoise waters of the Bosporus, a narrow waterway that connects the Black Sea to the Sea of Marmara and, beyond it, to the Mediterranean. Along those shores, on both the Asian and the European sides, Istanbul sprawled for miles with its crowded streets, modern high-rise buildings, and traffic jams. Narrow cobblestoned alleys choked with apartments and homes. Open-air bazaars, ancient museums, palaces, and towers built by kings from long-defunct dynasties spotted the landscape.

Roxanna got off the bus at the main station in the New City. She stood on the sidewalk, overwhelmed by the crowds and the noise, the language she did not understand, the faces and mannerisms of people who seemed so foreign—more European than Asian. She did not dare approach anyone for help. With the last of her money, she bought fruit from a street vendor and sat on the sidewalk to eat. Eight days had passed since she had left Van, almost nine months since she had left Tehran.

After a while she noticed the fruit vendor staring at her from behind his display, and realized the man might call the police to have her removed. So she stood up, disoriented, and began to walk in the direction of the sea. She had gone too far, she told herself. Like Alexandra the Cat, who had stolen her mother's money and abandoned her corpse, she realized the only way to survive now was to keep moving.

THE NIGHT BEFORE I was to leave, Sohrab gave me a bracelet—a thin gold band with my name engraved on one side, Roxanna's on the other. He told me he and I would see each other soon. I knew he lied.

He put me to bed, then went into his study to read. An hour later I got up and went into Roxanna's empty bed next door.

I lay on Roxanna's sheets, my head on her pillow, and prayed that she would come to save me before Sohrab could send me away. At four o'clock, when Sohrab called me, I was still awake and still waiting.

I washed my face with cold water, wet my hair and brushed it back. I wore a new dress, new socks and shoes. Sohrab went downstairs with my bags. I went into Roxanna's dressing room one last time.

She sat at her vanity, smiling at me with open arms. It was the day the doors had come down in the house, the day Roxanna had held me and said we would always see each other. I put my face on her shoulder and smelled her hair. I touched her pale skin, the fabric of her powdery pink dress. Roxanna laughed.

Behind her the table was cluttered with bits of makeup and fake jewelry, half-empty tubes of lipstick and blue and green eyeshadow broken into powder and gathered back into the case. A white leather handbag with a rounded bamboo handle rested near the makeup. To the side of the vanity, the oak-wood closet gaped open like a loose woman, the hinges creaking as the door swung slightly forward and back. Inside it, Roxanna's clothes, all faded and junked through the years of the robber ghosts, hung like bodies awaiting a spirit. Sometimes in the summer, during the long siesta time when everyone lay down with their eyes open and cursed the heat, I had put on those clothes and wandered the house, pretending I was my mother.

I searched for a keepsake I could take to America. Looking around, I realized that I should have gathered Roxanna's belongings long ago, that I should have locked everything away so no one could walk in on her memories after I was gone. I saw the box where Roxanna had saved Mercedez's address, quickly took the envelope, and shoved it in my dress pocket. Then I saw the green tear jar Miriam had given her, remembered what Miriam had said about Shusha drinking her own tears. I wanted to take the jar with me, wondered if Sohrab would object, if Roxanna would come back to look for it and become angry because it wasn't there. Sohrab was calling from downstairs. I rushed out.

At the bottom of the stairs, Fräulein Claude stood with a shawl wrapped around her shoulders.

"Be good," she told me dryly, not bothering to smile.

Teymur came out of his drawing room. His back was slightly bent. He put his hand on my head and said a prayer.

"Go"—he kissed me for the first time ever—"and may God take you away from all our lives."

Mashti opened the etched-glass doors and let in the cool night air. Momentarily quiet, the dogs began to bark again from the place where they had been tied to allow us safe passage to the car. Sohrab pulled my hand to make me move.

He sat with me in the back of the car, one arm around me, his eyes avoiding mine as if he knew he was committing a sin.

The car glided through dark streets. I listened to the sounds of the tires scraping against the asphalt, of Mashti's shoes hitting the clutch and the gas pedal, of Sohrab breathing next to me. As we drove north, the sky began to lighten, slowly revealing the contours of the Elburz Mountains. I rolled down the window and looked up. Nowhere else in the world would I see the color of Tehran's mornings.

It was six o'clock when we arrived at the airport. A woman with long red nails checked my passport. Sohrab was pale, his hand dead cold. We waited. A voice called the flight.

Sohrab walked me through customs, across the tarmac, up

into the plane. Handing me over to a stewardess, he showed me my seat and gave me a pillow and a blanket. Then he held me. He held me for so long, I knew he was giving me up for good.

When I looked up, he was walking away. Minutes later I found him in the frame of my window, standing behind a railing at the edge of the runway. I was not sure if he could see me on the plane, but he stood in the same place for close to an hour, until we began to take off. When the plane started to taxi, he waved blindly in my direction. I strained to see him, to keep his image in my memory. I tried to believe that he loved me, that I would manage without him, that I would not lose him entirely, as I had lost Roxanna.

Then I put my face to the window, in the place where he had been a moment earlier, and cried all the way to America.

The Land of
Choices and Chances
1972

SISTER ANA ROSE of the Saint Mary Magdalene Academy for Young Girls stood in her nun's habit and her black orthopedic shoes, peering at the crowd of passengers who were coming off the plane in Los Angeles International Airport. Her face was pale with worry, her lips pursed together as if to block a cry. She had been sent to collect me from the plane and take me to the school, but she looked lost and confused and badly in need of help. She did not notice the flight attendant who was holding my hand.

"You must be waiting for Lili." The flight attendant touched her arm.

Sister Ana Rose let out a sudden gasp and drew back in fear. Her eyes darted around for a minute, as if seeking the closest exit, then returned to the woman before her.

"This is Lili," the flight attendant said. My father had entrusted me to her at the beginning of the flight and told her a nun would collect me in Los Angeles. "I believe you are here for her."

The sister looked suspicious at first. Then her eyes focused on me and the color began to return to her lips. When she spoke, I thought she was going to fold in on herself—a puppet in a black habit at the end of a long and odious show.

"At last," she whispered. "I was sure I'd lost her."

The flight attendant mentioned my luggage.

"Oh yes." Sister Ana Rose became distracted again. "Of course. Luggage."

She turned around and started to walk away, but I remained in place, clutching the flight attendant's hand and refusing to let go.

I had sat on the plane for twenty-two hours—too nervous to eat or drink, too scared to get up even to use the bathroom, for fear I might lose my way back to my seat. The plane had landed once in London, then again in New York. The other passengers had gotten off and walked around the terminals. I had stayed in place, right hand in my coat pocket, clutching the envelope I had taken at the last minute from Roxanna's room. Every time some-one addressed me, I opened my mouth and tried to speak, but no sound came out. Finally, the flight attendant had sat down and put her arms around me.

"Don't be afraid," she had said, hugging me. Then I had felt a rush of anger so strong, I began to vomit on the floor.

It was fear—cold, white, unconquerable—fear that had para-lyzed me on that flight, and rendered me deaf and mute. I had known this fear all my life, inherited it from Roxanna the moment I was born. I had sensed it in her hands that held me but were always about to let go, in her eyes that looked at me but always reflected other horizons. I had known it in her bed—on those nights when I had gone into her room and found the sheets marked only by the memory of her skin. Once, in the days before they took the doors down, I had stood on the balcony of Roxanna's room and watched her in the yard: she was walking along the clothesline that ran from one end of the maids' yard to the other. A row of white sheets hung in the windless sun. Roxanna's small, fragile figure emerged between two sheets, vanished, appeared and faded again. Every time she vanished, the fear choked me.

The flight attendant smelled of pancake makeup and perfumed lipstick.

"It's all right," she tried to reassure me in the airport. She spoke with a clear British accent, the same one I had been taught in kindergarten, yet I barely understood her. "You are going to be fine. This lady will take you to your school and take charge."

I grabbed her hand tighter. I opened my mouth to tell her I did not want to stay here, did not want to go with the woman in the black habit.

Sister Ana Rose grabbed my elbow and yanked me off.

We stood side by side in the baggage claim area. Bags rolled up to us on the beltway, then rolled away and came back. We saw the same bags three times before Sister Ana Rose realized I did not know what we were doing.

"Pick out your bags," she said in her fast American accent.

I looked at her, looked at the beltway, did nothing. I had forgotten what my suitcases looked like.

"Which one's yours?" she asked me, and again I did not answer.

She sighed, shifted her weight from one leg to the other, wondered aloud what her next move should be. Then she grabbed my ticket stub and looked for the luggage tag.

"No one told me she couldn't speak," she muttered under her breath. Then it was a matter of finding our way out of the airport and back to the parking lot where Sister Ana Rose had left her car.

We went from one lot to another, crossed streets, climbed from ground level up to the roof and back down, retracing every step and checking every car. Sister Ana Rose had put my suitcases in a small metal cart, which she wheeled ahead without looking back to see if I followed. She pressed on, convinced every time that it was here, in this lot, on this floor, where she had parked her car. One hour and three parking lots later, she was beside herself with worry and about to call the police and report her car stolen. Suddenly, she let out a cry of relief and began running. There it was, the object of her agony and now her ecstasy: a dented yellow station wagon with a broken taillight and torn seats patched over with duct tape.

"I knew it was here all along." She exhaled.

We drove out of the airport and onto a freeway. Alone in the backseat, I sat motionless, my senses numbed by exhaustion and fear, my hand still clutching the envelope in my pocket. I was grateful that Sister Ana Rose had not spoken to me, that she seemed unaware of my existence. She threw a glance in the rearview mirror and felt obligated to break the silence.

"I heard your mother died."

The freeway was gray and long and mostly bare. We drove in the slow lane, Sister Ana Rose checking every exit and wondering if this is where she should get off, looking at the handwritten directions that she had taped on her dashboard but which seemed of little comfort to her now that she had to put them to practice. When we finally did turn off, it was onto a wide boulevard spotted with huge warehouses and large empty lots, then into a residential neighborhood with one-story homes and broken screen doors. Men in undershirts sat on junk-filled porches, playing cards in the afternoon heat. Little boys with dirt-smeared faces rode their bikes on the cracked sidewalk. We stopped in front of a one-story beige structure fronted by a statue of a forlorn-looking woman in prayer. I got out and saw the name of the school inscribed on a small plaque by the front door.

"I'll show you to your room." Sister Ana Rose took my suitcase out of the back of the station wagon.

A narrow entry hall led to a waiting area with a short table and a rotary-dial phone. To my right was an office, which I would soon learn belonged to Mother Superior. To my left was a narrow corridor that led to the classrooms. We crossed a yard and came to a smaller structure: a neighboring house that the school had bought and converted into a dormitory for boarders. I saw a mess hall, three bedrooms with two beds each, two bathrooms. The rooms were unoccupied and dark. My bed was next to a window that overlooked the yard and, beyond it, a small cemetery.

"You can start to unpack." Sister Ana Rose showed me my closet. "You've missed lunch. Dinner is at six."

The clock on the wall stared at me with its white face, but I could not read time yet. Sister Ana Rose started to leave, then hesitated and turned around.

"Do you understand English?" she asked.

I nodded, but she looked tentative.

"Does that mean yes?"

I nodded again.

"Good," she said. "School won't start for another two weeks. There is no one here but you and me and Mother Superior. Your father sent you to us early so you could become acclimated, and so I could tutor you a bit before all the other girls arrive."

I sat on the edge of the bed. She faded into the darkness of the corridor as if she had never been.

Days went by in the quiet of the empty school, with nothing for me to do but wait. I stayed in my room, floating in a fog of fear and insomnia, unable to rest at night, distracted all day. Every time I tried to close my eyes, the fear pushed them open.

Sister Ana Rose gave me a pile of picture books with English words in large capital letters and told me to look at them every day. I left them on the table, untouched. She took me into the chapel every morning and told me to repeat the prayers after her. I watched her lips move, but did not speak. In the mess hall, she sat at a table across from me and ordered me to eat. I put the food in my mouth but could not swallow. All day, every day, I prayed that my father would call.

He called on the seventh day.

"Bring me home," I cried into the mouthpiece of the phone outside Mother Superior's office.

Sohrab remained quiet at the other end. Sister Ana Rose watched me.

"Let me come home."

"You don't need to come home," my father answered. "You are six years old—practically a lady—and you have to stand on your own two feet."

I did not blame my father. Not then. Not yet.

I tried to believe him instead, tried to wait through the fear and the insomnia, the fits of panic that made my skin turn ice cold and forced my stomach to lurch out anything I ate. I tried to be obedient, helpful, patient. When he called, I told him everything I had done since I arrived in America, described for him the color of the drapes in my room and the smell of the paint in the mess hall, the prayers I had learned to say, the letters of the alphabet Sister Ana Rose had taught me to write. I told him everything and thought that through this he could see me—see my need, my desperation to go back to him—and that, sooner or later, he would let me go home because he did, at that time, in those years, still love me.

Distant and melancholic as he had always been, Sohrab was my only hope, and I did not—could not afford to—blame him yet.

It was only later that I would call him "Sinner."

Forty-eight girls attended Saint Mary Magdalene's Academy. I was one of four first graders, one of only two students who lived at the school. The other girl was in fourth grade—the child of a Mexican-American couple who traveled between the United States and Mexico and took their daughter home only for the holidays. She was dark and quiet, always writing letters, counting and crossing off boxes that represented days on a calendar she had hung above her bed.

"Sixty-four more days till I go home. Sixty-three. Sixty-two."

We hardly spoke.

The other students were Americans who came to school in the morning and left as soon as study hall was over. In the morning, they bounced out of their parents' cars and rushed into the school to find their friends. In the afternoon, they gathered on the front lawn and made plans to meet later at one another's homes. I watched them all—in the chapel, in class, at lunchtime. They talked in loud voices and traveled in packs, carried themselves with the kind of confidence that forced me to back away and graze the walls every time we crossed paths, laughed at jokes I never understood and was not let in on. When they saw me, they rolled their eyes, made faces, shrugged as if to say I was strange. When they spoke to me, they raised their voices and brought their mouths close to my face as if I were deaf.

"She's an orphan," they said to one another as I listened.

IT WAS NIGHT when Roxanna crossed the old pontoon bridge hanging above the Golden Horn—the inlet, surrounded by water on three sides, that linked the New City to Old Istanbul. On the fourth side, bounded by fifth-century Theodosian walls, was Istanbul.

A peninsula comprising seven hills, Istanbul had, for more than fifteen hundred years, been the seat of great empires. As Constantinople, jewel of the Byzantine Empire, it had been the most important city in the world for a thousand years. It had been the center of the Ottoman sultans, rulers of an empire that had lasted five hundred years and stretched from the Black Sea and the Balkans to Arabia and Algeria. It was the home of the Topkapi Palace and the Church of the Saint Savior in Chora, of the Blue Mosque with its cascade of domes, and the Covered Bazaar with its vaulted roofs and four thousand shops. Now it was crammed with inhabitants and tourists, with expensive restaurants and sidewalk food vendors, with wide, sunny streets overlooking the blue sea, and dark back alleys choking with clotheslines and antennas and piles of rubbish in every corner. Above the hills were the mansions of the rich Turks who drove European cars and retired to their homes along the Bosporus for the weekend. Farther down were the business districts and the tourist attractions—the many mosques and museums and open-air markets and restaurants. On the outskirts were the slums.

But the sea was everywhere.

And so Roxanna stayed. She had traveled to the end of Asia and could go no farther. She had also come to a place surrounded by water, and though it was not the sweet, blue-green water of the Caspian she had always dreamed of, the three seas around the Golden Horn provided an unobstructed view of the horizon with no memories or limitations.

She found a job wiping grease off the floor in a Turkish restaurant across from the Topkapi station, moved into an overcrowded building off a cobblestoned alley in the Kumkapi district along the Sea of Marmara. Istanbul's Armenian ghetto, the Kumkapi bordered the wholesale fish market and was populated almost entirely by Armenians. From her room on the third floor, Roxanna could smell the fish day and night, hear the sounds of Armenian women fighting with their drunken husbands and yelling at their many children, of patrons in fish restaurants eating *kalamar* and drinking "lion's milk." The plumbing in the building had long since gone to rot. The only light in Roxanna's room came from a single bulb that she had to screw and unscrew because the switch did not work. The hallways smelled of urine. The landlord came every Monday to collect his rent and then vanished.

Roxanna stayed in the building for a week, then a month, then a year. She took the bus to the restaurant and back, told everyone who asked that she was a widow from Iran with no family or friends. She learned incorrect Turkish by listening to the other waiters and dishwashers—all of them peasants who had recently migrated to Istanbul—and bits of English and French and German from the tourists who stopped to eat in the restaurant. But she never made any friends, never even got to know her neighbors in the building. Sometimes, when she was so alone she could feel her skin turn hard and cold like fish scales, she would take a man home and sleep with him in her narrow, creaky bed with the loose springs she could never quite cover. He would be a waiter from the restaurant, an Armenian teenager bored from working in the fish market, a tourist who had looked up, perhaps, from his plate of *biftek* and noticed Roxanna wiping the floor around the grill. She took money if they offered, made them Turkish coffee on her portable gas stove that doubled as heater.

"Tell me a story," she would say, and then close her eyes, through the long night or the short daylight hours, and listen.

———

Years passed and Roxanna the Angel remained in the same room across from the fish market. Slowly, she lost the urge to run, never dreamt of flying anymore. She spoke no Farsi, did not follow the news, purposely walked away from Iranian tourists or people who might mention the country in a conversation. She was not haunted by the fear of the robber ghosts, or even of Fräulein Claude anymore. Teymur's eyes still watched her in her bed, from across the distance that was safe and unthreatening, and she could lie naked all night under his gaze without being afraid.

Only sometimes, caught in a traffic jam in a crowded inter-section, running from the police when they came to search the building for felons and prostitutes, or else just standing on the street corner to smoke a cigarette, Roxanna would be struck by the realization that she was loose, and unknown, and that she was going to die in this town—free, it was true, but also alone.

MY ROOMMATE, Iliana, complained about me to Mother Superior. I was always up at night, she said. I vomited too often, sat too long staring at my books without turning a page. I bit my nails till my fingers bled, dug the tip of my pencil into my palms till I broke skin. I got violent headaches that made me moan, sat around with a pair of scissors and cut anything I could get my hands on—my books, my uniform, even my sheets. I drew on my hands and arms with an ink pen.

Mother Superior called me into her office and gave me a warning. Two weeks later, when Iliana complained again, Mother Superior called my father.

"Give her time," he told her. "She needs a few months to adjust."

She gave me a second warning, made me promise I would change.

"What's the matter with you anyway?" Iliana asked after I had left Mother Superior's office. "How come they sent you here?"

"I don't know," I said, and prayed she would not ask more.

"Well, how come they never visit?"

I shrugged and quickened my pace. She kept up.

"Who's that person in Beverly Hills?"

I kept walking. She realized I wanted to avoid her, and so she persisted.

"You know, that address on the envelope you keep in your pocket day and night."

I slowed down, then stopped.

"I've seen you hold on to that piece of paper ever since school started. I can't read the weird writing on the front, but the return address is to a woman in Beverly Hills."

My heart raced. I remembered the red circle around the words on the upper left hand corner, the words my mother had thought important enough to mark and save. I took the envelope out of my pocket and showed it to Iliana.

She made a face at how wrinkled and dirty it was. Then she stretched out the paper and looked at the return address.

"There it is: 1282 Sunset Boulevard, Beverly Hills, California."

I felt a door open and light pour in.

Late that night, as she sat in her bed counting the squares on her calendar, I asked Iliana if she would help me write a letter to the woman in Beverly Hills.

"Write it yourself," she said without looking at me.

"I don't know how."

"I don't care," she answered, and turned the lights out. "I'm not your teacher or your nanny."

I was too afraid of her to challenge her decision. For a while, I lay in the dark. When I thought she had fallen asleep, I got up and turned the light back on. She cursed but did not get up to turn it off again.

I sat at the table and tore off a page from my notebook. It was near Thanksgiving. I had had two months of schooling and did not know how to write more than my name and a few simple words. After a long while, I put the pen to the page and wrote the only things I could:

> Roxanna
> Lili
> Please

Iliana leaned over the edge of her bed and laughed at my letter. Then she got up and took an envelope from the drawer of her own night table.

"Here," she said, and addressed the envelope on both sides. "Maybe this woman will come take you away and then I can sleep at night."

MERCEDEZ THE MOVIE STAR had lived in Los Angeles for sixteen years—ever since she came here on the last leg of her honeymoon with Amin and sent him home alone. They had gone to Europe first—to Paris and London and Frankfurt, Athens and Madrid and Monte Carlo. He had bought her trunkloads of clothes, first-class tickets on airliners and cruise ships, booths at the opera. Mercedez had felt out of place at first, trying to feign confidence with her manners and her way of dressing, terrified that the other women at the expensive hotels and restaurants would take one look at her and know she was a poor girl from a distant ghetto, doomed to oblivion. She spent too much time setting her hair and doing her makeup, stepped with bravado into the hotel lobby, and, within five minutes, she would have that look of a wounded cat Amin loved so much. She had seen the other women look at her, and she realized that she looked wrong.

But she caught on fast, and Amin helped her. He would take her into the jewelry stores that catered to royalty, and let her try on anything she wanted. She would sit down and take off her coat, revealing her neckline, her resplendent skin. She took off her hat and let her hair fall against her shoulders, smiled faintly at the young men who waited on her and who would never recover from seeing her. Amin watched those men quiver with delight, heard them sigh with envy as the stones they hung around her neck touched Mercedez's skin.

He liked the way she bought everything without regard to how much it cost or how useful it would be, the way she spent his money as if it did not exist—as if Amin himself did not exist. Afterwards, she would walk out of the store ahead of him, never thanking him for any gift no matter how large or small. Men stopped and turned to look at her a second time. Women stared at her and wondered who she was, if she was famous, if they should know her name.

In their hotel room, he would take off his clothes and lie in bed, waiting. She let him wait, let him shiver with desire, call out to her. Then she would make love to him without taking her own clothes off, so that she left him forever hungry and only half-satisfied.

He always knew it would end. It was this—the sense that each time she made love to him, Amin had managed to escape the inevitable once more—that made Mercedez so precious. He was a man, condemned to death, who managed to evade the guillotine every day.

It was over in New York.

She dragged him through an endless succession of restaurants and clubs, smoky rooms full of bare-chested young women and cocky young men. They stayed at the Waldorf Astoria, shopped at Harry Winston. She never let him touch her.

Tired of traveling, on the phone every day with his son, who warned that the family business would fall to pieces without him, Amin felt the mounting panic blur his judgment but could not find the way to stop it. In Europe, where he had traveled every year for three decades, he had been a savvy old man empowered by the memories of the deals he had made and the women he had conquered. He had sat at the Ritz in Paris and told Mercedez about the businessmen and politicians he had known. She had listened, her eyes mocking him, and at the end of each story, she had raised her glass and toasted him because they both knew he had passed his prime and would never find his old glory.

But in New York, Amin was unknown and unknowing, pathetic with his refined French and correct German, powerless when people addressed him in their American English. His manners were outdated, his etiquette laughable.

She told him they were going to Hollywood.

It had been her plan all along—ever since she had been a young girl in the house of Alexandra the Cat, when she had looked at the pictures of movie stars in the magazines she bought at Blue-Eyed Lotfi's shop. Mercedez had always known she was going to Hollywood.

They arrived in spring, rented a suite at the Ambassador Hotel. She bought a white bathing suit, black sunglasses, a long cigarette holder. She lay by the pool all day, drinking martinis and eating caviar by the spoonful, oblivious to Amin, who sat next to her in his beige linen suit and large sunglasses, white shoes and gold cuff links. He looked like a deposed dictator who had lost his army and with it his manhood. He drank club soda with lime, read the paper front to back, felt his skin blister in the heat and his feet swell from the salt in the club soda.

There was an agent, a lunch by the poolside, a late dinner to which Amin was not invited. The agent arranged for other meetings, a screen test, a date with a movie man. Mercedez got two minutes opposite an unknown actor in a bad film. She came back to the hotel and told Amin he must leave.

He took the news with the resignation of a longtime servant who has known he will be let go. He packed his bags, paid the rent on a suite for Mercedez for the next six months. He gave her enough money to buy the house on Sunset Boulevard, opened a bank account into which he would deposit large sums every month. It was all hers, he told her. All he asked was that she not divorce him.

On the screen, Mercedez came off looking hard and edgy—not at all the sultry woman she played in person, not the kind of face the director had been looking for. She tried for other parts, slept with other agents and producers, but in the end, it was all in vain. The door that had opened so easily closed on her just as fast. Mercedez failed for the first time in her life.

She became more angry, more determined to prevail.

"Fuck the movies," she decided. She had managed to get away from Iran, to reinvent her life. If she could not conquer Hollywood with her looks, she would still own enough of it to make a difference.

With Amin's money, she bought large chunks of Hollywood and Sunset Boulevards—entire blocks of shops and apartment buildings in the mid-Wilshire district, rundown houses, burnt-out theaters on the East Side. She rented the shops to anyone who asked, let the apartments full of rats and roaches to large families of illegal aliens who did not dare complain about the health and safety violations. Year after year, Mercedez invested in restaurants where patrons got sick from food poisoning, and in buildings where prostitutes turned five-dollar tricks. She never felt pity for the children who slept in her drafty apartments, never batted an eye when she sent her manager to evict families who were late with their rent. She had been angry all her life, and she did not mind venting her anger on the weak and the helpless.

By the time Amin died and his wealth was divided among his children, Mercedez had become rich in her own right, and no longer needed the movies to make her.

FROM THE MOMENT I wrote to her, before I had even taken the letter to Sister Ana Rose and asked that she mail it, before I had seen the postman come for the day's mail and carry my letter away, I waited for Mercedez to call. I had never seen her and did not know what she looked like. It never occurred to me that she might have changed her address since she wrote that letter to Roxanna, that she might not understand the meaning of my letter, that she might not want to answer me. I never even realized that I had not given her the school's phone number. I waited through Thanksgiving and the weeks that followed, through Christmas Eve and Christmas Day, when I stayed alone at the school with only Sister Ana Rose and Mother Superior. I waited through the first week of winter break. Then she came for me.

Tuesday morning I heard a car pull up to the front of the school, then heard a woman talking to Sister Ana Rose. I was sitting in my room, drawing lines into the palms of my hands with a red pen. Sister Ana Rose always punished me when I drew on myself: I would have to skip dinner and my television hour. And yet I kept drawing on myself, driving the pen ever harder onto my skin, trying to create a shape, a figure that would make me real, make me visible to the girls in the school and the teachers in my classrooms, to my father far away, to Roxanna.

"I don't know anything about visitation rules."

The woman in the front hall was pacing around in hard shoes, talking loudly to the nun. I put my pen in my uniform pocket and went to the door.

"You need permission from her father," Sister Ana Rose said in a lower voice.

"I don't need permission to do anything."

Suddenly panicked, I turned and ran to my bed, sat on the edge with my legs crossed and my hands folded on my stomach.

The woman was walking ahead of Sister Ana Rose, opening

doors, stabbing the floor with her heels as she approached my room.

"This place is a fucking cellar," she said out loud. Sister Ana Rose gasped.

The woman opened my door, looked inside, almost looked away. At the last minute she noticed me in the half-darkness.

"There you are." She exhaled and walked in.

She was long and lean and more beautiful than anyone I had ever seen. She wore a black hat, a tight black dress that hugged her body and revealed only her perfect legs. She had on a red cashmere cape, high-heeled snakeskin pumps, perfume that announced her from far away. Her skin was peach colored, her lips red, her eyes bottle green and luminous. When she spoke, the words rolled from her lips and bounced in the air like red and yellow and orange hard candies.

"You can't be here." Sister Ana Rose caught up, panting and beside herself. She was dwarfed by Mercedez. "We have rules."

She melted under the green stare, shifted her weight, rubbed her hands together to wipe off perspiration. Mercedez didn't bother to answer her.

She came towards me slowly, carefully—a panther approaching her prey and trying not to scare it. She reached above my head, over the bed, and opened the blinds on the window. Light fell onto her face in straight rows, illuminating her eyes. She sat next to me on the bed.

"My God." She sighed. "She did have a girl after all."

Sister Ana Rose planted herself beside the bed as if to save me from the Devil. "You are not on the list of her approved visitors," she dared.

Mercedez didn't even raise her eyes to her.

"No one but her approved visitors is allowed to see her," she persisted.

Mercedez still ignored her.

"No one," Sister Ana Rose reiterated. "And that includes *you.*"

Mercedez raised one eyebrow and stared the nun up and down.

"Bring me the list. I'll put my name on it."

"You can't do that. Only her father can do that."

"Then go call her father." Mercedez looked away, dropping Sister Ana Rose from the edge of the world. She shuffled away, feet heavy on the parquet floor, intending to call Sohrab.

"Close the door when you leave," Mercedez called out.

She told me that she was going to take me away, to her house at the other end of town, and that she would bring me back in time to start school after the winter break. She said all this in English spoken with a soft, melodic accent, the sound dripping from her mouth like a stream, soft on my ears, sweet in my head.

I packed a toothbrush, a change of clothes—the last dress Roxanna had ever bought for me. It was a navy-and-white-check dress with pleats in the front, already too small when I had left Iran, and yet I had brought it with me as proof that Roxanna had existed. Mercedez looked at the dress and turned her lips.

"We'll have to buy you some decent clothes," she said. "Get a pair of shoes."

Sister Ana Rose came back.

"I can't reach her father," she announced triumphantly, then gasped at the sight of my bag. "What are you doing?"

Mercedez the Movie Star took my hand and moved through the room like a blade.

"Taking her away," she answered. "You'll see her Sunday."

A limousine waited in front of the school. It was silver-gray with tinted windows, driven by a stunningly handsome young man with dark skin and Latin eyes. He got out of the car and opened the back door as we approached. He took my bag, helped me into the car, held Mercedez's hand, and watched her glide in after me. He never took his eyes off her.

In the car, she sat facing the driver's rearview mirror, leaned back and opened her cape to reveal the deep opening of the front of her dress, from her neckline into her chest. She took off her hat and let her hair fall around her face in one golden wave, lit a cigarette, crossed her legs, exhaled a cloud of smoke. He was watching her in the mirror. She let him watch her.

Sister Ana Rose banged on my window and threatened to call the police. We drove away.

"What happened to your mother?" Mercedez asked when we were on the freeway.

I shook my head. "I don't know. She went away. Maybe she's dead."

Mercedez was surprised, uncomfortable with my pain. She opened a door in the side of the car and took out a glass and a crystal bottle. She poured a clear brown liquid into the glass, added ice, took a slow, deep gulp.

"Never mind," she said. "Things happen."

We drove on the freeway, then got off at the Sunset Boulevard exit.

"Look out the window," she told me, softened by the drink. "This is my town."

Then I saw an America I had not seen in my months in Pasadena—the America of long, tree-lined streets and shady sidewalks, of gorgeous mansions and larger-than-life men and women, of green lawns and shiny cars and endless roads leading to ever-wider horizons. As we drove down Sunset Boulevard, Mercedez showed me the house that had once belonged to Lucille Ball, the hotel where she had had lunch with Kirk Douglas, the street where she had seen Marilyn Monroe drive away in a blond man's car. We slowed down at the corner of Sunset and a street called Foothill, drove through a low wrought-iron gate, up a wide driveway. We stopped in front of a two-story house with a facade of smooth yellow stones, flower beds all around.

"Here we are," Mercedez declared.

There was a large entryway paved in marble, light blue carpet on the living-room floor, a winding staircase, a grand piano. The driver brought my bag and left it downstairs. A woman in a uniform the same color as the carpet showed me my room upstairs. It was all silk and satin, light blue and yellow and peach colors, magazines stacked on the night table, pillows with lace ruffles on the bed. Mercedez told me to take a shower and change. When I had finished, she came back into my room.

"It's almost noon," she said. "I'm going to take a nap."

She slept through the afternoon. I stayed in my room at first, listening to the quiet of the house, looking out the window at the enormous backyard with its black-bottomed pool and the many lounge chairs lined up on the grass. The maid asked if I wanted to watch television downstairs.

"You must be hungry," she guessed, and led me to the fridge.

There was a bottle of tomato juice, a bag of apples, a tub of butter on the top shelf. All the other shelves were filled with bottles of wine and vodka.

"Madame doesn't like to eat at home," the maid explained, and gave me an apple. From a cabinet, she extracted a box of crackers.

"I don't bring food because I don't live here," she said. "I guess now Madame will send me out to get you some things."

At five o'clock the maid left. At seven Mercedez emerged from her room resplendent in fresh makeup and evening clothes. She looked surprised when she saw me.

"I have to go out," she said. "I have plans. But I hadn't realized, I guess, how small you are. Can you stay here by yourself?"

"Sure." I tried to feign confidence. I did not want to be left alone but did not dare ruin her plans. Frowning, she examined me for a while, then shrugged her shoulders and gave up.

"I guess you'll have to," she concluded. "Just don't answer the phone and don't open the door. Watch TV and then go to sleep. I'll close all the doors and windows."

She went to the bar and poured herself a drink, checked herself in the mirror above the mantelpiece in the living room, came back, examined me one last time.

"Have you ever been alone in a house before?"

It was important that I not fail her, that she like me, that I not become a burden she would want to unload.

"Sure," I lied again.

Later that night, awake in the bed with the satin sheets and the ruffled pillows, I heard the limo pull into the driveway and the front door open. Mercedez came into the house, closed the door but did not lock it, climbed the stairs, went into her bedroom across the hall from mine. I saw her undress in the soft light from her bedside table lamp. Her movements were slow and calculated. She was waiting.

Then the front door flew open in a single, violent burst, and I saw the young man—the driver with the dark eyes and the restless stare—tear through the house and into the bedroom, where Mercedez took him into her arms and ruined his life.

AT HOME, Sohrab never spoke to his father anymore. They spoke at work, in Teymur's office, which was like a vast reception hall with antique chairs and gilded tables, dark Persian rugs and velvet drapes. A servant in a black-and-white uniform poured drinks into crystal glasses and offered them to guests on a silver tray. A secretary, hired by Teymur but planted there by the Shah's secret police, took two sets of notes—one for Teymur, one for her bosses at the police headquarters—from each meeting.

When the secretary left for the day, Teymur and Sohrab sat together to review their affairs. They spoke about their factories, their workers, the Shah's habit of arbitrarily introducing new laws—creating two problems as he tried to eliminate one. They spoke about the accountants who remained in the basement on Ferdowsi Avenue, buried waist-deep in paper, aging too fast and working too slowly.

"Send them away," Sohrab advised his father, but in vain. "You taught me yourself not to challenge the system."

It was the only reference Sohrab ever made to the past, this mention of that morning when Teymur had taken him to see the hangings in Freedom Square. In all the years after Roxanna's disappearance, after they sent me away and remained in the house together, Teymur, Fräulein Claude, and Sohrab never spoke to one another of what had happened. They went about their lives as if uninterrupted: Fräulein Claude caring for the house and for Mr. Jacob, Sohrab working at the office or reading at home, Teymur forever absent. Perhaps, Sohrab thought, the silence allowed them to stay together—consoled them even, as they drew comfort from each other's presence. Perhaps there was nothing they wanted to say, because they each understood the others' pain too well. In the end, all that mattered was to endure one's loss.

Teymur the Heretic knew he was tempting danger by trying to pay his taxes. He knew that the Shah's informants were watching him, that they had watched him since he had arrived in

Tehran some forty-six years earlier. The Shah had informants everywhere—in elementary schools and hospitals, army barracks and restaurants. His spies rode taxis all day just to listen to other passengers' conversations, took domestic jobs for the sole purpose of informing on household events. They followed Teymur, he with his Qajar ancestry and self-made wealth, his so-called German wife and Jewish father, the daughter-in-law who had disappeared without a trace—not even a burial—and the house full of ghosts no one could catch. They had followed Teymur all his life in Iran, and they would certainly not let the matter of his taxes go unnoticed, and yet . . .

And yet Teymur was tired. He was sixty-six years old and had lived long enough to know he was damned. He had abandoned his mother to her own bitterness, betrayed his wife, deceived his son, caused Roxanna's demise. Now, faced with a future without options, he was sick and tired of having to bribe dirty little men with green leather briefcases, of fearing overweight generals with diamond pinkie rings and emaciated mistresses, of bowing before the Shah and keeping his mouth shut in front of the street sweeper who informed to His Majesty. That is why Teymur refused to dismiss the accountants, even though he knew he was going to lose his life over the taxes.

THREE DAYS AFTER I returned from my visit with Mercedez, Mother Superior received a letter, stamped in Tehran and purporting to be from my father. In it, he gave the school permission to release me into the care of Mercedez the Movie Star on weekends and during school holidays.

Mother Superior had already placed Sister Ana Rose on probation for allowing Mercedez to take me out in spite of school policy, and Sister Ana Rose had punished me by taking away my dinner and television time for an entire week. When the letter arrived, Mother Superior examined it suspiciously, then pulled my file out of a drawer to compare the signature on the letter with one she had on my admission forms. She noted immediately that the two did not match at all.

"It's a sham," she declared to Sister Ana Rose. "Bring me the youngster."

She asked me about the letter—executed, she insisted, by the devil in the red cape who had left heel marks all over the parquet floor. I told her the truth: I knew nothing about the letter. I had never told my father about Mercedez.

Mother Superior dialed his number in Iran.

She told Sohrab she was calling to confirm the authenticity of a letter she had received, presumably from him. It was about a woman named Mercedez, who had appeared at the school without an invitation and insisted she had visitation rights. Mother Superior did not mention the five days I had spent with Mercedez over winter break.

She held the phone to her ear and stared at me triumphantly while she let Sohrab absorb the information she had just delivered. Then her jaw dropped.

He had not written or signed the letter, he said. He had never contacted Mercedez. And yet, if I wished, the school was to release me into her care on weekends and holidays.

Mother Superior was aghast.

"In this country we do not entrust our children to liars and crooks," she said. She was speaking to Sohrab, but looking at me.

The next thing he said made her give up. She put the phone down slowly, folded the letter, and put it away in my file. She sat in her chair and tapped her fingers on the edge of her desk.

"What a strange man," she whispered.

TWO YEARS WENT by without an answer from the basement on Ferdowsi Avenue. In 1975, the men finally emerged from their cave. They had grown overweight and loose-muscled and pallid, squinting in daylight. Their leader, the one who had worn white linen pants on the first day, placed a thousand-page handwritten volume on Teymur's desk, took two steps back, and remained at attention.

Teymur opened the book to the first page and stared at the numbers. The accountants expected that he would become angry, that he would slam his fist on the desk and object to their findings. No one in his right mind, they thought, would voluntarily hand over such a large sum of money to the government.

Teymur closed the volume, stood up, and shook hands with the men, then sent them home.

He stayed at the office that night and read the report. Sohrab came in and told him he should destroy the book, then pay off the accountants so they would not inform the Shah's people of their findings. Fräulein Claude called him to plead that he have mercy, if not on himself, then on her and Sohrab. In the morning Teymur walked alone to the bank and asked for the manager who had sold Morad the land that killed him.

The manager ran out of his office the moment he heard Teymur's name. He was smiling, but he talked too fast and his palms were sweaty with fear. He offered Teymur tea and dates, asked if he preferred Coca-Cola, insisted that he try some bitter English chocolate. He promised Teymur devoted service, ever-lasting allegiance, favors beyond the call of duty. Teymur took a pen and wrote a figure on a piece of paper.

"I need a cashier's check," he said, "made out to the Office of Taxes."

The manager went limp.

"I don't understand," he mumbled, certain he had missed a clue.

"You never have." Teymur laughed in response. "Do your job."

AT SCHOOL, I tried hard but barely achieved. My grades were low, my accomplishments minimal. I studied but did not concentrate, spoke but did not communicate. The teachers wrote me off. The other girls tired of picking on me and slowly forgot I was there. Mercedez, too, often forgot to call or send for me through an entire summer. I stayed in the dorm, alone with the nuns, immaterial and nonexistent.

Because that is what I had become in the years since Roxanna left, the way I had managed to survive and go on: I had become invisible to myself and to everyone else. I had vanished in the cloud of fear and anxiety that had surrounded me on the flight to America—or maybe before it, on the night Roxanna left, when I called her and she turned around, looked at me, and did not *see* me.

So I took the pen to my own skin and drew figures all over my palms and the insides of my arms. In the morning, I washed them out in the shower but then started again almost as soon as I had dried off, sat up nights drawing on my stomach, my thighs, the soles of my feet—anywhere I could cover with clothes so the nuns would not see. I drew fine, circular lines, arches and loops and long, narrow bridges above the palm of one hand, up over my arm, across my chest, down onto the other palm—a labyrinth of daily sorrow and endless longing that repulsed the nuns and made the other girls avoid me as if I carried the germs of a deadly disease and that, ironically, delighted Mercedez.

"You're a great artist," she declared every time she saw me half-dressed and bearing the results of the previous night's drawings. "You should put this stuff on paper, or else parade around in the nude and let me show you off at some galleries."

She did show me off to her friends—on those nights when I stayed with her and she decided to take me out to dinner. We went to Chasen's for drinks, Perino's for main course, the Polo Lounge for after-dinner socializing. Everywhere she went, Mercedez had her own booth, her own favorite servers and bartenders, her own group of devoted admirers who flocked to the booth and competed for her attention.

"My niece from abroad." She introduced me to the men who thought me "sweet" and to the women who, for the large part, never saw me. "Actually from Pasadena—but that may as well be abroad."

I would sit at the table for hours, eating my food and sipping the juice Mercedez ordered every half hour as she renewed her own drink. Reassured by the presence of others, by the sounds of music and laughter and incessant talking, I would fall asleep, usually sometime in our second restaurant, and Mercedez would call her driver to take me home. Then I tossed and turned in bed, fighting to overcome my fears, until at last I reached over for the pen and started to draw on my skin again.

Near dawn Mercedez would come home—sometimes walking, sometimes stumbling, but always with a man. She would make love to him in the living room or her bedroom, in the kitchen, out on the lounge chairs by the pool. Then she always left him alone and went to sit by the grand piano she could not play, teasing the keys with her index finger and humming softly as she drank herself to sleep. I came out of my room and watched her from the landing: her head would be resting on top of the piano, her hair spread onto the keys, and only I knew that she slept there because, like me, she was afraid to be alone.

THERE WAS A two-day interval between Teymur's handing over the cashier's check to the Office of Taxes and the visit from the man who introduced himself only as "His Majesty's devoted servant." He had an enormous jaw and thick, meaty lips, but his teeth were tiny and set apart, like a baby's.

"Take your jacket and come outside," the man told Teymur through those baby teeth. "A car is waiting for you at the door. Get inside and don't ask questions."

Teymur fought to keep his hands from shaking. He stood up behind his desk, tightened the knot on his tie, put on his jacket. He looked through the window at the street outside, turned to the door, and found himself hoping a familiar face would walk through it. He took too long to find his keys, stuffed two stacks of cash into his pockets. When she saw him leave with the man, his secretary, who knew where he was going, asked sarcastically if he expected to be back for lunch.

Teymur walked down one floor, to Sohrab's office, and gave him the keys. He wrote down two phone numbers—old friends in the air force who might intercede on his behalf should the need arise. Sohrab went with him to the street. It was two in the afternoon when they emerged from the building and spotted the cherry red Volvo parked across from the entrance. Teymur was terrified, suddenly wishing he could return to the life that until an hour ago had seemed unbearable. Somehow, he thought, he must have been moving towards this moment all his life.

The driver took him to an unmarked building on Persepolis Avenue, next to the theater. There was an office with an aluminum desk, one chair, no telephone. An overhead fan buzzed relentlessly without providing cool air. The doors had no handles. The windows were painted shut.

A man in a powder-blue suit and crocodile-skin shoes asked Teymur questions. He wanted to know about the factories, about Teymur's German wife, about the money Morad had paid for land already belonging to the Shah's sister. He said nothing about the check Teymur had paid to the Office of Taxes, made no charges, offered no explanation. They talked till eleven o'clock that night. The man with the crocodile shoes did not take notes.

They kept Teymur in the building for two days, then transferred him to another one. He asked when he could go home.

"Not for a while," they answered.

He asked what the charges were.

"Sedition."

Then they took him to prison.

In prison, he was beaten and interrogated, but never charged with anything more specific than sedition. State-controlled radio announced his arrest and counted among his crimes bribery and the illegal hoarding of basic supplies. Government-censored papers printed his picture on the front page and speculated about his possible ties with Nazi Germany during the war. His factories were shut down, his properties confiscated.

Even his house would have been taken over, emptied of valuables, and sealed. It would have been turned into a museum for tourists, or an orphanage that the Queen could visit once a year, wearing a diaphanous pink hat and a pink Chanel suit. She would have had her picture taken with grateful children who, contrary to rumors, were not—"see for yourself, Your Majesty"—tied to their bedposts or suffering malnutrition. The house would certainly have been taken over, were it not for the fact that it was haunted.

The Shah, who had decreed that ghosts did not exist in modern Iran, was nevertheless reluctant to touch a place so unlucky it had driven Teymur to ruin. He let the house go, allowed Sohrab and Fräulein Claude to continue living there with Jacob the Jello and Mashti.

Sohrab spent the next three years trying to obtain his father's release. He wrote letters and made promises, bribed high-ranking officials, requested visits with petty bureaucrats. He called the two men whose names Teymur had given him, then he called others—all of Teymur's old friends, all of his business associates. Everywhere, he was faced with a gray wall of fear—"Will I be next?"—and an apology that if they spoke on Teymur's behalf, they, too, would be considered "sympathizers."

"Sympathizers of what?" Fräulein Claude laughed bitterly every time Sohrab was turned down by another of their old friends. "Your father never sympathized with anything in his life."

Short of money, aware that the Shah's secret-service agents were watching the house all the time, she hardly went out at all. She paced the house alone, in her high-heeled sandals and sprayed-stiff hair, her ankles so thin even she could not help wondering how much longer they would stand her weight. She made dinner for Sohrab and Jacob, dusted the house, noted that since Roxanna's flight, the robber ghosts had not come back even once. Every afternoon, right before sundown, she went into the kitchen and asked Jacob what he saw.

"Nothing much," he answered with a child's innocence. "Just Roxanna in the window, wearing blue wings, looking at me."

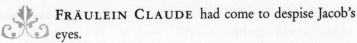 **FRÄULEIN CLAUDE** had come to despise Jacob's eyes.

She blamed him for what he saw, for telling her about it so easily, unaware of the pain it caused her. She hated him for seeing Roxanna even in death, for telling her that he saw Sohrab pacing the yard at night, his shadow long over the concrete floor, his eyes turned towards the sky as if praying to have Roxanna back. Most of all, she resented him for having seen those men she had brought home, in the days before Roxanna's disappearance—the ones she had paid to rob her, the robber ghosts who were not ghosts at all, only trained thieves she let into the house with her own keys and invited back every week.

She had hired the men soon after Jacob had told her about Roxanna and Teymur. Fräulein Claude had realized, in the white heat of the panic that blinded her, the precariousness of her own future: how easily she had lost her son, then her husband, and how easily she could lose the only part of her life Roxanna had left intact—the money that was hers, and Teymur's, it is true, but for which Teymur showed no regard. She needed security, she thought, in case Teymur turned on her, divorced her for Roxanna, or just left her. In a country where any man could annul his marriage unilaterally, with no obligation to shared wealth or spousal support, at a time when Teymur could simply have taken away what she had spent a life gathering, Fräulein Claude decided that her first obligation was to protect her own security.

She hired two Russians from the Caucasus, paid them to steal her own and Roxanna's jewels, sell them on the black market in the Soviet Union, and bring her back the money minus their own take. It was their idea to make it look like an inside job so the police would not be called in.

The men came in daylight, from the servants' entrance right through the kitchen, which Fräulein Claude had arranged to be empty except for Jacob. He saw them and thought they were gentlemen of class and distinction because they wore expensive suits and gold watches.

It was so easy, she fell in love with the whole scam: The men went through the house and misplaced a few objects. Then they took Roxanna's wedding band, Fräulein Claude's earrings, Teymur's cuff links. They waited awhile and came back for the sapphire necklace. After that, they went off and sold their booty. Fräulein Claude counted the money and, waiting to decide where she was going to hide it, stuffed it in an envelope that she taped to the back of her closet. She felt a power she had never sensed before: the ability to control everyone's life merely by the fear she spread—to accuse and condemn, to be heard and respected, and, above all, to be once again in charge of her own household.

She let the men in for the paintings, the antiques, the rugs. She kept the money in her own room, in the closet no one was allowed to approach. She did not count what the men brought to her; it did not matter anymore. She had stumbled onto something bigger and more empowering than money, and she could not stop herself even after she realized it was time.

That is why Fräulein Claude did not mind, deep down when she faced herself alone, to see Teymur imprisoned and tortured. Nothing he endured in prison could compare with the rage that he had instilled in her, the anger that poisoned her food and turned her nights into hell, that fought her like a fiend from within, that changed her, she knew too well, from the young girl who cared for all her brothers and their lives into an old woman bent on destroying everyone. It was Teymur's fault that Fräulein Claude had become mean and bitter and cruel, and if he suffered now, she was convinced he was only repaying his debt to her.

He was released from the Shah's prison in 1978, in the tumultuous months leading up to the Islamic revolution. He suffered from the aftereffects of a beating that broke his ribs and punctured his lung. He died at home, in the drawing room above the garden, in the house he had built with hope—the house on the Avenue of Faith.

ALL THROUGH sixth grade, I worried about graduation. Saint Mary's was only an elementary school. After sixth grade, anyone who still lived in the dorm would have to attend the public high school down the street. In the six years since I had arrived here, there had been a few other boarders— girls from Catholic families who stayed a few months, sometimes a whole year. I was the only one who had never left.

In March, I wrote to my father asking him what his plans were for me after elementary school.

"You will live at Saint Mary's," he wrote back, "and go to public school. I have already made arrangements."

In April, I sent him an invitation to the end-of-the-year festivities. He wrote back that he could not attend.

In May, I called him and begged that he take me home.

"Stop asking." He became impatient. "Your school is now your home. America is your country. You should accept this after all the time you've been there."

I went through graduation alone. At the end of June, Mercedez sent for me.

When I got to her house, workers were putting up Independence Day decorations on the front lawn. There were sequined flags, life-sized statues of Uncle Sam, bikini-clad mannequins wearing red, white, and blue top hats dancing arm in arm in a chorus line. Their legs were raised halfway, revealing black-and-red garter belts that flashed at night.

Mercedez the Movie Star was famous in Beverly Hills for the way she decorated her house on every major holiday. Tourists drove from faraway towns to look at her headless brides and flying witches on Halloween, or to hang trimmings on the arms of the men and women she hired to pose as Christmas trees. The Hispanic teenagers who sold maps to the stars' homes every few blocks along Sunset Boulevard always pointed to her house as the one destination tourists should not miss. At night, blond-wigged waitresses from truck stops in Bakersfield climbed over her fence in their high-heeled pumps and posed for pictures with naked elves. Tattooed young men wearing leather and high on speed drove down from the rock-and-roll clubs on the Strip to make love to the giant plastic bunnies on Easter. The mayor of Beverly Hills swore privately he would rather spend his birthday with Mercedez than with his own wife.

I got out of the car that day and carried my bag in. The Latin driver, having spent himself in Mercedez's bed and arrived at the point when she no longer wanted him, had long since been relieved of duty. For years he had come back, begging at her door—one last chance to hold her, one last kiss—but she had shut the door on him as she did on all the men who came before and after him.

The maid greeted me in the entry. "Madame is sleeping," she said. "I can bring you a glass of juice."

I took the juice and went out by the pool. It was hot. Quietly, so I would not wake Mercedez, I changed into a bathing suit and slipped into the ice-cold water.

I swam underwater, touching the bottom of the pool with my hands. I felt exhilarated by the cold, by my weightlessness, by the quiet sound of my body moving through the water. I opened my eyes and swam to the end of the pool, then back again without coming up for air.

This is what it must be like to fly, I thought.

I felt weightless and unfettered. Even when I ran out of air and sensed the aching in my lungs, I did not want to surface from the depths.

This is what it must be like to be dead.

One more lap underwater and I passed out.

The maid jumped in with her clothes on and dragged me out.

"You almost killed yourself," she yelled as I coughed water through my nose.

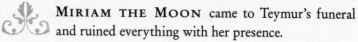 MIRIAM THE MOON came to Teymur's funeral and ruined everything with her presence.

She had not been invited, of course, and she knew, because no one could have made a secret of it, that she was the last person Fräulein Claude would have liked to see in her moment of grief. All the same, she showed up in her dark-brown jacket and navy-blue skirt, her useless old husband dragging three steps behind her and sizing up the crowd of mourners for potential customers he could unload his fake antiques on, and she had the nerve to go up to Fräulein Claude and try to shake her hand.

Fräulein Claude looked away so abruptly, all the eyes in the room turned towards them. Unfazed, Miriam patted Fräulein Claude's shoulder like an indulgent grandmother tolerating a child's immaturity and went on shaking hands with Sohrab and Mashti, Morad's wife and children, Fräulein Claude's brothers and their wives. If she was aware that everyone was watching her, she did not act as if it bothered her. If she knew what they were thinking, she kept it to herself.

After all, whether she acted like it or not, Miriam the Moon had already gone down in history as the woman with the most rotten luck God had ever handed a human being.

Her mother may have drunk poison and killed herself. Her sister may have run away with her husband's nephew and disgraced her family. Sussan, the youngest girl, may have married her only suitor—the man she knew would let her down—only to discover he was already married to a Muslim woman he had loved for many years. Rochelle's husband may have traveled to Hong Kong to look for trained whores and to Thailand for virgin girls. But nothing in this world, not even Fräulein Claude's tragedy with Teymur, could compare in magnitude with what had happened to Miriam.

Soon after Tala'at had run away from Iran, Miriam had decided she was going to become a businesswoman. For years she had sold fake antique silver to unsuspecting tourists, planned every expense down to the last penny, saved up all her earnings in wine jugs that she buried in the ground beneath her bed. Then she had counted her money and told Mr. Charles they should invest in an apartment house.

Her children were still small when Miriam set out on a quest to find the perfect investment at the best possible value. She had never owned a car, and she did not believe in paying for taxis. The buses in Tehran were too crowded, never ran on schedule, and broke down at every intersection. So she walked every inch of the city, from Cyrus Avenue in the south to the hills of Shemiran in the north. She talked to every real-estate broker, checked the books, scouted the neighborhoods. She sat for hours outside apartment buildings up for sale, just to observe the kind of people who went in and out of them. In the end, true to character, she decided on a building that was not for sale.

It was a narrow, three-story apartment house on Persepolis Avenue, across from the theater where her old acquaintance Cyrus the Magnificent had brought his schoolteacher girlfriend to watch American movies. The street was always crowded, choking with pedestrians and noise and the smoke of car exhaust, so densely populated Miriam was certain the building would never sit empty. In those days she was reading an American book, *How to Make Your First Million Without Working.* Mr. Charles always said that Americans made money only by the millions—smaller denominations not being worth their trouble because they were so rich—and Miriam wanted to follow the principles her book advocated:

"If you have the money, buy the *best* building in the *best* neighborhood for the *lowest* price. If you don't have money, buy the *worst* building in the *best* neighborhood for the *lowest* price."

The building Miriam selected was sandwiched between two taller structures, set on the street so that it received no natural sunlight. Shaped like a thin rectangle, it was so narrow, there was only one apartment on each floor. It had black iron bars on the windows, cramped corridors, confined rooms where air had not penetrated since the day they were built.

From the entrance, a foot-wide staircase led to the two upper floors. At the bottom of the stairs, a round wooden stool displayed the only telephone in the building. Shared by all the tenants, the phone was the object of endless quibbles and eavesdropping and had led to the breakup of at least one marriage since Miriam had started stalking the tenants. To the right of the staircase, the first-floor apartment was sunk a foot and a half underground, so that the living room, which faced the street, had a view of pedestrians' legs and cars' tires. Behind the living room were the kitchen, a bathroom, and two bedrooms displaying metal-frame beds and aluminum clothes racks. Behind them still was an enclosed patio that served as storage space for the whole building and contained everything from one-legged wooden chairs to a porcelain bathtub with holes in the bottom and weeds growing up the sides. The backyard was a tiny sunless patch of dry earth, enclosed on three sides by a brick wall, with only a round, empty pool, five feet deep and three feet across.

Altogether, the property was so flawed, Miriam figured it could be within her reach. She harassed the owner till he agreed to sell to her. Then she bargained with him over the purchase price till he was ready to give her the property for free, just to save his own sanity. She moved her family into the first-floor apartment. She was satisfied and triumphant, pleased with herself and her progress—the poor tenant from the ghetto a landlord at last.

She spent the first few weeks scrubbing the walls and the ceilings, putting rat poison and disinfectant in every corner, organizing the kitchen, and cleaning the yard. She bought used furniture for the living room, arranged the junk on the patio into neat stacks, but could not bring herself to part with any of it. Then she emptied the dirt out of the pool and, instead of water, replaced it with fertilized soil. She planted sunflowers in the pool, put grass in the yard, painted the brick walls a bright yellow that made the neighbors complain but that did—or was it, as she insisted, the sunflowers?—attract more light into the house. When she was done, she told Mr. Charles she was going to look for their second investment.

Mr. Charles, too, felt encouraged by their financial success, and devoted himself heart and soul to the business of expanding his client base. Illiterate and unsophisticated, he was blessed with an excellent memory that allowed him not only to keep his books mentally, but also to learn English just by listening to his American and British customers talk to one another. He was in awe of the British, but he loved the Americans because, he said, they were "large"—not necessarily generous, he explained to Miriam (some of them, in fact, resented having to support their own children past the age of eighteen), but so blessed with plenty, they radiated wealth without even trying. He stood outside his shop every day hoping to spot Americans before they entered another shop. He plucked them out of the crowd, grabbed them by the arm, took them to his own store with promises of tea and pistachio nuts and "Don't vorry. I have viskey if you vant." He gave them a tour of his shop, showcased every antique separately. He never pushed to sell to Americans. It was not their business he wanted; it was their company. More than anything else in this world, Mr. Charles liked to bring Americans home.

Once or twice a month, he managed to coerce some unsuspecting customers into accepting a dinner invitation, or else raised their curiosity enough so they stopped by for a drink. On those occasions he burst in through the front door earlier than usual, speaking his incorrect English laced with the American jargon he had picked up only halfway, apologizing for the humble surroundings as he went along. He was never embarrassed of his home and family except in the presence of Americans. Then his house seemed too small, his wife seemed too old and eager to talk to men about matters that should not concern a woman. His daughter had no poise, laughing the way she did at every chance, her voice so unconstrained, it had the ring of a hussy in heat. His son—worst of all, his son—looked as if he would never amount to anything more than his father.

To numb his own embarrassment and to seduce his guests into staying, Mr. Charles headed straight for the small wooden cabinet in the corner of the living room where he kept his stash of whiskey and the four crystal glasses he had bought over Miriam's vehement objections that "one can drink just as easily out of ordinary glass and it won't cost so much or break so fast." Assuming there were no Americans in this world who did not like whiskey, he poured generous shots, calling out to some-one—his children, Miriam, a tenant if she heard him and had the inclination to oblige—to bring ice. Then he lined the coffee table with appetizers: fried eggplant and garlic, peeled cucumber with raw onion and tomato, roasted pistachio nuts. He talked and drank, thrilled to have someone "large" under his roof, feeling his station in life elevated by the Americans' company. Some-where between his fifth and seventh shots, he always leaned for-ward, looked deep into the Americans' eyes, and swore he loved them, "for yourselves," he said, "not because you may buy some-thing from me. Just because of who you are."

It was one of those Americans, one night when Mr. Charles was bursting with love and admiration, who gave him the idea of filling the pool in the yard with water instead of sunflowers. They had been drinking since eight o'clock. Around eleven, Mr. Charles had decided to give the man a tour of the apartment house, taking him through the two upper floors, where he woke up the angry tenants and sent their half-naked wives into hiding just for the pleasure of leading a half-drunk American through their bedrooms and kitchens. Then he took his guest through Miriam's and the children's rooms, the bathroom, the patio, and ended up in the backyard with the bright yellow walls. The American, wearing a green safari jacket with red plaid trousers, was trying to figure out the most humane manner in which to free himself of Charles's hospitality. He remarked that he liked the color of the walls.

"It isn't much"—Mr. Charles accepted the compliment with pride—"but it's taken every bit of life I've had in me to get us here."

The American took another sip of whiskey and observed, in a gush of East-West brotherhood he would not remember in the morning, that since Tehran's summers were so unbearably hot, a landlord could benefit from having a pool at his house—"instead of," that is, "a giant pot of sunflowers."

Mr. Charles felt as if he had had an epiphany.

"And here I always say the *British* are smart!"

He called Miriam and told her they were filling the pool with water.

"Of course not." She was indignant, not only at her husband's naïveté, but also at the American's lack of foresight. "I'd have to watch the children all day to keep them from falling in and drowning."

On any other matter, Mr. Charles would have deferred to his wife's tenacity—if not to her twelve years of schooling and those English books she read. But the idea of having a real pool in the house had come from a person he regarded superior in every facet of life, and he could not, in good conscience, let it go. For weeks he argued with Miriam, asserting his rights as man of the house, drawing for support on his son's affirmations that there was nothing more pleasurable than to swim in ice-cold water in the middle of summer. His daughter, who knew her parents would not allow her to wear a bathing suit or get wet in front of the neighbors, kept out of the fight and busied herself studying for her final exams. By June, when her grades came in, Mr. Charles had decided he was going to end the bickering and take action.

One morning he brought two laborers into the yard, uprooted the sunflowers, and painted the pool. The next day he opened the hose into it.

It was such a magical moment—the water running clean and clear, the tenants coming out of their burning apartments to dip their arms and feet in the ice-cold water—even Miriam did not object.

Her daughter, who had been waiting for the right moment to ask a question, saw Miriam smile and ran up to her. Since she had ended the year at the top of her class, she said, would it be possible to invite two of her friends over one afternoon for tea?

"What for?" Miriam asked, almost insulted by the girl's frivolity. "Why would you want to sit around all day with a bunch of girls?"

Her daughter explained that she was only going to spend a few hours with her friends, that at seventeen, this would be the first time she had invited anyone over, that spending time doing nothing with one's friends could actually be enjoyable.

"Fine, then." Miriam shrugged. Appearances to the contrary, she had always secretly longed to give her children a happy life.

"But Joseph is out of school and I have things to do. You'll have to watch him while I'm gone."

Thursday afternoon, Sara's friends arrived in their miniskirts and high heels. Miriam stayed around for an hour, observing each guest's character and behavior, commenting that the girls' skirts were too short and that they were actually cheating themselves out of a healthy future with all the makeup they wore and the rollers they tortured their hair with every morning. She left at three o'clock. By seven, when she came back, the girls were gone and her daughter was reading a magazine on her bed. Miriam went into the yard to look for her son. He was floating facedown in the pool, already bloated.

Miriam the Moon would remember the events that followed that moment with the lucid objectivity of a bystander. She knew immediately that her son was beyond rescue. She also knew, from the weight of the silence behind her, that Sara had followed her into the yard, having suddenly remembered her duty to watch her brother, and that she was staring at the pool with her eyes bulging and her mouth open in silent horror. Then all of a sudden, Sara let out a monstrous shriek and ran to the water, throwing herself into the pool and calling her brother's name as if to raise him from the dead. Alerted by her screams, the tenants came to their windows, where they, too, saw what Miriam had discovered, and then pandemonium broke out all around as only Miriam stood, cool and collected, assessing the meaning of her son's death.

The tenants pulled Joseph out of the water and laid him on the grass. Refusing to let go, Sara lay on top of him, screaming till Miriam went up and separated them. She threw herself into Miriam's arms.

"Stop it." Miriam slapped her across the face. "It's *your* fault. *You* killed him."

For twenty-nine days following her son's drowning death that summer, Miriam the Moon did not speak to Sara. She let her lock herself in her bedroom, dressed all in black, sobbing into her sheets till she passed out. In the living room, Miriam and Mr. Charles sat shiva with the rest of the family. He cried incessantly. Miriam assured everyone that she was going to be all right.

A few times, Rochelle and Sussan tried to bring up the subject of Sara. They told Miriam that Sara was suffering horribly, that she blamed herself and would not stop doing so unless Miriam forgave her.

"It's not about forgiveness," Miriam answered. "She should know she's responsible."

On the thirtieth day of the shiva, Rochelle walked in to check on Sara and found her crouched on the floor, foaming at the mouth and vomiting Nile bleach. She died in the hospital, begging Miriam to save her.

Miriam the Moon sat shiva for another thirty days, then changed her black shirt with the torn collar and announced she was through mourning. She packed up all her children's belongings, even the toys, tucked them away in a corner of the patio, closed up their bedroom, drained the pool, and planted sunflowers once again. Then she went out hunting for properties as if she had suffered no damage. Her opinions remained as forceful as ever and her step was just as sure, but underneath her dark scarf and wide-rimmed glasses, her skin aged two decades in one year, and her face lost every trace of beauty it had ever borne.

"You have not broken me yet," she would murmur to God every Yom Kippur when she stood in temple, hungry and exhausted, pretending to pray so her friends would not know how much she hurt. When Mr. Charles declared he was too sad to go to work, she took over the shop and ran it by herself. When he said he was going mad with the silence in the house, she bought parrots and canaries and let them sing day and night to keep him amused.

Through it all, Miriam the Moon seemed to have forgotten her loss. She remained headstrong and impossible, so bent on denying God the pleasure of seeing her tears, she never showed her pain even to her husband. Her daughter's friends invited her to their weddings, and she went without bitterness. Her son's old classmates became the doctors and lawyers she would consult and insist on paying even though she never took their advice. But in her mind, her own children would never grow beyond their ages at death. Sara would remain the seventeen-year-old with the black, black hair and the too-easy laugh, Joseph the ten-year-old who ran around the yard with teeth missing, and Miriam could not help thinking that she could reach over, right there in front of her eyes where she saw them every moment of every day, and touch them in flesh and bones.

On rainy nights Miriam the Moon sat up in bed, horrified at the thought that her children were far away, soaking in their muddy graves, while she, who had wanted to give them happiness, stayed under a dry roof.

FRÄULEIN CLAUDE could smell the fires long before they were set, before, even, the first sparks had ignited. She could smell the blood and the smoke, see the orange reflection of the flames against the gray skyline of Tehran. Months before the first mobs tore through the streets of Tehran for the first time, Fräulein Claude could see the city burning.

It was summer 1978, and every day power went out throughout the city at odd hours. It happened without warning, for varying lengths of time. All at once the lights would go off, air-conditioning units would hiss dead, refrigerators would go warm. Television sets playing old episodes of *The Days of Our Lives* and *The Six Million Dollar Man* suddenly went black, and traffic jams, already miles long, became eternal. Drivers abandoned their cars on the street and walked home to have dinner by the light of kerosene lamps, came back hours later and found that the street was still packed. They were enraged and exasperated, overcome with a sense of impending doom, of a city bursting at the seams with frustration, an economy gone awry, a government out of control.

Fräulein Claude had heard rumors of strikes in the provinces, talk of the Shah's enemies coming together, joining forces to bring him down. Most of them wanted to replace his dictatorship with another, in their view, more benevolent one. The Shah, they said, had promised his people a return to the "Great Civilization," endless wealth, a political system that would be, in his words, more democratic than that of Sweden. Instead, he ruled by decree, arrested anyone who criticized him, appeared on television wearing his military uniform adorned with dozens of medals he had awarded himself, and told the people he was greater than God, more powerful than the president of the United States, more essential to the survival of his nation than bread or water.

All through June, Fräulein Claude smelled burning flesh. She walked around the house in a transparent summer dress, oblivious to the embarrassment she caused Sohrab and Mashti with her nakedness, and searched with her hands for what her eyes had lost long ago. Trusting no one, not even Jacob the Jello anymore, she spoke less and less, and spent hours at the kitchen sink, splashing herself with water that evaporated the moment it touched her skin. She thought about the news Mashti brought home from the street: Morad the Mercury's oldest daughter had converted to Islam and married a man thirty years her senior. His wife had borrowed three thousand dollars from one of Morad's old mistresses, and used the money to send her sons to America. Jacob the Jello's wife and children had gone to Israel, where his youngest son, Mateen, had lost a leg to a sniper's bullet. All the rest of Fräulein Claude's wealthy friends and neighbors, Teymur's old associates, and Sohrab's contemporaries were fleeing the country like rats.

By August, the heat was maddening. The asphalt on the street melted like soft rubber and gave way under pedestrians' shoes. Ants marched in foot-wide columns up and down the exterior walls of Fräulein Claude's house and into her bedroom. Lizards invaded the relative cool of the terrace, where, crazed by the heat and her own restlessness, Fräulein Claude chased them under piles of dust and cut them in half with a butcher knife, only to watch them tremble, then run again.

In the southern part of Tehran, the army drove bulldozers through the shanty towns made of tin and cardboard, holes dug underground, and tents erected on top of trash dumps, where immigrants from other provinces had come to search for the good life.

The evening paper, controlled by the Shah and his secret police, published a letter insulting the Ayatollah Khomeini. In protest to the letter, riots broke out in the city of Qom near Tehran. The Shah's soldiers opened fire. News of the shootings reached other cities across Iran, setting off fresh waves of riots, which in turn provoked more killings. The protesters—opposing the Shah's dictatorship, his family's corruption, the country's un-Islamic ways—set fire to banks and restaurants, government buildings and private cars, businesses owned by Jews.

In the city of Abadan on the Persian Gulf, temperatures were in the high double digits. Four hundred people, entire families, were sitting in a movie theater one afternoon when fire broke out. Exit doors remained locked. The fire department responded too late. Everyone burned.

The Shah accused his opposition of arson in the Abadan theater. The rebels, in turn, pointed the finger at the Shah. No one would ever know the truth, but the smell of charred flesh—of rotting, balled-up skin—rode north in the wind and spread the anger to every city in its path. All over the country, movie theaters went up in flames.

AFTER SIXTH GRADE I stopped calling my father, stopped writing to him except the few times a year when I had to inform him of my progress at school or ask about his plans for me. I let go of the hope of ever going home, and the conviction that I would see Roxanna again.

"He's doing you a favor, you know," Mercedez told me after my graduation that summer. "I had to cheat and lie and sleep with a dozen men just to get myself out of that ghetto and to America. Your father just handed you this freedom on a platter and let you be whoever you want. If you're smart, you'll thank him and never want to see him again."

I spent that summer at Mercedez's house. She was gone most of the time, on different trips, with different men. I stayed with the maid. We played checkers by the pool, went swimming. I helped her clean. In the afternoons, when she took a nap, I went out for walks.

Often, in those days, I saw Iranians who had come to Los Angeles to escape the riots that would turn into a revolution. They always walked in groups, the men wearing business suits even in the August sun, as if to prove to themselves and to others that they were not exiles, that they had had important work to do all their lives, that their jobs and offices were still waiting for them. They walked ahead of their wives, hands clasped behind their backs and heads lowered in conversation with their friends. They spoke of the latest news from Iran—the banks that had shut down, the companies that had burned to the ground, the exchange rate of the rial.

Behind them, the women walked in high heels and tight skirts, looking tired and pale, talking about the homes they had left behind: "just furnished," "just bought," "just built from the ground up." They sat on the benches in the park across from the hotel on Sunset, and wondered what they would do with their children who had been out of school for almost a year, worried about how their teenagers were bound to become "rebellious alcoholics" if they stayed in Los Angeles too long, how their daughters had already declared that, revolution or not, they preferred to stay in America for good.

Every time I saw Iranians, I followed them.

I walked behind them, sat on park benches next to them, watched them from across the street. I kept my head and my ears cocked, but as close as I got, they never suspected that I was one of them. Sometimes they spoke to me in their heavily accented English and their confused grammar. They asked directions, wondered how old I was, what school I went to. I wanted to answer in Farsi, but was afraid that they would not understand me, that after six years of speaking the language only to my father on the phone, I had forgotten how to speak it and they would laugh at me. I wanted also to tell them I was Iranian, ask them if they knew my father, if they had heard of Roxanna.

Instead I watched them—travelers in a foreign land, exiles waiting to go home. As lost and homesick as they were, they clung together and managed to re-create, every day that they spent away from home, a sense of belonging and community that I had never known. *I* was the real exile, I thought on those afternoons in the park—the traveler who would never find her destination.

But on other occasions, watching my compatriots and how they had brought with them not only their sense of home and community but also their pasts loaded with failed hopes and lost expectations—on these occasions I would remember what Mercedez had told me and think that perhaps she had been right—that Sohrab might have done me a favor by sending me away. He had taken away my hope and my family, it is true. But he had also taken away the fear I had of being haunted by greedy ghosts, the anxiety of having rabid dogs at the window, the anguish of wondering if Roxanna was buried under the concrete in our yard. He took from me the sadness that had tainted my mother's life, and the limitations of a destiny I could not have avoided in Iran.

Perhaps this was what they had done for me—Roxanna, who left me, Sohrab, who sent me away—they had sent me off across the ocean and, by so doing, given me a new destiny.

KHODADAD the Gift of God, Mashti's seventeen-year-old grandson, had dropped out of school to be a full-time messenger for the Ayatollah. He grew a beard and rode around town on a moped, carrying word from one mosque to another, distributing cassettes and leaflets bearing the Imam's word. After the movie-theater fire in Abadan, he forbade Mashti to work for Fräulein Claude and Sohrab anymore: the Ayatollah had sent word from Iraq that all the killings taking place at the behest of the Shah's regime—soldiers firing on demonstrators, spies setting fire to theaters—were the work of Jews. He, the Ayatollah, knew this without a doubt, as certainly as he knew God spoke to him in his sleep. He knew it because it was physically impossible for a Muslim to kill another Muslim: the bullets of a true believer could not harm another believer. The gun might shoot, but in the hands of a real man of God, bullets would be useless against a brother.

The soldiers who had been killing rioters, therefore, were not—could not possibly have been—Muslims. They were Iranian Jews who had long ago emigrated to Israel, and whom the Shah had brought back to kill the Imam's followers.

Khodadad the Gift of God told Mashti that all Jews were unbelieving enemies of God and worthy of death.

The Shah, nauseated by the smell of burnt flesh and by his own cancer therapy, turned against his allies and began to fire his ministers and intelligence chiefs. He appeared on television one night, looking gaunt and defeated, and asked the people's "forgiveness." Fräulein Claude watched him in horror. She and Sohrab were sitting in the first-floor drawing room, at the table where years ago Teymur had received Little Noori the Tax Man for the last time. Aware that they could become the target of an angry mob at any time, they had locked all the doors and left the lights out so the house would attract as little attention as possible.

"Mistakes have been made," the Shah said on television, and already Fräulein Claude knew he had lost the war. She turned from the television screen towards Sohrab. He sat upright against the bare background of the vast room, the light from the TV screen casting blue shadows all around him. He looked pale and sad, his hair gray before its time, his eyes a brighter yellow than she had ever seen. He was watching the Shah, but she knew his thoughts were far away, in the same realm of wonder and sorrow where he had existed quietly since he had lost Roxanna—before she flew away and left him, since that night when she slept with his father and told Sohrab with her own words.

Fräulein Claude touched Sohrab's hand as if to awaken him. "It's the end," she said.

He did not answer.

In September, an earthquake destroyed the town of Tabas, leaving fifteen thousand corpses for the Shah to bury. That same month, he declared martial law in Tehran.

The first night of curfew, the streets remained quiet. Lying in her bed with the windows open, Fräulein Claude could hear only the sound of army Jeeps and soldiers patrolling the streets. There was none of the usual roar of motorcycles and mopeds carrying demonstrators from one side of town to another, no burst of sporadic gunfire between the army and the anti-Shah forces. And yet, all night long, she felt a sense of imminent movement, of pervasive, almost overwhelming tragedy.

At three o'clock, she got up and went past Sohrab's bedroom. He was awake, at his desk, reading the paper. She went downstairs to check the locks on the doors.

She found Jacob the Jello lying facedown on the brazier, his mouth and nostrils filled with cold ashes, his limbs already dried and useless.

She went out the next day and bought Jacob a new suit. It was a tailored navy-blue affair, with wide lapels and six buttons on each side of the jacket. She had Mashti peel off the brown suit that Jacob had worn for the past twenty years and dress him in the new one. By the time they were done, Jacob the Jello looked better than he had on his wedding day. Then they laid him on the backseat of the car and took him to the cemetery, where the undertakers, impressed by his appearance, demanded proof that he was dead, before they took off his clothes and found the scrap of bones and yellow skin that Jacob really was. They washed and stuffed him with cotton, wrapped him in a shroud, and buried him as quickly as possible—and that, indeed, should have been the end of Jacob the Jello, but it wasn't.

Because when she came back from burying him, Fräulein Claude did not have the heart to throw out Jacob's old brown suit, and so she draped it instead on a hanger and hung it from a hook in the kitchen alcove above the place where Jacob had always sat. She also put his hat on the hook.

Maybe it was the suit, so worn that it had retained the shape of its owner's body forever, so familiar a sight that no one who saw it in the kitchen thought twice about checking if Jacob were still in it. Or maybe it was because the undertakers who had washed Jacob's corpse had not known to wrap his mad hallucinations along with him. In any case, the images never entered the grave with him. They followed Fräulein Claude and Sohrab home, walked through the house unabashed and unintimidated, talked to one another and to Fräulein Claude, told tales.

And so Fräulein Claude would turn around at high noon, when the sun blazed against the concrete floor of the yard, to find her husband licking tears off of Roxanna's lashes. Sohrab would wander into the kitchen to see Roxanna, young and lost and dressed in her old school uniform, laughing shyly at Effat the maid's exploits. Men in pin-striped suits carried rugs and paintings out of the house in broad daylight, and the Sponge Woman quietly offered to go down on Jacob, "as often as you want," in return for a drag on his opium pipe. He always refused.

At night, anyone who looked up above the house on the Avenue of Faith could see the slender creature in the luminous white gown open its wings against the sky and fly off.

In October, the workers at the National Iranian Oil Company went on strike, creating a shortage of gasoline. In November, the eleven-story National Gas Building was set on fire. Then the banks shut down, and the bazaars and government offices followed. The Shah ordered the dissemination of leaflets warning people that the red liquid stream they saw in their cities' gutters was not real blood, but red dye poured by the revolutionaries to scare law-abiding citizens.

In the days prior to the Muslim high holy days of Ashura and Tasuah, the tension in the streets was so thick, it smeared a film over the windows of Fräulein Claude's bedroom. She stood looking out: the gas workers' strike had not only shut down factories, but also resulted in a shortage of heating and cooking oil, and an almost total lack of gasoline. People pushed their cars down the street, slept all night in lines at gas stations, threatened to kill one another over a gallon of gasoline.

Men on motorcycles drove up to every house, announced a gun battle a few streets away, recruited anyone who was willing to stand behind a temporary barrier—an overturned car, a pile of rocks—and fight the soldiers. Short of bandages and first-aid materials, they raided Miriam's house and took all her sheets and towels, cut them into strips, and took them away to the wounded.

On Tasuah, two million people marched through Tehran. They walked quietly, carrying pictures of Khomeini, and there was no question they were going to destroy the Shah.

MIRIAM THE MOON spent the last months of 1978 trying to cash in her properties. She had closed the antique shop months earlier—because she had had no customers for close to a year and because all the other store owners on the street had obeyed the Imam's call to a general strike. Those who did not would be immediately branded anti-God and anti-Islam. Their stores would burn down, their houses would be ransacked. Now, she wanted to find buyers for the business and for her apartment buildings. She knew it would be hard, because anyone with any money to spare had already moved their cash out of the country, or else had had their assets frozen by the banks. But Miriam the Moon was tenacious and persistent and willing, just this once, to sell at a great loss.

"I know what I'm doing," she would tell Mr. Charles late at night, even though he never listened. "There is going to be a great war in this country, and anyone who stays is going to burn."

So she traversed the city—a lone woman dressed in a man's jacket and shoes, bearing no trace of the beauty that should have afforded her a charmed life but that had opened no doors, emerging at dawn against a red sky, walking all day through streets of fire and through moving, murderous mobs, stepping over the black carcasses of burnt cars, into shells of buildings, past bloodthirsty hordes who hunted down government officials, secret-service agents, wealthy Jews, brought them into the street, and beat them to death with their bare hands.

"Say 'Death to the Shah,'" they demanded of their victims. "Say, 'Death to America.'"

Miriam the Moon set her eyes on her goal and kept moving.

She called on everyone she knew, even Sohrab. She sat in their homes and told them why it would be wise to buy from her. She played on their sense of greed, told them that this was a once-in-a-lifetime opportunity, that she was selling at such a loss only because she had to leave the country.

"But you," she told her friends, "you are going to stay and see this through. Any day now the Shah is going to come to his senses, fire on a few thousand demonstrators, and scare them back into their homes. Then all my properties will go back to their original values. You will have made a monstrous profit, and I will be the fool."

One by one, in the fall of 1978, she sold all the assets she owned, even the basement apartment she and Mr. Charles were living in. She came home late one night and told him they had three months to move out.

"Where to?" he asked, completely beguiled, as if he had never heard her mention her plans for selling the apartment. His eyes had the blank expression of a blind man; his face was only half turned towards Miriam. In the years since his children had died, Mr. Charles had become docile and distracted, tending mostly to his birds and his plants, treating them more gently than he ever had his wife or children.

"We have to leave," she told him.

Mr. Charles, like Miriam, had never traveled in his life, never even crossed the boundaries of the city of Tehran.

"What do you mean 'leave'?" he asked innocently enough. "How does one 'leave'?"

Miriam sat down on the bed she had just sold, and took her shoes off. Her feet were swollen and blistered from walking so much. She reached under the bed for Charles's spare pair of shoes—men's wing tips—and tried them on over her thick black stockings.

"They're a little big," she declared, "but they'll be fine with a couple of socks."

She saw that Mr. Charles was staring at her. She sighed, put her hand in her pocket, and extracted a small package. It was a piece of butcher paper folded and refolded, then wrapped with a rubber band. Miriam put the paper on the bed and opened it.

"Look!" she said, suddenly beaming. There were five diamonds, eight carats each. They sparkled against the darkness of the room—all of Miriam's life, her hopes and achievements, her endless sacrifice, her eternal sorrow—sold half price in the back rooms of a burning city and bought again in the form of hard, brilliant stones.

"I bought them with the money from the sales I made. I figure they'll be easy to hide, because we're going to need to smuggle them across the border. But we can sell them wherever we are."

Mr. Charles was confused again. His lips had gone pale and his face was beading with moisture.

"What border do you think you're going to cross?"

Seeing his panic, Miriam felt sorry for him. She leaned across the bed and put her hand on his forearm. He trembled and pulled away.

"Things are going from bad to worse here," she explained quietly. She knew why he had pulled away from her—that without ever mentioning it, he blamed her for their daughter's suicide. Just as she blamed him for their son's drowning. She knew that part of him hated her, that in another time he might even have left her. In another time, she often thought, she might have taken a butcher's knife and slit his throat for filling the pool with the water that killed her son. But now they were old, and worn out by tragedy, and all they had was each other.

"Pretty soon the Shah is going to escape the country, and then the mullahs will take over," she explained. "Chances are, there will be a bloodbath. They're going to kill each other, but mostly they'll kill Jews. So we have to leave."

For the first time in his life, Mr. Charles realized he had no conception of the world beyond his own city.

"Where would we go?" he asked. "We don't know anyplace else."

The world beyond Tehran—America, England, that elusive and forever magical place referred to collectively as *Farang* ("the

West"), the places he had always dreamed of but never seriously thought he would see, the people he had always adored but never imagined he would live among—all of that world was suddenly staring him in the face like a black, hideous void.

"Rochelle has gone to America," Miriam said, trying to be brave. "My brother, Bahram, is there, too, in the same city. And Sussan's husband is sending her and the kids away this week. They're all packed, sitting in the airport every day. They even sleep there, just waiting for a runway to open and a flight to take off to anywhere. He's told her he'll join her in Los Angeles, but I know he's lying."

She realized she had wandered off her subject.

"So"—she looked her husband in the eye—"I figure if they can do it, so can we."

Mr. Charles shook his head, as if to confirm that Miriam had indeed gone mad, and turned to his canaries again. Grateful that he had lost interest in the subject, Miriam served a dinner of bread and yogurt, then sat down to strip the soles off of Mr. Charles's wing-tip shoes. She was going to glue the diamonds into the shoes—two in one, three in the other—then sew the soles back on with a cobbler's needle. It would be difficult, because her hands hurt from the early stages of rheumatism, but as she sat working that night, Miriam knew that the fight had only just begun.

She spent December waiting in line outside the passport bureau in Tehran. It was closed, of course—shut down by the strikes—and even if it had been open, even if the various other related agencies had also been open, the possibility of someone like Miriam obtaining a passport was nil: Like most other people of their generation, neither she nor Mr. Charles had ever owned a birth certificate. They had no identity papers, not even drivers' licenses, and the only way to prove they existed was to call on the testimony of friends and relatives. Still, Miriam stood in line every day, along with thousands of others, and went home only when the tanks rolled down the street every evening to enforce martial law. On the first day of January 1979, she went to see Sohrab.

Fräulein Claude answered the door, but refused to open it for fear that a mob was waiting outside.

"It's just me," Miriam tried to reassure her, "and I don't even have any cheap silver to sell."

But Fräulein Claude lived in mortal terror of being attacked by a mob—of her old servants, all of them now enemies, coming to stab her in broad daylight, or of ordinary thugs throwing Molotov cocktails into the house and setting her on fire. She had placed no less than five locks on the main entrance to the house, boarded the etched-glass panels in the door with planks of raw wood, and allowed only Mashti in and out.

"Go away!" she yelled at Miriam through the door. "You're attracting attention to us."

"Then open up, or I swear I'll stand here and scream bloody murder till someone hears me."

She found Sohrab sitting in his father's drawing room. His hair was entirely gray, his hands thin and pale. He looked like one of the ghosts Jacob the Jello had so often talked about— handsome, polite, transparent. When Miriam walked in, he got up and shook her hand.

She sat down, adjusted her scarf on her head.

"You know the Shah is going to leave," she told him without introduction.

He nodded and said he fully expected it.

"Once he's gone, the new regime will come after people like you," she said.

Sohrab's name had already appeared in various newspapers controlled by the mullahs. He was on a list of men accused of being "corrupt on Earth" and "antirevolutionary."

"At best, they will take away everything you own," Miriam went on. "Most likely, they will kill you."

He smiled again and nodded. His eyes stunned her every time she engaged them.

"You should think about leaving," she advised. "Take your mother and go away."

"And you," he asked, "are you going to leave?"

She crossed her legs and put her bag on top of her knees. He thought of how beautiful she had been, how she had looked that morning just prior to his and Roxanna's wedding, when Miriam had come to the house with her husband and many relatives, when she had looked at that place so filled with luxury and wealth and all of Fräulein Claude's ambitions, looked at it and declared it was doomed.

Did she know, early on, that Roxanna would leave him?

"I was hoping to get passports for myself and Charles," she said, "but that's not going to happen. The airport's closed and buses don't run because there's no gas. So I'm thinking of going east, towards Pakistan. I met a lot of people in line outside the passport office, and they all say that if I can rent a car and hire a guide to get us there, Charles and I can cross the border with no trouble. Once we're there, I'll worry about getting papers and crossing over to another country."

Sohrab was amused and perplexed at once.

"Why would you do that?" he asked. "Are you so afraid of the mullahs, you would give up your whole life here and run into the desert?"

She raised an eyebrow and studied him. Without wanting to, without even realizing it before, she and Sohrab had become friends over the years.

"It isn't just fear," she said. "I'm getting old. I figure this is my one chance to get out and see the world."

"Where will you go?" he asked, but he already knew the answer.

"To America. My sister Rochelle has had a green card for years and goes there every summer with her daughter. She thinks her husband's doing her a favor—sending her off like that so she can travel and shop. He only does it to get her out of his way so he can fool around with his girlfriends."

She saw Sohrab laugh and felt encouraged.

"Anyway, she's gone off this time, and taken all her rugs and antiques with her. They've bought a house, even, because her husband is so afraid of what is going on here, he figures she may never be able to return. They could probably arrange for a visa for Charles and me, if we ever get passports. That's why I'm here, because I may not see you again."

She leaned towards him.

"I know—I've heard—that Lili has been living with Mercedez in America. I want you to give me her address."

She held her breath and waited. He did not react at all.

"She's my niece. Besides, to find Roxanna I have to know where Lili is."

Sohrab narrowed his eyes, as if to focus better, and then shook his head in amazement. She was not feigning confidence, he thought. She had *decided* to believe, *decided* to have faith.

"You really do still believe she is coming back," he said.

"I know what I know." Miriam sighed, but stayed erect in the chair.

"It's been eight years," Sohrab remarked.

"It could be a hundred years for all I care," she retorted. Then she paused. She thought she saw doubt in Sohrab's eyes. When she spoke again, her voice was tired and bare and stripped of its usual confidence.

"You can only suffer so much loss," she said, and all at once her voice gave out. She stopped, caught her breath, dredged up the last bit of courage left in her to keep moving.

The only way to avoid surrender, Sohrab thought, was to forge ahead.

"I lost Roxanna twice—when she went to live with the Cat, then again when she escaped this house. I lost my mother, my two children. I've even lost Charles, who is here but doesn't know it anymore. Maybe I *need* to believe Roxanna is alive."

For a moment that day, Miriam the Moon almost overcame Sohrab's resolve.

Then he stood up and held his hand out to her.

"Good luck to you," he said.

His hand was warm. She held it, wondering if she should press on, if there was any possibility of changing his mind. Then she gave up.

"As you wish." Her voice was hard again. "But I want you to know this: you made a mistake cutting Lili off. She reminded you of Roxanna, and you couldn't bear that, so you sent her away and locked her up and pretended it was for her own good. Still, I am going to find her. Just as I am going to find Roxanna. And when I do, I will tell them that you love them and that your only sin was to not have faith."

The Shah left on January 16. That same day, an earthquake in eastern Iran buried thousands of people alive.

MASHTI'S GRANDSON appeared on television, talking about Jews as "Zionists" who deserved to die. Morad the Mercury's old butler, the one with the mouthful of gold teeth that Teymur had paid for, went every day to Sohrab's office, which had been closed for months, and delivered death threats. Bahieh the Sponge Woman rang the doorbell at midnight and, when Sohrab answered, cried obscenities at him.

Fräulein Claude tried to convince Sohrab that they should escape while there was still time, but he never responded to her pleas. So she swallowed her fear and put more locks on the doors, checked and rechecked them all night, counted her jewels and her money and hid them in ever more unreachable places. The fear tightened her throat into an impossible knot and traced its deadly path through her stomach into her intestines, where it lined the walls with a festering film that rose back into her mouth in the form of a yellow, noxious bile that made it impossible to eat. Her voice became garbled and broken, and her body was forever surrounded by a permanent cloud of stinking vapors she could not erase.

After the Shah left, his last prime minister, Shapur Bakhtiar, tried to restore order but gave up almost immediately. He had been told that Ayatollah Khomeini was on his way to Iran from Paris. He would fly in even though the airport was closed, and the only way to stop him was to shoot his plane down in midair. On the night of January 30, Bakhtiar opened the Tehran airport. Twenty-four hours later, Khomeini's plane landed in the capital.

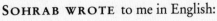 **SOHRAB WROTE** to me in English:

"I cannot call you because the phone lines are down," he said.

I saw him—the man I had known years ago as my father, who had been young and melancholy and gentle, who had kissed me in the morning and sat watching me over dinner at night. I saw him at this desk, hunched over the letter he was writing to me, his hands pale and refined and barely touching the paper at all.

"The new regime has confiscated our house and turned it over to the 'Organization for the Defense of the Weak.' Fräulein Claude and I have each been assigned one room. Five other families live in the house with us.

"I cannot send you money because our bank accounts are frozen. Perhaps your friend Mercedez will agree to pay for your school and other needs until I sort matters out with the new regime?"

It was just another mystery of her peculiar personality that Mercedez—the slumlord who never gave money to the poor and did not have pity on the children of her tenants living in her cockroach-infested rooms—agreed to support me entirely without any expectation of being paid back, and that she has continued to do so without ever making mention of it to me directly.

MIRIAM THE MOON arrived in Los Angeles in March of 1981, two years to the day after she and Mr. Charles left Iran huddled in the backseat of a rented Volvo that drove them across the land border to Pakistan. They had paid the driver one hundred thousand tomans to smuggle them through the country, and once they were out of Iran, they had to pay him again so he would not turn around and betray them to Pakistani authorities. He drove them three and a half days to a refugee camp in Peshawar, on the Afghan border. The camp had been set up by the United Nations High Commissioner for Refugees (UNHCR) to house refugees of Afghanistan's war with occupying Soviet forces. Dusty and overcrowded and receiving new arrivals every day, it would be a safe place for Miriam and Mr. Charles to hide from Pakistani authorities.

"Just tell them you're Afghanis," the driver said before he let them out of the car two miles from the camp. "They speak a variation of Farsi anyhow, and they look like us, so no one will know the difference."

Miriam and Mr. Charles would spend seventeen months in the camp, sleeping in tents and eating food that, Mr. Charles observed impartially, was better suited to the jaws of babies and toothless old men. At the first opportunity, Miriam called Rochelle in Los Angeles and told her she was going to need help getting to America.

"Find out the procedure for getting a visa, and look into renting a place for Charles and me," she ordered Rochelle. "In the meantime, I am going to find the right persons to bribe and coerce so I can buy a couple of passports."

She went to work immediately, asking questions and lobbying UNHCR workers, but all she got from them was more loose porridge and a pair of men's eyeglasses to replace the ones she had lost during her escape from Iran. So she looked elsewhere, among the other refugees at the camp, and slowly found her way to the man-who-knew-a-woman-who-was-related-to-a-man-who-sold-stolen-Iranian-passports. Unearthed during the rebel raids on SAVAK headquarters, the passports had belonged to political prisoners arrested by the Shah's secret police. They had been smuggled out of Iran and were selling at exorbitant prices on the black market in neighboring countries.

Miriam the Moon gave up her best diamond to arrange to leave Peshawar. They rode to Islamabad, then flew to Frankfurt. There, they stayed in a seedy hotel with no showers and cockroaches everywhere. Mr. Charles was too afraid to leave their room. Miriam called Rochelle every day.

"Get me a visa," she ordered. "Charles keeps threatening to turn himself in to the embassy and go back to Iran."

The American embassy in Frankfurt turned down their request for political asylum. They flew to Brussels and applied again.

"We had to leave our home with only one change of clothes," Miriam told the desk clerk every morning as soon as he opened the office doors. She was one of hundreds who called at the embassy every day. Their stories were all the same, their need obvious. And yet, Miriam managed to induce in the clerk a sense of panic and urgency he could not overlook. It was her direct manner, perhaps, or her strange clothes. It was the way her eyes focused on him when she spoke, the way she seemed to tell him, without actually uttering the words, that she had conquered greater enemies and overcome bigger obstacles than a lowly desk clerk in a crowded embassy in a quiet and cold city.

"My husband has worn the same shirt for ten months. He's going to die of depression if you don't help us."

She combed through the cheap hotels in the city for other Iranians sharing her predicament. She called her friends in Tehran, wrote to anyone she thought might bother to write back, and asked them all about the life she had left behind.

The Islamic government, they told her, had conducted mass executions on a scale unparalleled even by that of the Shah or his father. They had arrested Tala'at and her lover, The Nephew, who had been living in blissful sin for twelve years, and sentenced them each to forty years in jail. He wrote her love letters every day. One of the guards found the letters and reported him. He was executed after a ninety-minute trial.

Just as Mr. Charles was about to go mad, the embassy gave in.

In Los Angeles, Rochelle went to the airport to meet Miriam and Mr. Charles. She watched them get off the TWA jetliner— Miriam wearing the same brown jacket and wing-tip shoes she had put on at the start of her escape from Iran, Mr. Charles dragging his feet behind her, carrying all his worldly belongings in a brown-and-green-check carry-on bag he was ready to defend with his life. Instead of feeling excited to see them, Rochelle felt embarrassed.

In her Chanel suit and her snakeskin pumps, her lips painted amber and lined with brown pencil, her eyelashes weighted down by too many layers of mascara applied too early in the morning, she rushed up to Miriam, hoping no one she knew was at the airport that morning, and hugged her. Then she ushered her and Mr. Charles to the parking lot and squeezed them both into the one-passenger seat of her convertible Mercedes.

They drove to a rented apartment in a high-rise building along Wilshire Boulevard in Westwood. Here, Rochelle told Miriam, many Iranian Jews were living "temporarily" while they awaited the demise of the revolution and the return of the monarchy to Iran.

"They're going to have to wait a very long time," Miriam remarked dryly.

The building was crowded and badly managed and overrun by the smells of ethnic cooking and the noise of moving dollies loading and unloading on every floor. But Miriam moved into her apartment and accepted her exile without illusions. She made

a point of going from door to door and meeting all her neighbors—even the Americans, she said, because, after all, it was their
country she had come to conquer. The first week, she bought new
birds for Mr. Charles and turned their balcony into a small greenhouse where he could grow his plants and flowers. Then she allowed Rochelle to take her on a guided tour of Los Angeles.

In her man's suit jacket and with her shirt sleeves rolled up
halfway to her elbow, Miriam the Moon paraded up and down the
streets of Beverly Hills, through Rodeo Drive, where Rochelle,
who had spent a fortune trying to impress the store clerks into
showing her some level of respect, made the mistake of taking her.
Miriam fingered the clothes as if she were buying live sheep, asking prices only to tell the clerks everything was too expensive. She
demanded to see every manager in every store, warned them—
with their impassive faces and asinine looks—against the wrath of
the Almighty once He looked down upon "this street that's only
as long as a donkey's penis" and took notice of the kind of injus-
tice they were creating in this world: asking the sum of a country's gross national product in return for a shirt that was not even
silk, not even hand sewn, and that would cost eighteen dollars—
eighteen dollars at three thousand Iranian rials to a dollar, the
equivalent of a month's rent for a family of five in downtown
Tehran—every time the shirt needed to be dry-cleaned.

Mortified by her sister's attacks on the holy houses of Gucci
and Ferragamo, certain that she would never again be received
with anything more than a mocking smile anywhere along
Rodeo Drive, Rochelle nudged Miriam away from the street and
offered to buy her an ice-cream cone, only to have her lecture the
pot-smoking teenager behind the counter about the kind of
waste he was creating on this planet—selling thirty flavors of ice
cream when one would do just as well.

Rochelle took Miriam, with her ladderlike body and her Elvis
Costello glasses, to Westwood Boulevard, where the Iranian

grocery stores and restaurants were just beginning to open their doors and where Miriam declared she would not step because prices were so much higher than their competitors' on Pico and Fairfax.

Once Miriam settled in, she took two-hour walks on Ocean Avenue every afternoon just for the sake of running into other recent Iranian émigrés, and in no time at all she came to know every wino and drug dealer who ever haunted Santa Monica. Convinced as always that wasting food was the greatest sin known to man, she brought leftover food to her new friends: three-day-old rice with dill and parsley, sautéed lamb shank with onions and garlic and saffron, Cornish hens stuffed with currants and cumin. She carried the food in large pots wrapped in bleached-white cheesecloth that she tied in a knot, so that from far away the pots looked like coddled infants, or the heads of fat women wearing scarves.

Rochelle felt disgraced by Miriam's habits and Sussan complained that she was impossible to please, but no one who had ever known Miriam could deny her unequaled talent for studying people and discerning their secrets. With radarlike instincts, an incomparable memory, and a total lack of respect for the concepts of privacy or subtlety, she came to know the story of every Jew who lived on California's soil and, in time, that of his forefathers.

But neither her escape from Iran nor her takeover of Los Angeles would really grant Miriam any degree of satisfaction until she had achieved the task she had set up for herself before leaving Iran: to find me in America, nine years after my father had sent me away with the deliberate purpose of hiding me from my mother's family.

In the end, of course, she did.

WHEN SHE CALLED me that morning from the public phone opposite Mercedez the Movie Star's house, Miriam the Moon introduced herself as "your Dear Auntie Miriam. The one who raised your mother. You probably don't remember me, but I know everything about you, even things you never imagined could be true."

It was August 1981. I had spent three consecutive summers at Mercedez's house. I had come here in early June. Shortly after that, Mercedez had left on one of her spur-of-the moment trips to the Caribbean—the guest of a wealthy old man who claimed to have his own island. The winter before, he had taken her to his six-thousand-square-foot house on the slopes of Aspen Mountain.

"Go to your window and look outside," Miriam continued without giving me a chance to catch my breath.

My heart sank to the ground. I bolted out of bed and carried the phone to the window. There she was, at the phone booth on the corner of Sunset and Foothill—a long, dark figure on an empty street in the early-morning quiet, waving at me as she spoke.

"You wouldn't know this," Miriam went on, "but I've been traveling up and down the state of California searching for you."

She was looking straight at my window, as if she could see me standing there, trying to decide if she were a figment of my imagination.

"We had to escape Iran, Mister Charles and I. Mister Charles is my husband. He's from the ghetto, of course, like myself and your mother. But his mother thought she'd given birth to Moses, so she gave him a prince's name: Chaaarles. Never mind she could never pronounce it herself.

"Anyway, nothing doing. He can't even write his own name, much less run a kingdom."

She sighed, indicating this was an old wound she was not going to reopen at that moment outside Mercedez's house.

"During the revolution I went to see your father and asked him for your address and phone number. He wouldn't give them to me. You know how he is. I got to Los Angeles a few months ago. I figured you're of high-school age. So I've been going from school to school, every public and private high school up and down the state, asking if they have a student by your name. Didn't occur to me to look for Mercedez first, but once I did, there you were. Hang up and open the door. I'll be over in a minute."

With the receiver still in my hand, I watched as the woman hung up at the other end, then bent over and wiped her shoes with a handkerchief she had taken out of her sleeve. She picked up two green woven baskets—the plastic kind women carry to market in third-world countries—and crossed the street without once looking to either side for traffic. I waited till she had traversed the yard and stepped up to the door. Then I turned away, face flushed, and wondered what I would do if she ever stepped inside the house.

My first thought when I opened the door was that Miriam was old—much older than Roxanna—and that she bore no trace of a beauty that must have earned her the name Miriam—"as beautiful as"—the Moon. Then I remembered that I had seen her before, that day when she promised me she would find my mother, and even before that, on the few occasions when Miriam had come to the house to deliver bad news or to sit shiva. When I had asked, Roxanna had said yes, Miriam was indeed the most beautiful of all her sisters. She had been prettier than any other girl in their ghetto, outranked only by Mercedez the Movie Star, who had green eyes, but that did not count because Mercedez was the illegitimate child of a Russian aristocrat and an Assyrian phantom.

The woman before me now was unusually tall and thin, her legs so long she looked like a stilt walker in a skirt, her neck so bony I could see the movement of her Adam's apple as she spoke.

She had on a pair of men's wing-tip shoes, a long navy-blue skirt, and a brown polyester shirt. Over the shirt she wore a man's gray wool jacket—part of a suit, she would volunteer minutes later, that had once belonged to Mr. Charles. A black polyester scarf was tied in a double knot under her chin. Underneath it her hair, white at the roots, was a Clairol olive at the matted ends. She wore thick spectacles with wide black rims—a gift, she also volunteered, from the relief workers of the UNHCR in Pakistan.

"Miss Lili!" she declared as she walked in and kissed me on both cheeks. She smelled of soap and old clothes. She pulled away and examined my face, then my figure.

"How old are you?" she asked. "Fourteen? Fifteen?"

She shook her head in disappointment.

"You're too thin. You must be one of those girls who like to *diet.*" The word *diet* sounded like an insult.

Confused and searching for an introduction, I answered that I weighed pretty close to my recommended weight. As stupid as that assertion sounded, Miriam did not seem to find it strange.

"Whoever made that recommendation must be anorexic themselves," she answered. "No wonder you're so pale."

She picked up the baskets she had rested on the floor and headed for Mercedez's kitchen, where the stove had hardly been used.

"That woman must be crazy, leaving you alone in this house with only the maid."

As if aware she was being mentioned, the housekeeper suddenly appeared in the kitchen and stood staring at Miriam in shock.

"Who are you?" she asked.

"This girl's aunt." Miriam did not bother looking at the woman. "You can go mind your own affairs."

She put the baskets on the counter next to the sink, took off her jacket and hung it neatly on the back of a chair, and began to empty strange foods into the refrigerator.

I stood at the open door, one hand still resting on the knob, and watched in disbelief as bottles of rose water and cherry and quince syrup, bags of dried cumin and ground saffron, boxes of halva and dates, bunches of radishes and spinach and grape leaves lined the shelves. Miriam took out two fresh chickens—"Too expensive," she remarked, "but I don't cook if it's not kosher"—and a canvas sack of bleached white rice. "Basmati." She showed me the elephant design printed on the front of the sack. "From India. Persian rice is far superior, of course, but these days you can't get it, even in Iran."

She threw a glance at me from under her glasses and waved with the hand that held a knife.

"You can come in already," she said, motioning towards the breakfast table, where she wanted me to sit. "I know you're a brave little thing, staying in this house all by yourself at night. Don't tell me I scare you that much."

She was opening cabinets, pulling out drawers, rearranging dishes, and learning how to work the stove. She found a bowl and filled it with cold water, soaked a bagful of vegetables I had not seen since the days of my childhood in Iran, and began to sharpen the only kitchen knife by pulling the blade against that of a table knife. Only when she felt I was about to go to the phone and call for help did she bother to explain herself.

"I'm staying all day," she said. "I know that Mercedez wouldn't want me to, that your father doesn't want me to. But you're my niece, I raised your mother, and I intend to get to know you better. So, as long as I'm here and you look like you haven't had a decent meal in years, I figure I should fix you some lunch."

Hours later, we sat down to two kinds of stew and a dish of rice with sweet cherries and saffron chicken. The moment I raised the spoon to my mouth, Miriam threw a glance at my trembling hands and went on the offensive.

"I understand Mercedez has been supporting you."

She said this as a statement of fact, raising her eyebrows to indicate she was not too pleased.

"She and I go way back, and I understand she hasn't changed much since her youth."

Her eyebrows, like my spoon, were still raised.

"If I were your father, I would never have let you come live with her or let her pay your way."

She dropped her eyebrows and adjusted herself in her chair. Taking advantage of the momentary lapse in her assault, I swallowed my food and put the spoon back on the plate.

"Anyhow," she continued on a gentler note, "I am here now and we will see much more of each other, and I'll show you how people like us and your mother live."

I put another spoonful of rice in my mouth, swallowed without chewing, never took my eyes off my plate. The mention of my mother had made my heart race. The taste of that food, the smell of the eggplant and the sour raisins, had brought back memories of a place and a time I did not want to revisit.

"I'm still looking for her, you know. One of these days, I'll find her and bring her back."

I remembered Roxanna's hands peeling the thin, long Japanese eggplants, remembered walking with her to the grapevine at the end of the yard, picking the sour grapes coated in dust, eating more than we put in the basket. I remembered her face above the pot of steaming rice, her eyes watching me eat. She had loved me, I thought. I had mattered.

Miriam leaned forward and added some stew to my rice.

"That's why I had to find you first, you see: because I know, sooner or later, Roxanna is going to come back to you."

It shocked me to hear the confidence in Miriam's voice, as if she were speaking not of a fantasy held by an old woman from a strange land, but of a widely acknowledged fact.

"Do you still think my mother is alive?" I asked.

I could see my own reflection in the lenses of her glasses—a pair of tiny, identical faces, at once enraged and despondent, aware of their own impotence before this woman who had temporarily disappeared behind her glasses.

"Of course she is." Miriam did not skip a beat. "She's only forty-three years old. Why wouldn't she be alive?"

I felt my stomach turn with anger, felt the food poison my chest and burn through the roof of my mouth.

"Because she's not," I said.

The words had escaped my mouth against my will. It was as if I heard someone else speak, saying things I did not know.

"I know she's not. Everyone knows she's not."

Miriam was shaking her head, rock solid and confident. I realized I hated her.

"No one knows what I know," she said.

In one instant I forgot all the rules of discipline and all the manners taught to me by the nuns, forgot all the methods of self-protection I had learned while living alone, and I lashed out at Miriam hoping to destroy her.

"You are a stupid woman with stupid thoughts," I yelled, throwing the spoon back onto the plate and watching drops of red stew fly up at Miriam. They stained the lenses of her glasses. "You didn't know a damn thing even back in Iran when you came to see me."

Miriam remained still, her hands gripping the edge of the table, her eyes strangely calm.

"My mother is dead," I said, and shocked myself again. I wanted to stop, pull back into the same shell of silence and fear I had lived in for ten years. But Miriam was there and I could not stop myself.

"She killed herself," I screamed. "I watched her do it. She's dead."

The maid had heard my screams and rushed into the kitchen. I stood before Miriam, shocked by what I had said.

"So go away, and take your stinking food with you before Mercedez finds out I ever let you in here."

I walked away from the table, shaking, and leaned on the kitchen counter for balance. I prayed that Miriam would get up and leave, quietly, with the same suddenness with which she had arrived. I prayed that I would forget I ever saw her, that I would not remember what she had said. Most of all, I prayed that she would not find Roxanna.

Miriam the Moon drove the knife in deeper.

"And if she *were* dead," she asked, wiping her glasses with a tissue and not looking at me, "if your mother *were* buried somewhere like a dog, would it make it easier for you to understand why she hasn't come back?"

By the time she left that day, Miriam had managed to reinstill in me the same anxiety that had kept me awake all through my childhood. She had cleaned the table and washed the dishes, never allowing the maid past the door and into the kitchen, which had suddenly become Miriam's domain. Carefully, she had labeled the food in the fridge, written down heating instructions for the pots she left on the stove.

"You must come over and meet the family," she had said twice, clearly choosing to ignore my outburst, aware that she had me in her grip. "Rochelle is here, and Sussan, too—with the kids but minus the husband."

I made a face and turned away from her, indicating I was not interested in news of her sisters and their lives. She saw my reaction, but went on.

"I'll have a gathering and invite everyone," she went on as if she had not heard me. "Your cousin Josephine is just a few years older than you. Rochelle got her married off as soon as they came to America. She's got two kids already. There're also your great-aunts—your mother's aunts. Dear Auntie Light took a contract out on her husband. The FBI caught her."

For a minute I was stunned. I had seen her—this old woman who had paid to have her husband assassinated by her gardener. I had heard of the incident on the evening news but had not known she was my great-aunt.

"You have to leave," I told Miriam, aware that I was being rude, *wanting* to be rude. "Mercedez doesn't like me to let weird people in here."

Miriam picked up her plastic baskets and smiled.

"I look weird to you," she declared, again as a statement of fact. "You're going to have to get used to it."

She came back the next day, and the day after that. She took a bus from Westwood to Santa Monica Boulevard, then another to Canyon Drive, then a third up to Sunset. She knew how to drive, she said, but had not sat behind the wheel of a car since she had arrived in Los Angeles and learned that she would have to pay fifteen hundred dollars a year—at three, then five, then eight thousand rials to a dollar—just to keep insurance on a car. Always the entrepreneur, she had made a deal with the owners of a cab company whose drivers were predominantly Iranians: she would use them four times a week, for a flat rate of ten dollars a trip, regardless of the distance the cab traveled. She saved the cab rides for long drives or trips to the market when she had many bags to carry.

"You should ride the bus with me," she always insisted. "It's good to see how real people live."

Torn by doubt, afraid of letting her invade the peace I had so carefully constructed around myself, I hid out in my room when she came, and told the maid to send her away. The maid never succeeded. Miriam pushed past her and walked right up to my door, stood outside talking to me as if we were old friends, went back down and cooked a meal, and stayed—stayed until I gave up and saw her.

"Have some of this." She would shove a piece of food in my mouth. "It'll get rid of those dark circles under your eyes and put some meat on you."

She told me about my father, locked up in the house on the Avenue of Faith, reading books all day till his eyes gave out. She said that Fräulein Claude was completely mad, that Teymur had been a good man, a rare and honest man whose pride had killed him.

"He loved you," she said. "He loved you because you were his son's child—but more so because you were your mother's."

With my head down and my skin burning with rage, I cursed Miriam under my breath and hung on to her every word.

In August, Mercedez came back from her island getaway and found Miriam in the kitchen.

It was a Sunday afternoon. Miriam was barbecuing chicken breast on a skewer. She had marinated the chicken in saffron and lemon juice and olive oil, paprika and onions and crushed garlic. Because Mercedez had never owned a barbecue and regarded the whole act of barbecuing barbaric, Miriam was using the tiny grill on the stove. No matter how much I resented having her there, her presence made the house feel lived-in and secure. Around four o'clock I looked up from the chicken skewers and saw Mercedez in the doorway.

She was tanned and tall and dressed all in white, her arms lean and long, her hair pulled into a loose ponytail. She stared at Miriam as if at the scene of a disaster.

"Who's *this*?" she asked.

I groped for an answer but could think of nothing to say. Calmly, one eye on Mercedez and the other on her chicken, Miriam gave each of the skewers a turn on the grill, then spoke in Farsi.

"In this country you could get arrested for leaving children alone and not feeding them real food."

Mercedez went pale, shook a bit, looked from Miriam to me and then back.

For a moment, she looked almost defenseless—a lone woman come face to face with an old but unexpected enemy. Then she caught herself, stood up taller, narrowed her eyes, and bored their brilliant strength at Miriam.

Slowly, Miriam wiped her hand on a kitchen towel she had hung on the handle of Mercedez's oven. Then she went up to Mercedez and extended her hand.

"Figured we'd meet again. Never thought it would be here."

Mercedez did not take the hand. Miriam shrugged, then went back to the stove and filled a kettle with cold water.

"I've been coming around feeding this child every few days. She looks undernourished, not to mention depressed."

"What do you want?" Mercedez asked.

"Nothing from *you*." Miriam turned the stove on and put the kettle on to boil. From a red metal box, she took out two spoonfuls of black tea leaves and put them in a smaller kettle. When the water was boiling hot, she would pour it over the tea leaves and let them simmer for five or ten minutes before she served tea.

"Never did want anything from *you*. I'm just here for the sake of the child." She looked straight at Mercedez. "And to find my sister. *Your* friend."

I could tell that she was glad to have thrown Mercedez off, that she cherished having the upper hand, the sense of strength she got from confusing Mercedez. True to character, Mercedez did not let Miriam enjoy herself too long.

"Suit yourself." She walked away. "Just don't come back here anymore."

Miriam did, of course, come back—because she was a woman who had her own agenda, and because she took special care to offend and anger Mercedez. She found out Saint Mary's address and, when school resumed, turned up at the dorm every week-end. She befriended Sister Ana Rose and Mother Superior and brought them every kind of ethnic food she thought might agree with their Catholic palates. She offered to cook lunch for the whole school, shared with the nuns the Eastern secrets of keep-ing girls obedient and hardworking and away from boys: "Don't let them spend time in front of the mirror," she advised, and the nuns were overjoyed to have found a soul mate from the East. "Vanity is the precursor to sexual freedom." She told them of her own days as a schoolteacher in the alliance school, confirmed their suspicions that I did not have an ounce of Catholic blood in my body, that my father was indeed a strange man—"but then he's half prince and half Jew, and his mother poses as a German. What else can you expect?"

She told the nuns it was not true, what Sohrab and I had said about Roxanna being dead. "She's away, but certainly not dead."

By the time Miriam got around to asking Mother Superior for permission to take me away for a weekend, there was no doubt the answer would be yes.

"Perfect!" Miriam was genuinely thrilled. "I am going to have a family gathering and introduce her back to society."

SHE INVITED HER sisters, Rochelle's daughter Josephine, and her husband, who did not come, of course, but who would have taken offense if he felt he had been excluded from anything. She also called Mr. Charles's three great-aunts and his great-uncle Yaghoob. Then she took a cab to Pasadena on a Sunday morning to bring me to her house in time to meet everyone.

I went along against my own better judgment, half forced by Miriam, half compelled by a need to see for myself these relatives who, presumably, carried Roxanna's blood. Miriam's apartment was small but bright, filled with the sounds of birds and the heat of food cooking since early morning on the kitchen stove. Mr. Charles met us at the door.

"Shhh," he warned with a finger on his lips, "you'll frighten the birds."

The living room was furnished with odd, unmatched pieces. The dining-room table had been purchased from a Taiwanese couple at the Rose Bowl flea market in Pasadena. Persian-language magazines and newspapers were stacked all over the house. There was also a substantial pile of *National Geographic* and *Scientific American* issues that Miriam read regularly.

"I like to balance experience against science," she offered when she saw me leafing through the magazines. "Experience wins every time."

She left me in the living room and went to check on the food. I sat down, my stomach churning with nerves, my hands clammy, and watched Mr. Charles talk to his birds on the balcony. He was whispering to them, trying to warn them of the invasion of people about to occur. Something in that room, I realized, had made me especially anxious. Then the doorbell rang.

The first to arrive was Dear Auntie Light, who had come to America in 1977 on a two-month visit to her son and had ended up staying for good. She came with her husband, who refused to speak to her, and with her son, who spoke to neither one of his parents but still paid their bills and acted as their chauffeur and cook and nurse. Dear Auntie Light was short, with piano legs and an enormous hip that moved of its own volition in perfect semicircles every time she took a step. Her arms, too thin for her body, refused to let go of the imitation Chanel bag her daughter-in-law had bought for her downtown and told her was "probably" the real thing—a thousand-dollar bag sold from a street corner for thirty-three fifty by a man called Mustafa who had a dragon tattooed on his left cheek.

"Must be stolen, then," Dear Auntie Light had scoffed at her daughter-in-law's distorted generosity. But secretly she had been thrilled by the possibility that the bag might be genuine, and it pleased her to no end to own, for the first time in her life, an object of luxury she thought other women would envy.

Perhaps because they found her small attempt at vanity pathetic, or because they had recently decided it was not prudent to cross Dear Auntie Light, no one around her had bothered to point out that her daughter-in-law was making of a fool of her, and that if nothing else, the rusted letter G—not C—on the bag should have been a dead giveaway.

Two years earlier, at age seventy-one, Dear Auntie Light had hired her Mexican gardener to assassinate her husband.

She had paid the man three hundred dollars in cash and a bag of her husband's used clothing, and when the gardener had complained that he did not have a gun, she had personally taken the bus downtown, asked around till she had found a gun dealer, and bought the gardener a shotgun. The gardener was busy sawing off the gun's barrel in the garage of his tiny house in El Monte when his wife walked in on him and asked what he was doing.

"This old lady paid me three hundred dollars to kill off her husband and make it look like a burglary," he explained without interrupting his work. "They've been married fifty-three years, she says, and she still hates him."

Pregnant with her third child and always running short of cash, the gardener's wife thought Dear Auntie Light was short-changing her husband—paying only three hundred dollars for killing a man—and told him he must accept no less than seven hundred.

"Don't have it," Dear Auntie Light told the gardener when he showed up for his weekly service, "and he wouldn't be worth seven hundred dollars even if I could afford it."

The gardener told his wife he was going to go ahead with the killing anyway. "I gave her my word," he said. The wife went to the police.

That was how Dear Auntie Light, who had spent her entire life in obscurity, suddenly became front-page-of-the-"Metro"-section-of-the-*L.A.-Times* material. Arrested at her home and brought up on charges, she got to see her own picture on television and in the newspapers, and received requests for interviews from no less than eleven Persian-language publications just in Southern California. She spent two nights in jail before her son managed to post bail and have her released on grounds that she was senile and posed no real threat to society. Her husband, of course, was outraged by her treachery—"I never did manage to teach that woman to stay in her own place." He would have beaten her. How else was a woman going to learn the ways of civility? For two weeks he raved at her, promising to kill her himself before she was sent to the electric chair by the prosecutors in L.A. County. He called everyone he knew on the phone and told them that she was a whore, that she must have gone to bed with the gardener to convince him to do such a crime. Then he called his son and told him to bring her home because the dirty dishes had piled up and he could not work the dial on the clothes dryer.

Contrary to the general expectation, the affair resulted in a sharp improvement in Dear Auntie Light's relationship with her husband. Their neighbors reported fewer arguments after her arrest. Dear Auntie Light cursed her husband with every breath, but she took her responsibilities as a wife seriously. And the husband, who threatened to divorce her every day, never kept his word, because he realized she was all there was between him and the ever-widening gulf of loneliness that was old age.

Now they sat next to one another on the living-room sofa. Dear Auntie Light had crossed her arms but was still holding her bag, which now dangled over her stomach. Her husband was twirling a string of agate worry beads he had bought in Iran. Before them on the table was a green glass bottle with tiny blue flowers painted on it.

I had seen that bottle—or one like it—before. I knew this because it made me uneasy, because I had trouble keeping my eyes on it, because the very sight of it made me want to cry. I tried hard, but could not remember why.

Dear Auntie Light's entrance was followed by the arrival of Rochelle and Josephine, her infant son, her Guatemalan maid, and her Filipino nanny. Josephine, who had been named after the divan in Alexandra the Cat's parlor, had just gotten over a five-year spell of "bad mood" because her husband had kept "making" daughters. Having finally delivered the prized son, she had so blossomed with pride, she could not stop beaming even in tragic situations.

"As you see," Rochelle demonstrated to all present, while Josephine stood by smiling graciously, "we picked baby blue for everything—the stroller, the diapers, the help's uniforms. Young mothers have to pay such attention to details these days."

Next entered Bahram, who had changed his name to Bryan since he had come to America and discovered all the tall blondes of his dreams in one place. He owned a string of self-storage facilities around Los Angeles—an enterprise that, apart from producing a sizable income, also left Bryan with large chunks of free time to devote to playing golf. On that day, he was accompanied not by his wife, but by the woman who had been his mistress and secretary for the past ten years.

Behind him were Dear Auntie Power, who had spent two years in Khomeini's prisons for attempting to smuggle antiques out of the country, and her older sister, Dear Auntie Pride. Terribly wealthy, she was unanimously despised, envied, and mocked in the family. But Miriam had invited her anyway because she was, after all, a blood relation.

One by one, they filed into Miriam's tiny living room and found me.

"Here she is," Miriam introduced me, and they all sighed as if in the presence of a miracle.

It was an experience unlike any that life had ever prepared me for—those men and women who looked at me as if I were an item of extreme wonder, who came up with warm hands and vigorous hugs, kissing me on both cheeks and showing me their tears, who offered me food, kissed me as if to say I mattered.

"I remember your parents' wedding," Bryan told me twice. "Your mother glowed that night. The whole world was a new color."

At eleven o'clock, Miriam served her own version of brunch: fried Japanese eggplant with garlic and tomato; hard-boiled eggs with feta cheese and Lavash bread; peeled pickling cucumbers with raw spring onions and fresh walnuts and green peppers; baked whitefish with lemon and paprika; spinach baked with lettuce, parsley, onions, and eggs.

Dear Auntie Light's husband looked at the table in disdain. "No rice?" he asked. "What kind of woman doesn't make rice?"

Dear Auntie Pride, who was convinced that her relatives were going to try to poison her just to inherit her estate—valued at somewhere around ninety million dollars—refused to eat anything except bananas, which she peeled herself.

Miriam watched everyone eat. The American coffee she had made was so weak, they mistook it for tea, and her tea was so light ("Too much caffeine will cut your life by ten years and give you heart palpitations"), it tasted like plain hot water.

By one o'clock everyone had stopped eating—all except Dear Auntie Pride, who had taken a liking to the bananas and was working on her ninth. Rochelle had smoked her first pack of blue Dunhills, and Sussan had set about cleaning the table and doing the dishes. In the dining room, Dear Auntie Light sat clutching her bag, still without a word to her husband, sizing up the other two old women and the newest arrival—Sussan's eighteen-year-old Buddhist daughter, who never missed a family meeting, just so she could try persuading everyone to join her local chapter.

"You should try us," she was telling me now. "You may actually feel you've found your true 'home.'"

I had spent the morning thinking about how I was different from all these people, how, like my mother, I would never feel at home even among my family. I saw Miriam come in from the kitchen with a tray of steamed white rice mixed with parsley and currants. No sooner had we finished lunch than she had begun to prepare for dinner.

She put the tray down on the table and, with her fingers, scooped bits of rice onto thin sheets of onion skin, then tied them into perfect bundles that she would later fry.

I opened my mouth and asked the only question that came to mind.

"What happened to my mother?"

It was a moment of great consequence, one that even Dear Auntie Light's husband, senile and distracted as he was, would not forget till he died. For the first time in anyone's memory, Miriam the Moon was caught off guard and completely defenseless.

She stared at me for a moment, so stupefied she forgot the

onion skin in her hands and let the rice fall from it back onto the tray. Then she lowered her hands to her lap and wiped them on her apron.

"I'll get some tea," she said, and left the table.

I remained seated. Everyone else avoided looking at me.

I waited.

An eternity passed. Then Sussan spoke.

"She was different. That's what I remember."

Sucking on yet another blue Dunhill, Rochelle frowned and signaled with her eyes to Sussan that she should stop. Josephine said something about checking on the baby and left the room. Dear Auntie Pride reached for another banana.

"Why did she leave my father?" I persisted.

This time, Rochelle stepped in before Sussan could answer.

"We don't know," she said. "No one knows. Children should not ask such questions."

Quickly, she opened her bag and popped a small pill, an anti-anxiety medication she referred to as "my Xanax."

"That's horseshit!" Sussan blurted, but was silenced by a loud noise from behind. The same noise sent Mr. Charles's birds into a fit of frenzy, fluttering from one end of the enclosed balcony to another and then back, colliding with one another and becoming even more frightened.

In the kitchen, Miriam had banged the teakettle onto the stove and thereby delivered the message that no one should say any more.

"I made tea," she announced, with her back still to the dining room. She began to pour the tea into long, narrow glasses arranged on a cheap bamboo tray she had bought at the ninety-nine-cent store on Fairfax. She carried the tea to the table, along with a pumpkin pie that she had been defrosting all day and that still retained the smell of the freezer. The pie had been given to her last Thanksgiving, by Bryan's mistress, who had accompanied him to the family gathering while his wife was in Ohio visiting her parents. Miriam had taken the pie and immediately stuck it in the freezer—because she had too much dessert already, she had told the girlfriend, and because she found the whole idea of turning a vegetable into pastry rather revolting. Now, almost a year later, she forced the same pie onto Bryan's plate and delivered a stern warning.

"It's like ice-cream cake," she told him. "Finish it, or it will stay in the freezer for another year."

MIRIAM INVITED ME to her house many more times, called me every Friday night to help celebrate Sabbath with her, came for me in a cab and insisted that I go with her to the weddings and bar mitzvahs, the Brith Milahs and baby showers she was always attending. She had my other aunts call me as well, forced Josephine to invite me to all of her children's birthday parties. Twice, she even convinced Bryan to come for me in his Ferrari. He brought his girlfriend once, his wife another time.

"You can't lock yourself up in a convent all your life and think you're going to be a normal person when you get out," she said every time I refused an invitation. "You have to come out, socialize, get to know your family even if you can't stand any of us. In the end, you know, we're all you've got."

More often than not, I surrendered. I went along to one person's house or another, sat quietly in the clothes that Mercedez had bought for me, which I wore with great discomfort, wanting to look right to my aunts, certain I never could. Around me they moved and ate and talked to one another about everything but Roxanna, avoided the few questions I asked, panicked every time I tried to sway the conversation towards her. They inquired about my school, the health of the nuns, Mercedez's latest boyfriend. I answered in short sentences and hoped they would forget I was there. Then I listened to them go on for hours with all the tales that became familiar after only a few visits: the bad marriages and failed loves, the lost opportunities and squandered chances, the wasted youth and husbands gone astray—a thousand years of suffering stacked one on top of the other and pulled off the shelf, one year at a time, whenever two or more of my aunts got together to talk.

Eventually, I told Miriam I did not want to go to her parties anymore.

She thought I was grief stricken, from having been abandoned by my parents and thrown into the hands of Catholic nuns, and promised to double her efforts to incorporate me into the life of the family. It was December of my senior year in high school. With encouragement from the nuns, and with Mercedez's backing, I had applied to colleges in California and on the East Coast. My grades were not good enough to get me into a top university, but I knew I would end up somewhere, in a dorm, having to relive the loneliness I so despised and yet clung to because it was familiar.

"It's got nothing to do with grief," I tried to explain my decision to Miriam. "I am seventeen years old. I'm too young to sit around with you and your sisters. I want to go my own way."

It was Saturday morning. Miriam had skipped going to the synagogue to come see me, then spent half an hour lecturing me about how I should eat more and sleep longer because at seventeen, I looked like a survivor of the famine in Somalia. "And no man likes a woman who doesn't have flesh on her bones, I don't care what those magazines say."

Her words awakened in me an ever-present fear: that I would be alone for the rest of my life as I had been for so much of it already, that no boys would ever like me, that they would fail to see me—as the girls did—that I would be invisible and inconsequential to them, as I had been to my own parents first and then to the rest of the world. It had been a while since I had drawn on my own skin, but seeing Miriam that day and hearing her warnings, I felt the irresistible urge to reach for my pen again. Still, I could not afford to show her more weakness.

"I don't care if men don't like me."

She looked around my room, at the bare walls, the hard floor, the twin bed I had outgrown long ago.

"This place is too dark," she declared.

I thought then that she looked gaunt and tired, badly in need of rest, as if aware that if she stopped, she would never be able to move again. I knew that feeling. I had lived it those first few months after I arrived here from Tehran, when I was exhausted but unable to sleep, terrified but unable to speak. I had lived it then and had continued to live it ever since.

Except that Miriam always managed to move forward while I, forever trapped in my own loneliness, stayed still.

Right then she was making new plans.

"What you need is some natural sunlight to cure your depression."

"I am not depressed," I protested. "I just don't want to see *you* anymore."

She picked up her bag and said she was going to the nursery to buy sunflower seeds.

Two hours later, I heard her speaking to Mother Superior in the yard.

"What you do is plant these seeds," she was explaining with confidence, "right here where the sun rises in the morning, and once the sunflowers grow and bloom, they will attract light from the east and reflect it into the rooms. It'll bring you much joy, and great luck."

Mother Superior laughed in disbelief.

"Sunflowers turn *towards* the light," she said, unwilling to hide her condescension. "They don't create light of their own, and they don't reflect anything."

Miriam put her bag down on the lawn and started to take out the gardening tools and the seeds she had just bought.

"The trouble with you Westerners is you don't have faith," she lectured the nun. "In the East, we know things because we have been around longer and have experienced them. You people just read about life in science magazines."

Miriam often evoked the collective "we" to give her arguments added force.

"And we have paid dearly for our experiences. They have cost us our youth, most of our lives."

For every belief or suspicion Miriam ever held, there were half a dozen corpses and a legion of suffering men and women to serve as proof.

She was staring at Mother Superior now, daring her to disagree.

"It's different in the East, especially if you're a woman," she said and broke ground with her small shovel. "We get one shot at everything—marriage, school, work. If we blow it, there's no other chance."

She pulled out a small clod of dirt and threw it onto the grass. The force of her movement struck Mother Superior as odd, made her pull instinctively away as if to safety.

"Just like *that*." Miriam pointed with her head to the dirt she had just discarded. "One chance."

Two months later, I woke up and found my room inundated with light. I sat in bed, inside the liquid, golden warmth that filled my room and transformed it beyond recognition. The light was so dense, so palpable, I felt it in my hands when I closed my fist. When I stood up, I felt as if I could float. I opened the window. In front of the school, Miriam's sunflowers were in full bloom, having attracted a pool of light so strong, I had to squint to see past them.

I made the mistake of calling Miriam to tell her she had been right.

"I'm always right," she declared. "You and those nuns should know that by now.

"And I'll tell you something else, now that you are in your last year of high school and about to become a college girl: that light is going to bring good tidings your way. You'll see. It's going to take you out of the void you've been living in for so long, shine a path, and bring you back your mother."

Good tidings it did not bring. But maybe it is true, what Miriam said that day, about the light leading Roxanna back.

JACOB THE JELLO'S youngest son, Mateen, was still an infant when his father moved permanently out of their house and into Fräulein Claude's kitchen on the Avenue of Faith. He was a skinny child with large black eyes, and a head of hair so thick and shiny, his mother shaved it every so often just to ward off the evil eye of the jealous. Once a month, she took Mateen and her other children to see Jacob.

They went on Thursday afternoons, after school had ended and their mother had had a chance to take them all to the public bath and scrub them clean. Summer and winter, she made them wear the heavy woolen sweaters they had received as gifts from Fräulein Claude. She used the sweaters to cover up the holes in the children's shirts, even if the temperature was in the nineties and the children were suffocating from the moisture of the public bath and the warmth of the sweaters. Besides, she said, if Fräulein Claude did not see them wear the sweaters, she might claim they were not appreciated and stop giving them as gifts.

"Think about the winter," she whispered to Mateen every time he cried and complained that he was hot. "You're freezing on the way to school and there are no more sweaters."

She lined the children up by age, took the bus to Teymur's house and, all the way there, cursed her opium-addicted husband and his evil, rich sister.

In the days before the robber ghosts, Fräulein Claude had left instructions with the servants to bring Jacob's family in through the back—through the servants' yard, she had explained to Jacob's wife before her children, so they would not cross paths and get embarrassed by other, "sophisticated," guests and visitors. She greeted them with a half-frown and a condescending smile, always in those loud suits and shiny gold sandals, with the fake accent she had employed so long, it had become second nature. She had the servants bring them water— no ice, she said, because the cold might give the children a sore throat. In reality she wanted them to feel uncomfortable and un-welcome, and to leave.

They sat around the servants' table, sipping their water po-litely and staring at their father in the alcove. He blew on his pipe and exhaled the smoke in their direction. Sometimes he recog-nized his children. Sometimes he asked the servants who the vis-itors were and why they were looking at him. Once, as they were taking their leave, he pointed to Mateen and told his mother, clearly believing she was a stranger, "Nice-looking boy you have there, madame. My hat off to you and his father."

Their family was not invited to Sohrab and Roxanna's wed-ding, of course, because Fräulein Claude had kept them off the guest list. By the time Teymur found out about the omission and corrected it, it was three days before the event and Jacob's wife was too proud to accept a late invitation. She was so hurt by the insult, she stopped going to the Avenue of Faith once a month, forgoing the money Teymur gave her on those occasions, telling her children it was better to be poor and proud than to live on Fräulein Claude's charity. A few years later, the robber ghosts would take over the house and Fräulein Claude would close the door on Jacob's family for good.

Mateen, therefore, had only seen Roxanna a few times, in the days before her marriage to Sohrab, when she had lived in the house as a guest, and even then, she had been so shy and self-effacing, he could not imagine how she had ended up as Sohrab's wife. He remembered thinking that she was young, really just a child like himself, and that her eyes were strange. But she had a laugh, a fluid, melodic laugh that stunned everyone, even the children. Every time Roxanna laughed in the house, Mateen re-membered, his own mother would burst into tears.

Later, he had heard that Roxanna had vanished—"thrown her-self out the window to escape Fräulein Claude's cruelty" was his mother's interpretation, "even though your crazy father claims he saw her flying away with white wings." It had seemed plausible to

Mateen, when he thought of Roxanna's eyes, that she could indeed fly.

In the early 1970s, Jacob's wife had moved her family to Israel and lost all contact with Iran. They had lived in Tel Aviv, on government-subsidized housing, food, and education. The girls had served in the army, then gone off to live on kibbutzim. The boys had formed families of their own. Mateen had lost a leg and moved back home with his mother.

He finished engineering school, married a Moroccan girl, moved his wife and mother from Tel Aviv to Netanya, by the sea. He stopped speaking Farsi, stopped wondering what had happened to Jacob, even stopped feeling the sting of the wool against his skin on those hot summer afternoons when Fräulein Claude had refused them ice. In February of 1984, he took his wife and daughters on a vacation to Istanbul.

They stayed at a house they had rented along the Bosporus, went to the beach, the museums, the mosques. One afternoon, after a tour of the Topkapi Palace, he looked into the crowd and saw a woman waiting for a bus.

She was pale and small, her face full of lines, her skin dry and stretched tight over a bony face. When their eyes met she smiled at him, the kind of smile strangers offer one another on rainy afternoons in a crowded place when they know they will never meet again. Then she looked away without a second thought, and the smile faded from her face.

Mateen stared at her.

She wore a white cotton dress, flat, worn-out shoes with no socks. Her hair was long to her waist and tied in a ponytail. Her hands, clutching a plastic bag to her chest, were chapped and black. She kept shifting her weight from leg to leg as if to relieve the pain in her feet, leaned over towards the traffic to look for her bus. But she never looked at her watch or checked a schedule. The bus did not run on time, Mateen guessed, or else she had no one waiting for her. He turned away and went home.

That night, he dreamt of Jacob the Jello for the first time in many years: he sat in the kitchen alcove, smoking his pipe, telling his wife that the Sponge Woman had offered herself to him in exchange for some opium.

They went back to Topkapi the next day, because Mateen's wife wanted to see the Forbidden Palace, a four-hundred-room harem where the Ottoman sultans' wives had lived with their children and their castrated Sudanese slaves. The wives, mostly Christians from the Caucasus, had been brought to the palace as slaves, purchased through the Istanbul slave market, and forced to convert. They spent their lives fighting one another and vying for the sultan's attention, producing heirs, plotting the murders of rival wives and their children. After they had abandoned the practice of fratricide in determining the succession to the throne, the Turkish sultans in turn relinquished their throne to the eldest surviving son. To protect the heirs, the sultans held them prisoner within the Forbidden Palace. The heirs spent their lives in the "Gilded Cage," having no contact with other humans. If they survived their isolation and ascended the throne, they were almost invariably demented from a life of confinement, and unable to rule.

Mateen saw the woman again.

She was standing with two other women outside a dirty restaurant, an apron wrapped around her waist, smoking a cigarette down to its butt. The way she stood, he could see only her profile, and those shoes she wore—saddle shoes, they were called in his daughters' school—with little white socks that had turned gray from washing. So Mateen crossed the street, with his wife and daughters, and went towards the restaurant. His wife complained that she could not trust the children's stomachs with food from such a place, but Mateen did not listen. He stopped a few steps away from the woman.

This time, when their eyes met, she became scared.

She had turned her face half away from her friends to blow

the last of the smoke out of her lungs, and she saw him staring at her. Her eyes were tired and tight, with too many lines, but the look in them was vast and fluid like the sea. It surrounded him entirely, so that for an instant he was alone, on that street bursting with movement, immersed in a lightness from which he never wanted to surface.

A bus screeched to a halt three inches away from him. His wife screamed. The driver shouted obscenities at Mateen, then slammed his foot on the gas pedal and left him in a cloud of black exhaust fumes. When Mateen looked again, the woman was gone.

He kept dreaming of his father.

He called his mother in Netanya and asked if she knew what had become of Roxanna the Angel.

"She died, of course," his mother answered. She was in her eighties then, but her mind was as sharp as ever. "I think she killed herself. Her sister Miriam the Moon lives in Los Angeles."

For a week, Mateen stayed away from Topkapi. Then one afternoon he left his family at the beach and went back.

Roxanna saw him limp into the restaurant on his plastic leg. He sat at a table. She swept the floor, gathered dirty plates, wiped tables. When the cook yelled for her, she would serve the food he had prepared. She moved quickly, avoided Mateen's table, shied away from him. After a while, she went up to the cook and said something in Turkish. The next time Mateen looked up, she had opened her apron and was rushing towards the bus station.

"Excuse me," he called after her in English. She did not answer him.

He followed her out. She crossed the street and went into the line waiting for the bus. When she turned around, she saw that he was behind her.

"Excuse me," he tried again.

She would not look at him.

He tried Hebrew, then Farsi.

Roxanna remained frozen, eyes dead ahead, but he saw that her hands had started to shake. Mateen realized she was going to run away again, so he stopped calling to her. The other people in the line were staring at him.

She got on the bus from the front, he through the back. They rode to Kumkapi. She stepped off the bus and ran into a building.

Mateen went home and told his wife he had seen a dead woman.

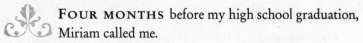

FOUR MONTHS before my high school graduation, Miriam called me.

"Come down Friday night and stay the weekend with me," she said without introduction. "I have prepared the guest room for you."

She had just moved from her apartment on Wilshire Boulevard to a house off of Veteran Avenue in Westwood. She had not wanted to leave her apartment, but Mr. Charles's birds had become a nuisance to the whole building. Often, they escaped through the front door and flew down the long and narrow hallways, into open elevators, where they frightened little old ladies with lavender hair just back from their hairdressing appointments. Or they flew off the balcony and covered people's windows with droppings. The manager had given Miriam ninety days before he served an eviction notice.

The house she had bought was a single-story Spanish-style creation from the late sixties. It had stucco walls painted bright yellow, an orange roof, and a mailbox in the shape of a giant African parrot. In the front was a narrow circular driveway, and a carport that Miriam had turned into a tiny grass lawn. There were three bedrooms: one for Miriam, one for Mr. Charles and his birds, and a third which she called the guest room. In the back was a courtyard paved with old yellow bricks and dominated entirely by an almond tree, nearly thirty feet tall, that cast its branches onto the roof.

I told Miriam I had to study and could not visit.

"Bring your books and study here." She sounded as serious as ever. "This is important."

"So is school." I tried my most sarcastic tone.

"Don't bullshit me," Miriam almost yelled, then stopped to catch her breath. There was an urgency in her voice I had not heard before, a sense of desperation that frightened me. "No one studies four months before graduation. You already got into college."

I had been accepted to San Francisco State University. I had never seen San Francisco, did not know anyone there. I was only going to go to college because Saint Mary's would not keep me after high school, and I could no longer impose on Mercedez.

"It's not bullshit," I told Miriam, proud of my own coolness, glad she had given me another opportunity to be irreverent. "I'm busy and I don't want to come."

An hour later, her cab pulled up to the school.

She was pale, I thought, and unsteady. She had brought no food with her, no bags full of clothes she had bought at various discount stores around the city and insisted I should wear. She went straight into Mother Superior's office and closed the door. Half an hour later, when the women emerged together, I knew I was in trouble.

Mother Superior ordered me into the visiting room, then left me alone with Miriam. I sat across from her in an old armchair, leaned back, and slumped down with my hands on the armrests and my knees spread apart. Miriam, I knew, hated the insolent manners of America's teenagers.

"So," I challenged her, my stomach already churning in waves at the prospect of what she had come to say, "what's new?"

She studied me from behind her Elvis Costello glasses. For once she was not rushing to speak, wasn't even eager to establish her own birthright to every truth in the universe.

I waited, trying to keep the ironic smile on my face, hoping against hope that Miriam would get up and go away, that she would tell me nothing, keep her news—this news that could only be hard and bitter and devastating—to herself.

And yet, as much as I anticipated the magnitude of the blow she was about to deliver, Miriam surprised me again.

"I have found your mother."

I heard her but at first felt nothing. I remained still, emotionless, so calm I thought I would never be able to move again. Then the rush of nausea forced me to sit up.

"Jacob the Jello's son called me. He says he saw her in Turkey."

I looked around for an exit, realized my legs would never carry me as far as the door, reached for the small wastebasket by the side of the chair in case I really did vomit. My face was covered with cold sweat.

"He saw her on the street and followed her home. He found out where she lives, but when he went to her, she wouldn't talk to him. He says she's very poor."

More than anything else at that moment, I wanted Miriam to vanish.

"We have to go there," she said. "You and I have to go to Turkey and see for ourselves if he's right."

I swallowed the bile that had risen to my throat.

"Go away."

Over the next few weeks, Miriam attacked the business of finding Roxanna with characteristic vigor. She applied for visas for herself and me, then set about arranging papers for Roxanna. She called an immigration attorney and told him he had four weeks to arrange a U.S. entry visa for a woman with no papers, no passport, and no birth certificate. She said that Roxanna could not sign an application or provide fingerprints, that she did not even know about or necessarily want to embark on the trip to the United States. The attorney suggested Miriam see a shrink or a magician.

So Miriam dug up her own dead daughter's birth certificate and paid someone to alter the date of birth—lowering it almost thirty years so it would match Roxanna's. She flew to the Iranian consulate in San Francisco, told them a story about how her daughter was an invalid, and had them issue a passport in Sara's name. She took the passport to the immigration office in Los Angeles with a stack of false letters swearing her daughter needed to enter the country for medical treatment. In four weeks, she managed to squeeze a thirty-day visa out of the U.S. immigration authorities.

"I've done it." She came back to my school and shoved the passport in my face. She was beaming with pride, out of breath with excitement. "I'm going to buy two tickets to Istanbul—for you and me—and a one-way ticket to Los Angeles for Roxanna. We have to leave right away."

"Go whenever you want." I shrugged. "Just don't think you can take me anywhere."

Miriam frowned, dead serious, and shook her head.

"I've had enough of your idiotic insolence," she warned. "I've told you this is serious. Now it's time you believed me."

I believed her all right. I had always believed her.

So I told her, in as calm a voice as I could manage, with words I forced out till my stomach began to bleed, I told her that I *could not* go with her because I did not—*could* not—afford to find out if Roxanna was alive. Because I had lost Roxanna a thousand times a day for twelve years and could not bear either to lose or to find her again.

"If she had wanted me, she would have stayed," I said. "She didn't want me then, didn't even see me when I stood behind her and called her name. And she won't want me now, even if I *do* go with you to find her."

For the first time since I had known her, Miriam the Moon put her arms around me and cried.

ROXANNA THE ANGEL was trying to chip the hard-water residue from the inside of her Turkish coffeepot when she heard two knocks on the door. It was early evening, and she had only one hour before she was due at the fish restaurant down the street where she had recently started to work. She had abandoned her job at Topkapi Station after eleven years of working there. It was that man, the one with the thick black hair so shiny you felt like touching it just to catch its glow on your skin, and the fake leg, who had scared her off. She never knew who he was or what he wanted, but after the day he followed her, speaking Farsi and calling to her as if he knew her, Roxanna never dared go back to the restaurant. Now she worked for Armenians, cleaning fish and barbecuing them for tourists who had read about Kumkapi in their Michelin Guides and felt compelled, once they had made the trip down to the Armenian ghetto and found that it was nothing more than another run-down neighborhood, to stop by and eat the local food just for good measure. It had been hard to make the move, even though in all her years at Topkapi, Roxanna had not developed any real attachments to the place or its owners. Maybe it was the force of habit, or maybe because her new boss screamed at her and threatened to fire her every time she was late or made a mistake. Maybe she was getting old and could not stand on her feet fourteen hours at a time without wanting to lie down, right there by the coal barbecue, and sleep.

She heard another knock, but did not get up. The wind had been howling for days, raising the garbage on the street into life-like, moving effigies, keeping her awake and shivering at night, driving the beggars into their cardboard homes. With the tip of a blunted knife, Roxanna kept chipping away at the black residue that lined the inside of the pot. After a while she put the knife down and submerged her hands in a bowl of water she had warmed on her portable gas heater. Her hands hurt constantly— a dull, rheumatic pain that throbbed under her skin till she wanted to moan. The heat from the water calmed them, but only temporarily. She had learned this from Alexandra the Cat, in the days of the ghetto when the old woman needed to relax her hands before a concert.

Someone banged on the door with the flat of their hand. Roxanna jumped, spilling the water to the floor. Quickly, she dried her hands on her skirt, then looked about for a rag to wipe the floor. She had had to go down three flights of stairs to get the water, and now she was angry that it had spilled.

"Stop!" she yelled back at the caller, still searching for a rag. The only people who ever came to her door were the rent collector and Christian women soliciting money for the Armenian Church.

"Stop knocking."

She opened the door just a crack, saw no one, opened a bit more. There were two women. One was tall, dressed in a man's overcoat, her head wrapped in a shawl. The other was short, wearing high heels and a full-length mink coat. Roxanna hated them.

"I have no money," she told them in Turkish. "And I don't believe in God."

She shoved the door back in their faces. Just when it was about to close, a hand stopped it.

"One minute," the taller woman said in Farsi.

Roxanna froze.

The woman pushed the door towards her, nudging Roxanna back an inch at a time, and when she had created a wide-enough opening, she squeezed through and walked into the room. Terrified, Roxanna stepped away from her. They remained facing each other, neither daring to make a move. From across the doorway, the one in the mink coat started to cry.

"I've been looking for you," Miriam whispered.

Roxanna did not breathe.

"I would have known you anywhere."

She realized that Roxanna was about to fall, and grabbed her arm.

"There," she said, and looked about for a chair.

Roxanna pulled her arm free.

"It's all right," Miriam said, but she, too, was trembling. Her lips had turned blue. She tried to speak again, but her voice failed.

"Go away," Roxanna finally said in Turkish.

Miriam shook her head.

"You know me," she said. "I know you do. And that's Rochelle crying outside."

Roxanna stepped farther back.

"Go away," she said again. "I don't remember you."

She realized she had spoken Farsi, and panicked. She should run away, she thought, eyeing the still-open door. She should run into the street and hide from this woman who had assaulted her so unexpectedly. She imagined charging out, throwing the short one with the long coat to the ground as she ran. When she looked again, Miriam had taken charge.

"Twelve years on the loose, and you still talk the same stupid talk," she said. She went to the door.

"Come inside," she told Rochelle. "And quit moping."

Rochelle took three steps into the room, hugging her crocodile-skin bag to her chest, crying in muffled sobs without looking at Roxanna. Miriam pushed her farther in. Sensing that Roxanna was about to run, she took the only chair in the room and used it to block the door.

"Sit down," she told Rochelle.

The room was gray and bare, the window painted shut. There was a bed—just a rusted metal frame placed on the concrete floor. On it were a mattress and a set of old sheets, two blankets, a beaten pillow. Next to it Roxanna had an aluminum table. On the other side was a torn yellow sofa with the springs showing.

Behind that was the sink, and Roxanna's portable heater. Cockroaches had crawled out of the drain and were scurrying around under the bed and the couch.

No one spoke. Roxanna stood with one foot behind the other, hugging her elbows, looking at the floor. Rochelle squeezed her bag so hard, her knuckles threatened to pop out of her skin. Miriam went to the couch and sat down.

She watched Roxanna.

"We've come to take you home," she said.

Roxanna did not look up.

"We live in America now," Miriam went on. "Since the revolution."

She paused.

"There was a revolution, you know. They threw the Shah out. It's the mullahs all over again."

Rochelle blew her nose, then sobbed some more.

"Teymur died," Miriam declared.

Roxanna shook so hard, Miriam became scared.

"It's all right," she reassured Roxanna. "It's over."

"I don't remember anything," Roxanna said, again in Farsi.

"Sohrab is still there, in the house. He's still waiting for you."

"I don't remember."

"Lili is almost eighteen."

This time, Roxanna did not answer.

"It's all right," Miriam said again. "You don't have to explain anything. No one holds a grudge. We've just come to take you back."

The answer was long in coming.

"No."

Miriam gasped.

"Don't come back," Roxanna insisted.

Miriam watched her for a moment. Then she reached into her bag and extracted a small vinyl folder with the passport and the airline ticket she had brought for Roxanna. She placed it on the edge of the table, then stood up. Her knees cracked like dried wood on a fire.

"We're staying at the Sheraton near Taksim Square," she said. "We'll be there another week, if you decide to call. The plane ticket is good indefinitely, but the visa expires in a year. My address is written down, and so is Lili's, with her phone number."

Roxanna did not react.

Rochelle stumbled to the door and opened it. Miriam followed her, then stopped and turned around.

"My children died," she whispered.

She waited for a reaction, waited in vain for Roxanna to look up at her.

"Joseph drowned. I killed Sara."

She thought she was going to gag on her own pain.

"I kept thinking about you after that. I kept thinking, I can't bring mine back, no matter what I do, no matter how much I want to. And I can't bring Charles back—though he's still alive and living with me."

She walked the length of the room towards Roxanna. Slowly, Roxanna raised her eyes to Miriam.

"But here you are, and all *you* have to do to find your child is turn around."

IN MAY, I wrote my last letter to Sohrab.

"School will end in June. I will spend two months with Mercedez, then move to San Francisco in the middle of August to prepare for the start of college."

I did not tell him how much I dreaded going through graduation alone, then leaving Los Angeles and starting a new life in San Francisco. I did not mention Miriam the Moon's expedition to Turkey to find Roxanna.

"The graduation ceremony is on the eighteenth. My aunts have said they will attend."

The ceremony was scheduled for eleven o'clock. From ten onwards, the high school across the street began to fill with the girls' families and guests. I stayed in my room, wearing only my school uniform, staring at the cap and gown that lay on my bed. Miriam had been back from Turkey for more than a month. I knew this from my conversations with Sussan, but Miriam herself had not contacted me since her return. My other aunts avoided talking about her and what she had found in Turkey. Had she not seen Roxanna? Was she so disappointed she could not bear to call me?

Someone knocked on my door.

"We're all waiting for you at the high school." Sussan braved a pale smile. "I came with Bryan and his wife. And Dear Auntie Light came with her husband. The kids couldn't make it. Josephine sends her love."

For once I was glad to see them. I was also relieved she had not mentioned Miriam.

She opened the door wider and gave me a box of flowers.

"The florist was asking for you outside," she explained. "I told him I would bring them to you."

My father had sent me flowers—two dozen pink roses that had been packed in a golden box and left in the delivery truck too long, so that by the time I received them, they were half wilted. I put the box on the table and began to pull on my gown. Sussan stood in the doorway watching me. I realized she had something to say. Our eyes met in the mirror above my bed.

"Miriam's here, too," she mumbled. "With Rochelle."

They were sitting in the fourth row from the back—quiet and serious and clearly not anxious to be noticed. Rochelle wore a hat, sunglasses, and a dress that should have belonged to a much younger woman. She kept puffing on her blue Dunhills and applying sunscreen to the area around her eyes. Miriam stared at me without a smile.

So I knew.

I knew what she had found and why she had not told me sooner, knew what she was thinking and how she was going to deliver the news. I knew it all through the graduation ceremony, through the hour and a half of speeches and handshakes, the thank-yous and farewells, the promises of bright days ahead and expressions of regret over what was being left behind.

Dear Auntie Light ambled up to me during the reception and complained about the heat.

Rochelle adjusted her hat once too many times and asked if the school served anything other than punch.

Miriam took a deep breath and charged forth:

"It's *her* all right," she told me. "And she doesn't want to know."

Back in my room when everyone had left, I threw the box of roses in the trash and changed into my pajamas. Then I closed the shades, slipped into bed, and with a shaver slit my wrist.

AFTER MIRIAM LEFT, Roxanna could not move. She remained standing, her eyes sewn to the ground, the door still open. Finally, she found her way to the edge of the bed and sat down. Night fell and the wind brought the smell of the sea into her room. People yelled and laughed on the street. Fights broke out in the building. Men got drunk, sang Georgian songs, made noisy love. Near dawn, it rained. Fishermen hauled their catch into the fishmarket across the street, sold it, and stumbled towards another sleepy day. Children came to Roxanna's door and peeked in without daring to enter. She remained on the edge of her bed, wondering.

She did think, absently, that she had missed the time she should have left for work, that the restaurant's owner would be standing behind his cash register when she walked in, yelling obscenities and firing her only so he could watch her cower and beg for her job before he hired her again. He might even fire her for good this time—not even pay her for the days she had already worked that week—unless she got up and went to work right then. But she did not move.

She had not recognized those women at first. Miriam had lost every trace of her beauty. Rochelle had changed her hair, her nose, her cheekbones. But then Miriam had spoken, and after that Roxanna had wanted nothing more than to make her go away. Now she tried to force her mind to focus, mustered all her strength in an effort to shove Miriam out of her mind, pull back the cover of darkness into which she had banished all her love and her memories, and go on as before.

But in the darkness she saw a light—the color of Sohrab's eyes—and she could not block it out. She looked away from it, towards the wall, and saw Miriam talking about her dead children, looked down and saw Alexandra the Cat at her piano, looked up and remembered watching Teymur through her wedding veil. And she did not realize—so terrified was she by the memories that had invaded her—that she had begun to do what Alexandra the Cat had warned her against: to look back, count the years and the events since she had left Iran, figure out her own age and then Miriam's, wonder what had become of Sohrab, and me, and everyone else.

Days passed, and Roxanna did not get up even to close the door. At week's end, the rent collector came and thought she was dead because of the way she sat erect and immobile on the bed, oblivious to the hordes of cockroaches that swarmed around her feet or the bits of garbage blown in by the wind. He went up to her and called her name, but when she did not answer, he told himself he was not going to touch her because she would only keel over and fall facedown onto the bugs and he would have to pick her up and bury her. He left and closed the door. The neighbors, he thought, would find her when the smell became bad.

After that Roxanna got up, suddenly feeling her hunger. She did not know how many days had passed except that the food in the icebox had grown mildew and the sink was crawling with roaches.

She took the folder Miriam had left on the table, and tucked it into her dress pocket. She counted her money, divided it in seven—enough to eat every day for a week—then went out to buy food and look for a job. For ten days she went around asking every shop and restaurant owner if he would hire her. She ended up hauling cartons of vegetables off trucks in a Lebanese grocery store. It was going to be all right, she told herself. She could still move on.

But there was the doubt.

It was Miriam's doing, the way she had talked about her own dead children and how Roxanna's daughter was alive and only waiting to be found. She got Roxanna thinking, for the first time in twelve years, that perhaps—perhaps—she had been wrong. Perhaps leaving had not been the best option, or the *only* option. Perhaps she should go back, *could* go back.

Roxanna began to wonder and she could not stop. Doubt seeped into every certainty she had held on to, kept her up at night, made her ask questions. For the first time since she had flown away from the house on the Avenue of Faith, Roxanna needed to know if she had made a mistake.

She was fired from her job at the Lebanese market because she was too slow hauling the cartons off the trucks. The owner's son was a twenty-three-year-old kid with frizzy blond hair, a wide middle, and a narrow mustache. He told Roxanna she was too old for that kind of work, and too fat. It shocked her, she who had always been so light, to hear herself described as fat. She went into the back of the store, where the employees washed and changed, and checked herself in the small mirror hanging above the sink: her face was swollen; her hands and feet were puffy. She came out, reached into the drawer under the cash register where the owner's son kept his wallet, and stole all his money.

She wrapped the money in a handkerchief and tucked it deep inside her pocket, found work pressing shirt collars and sleeves at a dry-cleaning store that catered to the rich Turks in the Old City. She worked from four in the morning till six in the afternoon.

After a few weeks, her manager gave her three dresses to take home. "You need a new wardrobe," the manager said, nodding towards Roxanna's dress. Roxanna followed the trail of the woman's eyes and saw that her own dress was tight against her belly, the buttons about to pop open.

Her shoes, too, had become too small. Her feet were so heavy, she could not stand on them for more than an hour at a time, and had to ask permission to sit on a stool while she used the cuff machine. Every time she looked in the mirror at work, she had become larger.

The manager told her that she should see a doctor, that she had gained too much weight too fast and her skin seemed sallow and watery. Roxanna said she would, but did not go because she wanted to save all her money. She had this idea—planted in her head by Miriam—that she should go to America and find every-one, look them all in the eye and see for herself if she had made a mistake by leaving. It was all she could think of: to go to America and find out if she had been wrong all these years, if she had banked her life on a mistaken assumption, if she had had a choice she was not aware of.

By June, she was having trouble fitting through the aisles of clothing that hung in the back of the dry-cleaning store, and the bus drivers sighed and rolled their eyes every time she stepped on board. The manager told her to stop gaining weight or not come back to work. So Roxanna walked into a clinic and told the doctor on duty she had been getting heavier for the past two months.

The doctor put her on a scale. A hundred and ninety pounds, he said. He gave her some diet pills and asked about the wheezing in her lungs. It was true she had been breathing differently, she said, that her chest felt heavier all the time. Sometimes, if she had to walk a long way, she felt as if she were blowing air through a tankful of water. The doctor gave Roxanna an inhaler and sent her home.

SISTER ANA ROSE went to my room to call me, she later told Mother Superior and the social worker assigned to the school, and found me asleep in bed. She thought there must be something wrong, because school regulations did not allow anyone to be in bed except in the evening.

"Wake up," she said. "That woman with the whiskey breath has sent her driver to take you away."

She saw me open my eyes, just a slit, then close them again. Then she saw the stains on the bedcover. She did not dare pull the cover off. Instead she ran out to Mother Superior, and screamed for an ambulance.

Mercedez's driver, a young man with green eyes and Harrison Ford good looks, wrapped his tie around my forearm, then picked me up and rushed me to the nearest hospital. Concerned about legal liability and her school's reputation, Mother Superior told the driver not to bring me back, dead or alive. She said I had already finished my last term at the school and was no longer anyone's responsibility but my father's.

I stayed in the hospital for seven days, told the psychiatrists and the social workers I did not know why I had taken the blade to my wrist. They asked for next of kin. I gave Mercedez's name and address, prayed that Miriam would not find out.

She showed up at the hospital on the second day.

"Foolish thing you did there," she said with her eye on my bandaged wrist. "God's in a big enough hurry to kill us all. He doesn't need help from *you*."

I turned away from her.

"But I know why you did it," she went on, "so I can't say I blame you for anything but being weak. I know a thing or two about loss, you see, so I know it's hard on you—this situation now with your mother."

"You must know about loss," I said. I wanted to hurt her back, drive in a knife as long and as sharp as the one she had stabbed me with, dig into her wounds. "Mercedez says you killed your own children."

Miriam bristled, turned to stone, began to crack. She had not expected this cruelty from me. She remained speechless for a while, then she picked up her bag.

"It's true," she said with only half a voice. "I gave them life, then I took it away."

Mercedez let me stay with her through July, never asked questions, never offered advice. In August I told her that I did not have the strength to leave for college, that I needed more time, a familiar place.

"Stay as long as you want." Mercedez shrugged. "Just don't let The Undertaker into my house." She always referred to Miriam as The Undertaker.

Through late summer and early fall, I watched Mercedez sleep with strange men, break a dozen hearts, drink herself into the blue dawn. One afternoon, I asked her what Roxanna had been like.

"Like you," Mercedez said immediately, and her words brought tears to my eyes.

We were sitting in the yard, soaking up the afternoon sun of L.A.

"Your mother was two people forever fighting each other," she said. "One was the runaway exile she was supposedly destined to become—the bad-luck woman everyone expected her to be. The other was going to be so good, she proved everyone wrong."

She saw me trying to swallow my tears and smiled.

"Enough with the melodrama," she said. "Your mother was like this, too—always dying to be miserable. I used to tell her even then that Destiny is horseshit. One good fuck, and you can change a million men's destinies. I hope she has realized this. I hope that's why she didn't come back with Miriam."

She shoved a glass of cognac in my hand. She downed a shot herself, then stretched out on the chair next to her black-bottomed pool. I watched her. After all the years of hard living, she was still beautiful—her teeth white, her body firm, her mind perfectly made up.

"So she had *you*"—she sighed, her voice dripping with irony—"in case the others had been right, that she really was bad luck and could not change it. She figured your life would fix what hers had messed up."

She leaned over the edge of her lounge chair and looked at me.

"Next time you feel desperate," she said, dead serious, "don't take it out on yourself. Destroy someone else."

IN SEPTEMBER, Roxanna went to the airline's office and reserved a seat on a flight to Los Angeles. She was to leave within the week.

She told the rent collector she could not pay him till her health improved and she could earn more money.

"I don't think your health is going to improve," the rent collector said earnestly. "You sound like you've swallowed a fish."

She was wheezing all the time, getting larger, slower. It was the doubt, she thought, the weight of all the thoughts Miriam had forced into her head, the sound of all the words Roxanna had not uttered that day when Miriam and Rochelle came to see her.

Her last day at work, Roxanna stole a few thousand lira—about fifty dollars—out of the cash register. She left her room in the middle of the night, without telling her neighbors or the rent collector she was not coming back. All her belongings—her new clothes, her Turkish coffeepot, the inhaler the doctor gave her in the clinic—fit into a small vinyl bag she bought from a vendor on her way to the airport.

On the plane, the flight attendants arranged for Roxanna to sit next to a small child. They had to show her how to use the seat belt because she had never been on a plane before, and even then, they had to stretch it to the very end before they could close it around her. The boy next to her wore shorts and kneesocks. Roxanna smiled at him. He told his mother he was scared of the fat woman.

Roxanna got off the plane in Los Angeles two hundred and eighty-three pounds and barely able to walk. The customs officers showed her to the booth where she could change her Turkish lira into dollars. The woman at the exchange booth told her where to find a bus that would take her into the city.

Outside the international terminal, Roxanna stood on the sidewalk and stared at the row of public telephones. She could call

Miriam, she knew, or me, or any one of the other phone numbers Miriam had given her. She could say that she was at the airport, that she needed someone to come for her because she barely spoke English and could not find her way around this town. It was the wisest choice, but she could not make it. What if, she thought, no one answered her? What if they said she should go away? What if they came—Miriam, at least, was certain to come— and saw her there, in that way, so fat and sick that she scared little boys? She would find herself a room and a bath, she thought. She would change her clothes, comb her hair, and maybe even buy some lipstick before she called anyone. She saw a bus marked "Downtown—Central" and got on.

The bus let her off on Central Avenue in Los Angeles. It was midday, and the streets were packed. Roxanna walked around in search of a hotel, something cheap and available where she could spend the night and prepare herself. From Central, she walked all the way to Pico, then up Santee into the heart of the clothing district. She saw Latinos selling food on the sidewalks, bumped into cheap clothes hanging on racks outside dusty, suffocating stores, watched West Africans selling counterfeit Gucci and Moschino scarves. At the cross section of Pico and Santee, a crowd had gathered around three men engaged in an argument. An Iranian man was complaining that his two adversaries, both Korean tailors, had ruined an order of three thousand pairs of blue jeans by cutting the fabric the wrong way. The Koreans explained that the mistake was made by the pattern maker, not the tailors, and that all they wanted was to be paid for the work they had done and to be on their way.

Terrified as always to come across Iranians for fear of being discovered, Roxanna looked down and tried to push her way through the pandemonium, but no one would budge. She decided to cross the street and use the other sidewalk. She looked up from the curb and saw the cars coming towards her, realized she was too tired and too sick to take another step. She remained at the curb, shivering and dripping sweat, terrified.

"Can I help you?" a voice asked in English. Roxanna heard the question through the surrounding cacophony but did not think for a moment it was addressed to her. The man who had asked it came up and touched her on the elbow.

"Do you need help?"

He spoke English with only the trace of a Persian accent. He was young, in his thirties, in a light-gray suit and shiny leather shoes. Roxanna stared at him through the film of sweat and panic that covered her eyes and found herself unable to utter a word.

The man gave her a pat on the shoulder.

"Wait here a minute," he said. He turned to the crowd and told them to take their fight elsewhere.

"This lady needs help."

Instantly, the crowd of onlookers turned away from the blue-jean controversy and towards Roxanna. They examined her from all sides, asked questions, made comments.

The man in the gray suit had the creeping suspicion Roxanna was Iranian.

"Are you Iranian?" he asked cautiously, afraid to offend if he had guessed wrong.

She did not answer.

"What language do you speak?" he tried again.

More and more people—Iranians and Asians who ran the shops bordering the street, Latinos on their way to or from the factories they worked in, housewives hunting the streets of downtown for bargains—were stopping to stare at her. Only the Americans did not stop. They slowed down long enough to take a look, then moved on without a word.

"Leave her alone, rabbi," one of the Iranians in the crowd addressed the man in the gray suit. "She's probably just off her rocker."

Roxanna realized she was about to lose the only prospect of help she had, and forced herself to speak.

"I just arrived here," she said.

The sound of the words, spoken in Farsi, startled her.

"I need a place to spend the night."

The rabbi nodded slowly and looked again at her body.

"Are you ill?"

"I have trouble breathing," she said, embarrassed. "All I need is a room I can stay in for a night. In the morning I'll be fine."

The rabbi was not so sure.

"Where did you come from?" he asked gently.

She just stared at him.

"What's your last name? What part of Iran are you from? Are you Jewish? How did you get here?"

She would not mention Miriam's name. Not now, when a host of people were looking at her, and not to this rabbi, who doubtless knew Miriam and would spread the word in the entire community about her obese sister.

She opened her mouth to tell the rabbi she did not want his help. Instead, she gasped, grabbed his arm for support, and it was all she could do to stare him in the eye and to keep herself from collapsing.

The rabbi realized he had bought himself a headache. He thought about referring Roxanna to any of the various Iranian social agencies established in Los Angeles, or advising her to get help from a homeless shelter or a soup kitchen. Normally, he would have done this, except that he had the misfortune at that moment of being watched by a host of other Iranians to whom he wanted to prove his leadership. So he gently pulled his arm away from Roxanna and braced himself for unwanted trouble.

"Stay here," he told her. "Let me see what I can do."

He left Roxanna on the sidewalk and went into the nearest shop to use the phone. It was a dress shop like any other, crammed with cheap clothes hanging from ceiling to floor. The owner was only too glad to make his telephone available to the rabbi, "so long as you don't want a donation from me," he said only half jokingly.

The rabbi stayed on the phone for a long time, dialing numbers, hanging up regularly to conduct discussions with the other men around him, then going through his pocket-sized phone book. The shop owner's wife, a middle-aged woman with varicose veins and a washed-out look, gave Roxanna a glass of orange-blossom syrup with rose water. Roxanna thanked the woman without looking her in the face, but did not drink. The woman looked offended.

"I have trouble swallowing," Roxanna explained.

The woman shuffled to the El Pollo Loco drive-in across the street, and came back with a straw.

"Here." She placed the straw in Roxanna's glass. "Try it this way."

The rabbi emerged from the shop looking satisfied, and stuffed his telephone book back into his pocket.

"I talked to the butcher at Tel Aviv Market on Pico," he was explaining to one of the men, who had appointed himself the rabbi's assistant in this matter.

"The ugly one?"

"Yes, the ugly one. His brother owns the pharmacy on Shenandoah. He has a room he can dispense with for a few days. It's upstairs, more like a storage place. There's no bathroom or stove. Just a small sink with running water. But it's better than having her sleep on the street."

A young Iranian boy, barely seventeen years old, drove up in a full-sized van.

"We're going to load you into this thing," the rabbi explained to Roxanna, "and take you up to a room I've found. There might also be a job"—he sized her up again—"if you find you're able."

Roxanna sat in the back of the van, the rabbi in the front passenger seat. They drove for twenty minutes.

—————

When they reached Tel Aviv Market, she stayed in the van and watched as Rabbi Joseph strutted into the store in his double-breasted suit. The market's owner, an Iranian, received him at the door. He was wearing a colorful cashmere sweater, the kind he had seen Bill Cosby wear twelve months out of the year on his TV show where he was a doctor with five children and a house that managed to remain spotless even though no one ever seemed to clean it. Having lived a poor man's life in Iran, the market's owner had only recently come into money, and now he wore the sweaters with the same kind of insouciance Bill Cosby emanated, hoping to signal that he had come out of his mother's womb wearing a four-hundred-dollar sweater with a tiger's head embroidered on the front.

Minutes later, the rabbi emerged from the market again. He was accompanied by an enormous, bald-headed creature wearing a bloody butcher's apron and talking incessantly as he climbed into the front of the van next to the rabbi.

The butcher turned around to stare at Roxanna.

"Is that her?"

He had one blind eye that was two-thirds closed, a scar across his right cheek, a harelip, no nails on his fingers.

"She looks bad." He nodded and smiled at her as if she could not understand what he had said.

He gave the driver directions.

"Nine blocks down. You can't make a left turn into the alley, so go up to the light and come around the back. The building is like a tower—narrow and tall—and there is a yellow sign in front that says PHARMACY. My brother couldn't think of a name for the place. He's like that, you know, not very imaginative. All he ever learned to do was read books and mix powders."

He turned around and looked at Roxanna again.

"She breathes like a whale," he said to her face.

The van stopped on the corner of Shenandoah Avenue. The

butcher took the rabbi inside a sorry-looking building that had once been white. The young man in the driver's seat never even turned to look at Roxanna.

The pharmacist was thin and disappointed looking, as quiet as his brother was talkative. He came up to the back of the van and sized up Roxanna.

"Are you sure she's going to leave soon?" he asked the rabbi.

"I'll guarantee it myself," the butcher interjected. "I'll get her a job at Tel Aviv Market. Today. My word."

The pharmacist looked through his brother towards the rabbi.

"She can stay two weeks," he told the rabbi. "On *your* word."

The Guatemalan and Salvadoran workers at Tel Aviv Market could not say a complete sentence in English, but they spoke Farsi with various Jewish accents belonging to different provinces in Iran. They argued with old Iranian women over the quality of the rump the butcher had just sold to them, and over whose fault it was that the eggs had fallen and broken all over the ladies' shoes as they were being loaded into the car. When Roxanna started working alongside them, bagging groceries on her feet twelve hours a day, the Latinos assumed she was their country-woman and spoke to her in Spanish. When she did not answer, they tried Farsi, and even the few words of English they could muster. She only looked at them and then looked down, and after a while everyone assumed she was either deranged or hard of hearing. They left her to her own devices.

She worked at the market for a week, getting paid three dollars an hour. Her greatest fear next to dying in her sleep was that one of the women who shopped at the market would recognize Roxanna from the past.

On her eighth morning in the pharmacy building, she woke up and found she could not move.

The pharmacist waited for her to come down the stairs and

go to work. When she did not appear all day, he realized she was in trouble. At seven o'clock that evening, he went upstairs.

"Are you all right in there?" he hollered through the door. "You didn't go to work today."

Roxanna tried to sit up, but could not move. She struggled, failed again, called back that she was fine.

The next morning the pharmacist knocked on her door again. He heard only the sound of her breathing, felt the tremor of the building under the weight of her body. He went downstairs and called the rabbi.

"That woman you brought here is going to die on my hands," he announced.

The rabbi was on his way to bury an Iranian boy who had been shot by gang members in Westwood. He promised he would come over and check on Roxanna as soon as possible.

"In the meantime," he advised, "have your wife feed her so she doesn't starve."

They found Roxanna lying on the mattress, clearly heavier than when they had last seen her. Her eyes were open but unresponsive, and as much as they coaxed her to talk, she remained silent.

The pharmacist wanted to call city authorities and have Roxanna taken out of his building. The rabbi insisted on contacting various Iranian charities first. He wanted to see if he could provide help without turning Roxanna over to uncaring government officials who would—this much the two men agreed on—park her body somewhere and let her die. For two days the rabbi consulted with community elders and religious leaders. On the third morning, the pharmacist put an end to his misery.

He called the rabbi at nine o'clock on Wednesday. "The city came over this morning," he said. "It seems the tower is leaning to one side, and that happens to be just where your lady friend has been lying the past few days. No surprises there. She's heavy enough to move the Empire State Building. Now, it seems, the tower is a public hazard because it may collapse right on top of Pico Boulevard traffic. The city is going to tear it down, and mind you, I have no insurance."

By the time the rabbi got there, the pharmacy had already been shut down. The owner stood on the sidewalk, looking as if he had just buried a child. His brother, the butcher, had parked his own new car in front of the building and was prancing around it smiling widely and using his shirtsleeve to wipe finger-prints off its shiny paint.

Upstairs, the rabbi found three men in Roxanna's room. They were inspecting the premises, trying to figure out how best to move Roxanna out without posing a greater danger to the building. In the few days since she had been lying there, she had grown so large, she could no longer fit through the door. Since tearing down a wall in a building with a shaky foundation was risky, they were talking about cutting a large hole around the window and using a crane to lift her out.

The rabbi went up to Roxanna and watched her. She stared back at him, her eyes wide open, yellow fluid dripping out of them onto the sides of her swollen face. She looked sad, and afraid.

"Tell me, madame, isn't there anyone in this world you could call for help?"

She did not move a muscle or bat an eye. On the floor next to her, he saw her bag.

"We've already searched it." One of the men read the rabbi's mind. "There is a sheet of paper with some foreign-language writing. Maybe you can read it."

The rabbi, of course, recognized Miriam's and Rochelle's names on the paper. He hesitated a moment with the list in his hand, wondering if he should call them. He would have loved to discover Roxanna's relationship to the women, of course. Back in Iran, he would not have wasted a minute before picking up the phone and calling them. But here, in America, there was such a rule as legal liability for one's actions, however altruistic and well-meaning they were. If Roxanna died, the rabbi knew, Rochelle's husband would not hesitate to sue him for not having taken Roxanna to a hospital or turning her over to the proper authorities earlier.

He stuffed the paper back into Roxanna's bag.

"It's Chinese to me, too."

That night, Roxanna lay on her mattress and, for the first time in twelve years, prayed to God for help. Over and over she recited the Shema—the prayer her mother had taught her to say before going to sleep—and it was an indication of her distorted and disturbed luck not only that her prayer was answered, but that it conjured to her door none other than the person who had caused her misfortune in the first place.

MIRIAM THE MOON was riding in a cab down Wilshire Boulevard, bound for Tel Aviv Market, where she intended to beat the rush of early-morning customers yelling at the Afghan manager of the produce department that the vegetables were too wilted and the fruit was too expensive. Since the market opened at seven A.M., Miriam had called the cab for six-thirty, calculating she would get there at ten to seven and be one of the first inside so she could take her pick of everything.

Two blocks down Wilshire, Miriam saw another woman—obviously Iranian, and probably Jewish, because she had that "disappointed victim" look—waiting for the bus. She had two empty shopping bags resting next to her on the bench. Miriam ordered the cabdriver to pull over.

"Tel Aviv Market." She stuck her head out the window. "We can take you."

Wide-hipped and suffering from swollen joints, the woman took a long time to get up from the bench. She dropped her bags more than once, and was panting by the time she traversed the sidewalk that separated her from the cab. The driver and Miriam got out to help her.

"Thank you." She exhaled so deeply, the driver thought she was going to faint in his cab. "I've been waiting for the bus since five o'clock this morning. They keep coming and going. People get on and off. But I don't get on because I don't know which number I'm supposed to take, and I can't ask anyone because they're all either Hispanic or foreigners."

Miriam smiled at the woman's use of the term "foreigners"—a generic phrase once used in Iran to designate Westerners. Arabs and Turks and Pakistanis each had their own nationality. The entire Western world—Americans and Europeans and even Australians—were called, reverently, "foreigners." Even in Los Angeles, men and women of Miriam's generation referred to Americans as "foreigners."

"My sons would kill me if they found out I've done this." The woman was panting away, sitting in the back of the cab with her legs wide open as if to facilitate the passage of air into her burdened lungs. "I have three sons. No daughters. They're good boys, but their wives are all modern and fancy and dye their hair yellow. They've locked me up in this apartment on the seventh floor, so high I'm constantly dizzy, and every time I complain that I don't like to live in a high-rise, they say I should be grateful because the whole world, apparently, is scrambling to move up one floor after another. I tell them it gives me vertigo, looking out my window to the street, so they say I shouldn't go out because I'll fall and hurt myself. Once a week they pick me up and take me for Sabbath dinner at their house. The rest of the time I'm alone, waiting for one of my sons to come by and take me out in his car. Today I thought I'd try the bus. Just my good fortune you should arrive." She finally stopped and examined Miriam.

"Which province are you from?" she asked.

They had turned right on Beverly Glen and were heading towards Pico. The woman was talking about her own experience, coming to America from a small town in southern Iran. Then she launched into a story about someone else who had recently arrived in Los Angeles.

Miriam calculated they would reach the market in a little over five minutes, and realized the woman would have neither the tact nor the experience to offer to divide up the fare. Since the rules of Iranian etiquette made it impossible for Miriam to demand payment, she opened her own purse and began counting ten one-dollar bills.

The woman was pointing towards a building on the right of the street, trying to impress upon Miriam the drama of her story.

". . . over three hundred pounds, can you believe it? And apparently, it's all water. They say she sweats salt water right onto the floor all night. A real whale."

They had pulled up in front of Tel Aviv Market. It was five minutes to seven, and a few elderly women, mostly Eastern Europeans who lived in the area, were already waiting outside. The cabdriver counted his money, realized Miriam had not tipped him, and therefore refused to get out of the car to help the heavier passenger. Miriam's new friend seemed to have made herself comfortable and sported no intention of getting out anytime soon.

"The worst of it is, you know, she won't tell anyone where she's from or which family, so no one can help her."

Something about that statement made Miriam stop and listen.

"My son would kill me if he knew I'd repeated this, but I feel I'm with a friend, even though I don't really know you, so I don't mind telling you," she said as Miriam helped her out of the cab. "My son says it's quite possible she's hiding from the law, or running away from a jealous, crazy husband."

Miriam waited with the woman till the market opened. She even walked inside and exchanged greetings with the young man who wore the Bill Cosby sweaters. Then she turned around and walked the nine blocks to the pharmacy tower.

The front of the pharmacy was boarded up, but the back door was open. Climbing the stairs, Miriam could feel the building move with the sound of deep, slow breathing. The staircase creaked and trembled under her feet, promising to collapse at any moment, and for an instant Miriam thought she should turn around and save herself.

But halfway up, she smelled the scent of moist air and sultry dreams, of cool nights and old, old memories. It was the same scent she had known in her childhood, in those years when she had slept on the floor next to Roxanna, and woken up many a night from the sound of her wings flapping in the wind. It was the same scent that had permeated Teymur's house in Tehran in the months immediately after Roxanna and Sohrab's wedding, the one that had made Miriam tremble with emotion the moment she had stepped into Roxanna's room in Istanbul and seen her aged and tired eyes. And so by the time she took hold of the broken handle and pushed open the door to the attic bedroom, Miriam had no doubt she had found Roxanna.

The room was dark. She saw a shadow at the far end, heard the breathing stop, then start again.

"It's me," she whispered, more to assuage her own fear than to warn Roxanna. "Don't be afraid."

She went towards the shadow, circled it, found the head. Two slits stared back at her from within a gigantic, bloated face. Roxanna's skin was beaded over with moisture, her eyes shedding a constant stream of tears. She closed them when she saw Miriam.

Miriam went to the window and tried to open it, but it was stuck.

She went back and knelt by Roxanna's bed.

"What happened?" she asked, her own voice choked with emotion. "How did you get like this?"

Roxanna did not answer.

Miriam watched her. Then she left the room and went downstairs.

She found a public phone, called Sussan and Rochelle, Bryan and his wife.

"Be here in fifteen minutes," she told everyone. "I have found Roxanna, and she is going to die if we don't save her."

AS MUCH AS Miriam had stressed the urgency of Roxanna's predicament, Rochelle took five hours to arrive at the scene of the rescue. She spent the morning trying to wake up after a night of parties, applied hot and cold compresses to her face and eyes, smoked cigarettes, and then sprayed herself with perfume so she would not smell like tobacco. Her husband, mercifully, had left early—"breakfast meeting," he had said the night before, but Rochelle guessed he was seeing a woman—and so he was not there when Miriam called. He had never liked Miriam, or any of Rochelle's relatives. He said that they had not left the ghetto—just carried it ten thousand miles with them to America—and that they were all a bunch of lunatics bent on spending every last dollar he ever made. Sometimes Rochelle agreed with him.

So he would not have been thrilled to answer the phone that morning and hear Miriam's voice, and he would certainly not have welcomed news of Roxanna's presence in Los Angeles. "Just another financial liability," he would have said of Roxanna. "If Miriam found her, Miriam should support her."

It was not that Rochelle did not love her family, or that she did not do her best to help them out. God knows she was always sneaking money to Sussan, or inviting Bryan's wife to her luncheons, even though the woman had nothing in common with the other guests and never made an attempt to blend in. But Rochelle had never really known Roxanna when they were children, and it was hard for her to feel a bond with a near stranger. It had been difficult enough, a few months back when Miriam had received word that Roxanna was in Istanbul, to adjust to the possibility that Roxanna might still be alive. To prove her goodwill, Rochelle had lobbied her husband for a week and, in the end, got him to pay for Roxanna's plane ticket. At the last minute, as Miriam was about to leave, Rochelle's husband had sent her along.

"Must be he has a new mistress he wants to be alone with," Miriam had remarked without concern for Rochelle's ego.

In Istanbul they had stayed at the Sheraton, Miriam refusing the five-star hotels that Rochelle had offered to pay for—"Waste is waste, no matter who makes it"—and the entire trip had been a nightmare Rochelle would never forget. The first day they had driven in a taxi up to Kumkapi, gotten out in front of Roxanna's building, stared at it without daring to go in. They had gone back and spent a sleepless night. The next morning, they had argued over the best strategy for approaching Roxanna: Miriam had wanted to go right into the building, give the tenants a description of Roxanna, find the apartment number, and knock on her door. Rochelle had sworn the tenants in the building would mug and rape Miriam before they helped her find anyone. As always, Miriam had prevailed.

And after all that—after twelve years of looking, that gruesome journey, all the anxiety—they had received nothing from Roxanna but rejection.

So Rochelle wondered, that morning sitting before her special makeup mirror with the fluorescent light and the quadruple magnification, about the wisdom of rushing once again to save Roxanna.

At ten o'clock, the maid brought up Rochelle's coffee and Xanax pills. After that Rochelle did her hair, applied makeup, and agonized over what to wear—what with the ghastly address Miriam had given her, there near that market Rochelle would not have been caught dead shopping at (even on the phone that morning, she had had the urge to tell Miriam again that she only shopped at Gelson's in Century City). By the time she was ready, it was twenty minutes to noon, and the coffee was cold. She packed the bottle of Xanax in her Prada bag and sat in her car, wondering how many of her very wealthy friends had already heard about her runaway sister turning up in Los Angeles, and what kind of excuses she was going to have to invent just to save face. There would be serious damage control to do, she thought, and somehow, she did not feel Roxanna was worth the trouble.

She took Beverly Boulevard all the way down to Pico, then made a left towards Shenandoah. She saw the crowd from three blocks away: elderly Iranian women gathered on the sidewalk opposite the pharmacy as if watching the aftermath of a train wreck. A fire truck was parked in front of the tower. Behind it were two police cars, an ambulance and a flatbed truck, Bryan's new yellow Ferrari, Sussan's thousand-year-old Trans Am, and assorted other cars Rochelle did not recognize.

She parked her Bentley on a side street behind a huge trash Dumpster, put on her Jackie Onassis sunglasses, pulled on the ten-thousand-dollar chinchilla coat she had bought last year in Canada (in the summer, of course, when the furriers' business was slow and they were willing to make deals). Then she stepped out of the car and tried to look inconspicuous.

Miriam the Moon was arguing with Rabbi Joseph.

"Who says these people know what they're doing?" she asked the rabbi, who was clearly annoyed by her interference. "Who gave you permission to let them move her in this way?"

Rochelle quickly spotted Sussan in the crowd and made her way over. She kissed her sister on both cheeks, looked around to make sure no one could hear her, then whispered, "How do we know it's her?"

Embittered by life's struggles and worn out by years of financial and familial pressures, Sussan was tired and cold and in no mood for Rochelle's theatrics. She looked at Rochelle without bothering to answer and, after a minute, moved over to let Bryan closer in.

Rochelle felt the need to explain herself. "I'm not being disloyal, asking a simple question," she told Bryan defensively. "I just want to know if anyone has checked to make sure it really is Roxanna before we spread the news all around the globe."

Bryan twirled the keys to his Ferrari and chuckled. Ever since he had had a midlife crisis and started psychotherapy, he had developed a habit of laughing at the most inappropriate times, telling people that everything would work itself out. Aside from making him annoying, his new approach to life had rendered him useless in crisis situations.

Miriam the Moon was threatening Rabbi Joseph with a lawsuit.

"Suppose she gets scared"—she was talking over the noise of the street—"and she has a heart attack midway in the air. Are you telling me you are willing to take legal and ethical responsibility?"

Bryan noticed Rochelle's mortification and chuckled again.

"It seems she's too large to fit through the doorway," he explained patiently, forgiving Rochelle for not being there all morning. "And they have to get her out because they're tearing the building down. So they've knocked a hole in the wall where the window used to be, and they're going to attach her to a crane and lower her to the street."

Rochelle went so pale, Bryan thought she would pass out in her chinchilla fur.

"A crane? What crane?"

But she was already looking at the contraption that had caused her consternation, gasping at the horror of it all—the sight of this machine used to carry massive objects, and a makeshift gurney, wide enough to fit three normal-sized people, hanging from the crane's arm with wide leather straps that would eventually deposit their load onto the back of the waiting flatbed truck. Not even a conventional rescue, Rochelle thought. Not even an ambulance. Josephine's mother-in-law would never forgive her this.

"I saw her only a few months ago," Rochelle moaned to Bryan. "She was skinny and small, miserable looking, it's true, but thin."

Bryan shook his head but offered no explanation.

They stood side by side and watched Miriam argue with the rabbi.

"Has anyone called Lili?" Rochelle tried again.

Bryan shrugged.

"Does anyone *plan* to call Lili?"

"All in good time." Bryan laughed.

"What's 'good time'?" Rochelle was furious. "What do you guys think you're doing?"

She noticed that Bryan was not looking at her. So she followed the direction of his gaze, looked up into the creamy sunlight of the early afternoon, and saw a great cloud in the sky. Gasping in awe, Rochelle took off her sunglasses and squinted to see better. Yellowed sheets, like the walls of a gigantic tent, flapped slowly in the wind. Underneath them Roxanna lay facedown, legs straight and head resting on one side, arms extended sideways, as the crane lowered her to the street and back into everyone's life, like a giant malediction.

They kept her strapped to the gurney and loaded her onto the flatbed. Two paramedics sat with her. Miriam wanted to join them, but she had interfered too much in the rescue effort, Rabbi Joseph told her, and she needed to back off. She drove ahead with Bryan. Rochelle watched them: a middle-aged man posing as a teenager, driving a woman in a headscarf and men's clothing down the streets of Los Angeles, ahead of a flatbed truck carrying an enormous creature who refused or was unable to speak, followed by Sussan, in the dilapidated Trans Am she had bought secondhand twelve years ago and had barely been able to maintain on her manicurist's income plus whatever Bryan gave her at the end of every month. Rochelle went last, suffering from a migraine headache and stopping three times along the way—to buy a cup of coffee, smoke a cigarette, pop a Xanax. Still, when she arrived at Miriam's house, the flatbed was just pulling up to the curb.

She stayed behind the wheel and watched the scene before her: Miriam got out of the Ferrari and led the firemen into the house. Bryan greeted his handyman, already there with his tools, ready to take down any door or blast through any window because Bryan paid him triple his rate if he showed up on demand. Mr. Charles was standing at the door, complaining that his birds would be frightened by all the strangers and never once asking the reason for the sudden descent on his house.

In the flatbed, Roxanna lay immobile.

"You're going to have to go up to her sooner or later." Sussan stuck her head through Rochelle's window and frightened her. "It's now or later." She smiled at Rochelle's nervousness. "May as well get it over with."

It was true, Rochelle thought. Roxanna was there. Miriam had made her everyone's problem. Whether she liked it or not, Rochelle was going to have to face her, help her, suffer with her.

She sighed and rested her forehead on the steering wheel.

"I just don't understand why we have to go through this," she confided in Sussan. "It doesn't seem fair. To any of us. And *she* doesn't even *want* this help."

Sussan opened the car door to help Rochelle out.

"Come on," she said, holding Rochelle's arm to keep her steady. "We can't let her die alone in the pharmacy."

They walked up to the flatbed together, Sussan still holding Rochelle's arm, leaning on her as much as supporting her. At the back of the truck, they smiled at the lone paramedic who had remained with Roxanna, then went around the side to where they could see her better. There she lay, an enormous creature of water and flesh, breathing slowly as if each breath were her last, looking at them without the slightest emotion, dead silent.

Rochelle went as close to the truck as she could. It *was* Roxanna, all right—defiant and unmoving and impossible as ever.

"It's nice to see you." Rochelle ventured, then broke down in tears.

MERCEDEZ THE MOVIE STAR walked into my room that afternoon and gave me a vodka martini. It was four o'clock. I had spent the entire day in bed, awake, unable to get up and face the day.

"Your aunt Rochelle called," Mercedez said, raising her own glass in mock salute. I had never liked alcohol before. The past few months, I had been drinking anything Mercedez offered. It was not the taste I enjoyed, it was the numbness the alcohol induced, the sense of "not being," not existing, that it brought on if I drank enough.

"Drink up," Mercedez urged, downing her own. "You're going to need a few more of these before this day is over."

So I came here, that evening in Mercedez's black Jaguar driven by her Harrison Ford look-alike chauffeur, whose very smile gives my aunts heart palpitations. I came because I had no choice, because I knew sooner or later I would have to give in to Miriam and my other aunts, because for once Mercedez encouraged me to come. I came that day and I have returned every day since then. For almost two months now, Harrison Ford has driven me here in the morning and picked me up late at night. Still, I know nothing of Roxanna but what I have seen.

At first, I just sat here, on this chair in Miriam's living room, across from the coffee table with the green bottle centerpiece. For a whole week I listened to my aunts go on about Roxanna and her frightening, deteriorating condition, heard them argue and fight over what should be done to save her. Doctors came and went. Nurses, too, and family members from as far away as Chicago and New York. Rochelle is certain her husband will divorce her once all this is over. Bryan's girlfriend no longer insists that he leave his wife and marry her. I watched and listened. I did not interfere. The one act I was not capable of was going to the room at the end of the hall, opening the door, and seeing my mother.

My aunts tried to force me, then backed down amid hushed whispers about what might happen if they pushed me too far, how I had surprised them all with the suicide attempt they never saw coming, how in retrospect it was inevitable that I would try to wipe myself out after all that had happened.

"When you're ready," Miriam assured me. "Just stay here and get used to the idea first."

Around me they went in circles, engaged in the impossible effort of divining Roxanna's illness and discovering a cure. Pending a firm medical diagnosis, they had put her on a drip IV and kept offering her small portions of food that she sternly refused. Because moving her was out of the question, they used all of their connections to bring the fruits of medical science into Miriam's house instead. They called on the best surgeons, paid X-ray technicians to make house calls. They brought in specialists, asked for more referrals. Day after day, a parade of doctors and nurses went through the house, making one diagnosis after another, pursuing various and often conflicting courses of treatment that were as brutal as they proved, in the end, useless. Through it all, Roxanna maintained her silence, and only kept gaining water. She never asked for me. I know this because I was here, and I listened.

Her sisters tried to break through to her. They sat by her bed and asked her questions, told her everything that had happened to each one of them since she had left Tehran. They brought their children in and forced them to look at Roxanna without showing the horror they felt, even allowed Mr. Charles to parade his birds before her in hopes of evoking a reaction. By the end of the third week, Roxanna had gained more weight, and the sound of her breathing was driving the dogs crazy up and down Miriam's street.

One night my aunts left earlier than usual. Harrison Ford called to say he was taking Mercedez to a premiere downtown, and would not pick me up until close to midnight. Suddenly, I found myself in the house with only Miriam and Mr. Charles.

And with Roxanna.

I sat there until Mr. Charles had put his birds to sleep and Miriam had gone into her own room and closed the door. I knew she was leaving me alone on purpose, giving me this chance to look in on Roxanna without having an audience. I sat there awhile longer, wondering if I could really do that—go up and see this creature everyone said was Roxanna but with whom I felt no closeness or even familiarity. I sat there so long, I thought I would never be able to stand. Then I got up.

Miriam had left the light on in the hallway, so I could see my own shadow approach Roxanna's door. The air around the room reverberated with the sound of her breathing. It was moist, like sea air, and heavy. Her door was unlocked. I pushed it back and walked in.

From the doorway all I saw was a large mass, like an animal lying upside down under a sheet. She was so different, so unlike the Roxanna I had known, I actually found it easy to go in for a closer look. She must have felt my presence, because she stopped breathing for a second, and when she started again, her breath was faster and more choppy—frightened, maybe. Her chest heaved up and down. Her stomach, like a monstrous tank, quivered under the sheet. I thought of the woman who had carried me, barefoot, on her shoulders one night, who had scaled the wall of our house and taken me through the cold, smoky night of Tehran and up in the Ferris wheel. I remembered how she told me she had flown with real wings. I remembered how she had called to me in our house on the Avenue of Faith, the sound of her laughter echoing down the hallways and the staircase and into every room.

I came up next to the bed till I could see her.

We remained that way—I standing at the side of her bed, staring down at her, Roxanna looking up through the yellow water that oozed out of the corners of her eyes onto her pillow. There was no emotion in her. If she saw me, if she recognized me, she never showed it. Then she closed her eyes.

This is how it is, I thought. *After all this time, after all the waiting, Roxanna the Angel sees me and, instead of everything she could say or do, closes her eyes on me.*

I bumped into Miriam on my way out.

"I hope she dies tonight," I said, certain Roxanna could hear.

She did not die that night, but her condition took a turn for the worse, and her vital signs began to slow even more. I know because I went back to Miriam's the next day, and the day after. And sometimes, in spite of myself and my anger, I even went into the room and saw her again.

Dismayed by the doctors who could neither diagnose nor cure Roxanna, my aunts accepted defeat on the scientific front and turned their efforts to older, more proven methods of healing.

Against the fervent opposition of her husband, Rochelle flew to Chicago in between two important wedding showers, and went to see the holiest of all holy rabbis—an American who did not speak to or look at her, but who did give her, in return for a hefty "donation," a red string blessed with prayer which she was to tie around Roxanna's wrist.

Josephine laughed when she saw the string.

"They sell these all over L.A.," she said. "All my friends wear them now. They're supposed to ward off the evil eye."

Not to be outdone by Rochelle, Bryan took his mistress on a scuba-diving trip to the Cayman Islands and returned with a man he called his "personal guru and spiritual guide." In exchange for a week's all-expenses-paid stay at the Century Plaza Towers, the guru came to Miriam's house every morning and afternoon and put his hands, warmed by Tiger Balm, over Roxanna's stomach. He claimed he was going to extract the negative vibes that had made her sick. The vibes cost Bryan ten thousand dollars and still did not go away.

After that Sussan's daughter discovered a Tibetan monk and moved him into Miriam's house. He spent two days chanting in Roxanna's doorway and burning putrid-smelling incense till everyone's eyes were swollen red and their hair smelled like damp towels. He was evicted when Rochelle, who had felt all along that she had known the monk in another life, suddenly recognized him as the old Filipino she had paid to clean her pool, who had shaved his head and eyebrows and donned a white robe.

Nine weeks and three days into the ordeal, Miriam the Moon sat me down before a glass of tea brewed with cardamom, and took stock of the facts: she had done everything she believed might work to save Roxanna, she said, and even much she knew was useless. She had lost face before the community and subjected Roxanna to pointless humiliation. She had spent an unconscionable amount of money, caused irreparable damage to her relationships with her neighbors, and, in the end, was only that much closer to seeing Roxanna die.

"Time to be honest," she confessed.

I bristled, but remained quiet. Miriam's honesty had always meant pain.

"The truth is, I have known it all along," she continued. "I knew we were going about this the wrong way. Rochelle knew it, too. That's why she didn't want us to bring her here in the first place."

"You didn't have to bring her." I shrugged, forcing the words through tight jaws. "I wish you hadn't."

"That's true." Miriam sipped her tea. "But there's more to it than your wishes or mine. To find the right cure, you see, one has to make the correct diagnosis."

She put down her glass.

"So you're a doctor now." I offered my sarcasm. "Maybe you can cure her on your own."

She was not offended.

"Not a doctor," she said. "Don't need to be. I just know what's wrong with your mother."

She leaned forward and whispered in my face. "I know what's killing her."

My tongue was dry and heavy in my mouth. When I moved it to speak, it scratched my lips and muffled the sound. Miriam leaned back in her chair and went on to deliver the coup de grâce.

"She's dying of Guilt, you see. Over what she did to you, and to your father before you. She's dying of Sorrow, over the life that she wasted, that she could have fixed but didn't. So much pain bottles up in you, so many tears, and after a while it has nowhere to go, and it begins to kill you. There is a word for it in Farsi: *Degh*, 'to die of Sorrow.' I figure Roxanna never got the chance— gave herself the chance—to go back and ask forgiveness. I figure if she did that—with you, at least, if not with Sohrab—she might release some of those tears and start to recuperate."

She was looking straight at me, suddenly pleading with me. It was as if she thought I had the power to save not only my mother but Miriam herself, as if I could say a word, commit an act, and suddenly restore to them everything they had lost over a lifetime.

"What do you want *me* to do?" I asked, more out of exhaustion than a wish to help. "She won't even look at me."

Miriam seized the chance and did not let go.

"I am going to make almond tears," she said, speaking slowly so as not to scare me away. "Right here in the house. It's an old ritual we used to do back home, whenever we were faced with a tragedy we couldn't resolve. It's a long process—takes at least two days—and at the end of it, you need someone with a pure soul—good karma, they call it here—to feed the tears to the afflicted person. I thought I'd get *you* to do this."

She stopped, but her eyes would not release me. Then she made an offer she knew I would not refuse.

"If you do this," she said, "I will tell you everything you want to know."

She sized me up, gauged my reaction, the extent of my need.

"All the secrets," she promised. "All the sorrow."

Roxanna

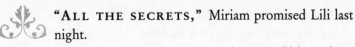 **"ALL THE SECRETS,"** Miriam promised Lili last night.

They were talking in the living room, but I could hear them as clearly as if they were standing next to me. Miriam has a high-pitched voice, but she knows how to moderate it, how to be louder or more quiet depending on what she wants me to hear at any given time.

"I will tell you everything you want to know," she said, hoping to coax Lili into her scheme, trying also to warn me, I think, that the time to speak is now.

As if there were such a thing as a whole truth. As if Miriam could possibly know every secret.

It occurred to me when she said this how much she has changed since I knew her last, how back in Iran she never would have contemplated airing any secrets. I think she realizes this: that she has come from a place where secrets lie in wait, ready to undo you if ever they see the light of day—that she has come from that place into a world where she can reveal any mistake, admit her own sins, and still have at least the illusion of a chance.

"This is the land of choices and chances," I hear Bryan say every day to my sisters. He is talking about all the girls he can date, even though he's married with a mistress on the side. "Dark and light and all the shades in between," he says. "Sizes two to twenty-four. Flat or busty. Single or married. I could even sleep with *men* if I wanted to."

I wonder if he has realized yet all the other choices, all the second chances he has here.

This much I know about living in exile, I who have done it all my life, even in my own home: You can love the old country all you want. Sometimes, exile is the best thing that can happen to a people.

After Miriam made her the offer, Lili called Mercedez on the phone and told her she was going to spend the night here. Lili has a sweet voice, a child's voice, and I can tell she is unsure of everything she says because she hesitates so much between each thought.

"I'm supposed to help make something with almonds," she said. "It seems I have to start early in the morning."

I think Mercedez laughed at the other end.

Lili doesn't need to know the whole truth. She only needs to know why I left her, and only *I* can tell her that.

I remember once when my mother made almond tears in the ghetto. It was when my brother was sick with smallpox and everyone thought I had brought them bad luck. They were going to make the almond tears to save his life and, even more important, to change my luck. I remember being thrilled—awed, even—at the prospect of impending miracle, or the possibility, however faint, that a handful of crushed almonds could alter the course of my destiny.

It didn't.

Still, you tend to get stupid when death stares you in the face. I never thought my life was worth much, but now that I know the time is close, I am so afraid of dying, I hardly want to close my eyes for fear I won't be able to open them again. So I was actually relieved when Miriam came up with the idea of making these tears. I am grateful she has not given up on me yet.

It's early morning, and I watch Lili in the yard, taking instructions from Miriam on how to climb the tree and pick the almonds by hand. The sky is a bright orange, the color of the ripe persimmons that used to fall from the trees in our garden on the Avenue of Faith in the spring. The almond tree is in full bloom, its leaves a bright green, its branches reaching all the way onto the roof, casting shadows all over the yard. Underneath it Lili stands on a step stool and, with her right hand, reaches into the pink flowers to pick the youngest fruit.

It is difficult work, and slow, because she has to pick one almond at a time and drop it in the box Miriam has left on the ground. Lili works diligently, consistently, and I wonder if she believes in Miriam's promise, or if she is just killing time, going through the motions to see me through to my grave.

I was always leaving her. Even before I actually flew out the window that night, ever since she was born, and before that, since I was a child myself, I had one foot on the ground and the other dying to fly. I tried once to tell her this. I don't know if she understood.

Before I left, she used to follow me around the house all day, with her little bare feet and skinny legs, afraid every minute that I would vanish before her. Every time I turned around and saw her, she would smile, but her eyes would be full of fear.

I did love her, it is true. But I did not love her enough.

The sun has come up, and I see Lili is uncomfortable in the heat. Every hour since nine o'clock the front door has opened and one of my sisters or relatives has come in. Miriam leads them all into the living room and tells them to stay away, to keep quiet. They sit on the chairs and talk in hushed voices. When they come to look in on me, I remain still. If they talk to me, I don't answer, but I do listen. I had been alone for so long, I had forgotten the comfort of voices, of this web of sound and feeling that surrounds me now, that coddles me in my isolation. It is filtered through the water that has filled my skin, through the sound of my own breathing that keeps me up even when I do try to sleep, through all the fears I can no longer control. I am back in the womb, and I can't help thinking this is how it will be when I die and they all come back to sit shiva.

Lili ignores everyone and keeps working the tree. Her hands have become black from the dust on the leaves, and her face is smeared with perspiration and the mark her hands leave every time she pushes her hair back or wipes her eyes. Twice, she stops to drink water. Then she looks over from the yard into my window and sees me staring back at her.

How do you begin to speak after thirteen years of silence?

By one o'clock she has filled the box almost to the top, and Miriam tells her she should stop.

"Come in and eat," Miriam says, but I know Lili won't.

For the rest of the afternoon, she sits in the yard, shelling the almonds by hand, shrugging off Miriam's invitations to various kinds of food. Inside the house, my sisters watch her and whisper about what will happen to her if I die, how she will undoubtedly try to take her own life again, how the only way to save her is to save me. Curiously enough, Miriam disagrees with them.

"Just because one person is doomed doesn't mean everyone else should be," she says.

At five o'clock, Lili has finished peeling all the almonds. She carries the box into the kitchen and leaves it on the table, then goes back into the yard to gather up the trash and throw it away. It's the hour of sunset, and the light bounces off the glass window in my room, so that although I can see her well from the inside, from where she is standing, all Lili can see is the red glare of the sun against the glass.

She comes up to my window then, puts her hands—her blackened, chapped hands—onto the glass, and peers in at me.

All night long, I see those hands in the dark.

The night I ran away she followed me through the house. I knew this. I had seen her earlier on the staircase. When I stood on the railing, she called me and I turned around. She held her arms out to me. She must have thought that she could stop me, that I would not leave her or, at least, would not leave *without* her. I think she was counting on that. I looked away and let her go.

That is what has bothered me most since I left her: that she could not *believe* I would let her go.

I did not love her as much as I loved Teymur, or my own freedom. I had tried to tell her this. She never believed me.

When it's morning again, Lili takes the box of peeled almonds back into the yard and stands at the table, crushing the almonds with a meat grinder. She holds the grinder in her right hand and bears down on it with all her weight, lifts it just a bit, then brings it down again. Slowly, she manages to crush all the almonds into a thick, grainy paste.

In the living room Miriam is serving tea and dates, peeled pickling cucumbers with salt and lemon juice, peeled apples, more tea. It occurs to me that these are the traditional foods served at wakes, and it makes me want to laugh—the irony of these women sitting shiva just as they are trying to save my life. It's the story of all their lives, I think. They are always hoping for the best, knowing they will be disappointed, mourning the outcome even before they have embarked on the battle. They sip tea and watch Lili in the yard, sip tea and discuss the benefits of early marriage, the risks of liposuction, the latest fads in clothes, the best ways to ensure that a pregnancy results in the birth of a boy instead of a girl—"have sex in the middle of your cycle," Dear Auntie Pride is telling Sussan's Buddhist daughter. "Have your man eat spicy foods and drink Chinese Royal Jelly. Have him wash himself with baking soda and water before you start."

Dear Auntie Light arrives with news that her brother-in-law, eighty-three years old and living alone in Tehran, has just been found dead in his apartment. The neighbors had smelled a dead cat. The coroner said he had been dead for at least two weeks.

"Imagine!" Dear Auntie Light tells everyone. "You live in the same town all your life, eighty-three years, and in the end, you die so alone no one finds you for two weeks."

Some people are born into exile. They take it with them even if they don't go anywhere.

Alexandra the Cat taught me that the secret to survival is to embrace your exile, move into it and move on. You must travel ahead in spite of what you leave behind, she said. You must not get tired, slow down to rest, diverge from your path. Bury a child and go on. Lose a war and go on. Above all, she said, you must not look back.

I did this for thirteen years. I did it because I was convinced of Alexandra's truth, convinced that leaving Lili had been my only choice, that it would be impossible for me to return. It worked until Miriam found me.

In the yard, Lili has cut a wide piece of cheesecloth into four-inch-square pieces. She sits at the table, still alone, and with her fingers scoops bits of almond paste into the squares. She wraps the cloth around the paste, ties the top with a string. In one hour, she has wrapped three dozen bundles, arranged them in rows on a tray. Then the doorbell rings and Sussan announces that Mercedez is here.

This is how I know that only a miracle is going to save me: because I know Mercedez, and I know how much she and Miriam despise each other. And I know Mercedez would not come into this house, not even to see me, unless she thought I was dying.

Miriam greets her in the hallway outside my room.

"Good of you to show," she says to Mercedez in her most sarcastic tone. "You should have waited a few more months. Maybe by then, she'd have fossilized."

Mercedez doesn't answer, but as she walks towards my room,

I can feel the air in the house tighten all around her, and I sense Miriam shrink away.

She's a storm—angry and fast and awe inspiring. In one instant she has crossed the room and looms above me with her cat's eyes and her ruby lips. She stops long enough to have a look, raises one eyebrow, shakes her head as if to say I have disappointed her. Then she turns around and heads for the sliding-glass door that opens onto the yard. She calls out to Lili at the table.

"Your aunts are right," she says, aware I can hear her, oblivious to any pain she might cause. With Mercedez, weakness was always the greatest sin. "Whatever magic you're supposed to procure, you'd better do it fast."

The first two weeks after Miriam found me, I lay here, waiting for Lili to come into the room so I could see her. I listened for her voice amid all the others, listened for the sound of her footsteps. And yet when she did finally come in, she managed to catch me by surprise. I had not heard her approach, hadn't even felt her steps on the floor beneath me. Even when she stood above me, I could not see her reflection in the glass window next to my bed. It was as if a ghost had crept into my room—a young, beautiful ghost coming to beg for a body.

I looked up and saw her.

My daughter.

She is tall. Taller than I ever was. Tall as her father. And she has Sohrab's yellow eyes. I had wanted her to have those eyes.

She stood above me, and I thought how beautiful she is—how fair her skin is, how fine her features are. I saw her and felt I was looking at myself—younger, it is true, and more beautiful. And smarter, no doubt. But she has the same air of isolation about her that I have always felt, the same sense of being removed and unreachable. With her frail, thin body, without the weight that I have gained, she still looks like an island alone in an infinite sea.

That is why I closed my eyes on her: I saw how alone she was, how invisible she felt, how afraid she was to look in my eyes and realize I had not seen her. I may have taken myself out of her life, I thought, but I left her my destiny.

In the afternoon, Lili begins to tie each bundle of almond paste onto a branch of the tree. She wraps the string around the branch, then places a small plate on the ground directly beneath it.

"We have to wait for the tears to fall," Miriam explains. "Then we'll gather them all in a jar and feed them to your mother."

Mercedez the Movie Star has other ideas.

"We're waiting for nothing," she tells Miriam. "You've promised this girl a story."

So they come into my room—Miriam, Lili, and Mercedez. Lili sits cross-legged on the floor at the bottom of my bed. Miriam takes the chair across from Lili. Mercedez stands in front of the sliding-glass door, crosses her arms, and watches them.

Miriam talks through the afternoon and into the evening. In the living room, my sisters speculate about what she is saying and how much she will actually reveal, pray that she will be restrained. In the end, they get tired of waiting and leave. Mr. Charles, too, puts his birds to sleep and goes to bed. As dusk sets in, Mercedez is still standing above me, her silhouette striking against the silver sky, then fading slowly into the darkness. She is still the strong one, I think, this girl who defied the ghetto when no one else dared, who broke every rule and got away with it all. She has kept her anger, her cruelty, and that is how she has survived. Except maybe now, she is tired of the anger.

That is why Mercedez has come here, why she is watching Lili, ready to protect her from the edges of Miriam's truth. It was I, back then in the Cat's house, who had wanted a child. It is Mercedez who has ended up raising her, who is raising her still.

Miriam tells Lili the whole story: from how our Lubovicher great-great-grandmother ran naked through the temple on Yom Kippur, to how my own mother tried to kill me, to how Mercedez whored around in the ghetto and I, the Jewish girl who had married the prince's son, slept with Teymur the Heretic inside my husband's house. I remember Teymur's hands on my skin. I remember how he watched me. Would I have acted differently had I known the damage I would cause? Would I have loved Teymur less? Feared Fräulein Claude more? Would I have been able to stay strong, resist temptation, stop the pull of Teymur's desire that tugged at me all those years like an incessant tide?

Near dawn, Miriam's voice trails off, then stops. Mercedez finally sits down on the edge of my bed, watching Lili, waiting to see if knowing has freed or destroyed her.

This is what dying will be like, I think: a dark sky, a quiet room, an unspoken word.

There is a sorrow within me so deep, I have not been able to give it a name, I want to tell Lili.

It is my mother's sorrow, and her mother's—the tears that they shed in the tear jar, that they drank alone, inconsolable.

I did not want my daughter to have this sorrow. I did not want to leave you those tears.

That is why I left: to take the sorrow out of your eyes.

It is not as if I sacrificed myself to save you. It was not your needs I was thinking of, but my own. More than anything else, more than the need to be with my child or the love I felt for Teymur, more than the instinct simply to live, I wanted to end the sorrow.

I came back and saw that I had lost.

———

Lili springs up and startles us all.

"Look at the tree," she says, bolting for the window. I turn my head.

Then I see it: that tall, beautiful tree standing in the new light of dawn, its branches wide and long and full, golden drops of oil falling from among them into the yellow and red and purple plates below, gathering there to reflect the red bark of the tree, the warmth of the rising sun, the promise of an unlikely miracle.

Even Mercedez cries with joy.

They wait till all the oil has dripped from the paste. At nine o'clock, they gather the plates full of almond tears and put them on the table in the yard. Then Miriam disappears into the house and comes back with a bottle and a cone.

"Pour all the oil in here," she tells Lili.

Lili goes pale. She steps back as if in horror, opens her mouth to gasp for air, covers it with her hand so she won't scream.

It's the bottle—old and green and chipped in one corner—that has shocked her so. She has seen it before. She must have just remembered where. I, too, remember.

It is my mother's tear jar, the one Miriam brought to me when she gave me news of Shusha's death. It was after Tala'at had left with The Nephew: "Mother cried into this for three days and then drank her own tears," Miriam had said. I kept the bottle in my room, but did not take it with me when I left. Lili, too, left it behind when Sohrab sent her to America. But Miriam went back and found it, carried it across the world, saved it in her house: the only gift my mother had to give me, the only one I am going to leave for Lili.

I open my mouth to say *No*.

Instead, I gag on the water in my lungs and start to choke. I try to breathe, but the rage stops me and I begin to cry in deep, noisy heaves, water spouting out of my throat and my nose. Before I know it, I am vomiting the yellow fluid from my lungs. Miriam hears me and rushes in to help. She brings her hand up to help raise my head. I want to push it back but I can't. For once she panics and screams for someone to help. Then everyone rushes in. They are calling the paramedics, shouting orders to one another, standing in the back of the room and crying helplessly. I cough harder, vomit more water, gasp for air, but my lungs are too full, my airway is blocked, and I flail about for one last breath.

"Mama!" Lili calls me.

It's the child's voice, the voice that called me on the balcony, the voice that still believed in me.

It shocks me to hear her call me. I look for her in midbreath, find her through the film of darkness that has descended all around me. She is peering back at me, terrified as she was the last time I saw her, when she was five years old and I was leaving.

Mercedez has pushed Miriam out of the way and is holding my head up, clearing the airway so the air can get it. When I inhale again, I am calmer.

Lili is still there, at the side of my bed, looking down at me, watching my every breath. I remember how she has called me, but now I see the difference between the child she was when I left and the woman she has become in spite of me. She is terrified, it is true, but she is also angry—demanding that I not die, not yet, not in this way. Her existence is no longer tied to mine: I tried to make her vanish while I was with her—all those years when I told her I was going to leave and refused to see her, when I thought only of my own need to escape. I made her vanish then, but now, in this town, in this house surrounded by my sisters and by Mercedez, I by my own death will no longer erase her existence.

The paramedics bring oxygen, empty out the room, leave instructions that I should stay calm. For a while after that, I lie on my back, breathing the oxygen that tastes sweet and dry and hollow, grateful I am still alive, wanting one more minute, one more hour. When I remember to look again, Lili is gone, but Mercedez is still there.

"They're going to do this thing with the oil," she says, addressing me for the first time. "Try to be helpful."

Miriam comes in with the tear jar and calls for Lili. She puts a spoon into Lili's hand, pours a few drops of oil from the jar into it, and motions towards me with her head.

"The first drops are the most important," she says. "Have faith."

Lili's hand is shaking, and she drops the oil on my chest. Miriam tries again. This time, my breath blows the oil right off the spoon.

Mercedez gets impatient.

"Can't you do this intravenously?" she asks sarcastically, but Miriam has not heard her.

Lili is still trying, still trembling. Tears well up in her eyes, run down her face, fall onto mine.

There was a time when I was young—your age, perhaps a bit older. Alexandra the Cat died in my dress, and I left her house and the ghetto. On the Avenue of Faith, in that house forever linked in my memory with magic, I met a man who loved me, who gave me the child I had wanted. At that time, in that house, I came to believe in the possibility of miracles.

The third time Lili tries, I can actually taste the oil.

It's warm and sweet, like something I used to drink as a child, way back in that ghetto so full of noise, you always knew you were alive. That's what I remember most about Iran: the voices of my family echoing under one roof, the sunlight in our courtyard, my mother always praying for a miracle, crying into her tear jar and drinking her own tears, then crying again.

I told myself when I escaped Sohrab's house that I was not going to regret anything, and to this day, I haven't.

Except now, looking at Lili next to me, tasting this oil and counting the years that have made her, my little daughter, into a grown woman, I feel a wall cave in, and I begin to cry—real tears instead of this cursed water that has been pouring from me like poison.

Lili doesn't notice this at first. Even Miriam, as vigilant as she is, mistakes my tears for the water my eyes have been shedding. She tells Lili to give me more oil.

Suddenly, I catch myself thinking—I who have never believed in redemption and would never allow myself to pray for miracles—that maybe all is not lost. Maybe *I* am not lost.

I cry quietly, my eyes fogged up with salt. My tears are so dense, they wet my pillow, and still I cannot stop. I feel lighter, as if with each tear I am shedding another pound, as if it is the tears, gathered up inside me through the years of living by the Sea of Marmara, before that in the house of Teymur's Desire, and even before that in the ghetto far away in the desert—as if it is the tears that have weighed me down.

Miriam is wrong. I am not sorry. It isn't about being sorry.

I can't take the sorrow out of your eyes, I want to tell Lili, *but the sorrow is not all I have to leave you. It is not how it started, how it was going to end. You were the miracle child—the hope of an enchanted life—and I was sure, in those years, that your journey would not end in sorrow. Maybe here, in this land of chances and choices, it does not* need *to end in sorrow.*

The next time she brings the spoon to my mouth, I take Lili's hand.

She goes stone cold, then panics and tries to pull her hand away, but I won't let go. I hold her small, fine fingers in my own now-enormous fist and I press with all the force of my rotting body and I don't let go until she stops struggling. Her hand softens. She stays there looking at me in the dark, and I think she understands, because she is still and waiting.

I stand up. I feel lighter, thinner, more weightless than I have felt in a year. Then I put my arm around Lili and, in one move, lift her off the ground.

We glide through the glass door, into the yard, across it, into the night sky. When my feet leave the ground, she holds on to me and looks down.

Turn around, I say. *Behind us through the dark. You can see us all now, even those I had forgotten.*

I show her the path that brought me to this house—the streets I traveled in the back of the flatbed truck that moved me here like a beast, the terror I felt hanging from the arm of the crane, the darkness of the pharmacy tower, the men and women who surrounded me that first day off the plane when I collapsed on the street in Los Angeles.

But then we go farther, and I show Lili the colors of Istanbul, the red and gold and green tiles of the mosques around my apartment, the painted arches in the palace of Topkapi, the blue of the Sea of Marmara.

I show her the mountains I crossed going into Turkey, the jungles of northern Iran, the brown, barren desert that conquers all.

Tehran is in ruins. There is war, and hunger. The trees have died along the Avenue of Faith. Our house—Teymur's house—is inhabited by strangers who are hostile and angry. Among them, Fräulein Claude walks distracted and disheveled, talking to her dead brother, asking him for Teymur. Sohrab is alone in his room, at the end of his life, still grieving.

But I do not stop here. I take Lili in my arms, the way I should have done years ago, and I fly her past the devastation, through the streets lit by torches for miles around, into the house I saw the night of my wedding.

Turn around, I say.

In the moonlight, the house on the Avenue of Faith lights up one room at a time as I move through it, dressed in my wedding gown, walking towards Sohrab, who waits for me, who will smile at me, hold his hand out and pull me into the sunlight of his promise.

This is how it started, I say.

We hear the music, the sound of Tala'at's laughter, the jingle of Fräulein Claude's bracelets as she walks through my wedding.

We go into the house that is once again furnished and bright and glorious, through it into the backyard.

It is spring. I stand in a sleeveless dress, crushed red and purple grapes on my hands.

Sohrab asks me if I will marry him, and all I can think of is the daughter I will have, the daughter with the yellow eyes.

"There is no such thing as Destiny," he tells me, and his voice—the innocence of his faith—makes me want to cry.

I am eighteen years old, barely out of the ghetto, and I have met Teymur for the first time.

He stands in front of the house, outside the doors with the etched-glass panels, refusing to look at me.

I would not—could not—have loved him any less. I could not have refused him, could not have resisted him any more than I did. But on this day, in this land of choices, I can see the possibility of forgiveness—the chance to sin and be absolved, to start again, as I should have done after I slept with Teymur. As Sohrab wanted us to do. As Lili *can* do.

In the beginning, I tell Lili, *there were many choices and I, believing I was doomed, let them go to waste.*

In her eyes I see it now: she has understood me. There is that same sparkle, that gleam I saw the night I took her out of the house for the first time, when we climbed down the wall outside her bedroom and ran into the street away from Fräulein Claude's tyranny. Lili was astonished—I remember this—shocked to find out that the world outside our house was not as dark and quiet at night as she had always assumed. Then she looked up and saw Pari-with-the-Boots laughing as she walked through the entangled web of cars and pedestrians, emerging from the fog and the steam of running engines—a fairy-tale genie come to life. Lili has seen the *possibility* of another truth.

I bring my lips to my daughter's cheek and whisper:

"Turn around. It is possible to know and, at last, feel at peace."

To my husband, Hamid, who has been my best friend, my greatest supporter, the shoulder I have cried on, the hand that has kept me from falling;

To my children—Alex, Ashley, Kevin—who surrendered their mother to the blue screen day after day, who have blessed this book with their good wishes and have blessed my life with the miracle of their laughter;

To my parents, Francois and Giti Barkhordar, who had the courage to seek "the land of chances";

To my friends, authors Adriane Sharp and Mary Stachenfeld, who drove the freeways of Southern California early Sunday mornings in the rain to meet me in middle-of-nowhere restaurants and talk about this book. The coffee was bad and the eggs had undergone many previous incarnations, but the advice I received on those mornings was invaluable;

To my agent, Barbara Lowenstein, who believed in this book from the outset and has worked on its behalf with unparalleled enthusiasm;

To my editor, Christa Malone, who told me she cried reading this book; to her daughter, Sierra, who inspired her to read on;

To publisher Dan Farley, who said yes on the eve of Yom Kippur;

To my sister, Gentille Barkhordar, who answered frantic six A.M. calls and who rushed over so often late at night when my computer crashed; and to my other sister, Jeannette Monfared, who watched over me in the years when we were at boarding school and who has continued to watch over me since;

To my friend Dr. Douglas Sears, who showed me the possibility of a different truth;

To my teacher, author John Rechy, who instilled in me the desire for excellence;

To the esteemed Dr. Raheem Cohen, who took me into his home and offered me the treasure of his memories, and to my aunt, Eghtedar Hanassab, for a lifetime of stories;

To the late Parivash Nahai, who has inspired me with her grace and courage;

Thank you.

MOONLIGHT ON THE AVENUE OF FAITH

GINA B. NAHAI

A Readers Club Guide

ABOUT THIS GUIDE

The suggested questions are intended to help your
reading group find new and interesting angles and topics for
discussion for Gina B. Nahai's *Moonlight on the Avenue of Faith*.
We hope that these ideas will enrich your conversation and
increase your enjoyment of the book.

Many fine books from Washington Square Press
feature Readers Club Guides. For a complete listing,
or to read the Guides on-line, visit

http://www.simonsays.com/reading/guides

A Conversation with Gina B. Nahai

Q: How much of *Moonlight on the Avenue of Faith*—a novel about the history of Iran, Jewish persecution, and the ambivalent intersection of Eastern and Western cultures—is based upon your own life?

A: "Moonlight" is not autobiographical, but it stems largely from my own memories of Iran and the people I knew as I grew up. Lili's story is not my own, nor is Roxanna my mother. As with all my books, I did a lot of oral history interviews in order to gather these stories, then transcribed them while trying my best to stay true to the voices and the tales I had heard.

Q: One of the things that strikes me most about *Moonlight on the Avenue of Faith* is your complex, highly ambivalent treatment of Iranian-Jewish exiles in America, a condition rarely dramatized in fiction. Tell us about what you hoped to highlight and emphasize about the nature of exile, and how you feel about the result.

A: More than anything else, the history of the 20th century has been one of exile: the two world wars, and since then the countless regional civil and border wars have created massive movements of people across national lines. As a student of oral history, I have always been fascinated by the idea of exile. My own life experience has also been one of perpetual living "on the outside." In "Moonlight" I pose the question: "What do we lose, and gain, when we go into exile?" My own conclusion has been that exile can be as freeing as it can be devastating.

Q: Do you ever go back to Iran? Do you still have family there?

A: I do still have relatives in Iran, and for a long time after the revolution, I wanted very much to go back and visit. So much time has gone by now, and so much has changed in Iran, that I fear the country I knew is no longer there. I still would very much like to go back and see the changes some day.

Q: What is the significance of the "Moonlight" in your novel's title?

A: Lili loses her mother in moonlight, and she finds her again, at the end when they fly together over Tehran and the house on the Avenue of Faith, in moonlight. It is a metaphor for hope, and for the sacrifices we make in the pursuit of personal choice: it is light that is possible to see only in darkness.

Q: In your novel, you manage to seamlessly combine elements of both reality and fantasy. Your depictions of Iranian political oppression and the rich heritage of familial obligation are imbued with and offset by the constant presence of magic, mythology, and the supernatural. What was behind your decision to tell your story in this manner?

A: Magic and mythology are very much a part of the Iranian sensibility. Many of the stories I tell in "Moonlight" were related to me in exactly the same way, and I thought it was important to stay true to the original version. Beyond that, I feel there is an enduring quality to fairy tales that the other forms of fiction lack. People of all ages and convictions can connect with fairy tales if only they are willing to suspend disbelief and enter the world the writer creates. So I wrote

"Moonlight" as a fairy tale, hoping women and men of all nationalities would relate to its universal themes.

Q: Reviewers have repeatedly compared _Moonlight on the Avenue of Faith_ to the works of Gabriel García Márquez, Jorge Luis Borges, and Isabel Allende. Were you particularly influenced by any of these authors? What other writers inspire you?

A: I admire García Márquez tremendously, but magical realism originates before him in the works of Yiddish writers, and even before that in the works of Iranian writers I read as a child. I think my work differs from Borges or Allende's in that I write about history and specific events and facts, that I do a tremendous amount of research for each book and try to portray the repercussions of political events on the lives of ordinary people. In this sense my main inspiration as a writer is Oriana Fallaci—a reporter who observed the world through objective eyes and then wrote about it as a story. I have also been influenced by Marguerite Duras and the early works of Toni Morrison.

Q: At one point, the characters in the novel tacitly blame the acceleration of Morad the Mercury's death on the shortcomings of Western medicine. Was this perspective of "traditional" medicine a common one at the time?

A: In the early decades of westernization in Iran, there was a sense among some people that everything western and new was superior to what the East had known thus far. Medicine especially was upheld as the great new answer to worldly ills, and American doctors were viewed as nothing short of miracle workers. With these unrealistic expectations, those who embraced western medicine at the expense of everything old and unscientific, were bound for inevitable disappointment when the doctors failed—as they did in Morad's case—to deliver miracles.

Q: Fräulein Claude is, perhaps, the most likely to elicit blame from readers. As you were writing, what were your feelings about Fräulein Claude? Did you struggle with her emotions and choices?

A: I was surprised by the reaction readers have had to Fräulein Claude. I saw her as a survivor, a woman who saw necessity to change her destiny and did so by reinventing herself. She was a devoted wife and loving mother, and I say of her, "she was not cruel, Fräulein Claude. She became that way only after she had lost everything that mattered." I can not blame her for her cruelty; it was her way of defending what was hers.

Q: Roxanna is, among other things, a woman struggling to cast off the weight of her past. How successful is she, and indeed any of us, in doing so?

A: I don't thing anyone can cast off their past, but I do think it's possible to reshape our future, and therefore our destiny. This is what Mercedez has done, and what, I hope, Lili will be able to do: scarred as they are by their past, they recognize there is a choice, and therefore avoid falling into the seemingly inevitable "fate" they have been assigned. In Roxanna's case, she makes the mistake of believing there is no choice—that to avoid bringing bad luck upon her family she must leave them all together. It's only at the end, when Miriam forces her to face her own past, that Roxanna realizes she had other choices.

Reading Group Questions and Topics for Discussion

1. In the particular emotional realm of *Moonlight on the Avenue of Faith*, one's ability to live and love depends entirely upon one's capacity for forgiveness. Without forgiveness comes tragedy and death, as in the case of Miriam's daughter, Sara. With it comes the potential for redemption and even physical healing, as in the cases of Lili and Roxanna. What effect does the act of forgiveness have on the lives of the rest of the novels' characters?

2. "That is how the world really functions," Miriam the Moon tells Lili at the beginning of the novel. "Human beings are nothing more than the instruments of a callous Fate. Free will and conscious decisions are mere inventions of minds too feeble to accept the reality of our absurd existence." How does Roxanna the Angel's first-person narrative at the close of the novel—in which she recognizes all of the choices she "let go to waste" in her life—complicate and even challenge Miriam's early pronouncement about the futility of faith in free will?

3. *Moonlight on the Avenue of Faith* has been called a novel of magical realism. While magical realism has been traditionally regarded as a regional literary genre—restricted to the Latin-American writers who initially popularized it as a literary form—it is really an international phenomenon with a wide-ranging history. Beyond Gabriel García Márquez, writers as diverse as Toni Morrison, Salman Rushdie, Derek Walcott, and Jorge Luis Borges have contributed to its far-reaching influence among the literatures of the world. Where does Nahai's brand of magical realism fit into the genre as a whole? What qualities does her work share with other works of magical realism? How is it unique?

4. Beginning in the eighteenth century with the Crow (the Lubovicher rabbi's wife), chart the course of the "bad luck" which Lili is assumed to have inherited from a long line of female ancestors. What was each woman attempting to take flight from? What do each of these women have in common?

5. In the process of describing Roxanna's life toward the end of the novel, Mercedez the Movie Star also offers an insight into her own life's modus operandi: "Your mother was two people forever fighting each other," Mercedez says. "One was the runaway exile she was supposedly destined to become—the bad-luck woman everyone expected her to be. The other was going to be so good....I used to tell her even then that Destiny is horseshit." To what degree is Mercedez the novel's most strong-willed, self-assured, and genuinely contented woman? On the other hand, what hints does Nahai provide to suggest otherwise?

6. Both Mercedez and Miriam are possessed as young women with bewitching physical beauty. But while Mercedez goes on to trade exclusively on her erotic power as a woman to succeed throughout life, Miriam plainly takes no stock in her beauty—nor in the conventional role of Iranian women—even to the point of wearing men's clothing. In spite of these differences—and in spite of the fact that they despise each other—what are the essential similarities that exist between Miriam and Mercedez?

7. How do both Mercedez and Miriam use the force of their characters to redress any cultural disadvantages they might have as women? How might one describe Nahai's vision of the balance between the sexes? Compare and contrast Mercedez's remarkable determination to transcend her ghetto childhood with Miriam the Moon's equally strong will to overcome a relentless string of tragedies.

8. One of the primary themes of *Moonlight on the Avenue of Faith* has to do with the nature of escape. Tala'at escapes by running away with Habib's nephew. Effat leaves for Kent with an Englishman. The steel-willed Mercedez, of course, achieves several escapes in succession before finally arriving on Sunset Boulevard and setting up house as Mercedez the Movie Star. By stark contrast, Shusha escapes her misery by drinking a glass of poison. How do the rest of Nahai's characters escape? Which attempts result in failure? Why?

9. Roxanna the Angel's role as a mother is clearly central, but what about her role as wife and lover? What is the legacy of her relationships with Sohrab the Sinner and Teymur the Heretic?

10. In the sense that a work of art is an expression of and an explanation for a particular identity, how might Lili's practice of taking a pen and writing upon the surface of her own body comment upon the nature and function of the artist?

11. In the years after Roxanna's flight, Lili tells us, "I had become invisible to myself and to everyone else." How does Lili react at different points in the novel to this constant feeling of transparency, of being "weightless and unfettered"?

12. Considering the fate of each of her characters, what distinctions, if any, does Nahai seem to be making between the meanings of 'escape' and 'exile'? Between the meanings of 'escape' and 'redemption'? Explain.

13. When Roxanna grows wings and deserts her family in the house on the Avenue of Faith in hopes of thwarting her unacceptable destiny, Lili notes that her mother is "upsetting the balance between dreams and reality." What does she mean? In what ways does the novel as a whole upset the balance between dreams and reality?

14. What is the significance of Shusha's tear jar? By giving the bottle to Roxanna—"It's the only thing Mother left us"—what legacy is Miriam symbolically passing on to her sister? Why do you suppose Roxanna's first instinct is to destroy the jar?

15. What other symbols and images emerge and tellingly recur throughout the novel? Consider, for instance, the Caspian Sea, feathers, sapphires, Pari-with-the-Boots, and sunflowers?

16. What are your own memories of 1979, the year of Iran's Islamic Revolution? Looking back after reading Nahai's book, what is your sense of the Western media's perspective on the riots, the movie-theatre fires, the Ayatollah's overthrow of the shah, and the seven-month hostage crisis?

17. If Los Angeles is truly the "land of choices and chances," then what would you say Tehran is the land of?

18. Explaining why she subscribes to *National Geographic* and *Scientific American*, Miriam says, "I like to balance experience against science....Experience wins every time." How does this arch statement comment on the entirety of *Moonlight on the Avenue of Faith*, and how does it inform and foreshadow the resolution of the novel's considerations of free will and fate?

19. Although Jacob the Jello sees things through a perpetual cloud of opium, how accurate is it to say that he actually sees more clearly than anyone else in the novel? And how does it happen that, even after his death, his visions continue to haunt the inhabitants of the house on the Avenue of Faith?

20. In the course of her novel, Nahai intimately acquaints us with the condition and status of women—particularly Iranian Jewish women—in Eastern society. What did you learn from Nahai's novel about Iran's gender politics? What details surprised you in particular?

21. *Moonlight on the Avenue of Faith* features a range of women who, dissatisfied with the limitations with which their lives have presented them, proceed to reinvent themselves. For instance, Fräulein Claude conceals her past by transforming herself into a worldly, platinum-blonde German who, through the entire course of her marriage, never once lets her husband see her out of makeup or high heels. What is the nature of Alexandra the Cat's transformation? Miriam the Moon's? Mercedez the Movie Star's? How do these various acts of reinvention serve to empower, imprison, or liberate them?

About the Author

GINA B. NAHAI was born in Iran and educated in Switzerland and the United States. She is the author of the award-winning and internationally praised novel *Cry of the Peacock*. A frequent lecturer on Iranian Jewish history and the topic of exile, she has studied the politics of Iran for the U.S. Department of Defense. She lives with her family in Los Angeles.

What book will you choose for your next reading group?

Visit

www.simonsays.com

to keep up on the latest new releases from Washington Square Press as well as author appearances, news chats, special offers and more.

Our WSP Readers Club Guides will help enrich your reading group discussions by offering more questions, better and more focused discussion topics, and exclusive author interviews.

To help choose your next reading group book and to browse through our vast library of available reading group guides, visit us online at **www.simonsays.com/reading/guides** today.